The Salvaged Summer Trilogy

All For Overalls

Dominique Allen

Book 1

Printed by Book Printing UK www.bookprintinguk.com

Remus House, Coltsfoot Drive, Peterborough, PE2 9BF

Printed in Great Britain

ISBN 978-1-3999-2831-1

All For Overalls

'Just because you're out of the way
doesn't mean you're not in the middle of it!'

The Salvaged Summer Trilogy:

Bk 1: All for Overalls

Also, soon to be available

Bk 2: If the Sock Fits! (late 2022)

Bk 3: Raids, Rallies and Reserves (early 2023)

Also, becoming available by the same author in spring 2023:

Three Sides Out, One Way Home (Malaya 1956-58)

Further information available from
queries@gertiespath.co.uk

With thankful acknowledgement to Karen Neale for her wonderful pen and watercolour cover artwork.

And with sincerest thanks to the encouragement and guidance from David, Bev, Sam, Jenny, Tim and so many more, who saw beyond my disabilities, to take these first few steps with me along Gertie's path.

And with the deepest gratitude to my mother and twin-sister, who didn't have a clue what they were getting into when they suggested: "you really ought to give everyone a chance to know Gertie … we'll help."

And, of course, to Granny, who always knew.

CONTENTS

CHAPTER 1

June 1940
A Rough Start

IT WAS A BEAUTIFUL SUMMER'S day in a small English village, and there was trouble brewing.

"Gerroff!" Gertie protested, as Al yanked at the bicycle saddle, snatching it out of his hands. "I'm not taking it, you idiot!"

"It's not mine, it's the butcher's second-best," Gertie pleaded. "He gave it me for the deliveries." The bullies were Al's elder brothers, he'd just been trying to catch the bicycle before it went down on top of Gertie, who'd already fallen.

The bullies were doing all the name-calling and kicking, but Al was trying to give as good as he got, whilst Gertie was desperately trying to stop the basket from tipping its precious cargo into the road.

Gertie was a year older than the bullies, but they were stronger than him. They'd never liked him, even at school. Gertie had always been a bit of a weed and somehow those glasses of his annoyed them, he'd never got to the bottom of why.

Al felt sorry for Gertie but didn't want to end up being clouted too. He knew how his bully-brothers operated; they tended to kick first, and he'd got quick at missing those attacks. He needed both hands to hold on to the saddle, but they'd started tugging, trying to get him to release his grip. At least they couldn't kick him anymore, there were too many people about. Instead, the bully-brothers tugged and shoved until Al lost his balance too, and plunged forward. If Al hadn't yelled a warning, he'd have ended up on top of the butcher's bicycle *and* Gertie!

Gertie scrambled out of the way as best he could, but was more scared of the parcels getting damaged than he was of the boots of the bullies. He was still trying to keep the basket at an angle that contained most of the deliveries, but sadly some items had already been rattled loose.

The bully-brothers didn't have bicycles, so why should Gertie have one? He didn't deserve it; he wore glasses!

Gertie was suddenly desperate, forgetting about the bruises on his knees and the scrapes on his hands where he'd taken the brunt of the fall. The bullies had succeeded in toppling the butcher's bicycle and Al was in the tangle too, there wasn't a hope.

Crumpled and battered, both boys now began scrabbling back to their feet, untangling their limbs from the frame of the bicycle and each other, in a fluster of rage and embarrassment, grabbing to recover the sprawling parcels of meat before their own clumsiness crushed them any further, dusting them off and trying to pack them unconvincingly back into the basket. Al looked over at the basket. "It looks OK. How about you?" Both knew if Gertie lost those parcels, then Brisket the butcher would skin him.

The two bully-brothers had taken a hasty step back once they'd lost any chance of snatching the bicycle, it was far too obvious who the culprits were for their liking. Time to do a runner. They didn't get the opportunity to follow through on that threat of more kicking.

Aggy's yell of, "Leave them alone. Get out of here. Why aren't you at school?" managed to confuse the bullies momentarily. They recognised her as the young schoolteacher and heard as far as 'get out of here', and got out of there!

Gertie knew who she was, too. When he'd heard Miss Aggy's voice he'd frozen. Thankfully, Al was too young to be so well trained and carried on with climbing off Gertie's leg.

Gertie had liked school, except for the bullies. He hadn't wanted to leave but was too old at fourteen. He'd never liked the headmaster; Mr Pegg was too old to make sense. Most of them had thought Mr Pegg was half-deaf anyway. He was always shouting at them to 'pay attention', then talking too fast for them to keep up, and smacking the back of their knuckles with his ruler. Miss Aggy was nice. She didn't talk too fast and even gave them a chance to ask questions. Gertie liked asking questions. Most of the time no one listened, but Miss Aggy did.

Mrs Parr was the other teacher at the village school. She was nice too, but everyone was sad for her because she was a widow. She'd got one of those telegrams. They'd all tried to be kind to her, but she still had red eyes and spoke softly.

Gertie was glad it was Miss Aggy who'd been doing the shouting at the bullies. He'd liked her classroom, but there was work to be done. The butcher had given him a job, so that's what he did. Everyone needed to pull their weight now there was a war on!

Miss Aggy's husband was the church warden, but he was in on the War Effort too. He'd got injured in a training accident, but still worked over at the local army camp in the clerking-office. Oh, Miss Aggy was adorable, but she'd married the church warden last year. Everyone knew she would, when he came home from leave, then he'd gone away again and got himself injured, but not so much that anyone could notice. Gertie didn't mind the church warden though, a regular sort of bloke.

Gertie would have happily married Miss Aggy himself, if he'd had the chance and been old enough. He always thought that had been a bit unfair; too old for school and too young to marry. That meant he'd had to stay at home with his mother, and his mother didn't seem to like it any more than he did!

Gertie could look after himself. He'd been doing it for years. By his reckoning he'd been about nine when his dad had finally stopped bothering to come home. His mother had done a lot of sighing about the place for a year or so after that. He'd asked her a couple of times about it, but only a couple. She'd lobbed a rolling-pin at him the first time and the bag of clothes pegs she'd been holding the second. After that his mother had started 'going into town' more, and not bothering to come home sometimes, but at least she'd stopped shouting at him so much!

Gertie had the whole of the attic room to himself. It was nice up there. If Miss Aggy had married him, she'd have liked it up there with him. If he opened the window and leaned out far enough, he could see all the way over to both ends of the village. Miss Aggy would have liked that. It was a very pleasant view from Gertie's attic.

He didn't have any money. Gertie had tried it and didn't like it. He'd watched some of Ol' Creak's customers. Ol' Creak ran the village shop and post office. Some of his customers would take the shiniest coin in their change and turn it through their fingers, like they were checking its balance. Ol' Creak would scowl at them, but they'd ignore him and put the coin in their mouths and bite it. The first time Gertie got his paper-round pay from Ol' Creak, he'd tried doing that. It tasted horrible and set his teeth on edge. Why did they do that? Ol' Creak would never give them anything dodgy, not with a post office under the same roof. His customers ought to know that. Even Gertie knew that much, and he hadn't even bought his own newspaper yet!

Gertie hadn't minded doing the paper-round on Ol' Creak's bone-shaker, but the butcher's second-best bicycle was better. Only Brisket hadn't need him then, so Gertie had tried working for Grouch, the village milkman, for a while, but had got on better with Nag, the milko's horse. Grouch just sat on the cart and grumbled mostly.

When he started working for the butcher, Gertie didn't even need to tell them about not liking the taste of money. Brisket's missus guessed and got it all sorted for him. Brisket just cut and wrapped the meat, his missus sorted out the deliveries and the pay.

Brisket's missus always put Gertie's money in an envelope. "For your mother," she'd remind him, before handing it over to him at the end of each week. He was only allowed behind the counter when she did that. Then with that safely tucked in his pocket, after he'd repeated the instruction back to her – "For mother" – she'd nod and get on with the next bit, reaching down under the counter for the small package of sausages, telling him the same thing every week. "I've cooked them for you, so don't bother your mother about them." Gertie took them and repeated the instruction back to her – "Don't bother Mother" – Brisket's missus would nod and mutter 'good boy', before shooing him away until Monday. He'd been working for the butcher every week since then.

Gertie had his own attic. He always left the envelope from Brisket's missus with the rest of the post for his mother by the front door, and sometimes she left him his supper under a plate. Apart from that he rarely saw her. If he needed clean clothes, he'd try the cupboard on the landing. If they weren't there, he just kept on wearing what he'd got.

Gertie liked Al, always had. They shared a dislike for Al's bully-brothers. And they were both grateful for Miss Aggy coming to their rescue. She had enough to be getting on with but had stopped to help them anyway. Gertie was wondering where her husband was. Somewhere between his church wardening, Home Guarding and clerking-office duties, or at the allotments, perhaps?

Gertie would have liked that, to have had a garden. He much preferred the taste of soil to the taste of money. He liked the smell of reading-book pages and sausages, too.

Miss Aggy's husband was still called 'Corp' out of respect for his injuries. He was a decent chap, but she shouldn't have married the church warden, to Gertie's way of thinking. He was always going off and coming back, and that must be unsettling for her. If she'd waited a few years Gertie would have been happy to marry her. He would have stayed with her and given her the sausages, too.

Ol' Creak always needed fresh paperboys. No sooner had he got them trained up then they grew out of the paper-round and got on with something else. He was always cross with his paperboys; it evened out the annoyance he felt when they left him stranded.

Everyone called Ol' Creak's shop *the* village shop because he ran the post office at the other end of his counter, even though he sold far more tobacco and newspapers than writing paper and stamps. But there was a war on, so maybe that would change.

Gertie had done Ol' Creak's paper-round until the milko needed a lad. From paper 'boy' to milko's 'lad' sounded like a step in the right direction to Gertie.

Grouch didn't mind Gertie working with him on the milk round, so long as the lad did the running about and looking after Nag. Grouch did the driving and the counting, and Gertie was happy with that.

Gertie had never minded an early start; it worked the right way round for him. He woke and got up, spent the day working, then got tired and went to bed. Why anyone would want to be out in the dark was beyond him. What was the point in doing that? They couldn't see anything. Gertie had always thought it got dark for good reason, to sleep. He'd been called 'stupid' by the bullies at school, but that was only because of the glasses, and they were borrowed, so that wasn't true either!

With the milko's deliveries, Gertie didn't need to trudge so far in the cold and damp; at least there was a bit of cover in the cart, and the horse did most of the walking. Gertie just did the running with the bottles from the back of the cart to the doorstep and returned with the empties. He had the legs for that. Except on Saturday mornings, when Grouch got off his backside and did a bit of work collecting the payments.

Gertie liked working with Nag when the round was finished. He liked the smell of the horse and when he rubbed it down; his hands smelt warm like summer earth. Gertie liked sausages and horses; he didn't like money and he didn't like newspapers. Books and the radio though? Oh, they were wonderful, like Miss Aggy and bicycles!

He'd met up with Al and the new city-quick evacuee, Walker, down at the village stables. They'd been playing football and he'd scolded them for startling the horse. No one had ever listened to Gertie's scold before. It had surprised the heck out of him and they'd been best friends ever since.

It had been Gertie's idea for Al and Walker to step forward and do the village paper-round between them. They weren't meant to, they were too young, but what with all the war shortages no one was really counting.

Ol' Creak wasn't going to grumble so long as the newspapers got delivered. Al and Walker did everything together, so the paper-round got done very efficiently. Al's family were old names and well worn-in locally, and Ol' Creak paid the boys fair, half and half.

Even with the newspapers and the radio, most of the village found reasons for coming into the shop to find out what was *really* happening.

Al and Walker had learnt all about salvage from school and they'd told Gertie. They seemed to be teaching much more interesting lessons since the war had started and the bullies had gone off.

Between the three of them they'd begun the Salvage Scamps. They would have preferred to have been known as the Salvage Squad, but Gertie and Al were used to being called 'scamps' and Walker, being from the city, was used to being called a lot more names than that. Walker had told them they couldn't be a squad because there weren't enough of them. Even if they included Al's little sister, Maze, so they'd agreed on the Salvage Scamps. They'd make-do with that. There was a war on, everyone was needing to make-do.

Gertie had found out more about the what and why of salvage from the leaflets that Over-Eager-Edith was getting with her Women's Voluntary Services paraphernalia. They were easier to read than the newspapers and kept nicely in his back pocket.

He'd heard the radio talk about all those bigwigs up in Whitehall, with their speeches about 'tough times ahead', talking about 'shortages' and 'sacrifices'. Gertie had listened carefully and it all sounded the same: 'Things are going to get more difficult.'

That's why Walker's parents had sent him to the village out

from the city. Everything happened in the cities first. They were bigger and busier. Gertie was hoping the bigger and busier 'difficulties' wouldn't have time to get to the village.

The cities were all about filing offices and sending out orders and making radio programmes. The towns were all about cars and factories and shops with big windows and houses with too many rooms. The village was all about being in the middle of the fields: working fields, training fields and airfields!

Right now, it was harvest time in many of those working fields and everyone was gearing up to help in one way or another. It wasn't any more difficult now than it had always been. War or no war. No matter what those bigwigs said, they couldn't make farming any more difficult than it had always been. The earth was the earth, and the weather was the weather, and the farmer did his best with whatever happened in between!

Everyone needed to muck in together and Gertie rather liked that way, so long as it included him being able to keep the butcher's delivery bicycle and the sausages!

'We've all got to do our bit. It's just the longer this goes on, our bit is going to get more difficult to do!' That's what Gertie had heard Miss Aggy tell some of the Sunday ladies. Gertie didn't go to church, but he liked to hear the singing. He missed the church bells ringing, but the war had stopped them. At least the choir still sang on Sunday and Gertie could sit out of the way on the church wall and listen from there. He learnt a lot on Sundays.

That 'doing our bit' made Gertie smile. That definitely included the Salvage Scamps. Gertie might not be able to do much, but he could still be part of the War Effort. If they were going to be able to bring in enough salvage, then they were going need not only Maze's old pram, but Gertie's bicycle basket, too.

Monday was the day for bringing the salvage to the collection point at the village hall. Gertie, Al, Walker and Maze liked the finding and the bringing-in bit. They didn't get involved in the sorting out, the church ladies and WVS took charge of that. They were only children; they weren't allowed to be in charge of anything ... and right now Gertie definitely was *not* in charge of the state of those butcher's parcels!

"For Gawd's sake, don't tread on 'em," Al was muttering across to him. "You and your stinky feet." His friend wasn't being unkind; they both knew Gertie's feet stunk. Gertie wondered if it had been his feet that had something to do with his mother telling him he could have the attic room? He'd worn through the socks his dad had left him long ago, but it was summer anyway, so socks didn't matter. Sometimes, when he was sitting on the church stone wall, he kicked his boots off too. It was nice grass in the churchyard.

Even if he was only doing the deliveries for the butcher, that was still doing his 'bit' for the Effort – that was, if the bullies let him.

The newspapers had been saying it would all be 'over by Christmas', but that had been after a year when everyone had been saying it wasn't going to happen at all. Now the war had happened, good and proper, and Gertie couldn't see any sign of it stopping soon.

"BULLIES!"

Aggy shouted, then looked down at the forlorn figure, as Gertie looked up adoringly, unable to focus on what the schoolteacher had just said, distracted by her shiny hair and strong eyes. Al was fully occupied not-listening, too. He was trying to extricate himself from the bicycle pedals, whilst Gertie forgot completely what he was meant to be doing with the butcher's parcels in his arms.

"It's all right, it wasn't your fault," Aggy was telling them both.

Al knew his older brothers; they weren't going to admit it was their fault. No matter what the schoolteacher said to their parents, it wouldn't matter. They were farm boys now, no longer under her jurisdiction. "They don't go to school no more, Miss. They're working over on Tuckly's farm."

Aggy sniffed, then tutted before she spoke again. "No harm done I hope?" recognising the sprawling figure. "Gertie, have you grown since I saw you last?"

It was the kindest most encouraging thing she could think to say in the moment. It was obvious she couldn't say anything about the state of the butcher's parcels!

Gertie smiled, brushing off his scuffed knees. "I'm OK, Miss. I think I'm growing out of my dad's old trousers, though."

Poor Gertie. Truth be told, it was the state of his trousers that had first prompted the teasing from the bullies, not really the butcher's second-best bicycle's fault at all. They'd only started on the bicycle when they thought they could get away with it. The trousers had always been too big for Gertie's middle. He couldn't go back to his mum and ask for another pair. The last time he'd tried she'd given him a lecture and earache. She'd even threatened to have a word with the butcher's wife to stop giving him sausages, because they were making him grow too fast. That didn't make sense; if they did, then the butcher wouldn't be so short.

Gertie had managed to drop the hems to his ankles by himself, but the trouser legs tended to flap about and catch in the bicycle's chain. Unfortunately, he'd got a wobble going trying to kick them out of the way, and then twitched the handlebars. He needed to see the kerb, but the glasses were for reading the parcel labels only. Then with the trouble with the steering and trying to wiggle the glasses down his nose to look over the top of them, and then the sudden jeering from the bullies, he'd started to lose his balance and been scrambling to save the contents of the bicycle basket ever since.

Gertie's knee was scraped and the trousers torn. No, he wasn't going to start crying, not in front of Miss Aggy.

One of the young nurses getting off the bus at the church stop had heard the young schoolteacher's shout. It sounded as if she had her hands full. Florrie hurried over to help. She was only in training but *was* in uniform and it wouldn't have been right to leave an accident.

Florrie came to the aid of the lanky boy still struggling to his feet. His face was flushed, but his knees and palms had evidently taken the brunt of the damage. The smaller boy seemed to have tucked and rolled rather well, seeming none the worse for wear.

Gertie had been trying to hold all the parcels, but the loops of string kept catching on his fingers and wouldn't stay in the basket.

"Your bicycle?" Florrie asked him. Gertie grinned. "Nearly."

Florrie persevered. "Any damage?"

Gertie looked at her, a bit nonplussed. He rubbed his elbows nervously, then rubbed his knuckles. Sniffed, and brought his sleeve up to wipe his nose before answering, looking at the parcels of meat. "The butcher's going to have a right go at me if there is."

"Then we'll make sure there's no harm done," Aggy told

them briskly, picking up the last few parcels and checking for leaks or loose string, before inspecting the labels.

The farm-bullies were long gone, Al and Gertie could name them, but that wasn't going to make any difference. They hadn't seen Gertie cry and they hadn't taken the bicycle off him.

Gertie wanted to imagine Miss Aggy had another of those library books in her bag. He rather hoped she'd got within clipping distance of the bullies and swung her book-laden bag at them. Oh, it would have been worth tempting the wrath of the butcher to have seen that!

Florrie was looking for one particular address. "You look like you know your way around here," she asked Gertie.

Aggy took charge of the parcels of meat, ensuring all were safely returned to the butcher's basket. "Come on, let's get these delivered before any more mischief finds them."

Florrie wasn't quite sure if the schoolteacher was referring to the two boys in the middle of the village street, or the parcels of meat.

"I'll make sure the butcher knows what happened and take Al with me into school." Aggy turned to Gertie. "You'll have to finish your round for the butcher. Do you think you can?" Gertie nodded. "Good, then you can show this young lady to her billet whilst you're at it."

"Yes Miss."

Florrie smiled and did a little curtsy to Gertie. "So, you're going to escort me home?" she teased him gently. The young trainee nurse had been in the village no more than five minutes and already she had an ardent admirer. Gertie was smitten.

He watched the way the schoolteacher's bag swung on her arm as she took Al to school. It did indeed have a library book in it, he knew it would. Florrie waited for his distracted gaze to return to the moment.

"Where to first?" she repeated.

He grinned and blushed. "Oh, butcher's delivery."

She nodded and smiled. "The butcher's delivery indeed. Where do we begin? I'm not due to report in to Matron until tomorrow, but Mrs Tweeny is expecting me today. I've been stuck on that bus far too long. A bit of a walk will do me good."

Gertie grinned. "Then this walk'll do you wonders. There's a lot to get round."

"Then we'd best get started. Who's who around here?" Florrie got the chatting started, giving Gertie a chance to regain his composure.

Gertie wasn't sure whether to disclose his nickname, so began cautiously. "I'm Gert! Are we meant to be talking? Me and Al we do it all by code you know, safer that way."

Florrie thanked him for his consideration. "Quite right! I'm Florrie. I'm going to be working up at the RAF hospital." She really hadn't needed to explain that part; even Gertie could recognise the uniform. He apologised. Of course, he could tell Florrie everything. They wouldn't allow anyone in uniform who wasn't trustworthy. That's why if you put one on, and you weren't meant to, they shot you. Blurting out a bold, "Sorry Florrie!" then giggling, because it rhymed.

"That's better. Now where were we? Ah, yes, we were going to finish your deliveries, then you were going to show me which door is next to the doctor's house. That'll be where Mrs Tweeny lives and that's where my room is going to be for a while."

Gertie knew Mrs Tweeny very well. The Scamps hadn't needed to think of a codename for her. 'Tweeny' would do nicely, no one would guess that. She was the doctor's housekeeper. Dr Hastings didn't wear a uniform, but he was a fellow of standing in the village, so Gertie and the other Scamps decided it might be disrespectful to give him a codename. "We thought 'Doc' would do. That doesn't tell anyone listening too much does it?"

Florrie thought not, as they went from one door to the next with the butcher's deliveries. As they made steady progress Gertie was happy to explain to the young nurse how the Scamps had figured out the codenaming system soon after Walker had come into the village.

"He's city-quick and wasn't used to calling things what they are."

Florrie got a bit worried at that point. She also came from a large town, not quite a city, but large enough to perhaps struggle with some of the country names. "I think we all work for the War Effort now," she offered.

"Then if we get caught it's got to be name, rank and number and nothing else," Gertie agreed solemnly. He knew that much. Gertie was the butcher's delivery boy, maybe that counted as 'rank'. As for the 'number' part, that probably meant their house numbers, except they didn't have many of those in the village, either.

Al and Maze lived at the cabinet maker's. Everyone knew where it was and it hadn't had a number on the door for years. Walker came from his parent's house in the city, so if anyone went looking for him there, they'd be out of luck. As for Gertie, he lived in his own attic and they weren't going to get that out of him!

By then, Gertie had brought Florrie and the butcher's bicycle to the doctor's house.

"Mrs Tweeny'll likely be in there. She's only home after she's made sure the doctor's got himself sorted."

Florrie would have rather preferred to continue walking with the entertaining and informative young fellow, but she had also guessed she wouldn't be the only new arrival that morning. If she was going to get a half-decent bed, she'd better not waste any more time chatting.

"If I see you later, once I've got settled in, will you tell me more about the village? Nothing too sensitive, of course, but as a nurse I ought to know. So I can help, don't you think?"

Gertie considered this and decided, as a nurse she ought to. Being in uniform, anyone seeing her would expect her to know what she was doing. If he could help her with that then he ought to. All part of the Effort.

Florrie soon discovered Mrs Tweeny didn't *do* answering doors. Florrie knocked on both the doctor's and the house next door. That was when one of the upstairs windows flew open and a shout came down.

"Let yourself in. She's next door and she doesn't do doors!" One of the other new nurses had got there before her.

"Bother!" Florrie grabbed her bag and marched in, not missing the list of rules posted squarely just inside the door.

According to Pru, the earlier arrival, "She doesn't *do* the doctor's books, nor his telephone neither. Mrs Tweeny keeps the doctor's house presentable, and she intends to keep us all in similar order!" Pru sounded rather proper, but at least she kept her unpacking to her side of the room.

"Mind if I share with you? I don't really want that small room on my own."

There were three bedrooms in Mrs Tweeny's house. Pru and Florrie would share the largest bedroom, there was a small bedroom for the third girl to have, when she arrived, and Mrs Tweeny kept the middle bedroom. Pru had already discovered that there would be breakfast. If they had time to wait for Mrs Tweeny to get it ready for them before they needed to get over to the hospital to start their shift. There was supper for them too, if they got back in time.

"Mrs Tweeny doesn't like to leave any food out in the kitchen overnight and she doesn't like anyone going in to help themselves."

"Maybe we'd have better luck staying up at the hospital and having our meals there, before coming back after our shift?" Florrie wondered.

"I think we'll have to wait and find out. At least I brought some sandwiches with me. How about you?"

Florrie hadn't. Pru didn't mind sharing, which was nice of her. Whilst Florrie told her about the earlier incident, she couldn't quite work out why the lad had introduced himself as 'Gert'. She was sure the schoolteacher had called him 'Gertie'. There was something about that boy that rather suited the name.

Florrie had also taken an immediate liking to the schoolteacher. "Local, seems very capable," she told her colleague confidently. "Just the sort you'd like as a schoolteacher. Her name's Aggy. They do have some strange names in this village."

By the time Mrs Tweeny returned to check in on her girls, there were two of the three she had been expecting. At least the pair that had arrived seemed duly settled in and presentable. "Supper will be at seven o'clock. I shall keep it for one hour, but after that it won't be there. If you're not back before nine o'clock I lock the doors. Is that understood?"

"Yes, Mrs Tweeny," Florrie and Pru replied in unison.

"What if we have to stay behind because of emergencies?" Pru asked, being practically minded as ever.

"Then you will let me know beforehand," Mrs Tweeny

informed them briskly.

"I shan't keep your supper any later. It'll be spoilt by then and I don't waste food, and I don't leave my doors unlocked after nine o'clock. If you're working past nine o'clock then I shan't expect the hospital to allow you to be out on your own. They'll put you up overnight in one of the spare beds with the senior nurses. Behave yourselves and I'll have breakfast ready for you. If you're back in time."

"Yes, Mrs Tweeny." The girls responded as one, which seemed to satisfy Mrs Tweeny's requirements.

"This is going to be an interesting summer, isn't it?" Florrie wondered across to her colleague.

Pru grinned, "Oh, I do hope so!"

CHAPTER 2

Getting Their Bearings

WALKER HAD GOT HIMSELF A bucket.

"Where'd you get that from?" Gertie was curious but hadn't meant to startle his friend. He'd been walking his bicycle, looking for the next errand to arrive.

"I got issued it!" Walker informed him proudly. "They said at school, 'cos I'm not from around here, I could collect the pig food from the houses, then I'd be able to find my way better. I think they forgot I already help Al with the newspapers."

"Should I tell 'em?" Gertie teased him. Walker didn't mind. He liked the way Gertie teased; it wasn't like the bullies or those at school that didn't like him just because he wasn't local.

"Not if you want to come along with me," Walker challenged him boldly. Gertie was twice his age, but Walker had all the confidence. Gertie was waiting for an invitation and that sounded close enough.

"Hang on then, do you know where the pigs are?" Gertie was betting Walker didn't.

"No," Walker admitted. He'd actually been hoping Al had finished taking his little sister home from school and would be able to catch him up.

Gertie looked around to make sure no one was listening. "One of the back sheds, out beyond Jeepers' Yard. No one's meant to know about 'em."

"Then how does the whole school know?" Walker reasoned. "It's a pig-bucket. Doesn't take much working out!" He might be an evacuee, but he was a sensible lad and bright for his age.

"We can't put that bucket in the butcher's basket, so how are you meant to be taking it all the way over to the pigs?" Gertie might not be as quick as Walker, not city-quick, but he was village-smart. It was a long walk to the Out-Back sheds.

"We could borrow Maze's old pram. She won't mind," Walker suggested.

The pig-bucket was 'priority', they agreed. That meant the errand was definitely War Effort, and that meant it wouldn't matter if Maze minded or not, but she wasn't there and nor was her pram. They needed to keep the pigs healthy; the village was depending on them.

Walker nodded. "I'll fetch Al. You'll wait for us, Gertie, and look after the bucket?"

"Of course I will," Gertie grinned.

Aggy had briefly attempted to insist on calling Gertie 'Gerald' whilst he'd been in her classroom. She'd noticed the lanky lad mostly because he was getting picked on. His name had been perilously close to getting shortened to 'Gerry' and that wasn't a good name to have ringing about your ears these days. Thanks to Maze's suggestion, Gert had stuck soon after and Gertie seemed to come naturally after that.

"GERTIE!" The voice came through his thoughts like a hot knife through butter.

"What ya doing?" The hot knife turned into daisies opening in the sunshine, and the butter was melting.

"Hey, Rusty!" Gertie spun round, almost forgetting he was still holding the bicycle.

The truck stopped and she leaned out the window. "Finished for the day, have ya?"

Gertie sighed happily. "Almost. Gotta help the little'uns with the pig-bucket. They don't know where to go."

"Ah, bless 'em! That's a bit of a way for them. You'll see they get back safe?"

"Sure, Rusty," Gertie smiled. It was easy to smile at Rusty. She was a local lass and as gentle and as kind-hearted as those freckles of hers supposed. She could have gone on up to school in town, but she'd stayed with her dad after her mum died to look after him, the farmhouse and her grandfather.

Today she was in one of Jeeper's trucks. Rusty always drove her dad's third truck, he was all right, just a bit loud.

Bless her, poor Rusty had her hands full. She was just about all that was keeping that farmhouse from falling down around their ears. Whilst her dad, Jeepers, did his dealing out front in the Yard, and her grandfather, Old Spot, did his pottering around back in the garden.

Old Spot needed to have someone to talk with and Jeepers wasn't interested. Gertie went over there sometimes, to help Old Spot with his shed. Rusty's grandfather liked his garden, his roses and his strawberries; he just didn't like his son Jeepers so much! He liked his radio, too, although Gertie was never quite sure what Old Spot actually heard, they always seemed to get on well enough together.

Rusty hadn't noticed when it had begun, but knew Gertie had noticed it, too. It hadn't been anything definite, nothing she could put her finger on and say 'then', only looking back she and Gertie had noticed Old Spot sounding a little odder.

As far as Jeepers was concerned, anything to do with the

farmhouse and the back garden was down to Rusty, Old Spot included.

Rusty's grandfather was well aware he was muddling along, but wasn't everyone? There was a war on, and if it exasperated Jeepers, then all the better. Jeepers exasperated him often enough!

Old Spot liked his granddaughter. Rusty never forgot to bring him back a newspaper and always had time to chat with him. If she was going out in her truck, sometimes he even went along with her. He liked that. Not too often though, it was getting a bit hectic out there.

Anyway, Old Spot had plenty to be getting on with, his strawberries were almost ready. It was nearly strawberry-picking days. He'd done it every summer all his life. He'd go into his garden every day just to watch them growing, to remind himself they still grew there. Rusty had inherited her freckles from him, but Old Spot's nickname hadn't come from his freckles.

Years before, when Old Spot himself had been younger than Maze was now, when he was helping to grow the strawberries then, it was his duty to go out and 'spot' any with slugs lurking. He'd had the quickest picking fingers in those days, small and nimble for plucking those slugs off from the strawberry plants. His name had changed over the years, but 'Spot' had stuck. He'd been Old Spot for as long as Rusty could remember; 'Odd' Spot had only begun recently.

"You're not going to be taking the pig-bucket on those handlebars, are you?" Rusty queried.

Gertie assured her he wasn't. "Just taking the bicycle back to Brisket. Al and Walker will be back anytime. Of course, it would be a *lot* easier if you gave us a lift. Going that way?"

Rusty grinned. It didn't matter. It wasn't that far in the

truck and it wouldn't make much difference to her load, at least she'd be sure they all got back home before blackout.

Rusty liked driving the truck and everything needed to be moved these days; the farmers needed to supply the towns and cities even more since the ships were needed for more important things and the farmers needed their tractors. Rusty could have driven a tractor, but she liked the roads better. It also meant she could keep an eye on Jeepers and Old Spot and, for that matter, Gertie too. Someone had to!

"Jeepers will expect me when he sees me. Come on, jump in the back. He never gives the third truck any of the urgent errands. If I let you in the cab then the rest of your crew'll want to jump in and I'm not having that pig-bucket up here with me."

That sounded reasonable. Gertie lifted the bicycle up into the back of the truck. Rusty shook her head but didn't ask him to explain. As Gertie began clambering in the rest of the Salvage Scamps arrived, including Maze with her pram.

"Just in case we need it!" Al told them all, in answer to the unasked question.

The Out-Back Farm wasn't the easiest of places to get to for good reason and it wasn't really a farm either. That was where the pigs were kept. Most of the village knew about the pigs, but when it came to knowing the whereabouts of those sheds of the Out-Back Farm? Ah, then you needed to be in the know!

The Out-Back Farm belonged to Mr Tor, and he didn't like getting unexpected visitors, even when they had come to feed his pigs. There were farm paths and a few rutted lanes between the various barns and yards, but it was a rather loose arrangement, quite remote, between Jeepers' Yard and Tuckly's Far Fields Farm. Even the two farm-bullies who worked for Tuckly didn't bother Mr Tor.

Mr Tor was of obscure parentage, historically linked to the village. That much Gertie knew. He came into the village only occasionally, seldom even bothering to attend market day and even Ol' Creak was a bit nervous when Mr Tor was in his shop. That was telling.

Al, Walker and Maze were too young to know any of this. They were just enjoying the ride in Rusty's truck, keeping the bucket steady between them and looking to see what else Rusty kept back there.

The children knew what pigs were like. Pigs were muddy and grew fat and made bacon and sausages. Walker might be a bit confused on that part but Al was putting him right on a few of the details en route. Both boys checked for verification to Gertie.

"True. Mr Tor does all the work that don't fit on Brisket's shop block."

Rusty wasn't any more comfortable with Mr Tor than Ol' Creak was but Gertie seemed completely immune to his intimidating stare, so if the children were going to feed the pigs, best she took them and Gertie came too.

Mr Tor was dark in mood and complexion, and although he wasn't especially tall, he gave that impression from the way he loomed, with broad shoulders, heavily muscled arms and no neck. He never wore a jacket, only a leather waistcoat over his shirt, and moleskin trousers and boots. He might have looked quite smart if it wasn't for his face. It was like his waistcoat, tanned and weathered. It was impossible to tell Mr Tor's age, unless he had you in his grasp. Then you'd have thought him in his twenties from the strength of his grip.

Mr Tor never seemed to run, but you wouldn't want him chasing you. He could move fast and hit faster. Rusty hadn't seen it for herself, but her father had told of the night a while back when someone disagreed with a deal they were doing, Jeepers had wanted to walk away, but the other guy hadn't, and Mr Tor didn't argue. He never argued, he just 'settled it'. As far as Rusty could tell, the other guy never did get all the feeling back in a couple of those fingers.

Mr Tor liked his pigs, his guns and rabbits and pies. He didn't like people and he wasn't especially fond of trucks, either.

"OY!" he bellowed from the gate, as Rusty almost missed the turn.

Rusty slammed on the brakes, throwing Maze and Walker forward. Gertie was ready and grabbed Al just in time to stop him and the bucket following Walker in the tumble across the bed of the truck.

"Oy yourself!" Gertie called out. He could feel Rusty's face going red all the way back from the cab. He could feel the heat of her freckles prickling in nervousness. Rusty shouldn't be nervous, not with Gertie about.

Mr Tor peered into the back of the truck, ignoring Rusty completely, which gave her a moment to compose herself. "Pigs?" he checked.

"Pigs!" Gertie told him. "You want it here or over to them? We'll have the bucket back and have you got anything that needs taking whilst we're at it?"

Gertie knew the right questions to ask. Mr Tor didn't like going into the village if he didn't have to.

"New kid?" Mr Tor looked sideways at Walker, who was still trying to rub the bruises away for Maze, who was tearing up.

Walker was trying to hush her to 'keep it quiet'. "If you show him you're scared, he'll only growl at you. You remember the lion."

"What?" Mr Tor duly growled.

Walker wasn't going to be growled at and he certainly wasn't prepared to let this bloke scare little Maze. "The lion with the thorn. He growled a lot too but he just needed someone to take the thorn out from his foot, that's all. You got a thorn bugging you, Mister?"

Mr Tor liked a bit of spark. The new kid was alright. Not from around this way obviously, but he seemed to have the right instincts, protecting Maze.

"You are?" Mr Tor half looked at the new kid and half at the bucket.

"Walker. Pig-feeding duty. We were going to bring it in the pram, but Gertie said it was too far. So, we put the bicycle in the back and came this way."

That took a moment to digest. Mr Tor didn't bother. "Walker, hey?"

"Pig-feeding duty. We're in the right place, ain't we?" Walker queried.

"Who wants to know?" Mr Tor wasn't convinced. He didn't like strangers, no matter what their size.

"Them that's waiting to feed your pigs!" Gertie suggested fearlessly before adding, "And whilst we're doing that, d'ya wanna get ready whatever we need to be takin' back with us? Can't be leaving the truck idle for too long, there's a war on!"

Rusty had climbed down to check on the state of Maze and Walker. Both were OK. As she lifted Maze out from the back of the truck, Gertie was already following Mr Tor to the pigs, Walker had the bucket and Al was keeping up.

"We'll leave the pram?" Rusty suggested. Maze nodded and blew her nose. "Probably safer."

Walker hadn't seen pigs before and was curious. He knew what horses smelt like, since he'd spent time round past the village stables playing football. The local farmers didn't like using the fields that way, too soft and lumpy, but they were OK for the horses to do their rough grazing. Not so easy to score goals when the ball bounced between ruts and humps, but he'd learnt what stables smelt like over there. Walker liked Gertie, bit lanky and smelly, but brave.

Walker had thought he knew what to expect from a pig-yard, something like a horse-yard only a bit smaller and probably muddier, but he wasn't prepared for Mr Tor's pig-yard. It was massive and seemed to come out of nowhere. There were high dense hedges all around the place, with sharp-sprigged, raggedy trees that grew from every angle.

The pigs were louder than the horses and they stank worse that Gertie's feet, but they looked sort of happy about it.

Mr Tor let the boys go in by themselves. There was a large barn on one side and two smaller barns ahead of them and to the other side, whilst the trees and hedges combined to form a natural barrier beyond them. Down between the sheds were further obstacles, felled timbers and pieces of machinery with a few old blankets thrown over them. Only the larger of the three barns had doors and they were firmly shut.

The pigs had the run of both the smaller barns. Walker wasn't sure what to do from this point. He had the bucket and there were the pigs, what was he meant to do?

Gertie whispered, "Rattle the bucket."

"Do what?" Walker checked.

Al hissed, "You rattle the bucket."

Walker looked down into the bucket, it was all sloppy. That wasn't going to rattle. "What?"

Al realised the problem. "Slap it with your hand. They

need to know the bucket is for them or they'll charge at you. You need to give them a chance to know you're going to feed them, not butcher them. They'll be happier that way."

Walker couldn't disagree with that argument, he'd be a lot happier knowing that, too! He assumed when it was time for Mr Tor to come in and butcher the pigs he did it quiet-like, not rattling or slapping a bucket, that made sense.

Gertie came over leaving Mr Tor with Rusty and Maze, safely on the path side of the gate. "Go on, it's your job. We're just observers," He reminded Walker, as Al took a step back.

"You mean I need to get nearer than *this?*" Walker was looking down at his boots. This wasn't like the stables at all, this was like the bottom of the football field after it flooded, only this smelt worse. He kept a hold of the bucket and called out, not very loudly, admittedly. One of the pigs looked in his direction, which unnerved Walker, but he wasn't going to let them know that and started slapping the side of the bucket like Al had told him.

"Feeding time. Come on. Grub up."

Al stepped up beside him again, as more of the pigs started showing an interest.

"Put it in the trough!" Gertie called out helpfully.

"Right-ho!" Walker took the instruction and started looking for something, anything, that might remotely look like a receptacle for pig food. "This?" he checked, moving to start tipping the contents into the container.

"Don't you dare!" Mr Tor growled over the gate. "That's my guttin' bucket. I leave it there so's they gets used to it. Don't want to startle 'em with it."

Walker froze, holding the bucket close by his hip, still searching. All he could see were pigs with snouts and trotters and massive backsides that all seemed to be wanting to get into his bucket.

Al found the trough, but it was too far. Between Walker's bucket and the feeding trough were all the pigs. Both boys seemed stuck at opposite ends of the yard, one being muscled into a corner with the bucket and ravenous pigs, the other over at the far end, desperately gesturing for Walker to get over to him.

"DROP IT!" Gertie shouted.

"Drop the bucket! If you keep a hold of it they'll have you over," He shouted, already starting towards him.

Al tried to help, wading through the mud back to Walker, with Gertie approaching from the gate angle.

"Come on, drop the bucket and do a runner. We'll come back for it when they've finished."

Walker had heard enough and dropped the bucket. Taking hold of Gertie's hand reaching over to him, and was instantly yanked to one side, just as the pigs scrummed into the spillage.

Rusty caught the expression on Mr Tor's face, he seemed surprised by Gertie's strength. She'd seen it before. The village tended to underestimate Gertie. She didn't.

Mr Tor muttered something about "to the victor the spoils." Then turned to Rusty, "You making tea?"

"You got any?" she asked him straight back.

He thumbed over to the farmhouse. "Kitchen's there. Help yourself. We'll load up the truck and be over when we're done."

Rusty didn't ask what he was loading. Mr Tor knew who she was and that she'd be heading back to Jeepers' Yard as soon as she'd taken Gertie and the children back into the village. That was good enough for him.

He stepped aside to let Rusty and Maze get on with it,

whilst he went over to open the larger of the barns, all the while completely ignoring the pigs, the bucket and the three boys trying to retrieve it.

"When you're done with that, get yourselves over here. Make yourselves useful."

Walker managed to grab the bucket, whilst Al kept hold of his belt. Gertie very sensibly had taken a step towards the broom and had begun sweeping the yard clear of pigs and spill, away from the doors to the barn, into which Mr Tor had just disappeared. Gertie knew how to sweep a yard. He'd learnt from experience, if you want a job then start working!

There was a grunt and an oath from the large barn, before Mr Tor emerged with the first piece for loading. It looked like a part of an engine.

"Tractor?" Rusty heard Walker ask excitedly.

Mr Tor snarled in disdain. "Motorbike."

That made sense. Even Rusty knew Mr Tor had a reputation for motorbikes. "Yours?" she called over, immediately wishing she hadn't been so presumptive. The look on Mr Tor's face was thunder.

"Recovery job," he explained.

Rusty and Maze left the boys to it after that and headed for Mr Tor's kitchen. Walking always helped Rusty think, she didn't like thinking too far forward, unwise in war-time. For the moment she was trying to remember if the summer before had been anywhere near as challenging as this one? Her grandfather had seemed a little more reasonable then, but so too had Jeepers. Thank goodness for Gertie, he always managed to cheer her up.

Farming didn't really change, Rusty decided, as she looked around Mr Tor's kitchen with Maze. War or no war, a farmer's kitchen looked pretty much the same as it had always done.

Mr Tor's kitchen wasn't lacking in food. There was tea in the caddy and water in the kettle. There was bread on the board and a knife beside it. No butter, but some cheese and apples. That would do.

"Can you find me a jar of pickle in the larder?" she called cheerfully over to little Maze. Maze had sat herself down at the kitchen table. The five-year-old wasn't used to being given something to do in the kitchen all by herself. She was too small for her mother's cupboards and too young for the stove, and she could only wash up when she stood on the chair at the sink. Searching for a jar of pickle in the pig-farmer's larder was something she'd never tried before. She felt very brave.

It wasn't long before they could hear Al calling for his little sister. Maze called back from the larder. It sounded loud for such a small voice. Gertie must have been ahead of the boys and responded, "Is tea ready yet?"

Mr Tor didn't say anything but when he filled the doorway to the kitchen it startled Rusty. She almost missed pouring the tea from the pot.

"Don't stand there! Come and slice the bread up and you'd best be slicing the cheese too, or you'll have some very unfair sharing between them."

It was a timely warning from Rusty and Mr Tor could see the wisdom of it. He thumbed over to the larder with a question between his brows. Rusty looked over that way as she handed him his mug.

"She's looking for the pickle."

"Second shelf up," he directed Maze, who giggled in reply.

"The labels are all funny," she informed them. No wonder she'd missed it first time.

"Funny labels? What, like a cartoon?" Gertie asked, taking

his mug from Rusty as he counted the apples on the table. "One each, OK?"

Mr Tor checked. No, there weren't enough for that. He had more apples but wasn't going to get them.

"You'll have to share," he decided.

"No need. Always bring a spare with me," Gertie informed him, producing one from his pocket. Mr Tor knew very well Gertie hadn't had that apple in his pocket when he'd been feeding the pigs. If he had, they'd have gone for him too. Damn! Gertie had found the apples he stored in those trays in one corner of that large barn, smart lad.

"Deal?" Gertie checked, taking over the bread slicing.

Mr Tor nodded and got on with the cheese. "Done!"

"What's funny?" Al asked, ahead of Walker.

"Funny? What is?" Walker echoed the query bringing the bucket in with him.

"Leave that outside, we're eating," Rusty reminded the pair of them.

"We are? What's funny about eating?" Walker challenged them.

Maze came out with the jar. "This is, look. The label's funny."

Rusty took the offered jar and twisted the top to take a sniff. It was pungent, but definitely pickle. Pickled *what* was not so clear. She returned the lid and tilted the jar to read the label.

Passing it over to Mr Tor at arm's length she asked, "What is it?"

"Danish!" he informed them and if they didn't like that there wasn't anything else.

Maze decided she'd rather just have the cheese and apple

on their own, with the bread.

"Any butter?" Al asked, on her behalf.

Walker scoffed, "You've gotta be joking!"

Mr Tor didn't reply, so Al took Walker's word for it and handed the piece of bread to his little sister. Looking over to Rusty, "Do you know when Old Spot's strawberry jam'll be ready?"

Gertie knew all about Old Spot's strawberries. Everyone knew about them, except Walker. Al wasn't even sure if Walker knew where strawberries came from.

Gertie knew the only thing Mr Tor liked less than visitors was when visitors outstayed their welcome. They'd finished the tea in their mugs.

"We'll take the sandwiches with us and get started," he suggested.

Mr Tor grunted, glad to see one of them had the instinct to recognise they were keeping him from his work.

"Yes, time to go. Jeepers is expecting the load?" Rusty checked, with a glance to Mr Tor, before shepherding the children out of the kitchen and over to the waiting truck.

"Jeepers'll know what to do with it," was near enough.

Mr Tor didn't follow them out.

The boys returned to the back of the truck with the bucket, while Rusty let Maze climb up beside her in the cab. She hadn't gone into the pig's yard.

High summer seemed to unravel ahead of them. The paths and lanes and hedges and gates stood where they had always been. They didn't change their ways. Tuckly's sugar beet over in the Far Fields would remain until winter. It would be needing the frosts before harvest. Not Old Spot's strawberries though; such fragile fruits needed more gentle handling. Rusty found herself wondering about the children helping Old Spot with his strawberry picking.

"I know he'll want to send a basket of strawberries over to the House; he always does. I'm going to try and take him over in the next day or so." The children were already beaming at the prospect. "You can come if you're ready in time," Rusty offered them, as she turned back into the village.

The 'House' Rusty was referring to was the RAF hospital, but everyone except Walker knew where she was talking about. Rusty couldn't be sure which day it would be but guessed she'd find the Scamps when Old Spot was ready.

As Rusty saw the children and Gertie on their way, she saw Aggy struggling to shut the school doors with an armful of books. "I hope those aren't for salvage."

Aggy looked shocked at the thought. "Gracious, no! Saving them, more like it! If I leave too many books on the shelves, the children get ideas into their heads. I have to keep them locked away in the cupboards. We've had one salvage raid already this month."

Rusty had heard all about how important the salvage was from Maze. Even the youngsters knew the 'phoney war' of last year was over. This was it, the *real* war now!

It sounded ominous, and yet it was summer in the village, and they could hear the farmers getting busier in their fields and the children laughing. The women were grumbling about queuing and the men shouting about something not being where it had been the day before. Nothing had changed and yet *everything* had.

Just a few years ago Aggy and Rusty had been girls. They could have gone to grammar school in town. They could have learnt so much more. Now all they knew was here. They weren't unhappy, they had each chosen their own course, and now it was up to them to make the best of it.

They could both recall that Sunday when they'd been called into church to listen to the vicar's radio. Even those that had their own radios had come to church that day, not wishing to hear the announcement on their own, even those who didn't usually come to church. It had been a lovely summer's day. They'd been warned what to expect. 'Britain is at war.'

Most of the older village residents sat sedately in the church pews and had listened in silence to the radio placed on the chair in front of the altar. Then, when it was done, they'd stood up, straightened their backs, lifted their heads and squared their shoulders as best they were able.

"We've been here before. We know what to do and we're ready to get it done." Some of the younger women had wept quietly and some of the children had got scared, but their older brothers soon put them straight.

"We'll sort it out, you wait. We'll get over there, get stuck in and soon have it all sorted!" So many of the young men had already gone but more would be needed before this war was over. The local reservists went first and more had been eager to beat the call-up, they wanted to enlist properly, not wait to get their papers.

Those in the village old enough to know what it had been like the first time had prayed the others would never find out. But now it was done, there was no going back. They were all in it and everyone, young and old, would need to be doing their bit towards the War Effort. To fight for King and Country.

The issuing of the identity cards had been quite an event. Perhaps that had been when Rusty had first felt really grown up, old enough to be told she had to have her own identity card, not just Jeepers' daughter, not just Old Spot's granddaughter.

Her mother would have known where her birth certificate was but they couldn't find anything like that these days. She'd just written down 'Rusty' on the form and that's what it had on her card. That was her name, she'd decided that. If she was old enough to look after the farmhouse and Old Spot and drive third truck for Jeepers, then she was old enough to decide what name she wanted on her own identity card.

Then had come the petrol rationing. Jeepers hadn't been happy about that at all. He was in the surplus and hoarding business, so that wasn't convenient for him. Rusty had kept herself out of the way the week after that. She almost went to stay with Aggy for a few days but couldn't leave Old Spot. She'd managed to persuade him to 'have a go' at his back shed, and Gertie had helped.

It had been a week or so before the dust had settled in Jeepers' Yard, but he'd got it sorted. No one asked how he'd managed that but the arrangement kept his trucks fuelled and busy. He kept the paperwork in his office, a small caravan out in the Yard, seldom coming into the farmhouse anymore except to sleep or eat or to fetch one of his boxes down from upstairs.

There'd been another announcement about the start of food rationing earlier in the spring, again, it hadn't been news to the village residents. They'd seen that coming, too. They'd always kept their stores well stocked, they'd been doing it since before the Great War, it just came natural to a village.

This was the first summer harvest since the rationing had begun and everyone was ready for it. Everything would be gathered-in, nothing would be wasted. No change there then. Just the same as it had always been!

Chamberlain had resigned. Winston Churchill was Prime Minister. That would make a difference, Chamberlain had been anything for peace, Churchill was all for taking action.

War.

"I'm just glad they've decided to get on with it!" Old Spot had told Rusty earlier, when she'd brought the newspaper out to him in the back garden.

It sounded like he was ready for an argument, but she knew how to distract him. "It's looking lovely out here." She admired his handiwork with the strawberries on the one side of his garden, down to the sheds, with his yellow roses on the other side, down to where the vegetables started until the rhubarb and the compost heap took over at the bottom. Old Spot didn't need much but he liked to know he'd got everything he needed, he missed his working yard, but his 'ruddy son' had known better!

Rusty's grandfather had still been out in the back garden when she'd returned from Gertie's pig-bucket 'run', Old Spot didn't usually work that late in the day, but no one had come out to remind him to come in for tea.

Jeepers didn't keep a schedule. If anyone asked, he'd say he'd get there when he got there, unless it was a 'sensitive' pick-up. Then he'd send over the 'first truck' which was usually him. If it was that sensitive, it meant there was more to it, some dealing to be done. Jeepers' third truck was rarely important but Rusty was reliable for that, she'd been late coming back and he'd been considering sending her out again. Jeepers had been getting ready to be annoyed, until Rusty showed him the motorbike 'spares', Jeepers hadn't been expecting them and it was always useful to do Mr Tor a favour.

"About ruddy time," was the nearest to a thank you she got from her father. That was good enough. He'd be happy with that for the next hour or so, time enough for her to get something on the table for them to eat and make sure Old Spot got himself cleaned up. The radio sounds were soothing for exhausted heads too tired to think of anything else.

Rusty's grandfather was yelling over to her. He wasn't going to start making a pot of tea; she always told him off when he did that. "And don't forget you're meant to be taking me over to the House with my strawberry baskets. I haven't forgotten."

Rusty knew she'd have a few more days yet before enough of his strawberries would be ready, if Old Spot was going to be taking them over to the RAF hospital, then he'd need enough ripe and ready to fill those baskets. It was an easy promise for her to make.

"You give me a day's warning and I'll make sure there's room on the truck for them *and* you," she teased him. She knew her grandfather liked riding in the back of the truck, country lanes and sunshine, watching the fields go by. Old Spot would look forward to that.

"I'll need a couple of days to get my baskets ready," he warned her, "so don't go rushing me. Nothing good came of rushing strawberries!"

Rusty sat with her grandfather with their mugs of tea, waiting for the sound of Jeepers' slamming shed doors. There was slamming, then his thumping boots on the hallway stones, then thudding up the stairs, a bit of scraping and harrumphing, and then some stomping back down again.

He always thudded then stomped. Old Spot was wise and knew his son. Jeepers just wanted to be like Mr Tor, to have that sort of a reputation, that was something to aspire to. The problem was Mr Tor genuinely didn't want anything to do with anyone whereas Jeepers actually *needed* to be able to 'do business' and that needed him to be at least approachable.

"Could you be a little less lead-footed about coming down those stairs? One of these days they're just going to give up and fall down," Rusty told her father as she handed him the mug of tea.

"That would suit me just fine!" Jeepers grinned, winding up his father. "This old farmhouse takes up far too much space for my liking. I could double the size of my Yard without it." Old Spot was starting to go red in the face. Jeepers laughed. "Calm down. Why are you getting so hot under the collar? It's not like you even go upstairs anymore."

"Good thing I don't. Don't know what you've got up there. Don't want to know, neither," Old Spot told him roundly.

"That's good, because I don't want to tell you." Jeepers turned back to his daughter. "Your truck'll be loaded for you first thing tomorrow. I'm waiting for a pick-up that way, but nothing definite." He didn't want to go into details. That wasn't the way Jeepers worked.

Rusty simply handed him the breadknife, whilst she took charge of the butter. Jeepers turned to his father again.

"Got any strawberry jam ready?" That was guaranteed to send Old Spot into a fury of splutters.

"Never going to happen! Not in this house!" he shouted, reminding Jeepers and Rusty his strawberries were the best in the village. "They're for eatin' proper, fresh and whole, cream-scone-quality they are, fit for the finest sponges," he informed them proudly. Then he grimaced at Jeepers. "All that delicious sunshine stewed down with sugar. Phah! We all got to do our 'bit' and them strawberries is mine!" Old Spot informed them.

Jeepers wasn't impressed. "What? We're going to win the war with strawberries? Come on, Grumps, you know better than that. It's going to be boots and bullets that win this one, just like the last one. You told me that yourself!" Jeepers always called his father 'Grumps' when he wanted to annoy the old man, which was more often than not. Rusty's grandfather much preferred Old Spot. It was a term of endearment as far as he was concerned: 'Almost respectful,' he'd told her.

Old Spot liked 'that Churchill fellow'. "Knows what he's talking about, he does. Been around a bit and not afraid of a fight neither!" he'd told his son and granddaughter by way of a response. "Made a few mistakes early on, but you gotta do that to learn how to do it right."

Jeepers didn't have time to talk speeches; he had work to be getting on with. Taking his share of the bread and butter and his refilled mug of tea, he walloped his boots down on the kitchen tiles, making his grandfather start.

"See, told ya! Boots'll do the business, every time."

"So, what's Mr Churchill been saying then?" Rusty ignored her father and turned back to Old Spot, putting the supper plate down in front of him.

"He's been talking about Our Lads over in France, shouldn't be over there, they're not doing well. He's talking about blood and sweat? Aye, he's right enough about that, bound to be. Just as surely as there's tears and toil over here."

"Is he going to send them some help, d'you think?" Rusty wondered, as she sat down beside her grandfather.

"He ruddy well better or I'll have something to say to 'im!"

They spoke of the war and their boys-over-there, but before the tea was cold in the pot they were back onto Old Spot's strawberries. Everyone liked his strawberries. He never picked them until they were ready and never allowed any to remain that weren't fit for picking.

Rusty had promised she'd be taking him over to the House soon, he'd need to be inspecting them. "Got to get my best ready," he reminded her happily.

She'd told him all about the village Salvage Scamps by then.

"Good luck to 'em." He agreed with her, before returning to an earlier subject. "Gardens are like battles. No foolish haste, just a clear intention and plenty of resolve to get it done."

Old Spot didn't like talking about winter, not until after summer, and it was summer for as long as there were strawberries growing.

"We need this summer," he told her steadily. "We need it to get our boys back over from France. They're too far out. There's going to be a lot of salvaging this summer. Shouldn't need to remind you of that!"

Rusty knew he'd make sense of it all. "A salvaged summer, hey?" she asked him.

"Oh yes! We're good at that, you know." Old Spot got to his feet and walked over to the window, looking out across the fenland fields beyond his back garden, speaking as much to himself as to his granddaughter.

"Getting ourselves stuck? We're an island. It happens more often than you'd think. Plays to our strengths, you see. Sleeves up, head down, and muddle-on through!

CHAPTER 3

Small Mercies

THEY'D ALL HEARD THE NEWS, they'd all known something had to happen about France, but they hadn't expected that!

Mrs Tweeny had let the new girls into her sitting room to listen to the radio. They'd sat in stunned silence, to begin with. They'd sent so many men over there. It had begun so well. Losing ground? They couldn't be? Then Churchill's voice was telling them:

"We shall go on to the end ... we shall fight on the seas and oceans, we shall fight with growing confidence and growing strength in the air, we shall defend our island, whatever the cost may be. We shall fight on the beaches, we shall fight on the landing grounds, we shall fight in the fields and in the streets, we shall fight in the hills; and we shall never surrender ..."

"Then that's what we're going to do," Florrie declared, impulsively standing up in the middle of the room.

When Mrs Tweeny came into her sitting room she came to sit down and listen to her radio. She wasn't used to such outbursts but couldn't fault Florrie for her patriotism.

Pru had been the quickest amongst the three of the young nurses to get settled in at Mrs Tweeny's. She'd made a good impression, with her tidy manners and polished shoes. Florrie had managed to just about stay on Mrs Tweeny's good side, but neither of them were quick enough to stop Dotty putting her foot in it, even before she'd stepped over the threshold!

Dotty arrived late that first day; supper was already on the table. By the time Mrs Tweeny had supper on the table, she had been expecting there to be three young nurses, clean and present. Dotty wasn't.

She'd knocked on the front door just as Mrs Tweeny got herself sat down at the kitchen table. Florrie took the initiative and dashed out to wrench the front door open, out from the startled Dotty's hand.

"Come in, you're late. She's mad at you and don't mention the front door. She doesn't do doors!"

By the time both girls got back to the kitchen table, Dotty knew everyone's name.

That hadn't been the best of starts, but Mrs Tweeny had given her the benefit of the doubt and disregarded it. Ignoring Dotty's tardiness, instead addressing them all as one.

"You'll be needing breakfast tomorrow. It'll be on the table at seven in the morning. I do breakfast at 7 am and I do supper at 7 pm. I'm regular in my habits and I'll expect you to be likewise. Is that understood?"

"Yes, Mrs Tweeny."

All three young nurses were nervous. It was all very well to attend the lectures and practice amongst themselves, but they had their uniforms now. All they had to do was earn the respect they imagined those uniforms warranted!

Within those first couple of days their heads were spinning with instructions coming at them from all angles and then there was the exhaustion on top of that.

She would be inspecting the nurse's bedrooms at the end of the week, Mrs Tweeny had warned them, and expected them to be appropriately anxious. It seemed to have worked on Pru who had re-tidied her half of the bedroom for the third time in as many days, whilst Florrie had begun to make a little more effort with the state of her side. Dotty was in the small bedroom on her own and Mrs Tweeny couldn't even see the rug from the door for all her clutter. She had given Dotty a clear 'tut' of forewarning from the landing when she'd walked past. It had made Dotty look over to her and smile.

"Oh hey, Mrs Tweeny, just getting myself settled in."

Thank goodness Mrs Tweeny had pinned the bathroom times on the door. The girls were allowed to use it from 6 am to 7 am and from 8.30 pm to 9.30 pm. Baths were permitted on Wednesday evening only, unless by prior agreement with Mrs Tweeny. She had given them a basket and told them they were allowed to keep their washbags and towels in there. Anything else left in the bathroom would not be tolerated. Mrs Tweeny didn't like to have a cluttered bathroom. There was a washing line in her back garden. They could use the kitchen sink when she was not in the kitchen, and she didn't like to see any washing left out overnight. Apart from that she expected the three girls to make themselves useful.

Mrs Tweeny had reminded them they were 'in uniform now and will act accordingly'. She hadn't asked them about their first few days working up at the RAF hospital, wisely gauging they would be in no fit state to make sense of the place for at least a week.

As far as Florrie could tell, the hospital was a never-ending warren of great, heavy, wood-panelled doors that gave no indication whether they opened into a broom cupboard or another corridor of more great, heavy, wood-panelled doors. There were some rooms with exotic carpets and ornate ceilings, but most of the rooms had been stripped of all their pomp. There were other rooms higher up in the house, reached by stairways that twisted inextricably, that had low beams in the most unexpected of places. The main entrance was intimidating and the cupboards in the downstairs treatment rooms utterly confounding.

The one thing Florrie liked was the way the house gave the impression that for as many rooms as there were with beds and baths in, there were just as many with easy chairs and bookshelves. It was easy to see it had once been a very imposing house. It still stood grandly, with its windows gazing out across the grounds and its columns standing sentinel at the main entrance steps, and there were those carvings up at the eaves, haughtily looking down. Florrie was surprised how their presence felt reassuring, somehow reminding her the house had stood through worse times. She couldn't imagine *what*, but somehow she knew it had.

No matter who shouted what at her, or what they told her she should *already* be doing, it was the House itself that made her feel she was going to be useful. The grand old house had become an RAF hospital. It was a hospital, and she was a nurse. Florrie could already look back at some of her training days with a half-smile.

She'd thought nursing was all about nursing, but in the past week it seemed to be far more about walking and washing. Florrie could hear a grumble in her thoughts but shook it off. If it was going to be a matter of walking and washing to begin with, then so be it! She knew she could do more but would just have to do her best until someone else noticed that.

Florrie was glad to have had that time getting her bearings about the village with Gertie. That was about as much of the village as she'd got to know so far. She'd only managed to get over to the village shop and post office since then, where she'd met Aggy again, which had been very helpful. Florrie had got the impression that if she only ever got to know a couple of the locals, then Gertie and Aggy were excellent choices.

It had been Aggy who'd told the young nurses about the bus times. If they got up in time they could catch it, but that meant almost certainly missing Mrs Tweeny's breakfast schedule.

Mrs Tweeny's schedule was a little stricter than the bus driver's. They might be able to grab breakfast first and then run, or they could walk all the way. It wasn't as far as Florrie had first thought, by the time she began walking the distance regularly the second week.

It felt different walking along a rough grass verge than the pavements she'd been used to. It was a nice time of year to be walking, though, once she gave her thoughts the chance to appreciate it. When Florrie walked, apart from the way her shoes felt, she could almost imagine she was just going for a pleasant stroll beside a long, quiet road going into town, beside an ancient high stone wall, out from a charming little village. She'd managed to persuade Dotty to join her in the walk by then.

"It helps you get your head and feet connected before the shift." Florrie had actually been meaning to say, "the calm before the storm," but that sounded a bit melodramatic.

Pru didn't like walking so much. She preferred to miss Mrs Tweeny's breakfast and catch the bus. They would all manage to get to the gate about the same time. That morning Rusty had picked the walkers up going out of the village. Her truck was heading the same way.

"You're early, aren't you?"

"We're walking over to the hospital," Dotty explained unnecessarily.

"I'd guessed you might be," Rusty agreed obligingly. "I've got some timber to pick up for Jeepers, but I can drop you off at the gate. It's on my way."

"You're going into town?" Dotty asked, eager for any news. She was missing town, but could feel the charm of the village drawing her in. It was like there were only two paces to life in these parts: that slow, steady plod of the village or the hectic scurry of their shifts at the hospital. Town came somewhere in the middle, with a lot more colour and less barking of orders.

It wasn't far, only a few minutes the way Rusty drove her truck. They were at the bus-stop long before the bus got that far.

"How's it going?" Rusty asked, whilst they waited for Pru to catch up.

"How's it going?" Dotty repeated the question, before answering honestly. "I haven't got a clue! I thought I knew what we were getting ourselves into, but it's nothing like that. They give you books to study and lectures to listen to. I thought we'd had plenty of practice, but it feels like we were practising for something else entirely. We're not ready and I'm just waiting for them to notice!"

Florrie had to smile. That was *almost* the same thing she'd been thinking. It was rather comforting to know she wasn't the only one feeling that way. Maybe all the nurses had, when they'd started.

"There's just so much more to learn and no time to learn it. They just expect you to know what you're doing and get on with it. If you don't, then they start barking at you again," Florrie added.

"You mean the doctors bark at you?" Rusty asked.

"Oh no! The doctors don't talk to you at all! The doctors tell the senior nurses and it's them that bark at you. If you're too slow they shove you out of the way and do it themselves," Dotty confessed.

"You'll learn," Rusty reassured the young nurse, looking over to Florrie. "How about you? How are you getting on?"

"It's a bit unnerving," was the best Florrie could do on the spur-of-the-moment.

"Sounds like it," Rusty agreed, not for the first time thankful she drove a truck. She would have been happy to drive an ambulance and maybe she would one day, if the war went on for much longer.

The radio hadn't sounded good in recent weeks. She knew they couldn't give too much bad news, but sometimes there was no avoiding the truth!

"The Battle of France is over. The Battle of Britain is about to begin. The whole fury and might of the enemy must very soon be turned on us. Hitler knows that he will have to break us in this island or lose the war," Churchill had told them.

Rusty had been late getting back the day that had come over the radio. She remembered it particularly, because her grandfather was cross with her. Old Spot wasn't talking to her, because his strawberries were ready, and she'd promised to take him and them over to the House.

"I will, but the timbers Jeepers had got lined up fell through and he's been waiting for another delivery. The idea is that I take you and your baskets over with them. You wouldn't want me to take you over with only half a truckful, would you?" Old Spot hadn't answered her but had taken the mug of tea and newspaper she'd offered him.

That radio report had had quite an impact on the village residents. Rusty heard more about it the following morning.

"Now it's just us," Florrie had confirmed to Aggy, when

she'd next caught up with her outside the post office.

"Oh, that doesn't sound good!" Gertie had blurted. They hadn't noticed him walking over. Mrs Tweeny had sent him to post a couple of letters for Dr Hastings. Mrs Tweeny didn't do errands.

The young schoolteacher had turned and swung her hand up to clip his ear, then just flicked it instead.

"I wasn't listening in, you were in the way," Gertie protested with a grin. He didn't have a radio and never got round to reading the newspapers until they were tied up in heaps on the doorsteps ready for the Salvage Scamps.

Florrie had heard Gertie's concern. She was a nurse. It was her job to comfort those who were alarmed or afraid. Instinctively Florrie had tried to reassure the lanky lad.

"It'll be all right. You haven't missed the post!"

Aggy smiled at the pair of them. "We've all got to step up to the challenge now. There's no one else coming to help. We can *hope* they might soon, but until then, it's just us."

Florrie and Gertie both guessed Aggy might be worried about her husband. Although he'd been injured out of the regular Army, he still worked over in the clerking office at the local camp. He'd been able to resume his church wardening duties, but tended not to use his bicycle so much anymore, and the Home Guard was taking up the rest of his time.

Walker had caught up with them there. He'd left Al looking after little Maze and had recognised Florrie from her nurse's uniform. He couldn't remember which of Mrs Tweeny's girls she was, but he'd narrowed it down to one of three. Gertie was much better at faces than he was. Walker had grown up in a city and didn't recognise faces the same way. It took some getting used to, but Walker was a quick learner.

"They'll be sending more of 'the Lads' your way now.

You'll be in the thick of it," Walker told the young nurse.

Florrie hadn't thought of that. She *had* learnt that everyone seemed to refer to all the patients and servicemen stationed up at the hospital as 'the Lads', officers and men alike, it didn't matter, if they were 'up at the House', then they were 'the Lads'. As a junior nurse, Florrie seldom got to see the new patients when they first arrived at the hospital. It was only later, after the doctor had looked them over and the senior nurses had assisted him with any emergency procedures. Florrie had become proficient in cleaning, bedmaking and changing dressings and bandages. Even so, when she had been allowed into some of the side rooms, the injuries had shocked her.

What had been most shocking to Florrie was that a man could survive such injuries and not be driven mad by the unrelenting pain or broken by the despair of the damage done. She didn't talk about that; none of them did.

There had been a couple of Lads she'd thought might have been close in those first couple of weeks. One hadn't made it through the night but had never once shouted out. He'd cried when she'd taken her turn to sit beside him. He'd tried to speak at first, but instead he'd cried. Florrie had cried with him because she hadn't known what else to do. There was nothing else they could do, so she had sat beside his bedside and held his hand. Neither spoke, until they heard one of the other nurses approaching, starting to move the curtains aside. The nurse had whispered a warning ahead.

"I'm bringing you a cup of tea."

Florrie had sniffed and wiped away her tears and the Lad had looked up and winked at her.

"Don't worry."

Those had been the only words he'd spoken. She'd been

told her shift was finished before he ever spoke again, and the next time Florrie had walked past that room his bed was empty.

The other man she thought about now wasn't English. She'd heard him speaking. He was soft spoken, there was something in the way he spoke, it was English but with an accent she wasn't familiar with. She'd found out later he was Canadian, and his name was Joe. He'd been blinded. Florrie didn't know if he would regain his sight. No one had told her that. She'd been allowed to help bathe him and guide him from his bed to the table in the middle of the room. He'd sat down obediently and thanked her.

She'd asked him thoughtlessly, "Would you like anything to read?" Her next breath was a gasp of astonishment at her own stupidity and the breath after that an apology, but he was already laughing at her.

"Thanks. I'll manage."

He'd asked her for the box of dominoes, when she next came over to the table with another of the patients. She'd moved it to within his reach, without another thought.

The other Lad asked him, "You gonna play?"

"I will, when I get to working out my fingertips. Gotta practise working out which is which, but I'm getting there."

They seemed to think that was funny. Those Lads found a lot of things funny, in ways that had brought a lump to Florrie's throat, but she'd only cried the once, that time by the bedside of that young man who'd told her, 'Don't worry.'

He'd offered her comfort, but that was *her* job; she was the nurse! Sometime during that night so much had changed for Florrie. She wondered, perhaps so much was changing for everyone.

Those thoughts had come back to her in front of the

village post office, when Walker had said something about her being in the 'thick of it' at the hospital. They'd heard someone coming out from the village shop starting to talk about, 'if we fail.' But Gertie had stood firm, "We're not going to. I'm not having it!"

Rusty calmed Gertie with a smile. "That's just the sort of thing my grandfather says." The lanky lad grinned at knowing that and returned to his bicycle.

"Seems like we've got some spirit in us yet, then!" Aggy chuckled, as they watched him pedal on his way, but there was a determined set to her jaw.

The radio had mentioned América. They were meant to be helping. Rusty had overheard some talk between Jeepers and one of the incoming truckdrivers. He wasn't local or one of the regulars, so it was difficult to tell what he was saying, but she'd been able to hear 'the Americans' mentioned amidst the swearing.

Aggy seemed quite clear in her opinion. "That's the whole point, isn't it? We're not meant to like it: we're meant to stop it. We're meant to brace ourselves for worse to come!"

That morning as Rusty brought her truck up to the bus-stop for Florrie and Dotty to wait for Pru, she'd caught up with the news from the hospital and watched in admiration as the three young nurses made ready for their dash over to the gate to start their shifts.

"I should be seeing you later, once I've picked up this delivery. I'm meant to be bringing my grandfather over with his strawberry baskets. If you get a moment, let Mrs Toombs know to expect us, won't you?"

"If we get a moment?" Dotty asked her colleagues. "She's got to be joking!"

The senior nurses, fully qualified and able to take care of

themselves, had their own quarters up in the hospital. They were known as the 'Graces' by patients and visitors alike. The doctors just called them all 'nurse'. The porters called all the nurses all sorts of things, but only when they were sure they couldn't hear.

The junior nurses were generally referred to as the 'Little Graces'. Pru had thought that rather quaint the first time she'd heard it, until one of the porters had explained the actual form was 'small mercies.'

"Oh dear, we're not that bad, are we?"

The porter's name was Andy. He seemed to have a little more time for them than the other members of staff.

"You're just going through the clumsy stage at the moment. Most of the new'uns go through three stages. The first one is the soppy one." Florrie knew what he was referring to. She'd got over that one.

"The next is the clumsy stage," Andy explained, "when you're feeling overloaded by the different directions you're getting given."

"I think that's where we're *all* at!" Dotty agreed, then asked, "What's the third one?"

Pru would have preferred to know how long the second stage was meant to last. She didn't care for it much.

"The third stage is when you get to where you think you know what you're doing and really start making some clangers of mistakes!" the porter informed the three young nurses candidly, before wisely suggesting, "much better to stay around the edges of the clumsy stage. Be ready to listen to everyone, including the Lads. They'll tell you if you're doing something wrong. With any luck you'll skip over the third stage quick enough and start proper nursing."

Dotty wanted to know, "Will they ever stop barking at

us?"

"They only sound like they're barking because you're not used to the way sound travels around these parts," Andy told them.

Florrie could appreciate that; she'd thought something similar. "It's the stairways and the doors, isn't it?"

Andy didn't try and make sense of that one, instead offering them just a little more advice. "Matron gives orders. Doctors make demands. You'll do well to follow the first, abide by the second, but attend to what the senior nurses tell you, 'cos they're the ones that really know what they're talking about!"

It was good advice. Rules for the hospital. Rules for Mrs Tweeny's house. Rules for the village even. Cripes! Florrie wondered how she was meant to know them all. Maybe, if they had more time. That was what they'd been talking about on the radio, wasn't it? They needed more time. To salvage their strength? The radio had said 'strength', but what it had meant was 'men'. Like those she was looking after in the hospital. Those Lads, how much time did they have left?

"Small mercies," she had repeated under her breath. "We're all going to be needing those before we get to the other side of this." Even as she sounded those words, she could feel herself relaxing. 'The other side of this'. Yes, she really believed that.

Florrie had no idea how she knew. Maybe it had been that night when the Lad had told her, 'Don't worry.' She was still scared, but it wasn't the same tearful trembling fear. Now it was more determination. She knew she didn't know enough, but she would do her best, regardless. That was all she could do, that was all *any* of them could do, and that was just going to *have* to be enough!

Florrie didn't have time to deliver Rusty's message to Mrs

Toombs until a few hours later. She was heading across to the kitchen when one of the doctors called "Nurse!" She'd been the only one there.

Florrie had stopped, turned and waited for the doctor to tell her what he wanted.

"Take this out to the messenger. He's waiting for it."

It was only a few paces to the main entrance. She could feel the air change and the sunshine already finding her face. There was no one else in the hallway and the doctor had already disappeared.

Just as the doctor had told her, the messenger was waiting down at the bottom of the entrance steps, beside his motorbike. Florrie handed the note to the man.

"You're waiting for this?"

She'd been expecting to see the man and the motorbike, but not Gertie there too with his bicycle. Florrie didn't say anything until she'd delivered the doctor's note to the messenger and thanked him. Then turned to the grinning Gertie. "And what are you doing here?"

"Oh, I got a message to deliver, too," he returned brightly.

She couldn't see any paper. "A message?" Florrie queried.

Gertie wasn't going to tell her, not this time. The message wasn't for her. "It's for the cook."

"Oh yes, the strawberries. Old Spot's strawberry baskets?" she guessed.

"Oh, you know." Gertie felt slightly disappointed. He rather enjoyed delivering messages. If he was delivering them that meant he was the first to know. It didn't happen often.

"I only know because Rusty gave us a lift in her truck to work this morning. I haven't told anyone else. I haven't had the time. You can still deliver your message properly," Florrie told him in a whisper.

Gertie resumed his grinning and got back on his bicycle to pedal around to the kitchen entrance.

He found Mrs Toombs easily, she wasn't difficult to find. Mrs Toombs had a habit of filling the kitchen, either with her own bulk or with the bulk of what she was cooking.

Gertie had always thought whenever he'd been sick, which admittedly had only been the once that he could remember, he hadn't felt much like eating. Mrs Toombs was the cook for the whole hospital. To Gertie's thinking a hospital took care of sick people. If that was the case, then the Lads here couldn't be as sick as Gertie had been that time, judging by the amount Mrs Toombs was preparing.

There was another question Gertie had been hoping to have the opportunity of asking Mrs Toombs, about the hospital kitchen. It was an RAF hospital, Gertie knew that much. It couldn't be a secret because it said that much on the board outside the gate. If this was a kitchen meant to be feeding RAF personnel, air force meant flight. Gertie knew that birds needed to be very light to be able to fly. He could remember his mother talking about one of the little old ladies in the village: 'Oh, she's eats like a bird, hardly nothing of her.' Not according to Mrs Toombs' stodge!

"Wow, Mrs Toombs!" Gertie was about to blurt a few words on the weight of her pastry. Except it wasn't pastry, it was potatoes. Then he remembered where he was, a kitchen and why he was there, an errand to deliver a message. If he foolishly blurted before delivering the message, it was unlikely he would get anything to eat from the kitchen. Gertie wasn't stupid.

It wasn't the only reason why he'd agreed to deliver the message. He would have done it anyway. He liked Rusty's freckle-face. She wasn't beautiful like Miss Aggy, but she was kind, and he liked the way she laughed so loud.

"What?" Mrs Toombs looked sharply over to where the scruffy lad was disturbing the flow of her efforts. "Yes?" she demanded with fresh gusto.

Gertie got flustered. "Strawberries! Old Spot's coming over with your strawberries and I was meant to let you know."

"Yes," Mrs Toombs acknowledged she had received the message. "I haven't got any biscuits," she briskly informed the loitering lad.

"No. You won't be needing any biscuits for Old Spot's strawberries. He said you'll be needing scones for 'em."

Gertie was happy to correct her on that assumption. He didn't often get a chance to do that either.

"Oh, did he?" Mrs Toombs asked the bold young fellow. "Did he indeed!"

She was annoyed, but only with herself. She'd heard about the strawberries coming and hadn't allowed for them in her weekly order.

"Shall I tell him?" Gertie offered cheerfully.

"Tell him what? Who?" Mrs Toombs took a massive step towards Gertie's position and he shuffled back a pace.

"Old Spot. I can cycle up over that way, if you like, and tell him you don't want his strawberries," Gertie repeated his offer.

"I didn't say that. Don't you go putting words in my mouth."

That sounded dangerously like a scold. Gertie was getting out of there sharpish, ducking back to the kitchen door.

"I'll just tell him you know he's coming then, shall I, Mrs Toombs?" He decided it might be wiser not to wait for an answer to that.

Gertie was within arm's length of his bicycle, grabbing at it even before his back foot was out of the kitchen, swinging it forward and over, pushing off with the other, lifting himself up with the same movement and settling back down on the saddle. Safe.

CHAPTER 4

The Wrong Berries and
Al's Scrap Bucket

NOW WHERE WOULD HE FIND Rusty and her truck? Gertie didn't want to miss out on the other end of this.

He'd already promised to help Al and Walker with their salvage collection, maybe he could put the two together and take the Salvage Scamps up to Jeepers' Yard? Al had heard about it, but Gertie doubted he'd actually been there. Walker definitely wouldn't have, not yet, and Maze would be too young to know anything about it.

If they walked up that way, more than likely Rusty would find them and take them the rest of the way in her truck. Gertie liked that idea. He liked cycling, but if he could get a ride on Rusty's truck then all the better. He liked lying on his back in it, looking up at the sky. He could imagine that was how it felt to fly up there in the sky, only the other way up!

Al and Maze were already by the village duckpond.

"We've lost Walker!" they told him. "He's walked off again, something to do with the milko's crates!"

"Oh, I know where they are," Gertie offered helpfully. He used to work for Grouch.

"He's not looking for them. He's found one and wants to make a cart out of it with Maze's pram wheels, and she's been crying because he says he can," Al explained quickly, before Gertie set off in the wrong direction.

"No, he can't do that," Gertie knelt down to comfort the little girl. "Walker's not allowed to have the milk crates. They're 'essential' and prams are 'essential' too," Gertie assured Maze. "The cart can wait, we're looking for a truck!"

That got the two children's attention in double-quick time. They soon found Walker, and with all their chat about going over to Jeepers' Yard the young evacuee forgot the idea of a cart for a while.

"Do we need to bring the buckets?" Walker asked, showing them he'd got his at the ready.

"We taking two?" Al asked. He'd forgotten his. He only had Maze and her pram. Al did some quick thinking.

"One bucket should be enough, two would be obvious! If we're going over to Jeepers' Yard, there's bound to be plenty of old nails and bits about the place. If we do the sweeping, he won't even notice."

Gertie couldn't find fault with that idea.

"Then we'd better hurry, because Jeepers might not notice, but I bet Rusty will, if we don't get over there before her." He took a breath before adding, "and if we get there before Rusty, we might even be able to help Old Spot with his strawberry picking."

That decided the pace, with Maze piping up, "Oh, yes please!"

Only Gertie knew how far it was; too far for such short little legs as hers, to get to Jeepers' Yard. He was soon pushing his bicycle with Maze sat on the saddle, with her legs dangling and her hands around his neck. Gertie didn't mind.

They were walking along the back lane hedgeways, he never minded walking that way.

"Hedges mean berries, don't they?" Walker asked eagerly, starting to pick at the first berries he found and lobbing them into the bucket, that was by then trundling along in the old pram Al was pushing.

As quickly as Walker was picking and lobbing, Al was pinching and tossing the berries back out of the bucket again.

"What you doing that for? We could make a pie out of that lot!"

"No, we couldn't," Al told him, not turning around, but pushing a little more assertively, keeping up with Gertie's long legs striding on.

"No, I know *we* can't, but someone who can make pastry could!" Walker continued picking and lobbing with ever greater insistence. If Gertie didn't stop this soon, he was going to have a full-blown scrap in the middle of a working lane, and there was no telling what sort of driver would be coming up the lane heading for Jeepers' Yard.

"Come on you two, knock it off, will ya? Look, Maze's being better behaved than you two and she's half your age."

"No, I'm not," Maze chirped up. "I'm three times his age!"

"Ya wot?" Gertie swung back to stare at little Maze.

She'd taken her arms away from around his neck and was now balancing a little precariously on the saddle of his bicycle, with both her chubby little arms crossed over her chest.

"Yes, I am. He told me so."

"I never said that. You're *not* three times my age." Al halted the pram's progress and stomped up to face his little sister. "I *never* said any such thing!"

Gertie now felt like he had two scraps developing, neither

of which he felt qualified to mediate, both of which he was hoping to get to the bottom of.

Gertie started with Maze, she seemed to be the most reasonable. With one hand on the middle of the handlebars to keep it steady, he stopped the bicycle. With his other hand, he stopped Al approaching his little sister any more menacingly. Not that any of Al's menace met their target. Maze was utterly unphased.

Maze had it all worked out and was ready to explain. "Three times. I know that. It was a two and a three. That's three times. I know that. That's what you said."

Al grinned and calmed down. "There *was* a two and a three," he conceded, "but it was a fraction, not a times table, Maze. I said you were two-thirds my age, just about. I know you like your twos and threes, I thought I was helping, but I never said you were three times my age. That would make you bigger than Gertie."

"Oh, yes please. Then I can keep the bicycle?" The little girl had uncrossed her arms and leant forward to hug Gertie at that. Gertie went to mush.

"How about when you are three times my age, you can have the bicycle? How about that then?"

"OK. I can do that, can't I?" Maze looked to her elder brother for approval, who was trying to figure that riddle out.

"Oh, yes? How long d'ya think it'll take you?" Al teased her.

Maze went on blithely hugging Gertie. "Don't care. You'll tell me. You're better at sums than me. I've only got as far as twos and threes. I think we're doing fours and fives next week."

Gertie smiled with relief, unhooking Maze's arms from his neck and putting them safely back on to the handlebars, so he could start pushing again. "Heaven help us! Fours and fives, hey?"

Al wasn't sure if he'd won that round, but if Gertie was happy pushing the bicycle and taking care of Maze, then he'd go back to his pram and stop Walker throwing any more of those ruddy berries into the bucket.

"How about you stop that? I'll just tell you when we get to some we can eat."

"We can't eat those?" Walker asked, suddenly hesitating mid lob. "Why?"

"We can't eat them because they're inedible," Al explained. "At least they are for us. I dare say there's a few birds and animals about here that'll polish off all those I've taken out of the bucket. It's just our guts don't take kindly to them."

"It don't?" Walker asked, slowing his pace a little. "Why?"

"Well, for starters they taste like turps!"

"They do, don't they?" Walker agreed. "Hang on how d'you know!?"

Al blushed. Gertie knew the answer to that too, but Al's little sister didn't and Al didn't want her to, so gave the best answer he could offer that might just go over her head with its eloquence.

"'Cos I do."

Al winked at Gertie, then turned to stick his tongue out at Walker, only then taking a closer look at his friend. He didn't look well.

"Walker, you haven't?" Al suddenly let go the pram and stepped to his friend's aid. "You didn't?"

"I did! I thought all berries tasted like turps 'til they get baked into a pie. I thought that's what they're *meant* to taste like, and I was hungry, and … well, you shouldn't have tossed my berries out and you should have told me sooner!"

"Oh cripes!"

Gertie realised what was happening, he'd been listening and acted immediately.

"Al, take the bicycle and your sister. I'll sort out Walker. You idiot!"

"What you telling me off for? I didn't eat the berries," Al protested, as Gertie handed over the bicycle and small girl perched on its saddle into his half-sized care. Al just about managed to hold it steady, but there was no way he was going to be able to walk with it. Bracing both his legs and leaning into the bicycle. Maze wasn't the slightest interested in hugging her big brother's neck.

"If you don't hold on to me, you're going to fall off. You do that and you'll never get to three times Gertie's age, not even with all those fours and fives!" Al shouted. Maze begrudgingly obeyed the order.

Gertie was already at Walker's side. "How many do you think you ate?"

Walker hadn't got a clue. Only that his mouth still tasted like turps, and he wasn't quite sure how his stomach felt yet, but his legs didn't feel too good.

"It would help if you could be sick. You could sick the berries up. I do that all the time when I have to eat something horrible and green," Maze shouted over, trying to be helpful.

"I can't be sick. I'm from the city, we're taught not to be sick. You're not allowed to be sick in the city. If you get sick in the city they make you wash every day and you get sicker," Walker began to wail.

Al was about to suggest his friend try the alternative end of the problem.

Gertie could see Walker going greener by the moment. "That'll happen naturally, but not soon enough."

"We need to get help."

There was genuine concern in Gertie's voice. He'd never been responsible for three children before. He'd never even considered he was responsible for them until now, but there was no one else.

Whenever he'd taken them round on their salvaging errands, Gertie had just thought he was helping. Now it dawned on him he was twice their age and almost three times Maze's. Not only was he fully responsible for them, but he also needed to get urgent help for Walker *and* keep Al and Maze safe whilst he was doing it.

"Al, can you ride my bicycle?"

"Oh, yes please!" Al blurted.

"No, you idiot! Can you *really* ride my bicycle? I mean over to Jeepers' Yard and get some help?" Gertie explained as calmly as he could, which sounded more like a startled duck.

He scooped Walker up in his arms and started darting across the narrow width of the lane, looking up and down it, desperately hoping to catch a glimpse of another vehicle approaching. Any vehicle, from any direction. Right now, it could have been a German tank. Gertie didn't care. He'd flag it down and ask for help! It could even have been Mr Tor on his motorbike!

"Can you?" Gertie asked him again and Al realised the seriousness of the situation.

"I think so, but not with Maze in the way. She'll have to get off."

As Al confirmed his acceptance of the perilous mission, he moved to grab Maze and lift her down from the saddle.

"Shan't! No." She straightened up, taking her hands off the handlebars and bringing them down to clamp under her seat. "No." She'd intended to stick out her chin in defiance, but only managed sticking her tongue out the side of her mouth and going cross-eyed. It was the best she could muster.

"If you don't get off that bicycle this instant, you'll never see those four and fives and that's a promise," Gertie shouted over to her, surprising himself with the volume. Maze promptly let go and fell into Al's unsteady arms.

"Wow!" Al was impressed both with Gertie's assertiveness and Maze's weight. "Cripes! You really are nearly three times me, aren't you?"

Maze wriggled out from her brother's arms and found the ground.

"There!" She stamped her feet, then kicked her big brother in the shins. "There. And that's for dropping me. You were meant to lift me off. You said you would!"

"No, I didn't," Al started, then caught sight of Gertie's face and shut up. "Come on, get out of the way and let me get over to Jeepers' Yard. You look after the pram and the bucket for me, will ya?"

Maze was satisfied. She had full responsibility for the pram *and* the bucket, with or without the poisonous berries; that was almost as good as sitting on the bicycle!

Al climbed up on to the bicycle. On the second attempt he managed to get both feet on the pedals and started pedalling. He couldn't quite manage to stretch his legs long enough to reach the saddle as well, so straddled the bicycle with the saddle somewhere behind his back, leaning his chin towards the middle of the handlebars, still pedalling resolutely. It wasn't pretty to watch, but at least it distracted Walker from the way his stomach was starting to feel horrible.

Maze followed the bicycle, almost keeping up for the first twenty yards, which impressed the heck out of Gertie.

"Right little sprinter there," he murmured, before remembering he still had to get help for Walker, whether or not Al got as far as Jeepers' Yard. Gertie began running with Walker in his arms.

Al got to Jeepers' Yard just as Rusty swung her truck round the last top bend before the gates. She screamed at the brakes, wrenching at the steering wheel and burning rubber.

"What the hell!?" she shouted angrily at Al, who prompted squeezed the brakes and fell off the bicycle.

"Why d'ya go and do that for?" he shouted right back at her.

"Al?" Rusty asked, realising there must be something very wrong for him to be this far out from the village and on what she immediately recognised as Gertie's bicycle.

"Gertie?" she asked, already climbing down from the cab, leaving the truck in the middle of the lane.

"He's all right," Al told her. "It's Walker, being an idiot!"

Rusty wasn't sure being an idiot warranted Al pinching Gertie's bicycle and cycling in such a fashion all the way out to Jeepers' Yard to tell her. She waited for the rest of it.

"Walker's gone and eaten those berries you said was bad. I told him that."

"You did? Then why did he eat them?" she asked, immediately suspicious.

"I didn't tell him quick enough."

Al looked at her as if she was an idiot, too. Maybe it was catching. He picked up Gertie's bicycle from where it was sprawling across the lane. Thankfully, Rusty had got the gist of the situation.

"Come on, bring that with you. Let's go get 'em."

"Al?" Rusty's voice softened. She could see him starting to shake. "It's going to be all right. Gertie knows what he's doing. He's eaten poison berries himself enough times."

Al was chuckling by the time he'd got the bicycle round to the back of her truck. Rusty climbed into the cab and waited for him to follow.

"What about Old Spot's strawberries?" Al suddenly remembered.

"Damn! Forgot that," Rusty remembered. "You'd better go and fetch him and his strawberry baskets. We're going to be heading for the doctors. It might as well be the hospital. They'll know what to do."

The bicycle was in the back and Al was already halfway into the truck's cab by this time. Being allowed into the cab was one thing; being told to get back out and go into Jeepers' Yard on his own, gave him cause to hesitate. Never in his worst nightmares did he ever imagine a time when he would turn down the opportunity to help with the strawberry baskets, but Al was seriously considering doing just that.

Rusty sensed the reluctance.

"Go on. You can do it. We've all got to do our bit. This is yours!"

That was it; that was all Al needed to know. If this was his bit, then so be it! He was ready, even if it *did* mean braving the entire length of Jeepers' Yard uninvited, on his own, and looking for Old Spot all the way down to the bottom of his back garden. He slammed the truck door behind him and faced his fears, the gates to Jeepers' Yard.

"Just walk in and look as if you know where you're going. The side path is on the right," Rusty gave him directions.

"Right!" Al told himself, as much as to let Rusty know he'd heard her.

He didn't look back but marched on. This was for his best friend. This was for Walker. He could do this. This was his 'bit'!

"Good boy."

Rusty watched enough, then started her truck engine up again and set off in search of Gertie, Walker and Maze. Rusty hadn't far to go.

Gertie had overtaken Maze, but she was almost keeping up. Gertie had the expression of a shattered man about him. He was staggering forward with an ashen-faced Walker in his arms, almost dropping out of them. Every few paces Walker was starting to retch, and Gertie was losing his hold. Maze was sobbing loudly behind him, pushing the pram with the bucket rattling in it.

Rusty stopped the truck, scrambled down and ran forward in time to catch Walker just as he began to spasm into a fresh batch of stomach cramps. He fell forward, this time beyond the strength of Gertie's arms to hold him.

Looking to Gertie, Rusty spoke calmly.

"I've got him. I know what happened. Al got the message through. Come on, everyone in. You'd better bring the bucket with you, Maze. They'll need to know which berries he ate."

Walker groaned as Rusty put him gently in the seat beside her.

"Now, try not to be sick, but if you have to, do it out the window, there's a good boy."

Walker groaned again. Then whimpered as another spasm clenched his guts.

"You all in back there?" she called over to the back of the

truck before starting to move. Two shrill voices squealed back.

"We're in, bicycle, pram and bucket!" Maze counted.

"Berries and all!" Gertie assured her.

"Any idea what those berries were?" Rusty asked, turning again to the pale, squirming child on the seat beside her, as she headed back up to the Yard.

"The wrong ones," Walker whimpered, then groaned and lurched over to lean out of the cab window to throw up.

"There, good boy. That's better, isn't it?"

Walker didn't answer, Rusty was approaching the gates to Jeepers' Yard. There was nothing coming, and the gates were open. She was hoping Al had done his part.

"Better out than in. Go on, get it up," she patted the boy's back gently.

Walker's response was to promptly oblige by heaving up the next spasm through his guts down the outside of the cab door.

There was a shout from the yard, it was Al.

"Don't worry we've got a bucket ready."

Rusty grinned, shouting back over, "Bit late for that. Fill it with water and bring me a cloth, will you?"

Al obeyed the order, leaving Old Spot standing in the middle of the Yard enjoying the entrance. His arms full of baskets of straw and strawberries, each handle neatly hooked over and balanced along the length of his arms. He could see two more heads bobbing up from the back of Rusty's truck, as well as the sad figure slumped in the seat beside his granddaughter.

"Oy! You two, get down from there and give me a hand with these. Or d'ya want me to put you on clean-up detail, too?"

Gertie scrambled out first, then helped Maze jump down. Old Spot had expected Gertie. Gertie was always about the place somewhere, but the little girl shocked him.

"What d'ya bring her along for?"

Gertie grinned and answered, "The strawberries."

Old Spot smiled. He appreciated the honesty.

"What about him, then? Did he come for the berries? Because if he did, he picked the wrong ones!"

"He came for a crate to build himself a go-cart, but we weren't going to let him pinch Maze's pram wheels and thought maybe we could salvage enough spare nails and stuff from around here to do a deal," Gertie blurted.

Old Spot had a liking for Gertie's blurts. Never could find anything wrong with them. Even if some of the others around the village found him awkward and in the way sometimes, Old Spot thought Gertie rather refreshing.

Rusty hadn't heard *that* part of the plan until then.

"You were going to do what? I hope you didn't expect to get away with that whilst Jeepers was in the Yard."

"No. We were trying to dodge him until we'd filled the bucket and hid it in my pram," Maze informed Rusty squarely.

"Sounds like a good plan. What went wrong?" Old Spot asked, finding himself slightly disappointed he'd missed the opportunity to watch them in action.

He was handing the baskets of strawberries up to Maze who'd decided she didn't like the state of the Yard and preferred the back of Rusty's truck.

"Walker went wrong," Gertie continued the explanation.

Old Spot took a closer look at the boy.

"I should say so!"

Rusty got Al to help her clean the door of the cab first, before she came back with fresh water in the bucket and a towel to start cleaning up Walker.

"He'll feel better with that out of his system," Old Spot observed sagely.

"I still think we ought to take him with us," Rusty informed her grandfather sternly.

"What, you mean I'm not sitting up front with you?" he challenged her decision.

She gave him that same stare he'd taught her. Old Spot had taught it to her for using on Jeepers, when he asked her to take the truck through the village on market day. It was the 'you're an idiot if you think I'm going to change my mind just because you say so' look.

Old Spot appreciated Rusty had mastered it to perfection.

"All right, I'll stay back with me strawberries then."

"If you want your strawberries to survive the journey, with those two Scamps in the back with them, I think you'd better," she reminded him, as Al came back across the Yard with the last few baskets, "and me makes three."

"We're taking them *all* up to the House?" Old Spot queried, wondering how he was going to manage to keep the cargo steady in the back, not only the delicate baskets of strawberries, but also Gertie and his bicycle, Maze with her pram and Al with his bucket, not to mention the timbers Rusty had already got loaded back there.

"The House is the RAF hospital. That's why we're going over there, for you and your strawberries for the Lads, and for Walker and his gut-ache. They'll know what to do. As for Gertie, Al and Maze, well, they're up there now and I don't want to waste any more time taking them home."

Old Spot couldn't fault that argument, so settled back to enjoy the scenery. Gertie smiled and handed him some of the strawberry baskets to hold.

"Nice up 'ere, ain't it?" The elderly gentleman returned the easy grin. It was going to be an interesting journey.

Rusty climbed back into the cab of her truck. She didn't shut the gates. No one else was there. When Jeepers and the rest of his trucks came back they liked to be able to swing in and off the lane as quick as they could. No doubt he'd yell for her a couple of times before realising she wasn't there. Jeepers never went around to check the back garden. He would just have to expect them when they got back and that would take as long as it took.

She could hear her grandfather chatting away to Al and Maze, and Gertie's laughter. There was some feeble muttering under Walker's breath in the seat beside her. At least he'd stop being sick, although he still looked rather green around the gills.

"Best place for you, to see a doctor."

Walker began to protest. He was scared, genuinely scared. She could hear it in his voice, even though his head was turned away from her, and she was concentrating on getting the truck through the narrow lanes unscathed by the summer hedgeways' overgrowth.

"Tell you what, how about you look out your side and see if you can see any of those nice young nurses, staying with Mrs Tweeny. A nurse is all right, isn't she?"

That seemed to calm the boy for a while, long enough for Rusty to get her truck into the village. She was scanning the footpaths for anyone who might be able to help her, too.

"Aggy!"

Walker perked up immediately

"Miss Aggy!" he cried out.

"Oh goodness, what *have* you been doing with yourself?" The young schoolteacher dashed over with her bag of books and more under her arm. "Oh dear, you do look poorly."

Rusty explained, "He *is* poorly, and I've got a full load." She thumbed back behind her. "We're heading over to the hospital. Are those for the library? If so, hop in. I could do with some help with this lot."

Aggy peered into the back of the truck.

"I should say you could!"

Gertie was eager to offer a hand down to help her up into the back of the truck. Al wasn't sure there was enough room, what with everything else. Aggy decided along similar lines.

"I think I'd better sit with Walker in the front, but you can look after my books up there, if you would? I can put Walker on my lap, he'll feel better that way."

"You'll smell sick, Miss," Maze cautioned the schoolteacher.

Aggy could already smell sick, even if Rusty had washed down the door of the cab, Walker reeked of it.

"Poor chap. Come on, just hold on now. We're almost there."

Walker didn't resist the cuddle, but rather allowed himself to be picked up and sat on her lap like a baby. He just wanted to hang on and stop his guts from grinding their way through his innards. He didn't know what was happening in there, but it reminded him of the way the tractor wheels churned through the mud.

"Wrong berries," he murmured.

Aggy held him a little closer and nodded to Rusty that they were 'all ready' for her to proceed.

"I know dear. We've all done it. Got to learn."

"You've *all* done it?" Walker repeated in amazement.

She smiled down at him.

"Oh yes. Best way to learn. You'll not forget it now, will you?"

"Not ruddy likely!" he muttered and wiped his nose and mouth.

"They'll make you a nice cup of tea when we get there. They always make a nice cup of tea over at the hospital. They'll give you a biscuit to take the taste away from your mouth, too."

She talked softly to him and he calmed down, whilst Rusty continued driving through the village, hoping the rest of her passengers and load were behaving equally well.

Rusty got out on to the Long Town Road. It would only be a few minutes now before they got to the gated entrance to the drive up to the hospital.

There'd always been proper little gatehouse there before, when the house had been a proper grand old house, the way her grandfather remembered it. Since the RAF had taken it over and made it a hospital, they'd put a little shed and stationed a guard by the gate.

Rusty was ready for the questions, but her grandfather was quicker. Standing up to his full height in the back of the truck and bending down, to get face to face with the soldier about to check the 'load' arriving at the Gate.

"Strawberries for the kitchen!"

"Right-ho, Sir."

The young man took a startled step back. Then up popped Maze.

"And my pram, too."

This got the soldier nonplussed. He didn't have any prams

on his list that morning.

"Um!"

Whilst he was trying to find a suitable response to that declaration, or better still, stall long enough for Sarg to come over and sort it out, Al stood up beside his little sister.

"And my bucket!" he said, holding it ready for inspection.

The soldier instinctively stepped forward again at this point, just to look in the bucket. That didn't help, but gave a moment more for Sarg to reach them.

Gertie wasn't going to be missing out on this, so scrambled to his lanky legs, grabbing at a couple of Miss Aggy's library books and his own bicycle.

"Me too, I'm here!"

"So you are. Weren't you here earlier?"

"Yes, Sir. Sarg!" Gertie called over confidently, as Sarg marched up to see what all the delay was about at his gate.

"What have you got there, this time?"

Sarg relaxed. It was only Gertie and his bicycle in Rusty's truck. Rusty's truck had been scheduled over a couple of days ago, but better late than never. Sarg hadn't been expecting her to be bringing passengers, only timber.

"What you got here?" he questioned the young soldier. "Um!"

"You've got a sick child here, Sergeant!"

Aggy called both men's attention to the obvious. Sarg stepped forward to see for himself, then immediately coughed and stepped back again.

"Is he contagious?"

"No," Aggy informed him. "He's just eaten the wrong berries and we need one of your nurses. I think he's been sick enough to undo any serious damage."

"I think he's been sick enough, too," Sarg muttered, trying to hold his breath at the same time, waving them through.

Everyone in the truck knew Miss Aggy was in charge from now on. Al climbed down quickest as they came up to the main entrance, helping Walker down from the cab, then waited for the young schoolteacher to steer the sick boy up the entrance steps.

Rusty knew where she needed to unload her timber. She and Al could sort that lot out. Old Spot knew where he needed to go with his strawberry baskets. He'd take Maze with him.

Gertie had Miss Aggy's books. He knew where to go with those, because of the sound of the clatter of the table-tennis bats coming from the library.

He'd seen the kitchen. That would be where Old Spot would be taking Maze and the strawberry baskets. Gertie could guess that much. He could also guess that Rusty and Al would be taking the timbers out past the lawns, over to where they'd been making the new vegetable beds. Someone had told him about the timbers raising the vegetables up to meet the reach of those Lads who couldn't bend down so well.

Gertie liked the hospital library. It had so much more in it than just a lot of books.

Rusty had been happy to bring the timbers over. It was one of her easier deliveries. There was always help at the other end and no one gave her any problems. She rather thought she'd brought the problems with her this time!

Thank goodness she'd come that back route round to Jeepers' Yard. Thank goodness it had been her that had caught up with the Salvage Scamps. She was still cross with Al, he should have known better, but there was too much to do for any scolding.

"Come on Al, give me a hand or we'll have the Lads taking pity on us, for not keeping up with their share of the unloading."

There was already half a dozen of the timbers down from the back of the truck, being taken over to where the new raised beds were being prepared. Old Spot would be coming out to inspect them as soon as he'd finished in the kitchen.

Rusty didn't want to think about the 'what if': if Walker had got sick further back along the lane, or if she hadn't been the one to find them, or if Jeepers or one of his trucks had swung along that way at the reckless pace they usually did.

She'd seen a couple of the nurses by then, out in the grounds with a few of the Lads who needed helping. They all looked very smart, very clean. Rusty had cause to look down at the state of her own 'uniform', rolled up surplus overalls and one of her grandfather's belts.

The boots were her own, but the socks were a clean pair of Jeepers' that he never bothered with, and Rusty wasn't going to waste them. Her mother's clothes were in the chest of drawers in one of the rooms Jeepers kept for his boxes, and neither Rusty nor her grandfather bothered to know what was in them. Jeepers kept the doors shut, so they stayed out. Everyone was happy with that arrangement.

Old Spot slept downstairs; he preferred it down there. It also meant Jeepers couldn't take over that room, too. Her grandfather didn't like to make it too easy for his son. Rusty had always had her own room.

Since starting to drive third truck, Rusty had learnt to walk a little more boldly. The overalls let her blend in as just another 'working bloke' most of the time. She'd even kept one of Old Spot's caps tucked down the back of her seat. She could put a decent stomp in her step when it was called for and a swagger with her arms, though she wished they were stronger. They were getting stronger now, with the timbers, and Al was keeping up.

She hadn't seen Old Spot or Aggy or Walker yet. Rusty was starting to get concerned about them. Old Spot would keep an eye on Maze. As for Gertie? Heaven only knew where he'd got to!

Aggy had found one of the porters trying to get out for a cigarette, commanding him to fetch her a nurse. The porter wisely searched for the most junior amongst those within his range. They wouldn't know any better than to follow him. It was Florrie.

"Oh, thank goodness. Give me a hand, will you?"

"What's he done?" Florrie asked. She'd been half expecting it to be Gertie again, but this child was smaller. "Oh, bless him, it's that little city boy. He doesn't look too bright. Nothing broken?"

She could assess that much from the fact he was walking beside the village schoolteacher, admittedly none too steadily. The smell was enough for the porter to diagnose the problem.

"He's sick."

Florrie knew enough to ignore the porter's help and steer Walker over to one of the smaller sluice rooms.

"Come on, let's get you cleaned up. You need to drink lots of water and tea, to flush everything out the other way. How does your stomach feel?"

"Empty and raw," Walker decided.

Florrie was satisfied with that.

"Good. Then you're already on the mend, aren't you?"

Aggy took another look at him.

"He does seem to have a little more colour in him than

when I first saw him."

"How did you get over here?" Florrie asked, chatting to the schoolteacher over the boy's head, as she got him sat down in the white tiled room, with hard shiny surfaces that made Walker very anxious. "Don't worry all we're going to do is give you a wash and some fresh clothes. Nothing else," the young nurse began to explain.

That was Walker's biggest fear. He'd heard about that from some of his older city friends, before he'd been sent out to the village. They'd told him, "If you get sick, they take you into hospital and they wash you until there's nothing left, and you die."

"Please Miss, I don't want to be washed away," he whimpered.

"We're just giving you a jug and bowl wash. Look, nothing else, I promise."

Florrie spoke softly, but firmly. Walker listened. Florrie was a nurse. She worked in a hospital every day and she hadn't been washed away.

"We can't send you home stinking like that. I'm surprised you didn't spoil all those strawberries!" she teased him, as she began to help him undress.

Walker chuckled. "I was sitting in the cab next to Rusty. They wouldn't let me sit in the back with the strawberries."

"How very wise of them," Florrie agreed winking over to Aggy. "Did Rusty manage to get everything else sorted?"

Aggy couldn't be sure of that, but guessed they'd be able to find out, as soon as the porter came back with some fresh clothes for the boy.

"They're a little on the large size," the porter smirked as he handed them over through the gap in the door. He could see the boy shivering under the towels. "You look better, mate. You sure as heck smell better."

With Walker duly washed and dressed, Florrie took him and Aggy over to the kitchen. Maze had made herself very comfortable there and Old Spot seemed to be on amicable terms with Mrs Toombs. They could hear Rusty and Al getting on with the Lads out in the gardens.

"So, where's Gertie?"

"The books!" Aggy suddenly recalled.

Old Spot was still teasing Walker about his idea of collecting a bucket full of nuts and bolts and nails from Jeepers' Yard without anyone noticing.

"You don't look strong enough to carry a bucket full of nails!"

Mrs Toombs would soon remedy that. "What the boy needs is a good strong cuppa and maybe a couple of my medicinal biscuits. They'll put some meat on his bones."

As she spoke, the enormous cook turned her back on Old Spot, to face the small child standing a little shakily in front of her. Walker was somewhat drowned in the kit he was wearing. She tutted and motioned towards the biscuit tin.

"Go on," she whispered.

He reached over and wrestled the lid off. He'd never seen meat-making biscuits before. They didn't sound so bad, and they certainly couldn't taste any worse than those berries. The tin held wedges of thick shortbread. Walker could smell them as soon as he lifted the lid, sugar, butter and all things nice and wonderful.

"Ohhh!" he beamed.

Mrs Toombs informed him confidently, "Best thing I know to settle a raw stomach."

Walker hadn't told her, but the cook seemed to know exactly what the problem was. He sat himself down on the nearest chair, with the legs of his trousers flopping way past his ankles and the sleeves of the shirt threatening to drown his hands in their folds.

Holding the bottom of his teacup in one hand and clutching the biscuit tin with the other, "Oh. Thank you, missus."

"Not too fast. That's the trick. You sip the tea and nibble the biscuits. Nice and slow there," the cook instructed him.

Whilst Aggy poured more tea for the rest of them, Florrie listened long enough to see Mrs Toombs had it all under control.

"I'll come by later; I've got to get back to the wards. I shouldn't be down here."

Aggy thanked the young nurse and was about to shoo her, before remembering, "You'll bring Walker's clothes back for him? I've no idea how he's going to explain what he's wearing now."

"Oh, don't worry. Al will do that for him. He's looking forward to it!" Maze informed them, cheerfully dipping her finger into the mixing bowl Mrs Toombs had been attending to.

It was time for Old Spot to get out of Mrs Toombs' kitchen. He wanted to get over to the gardens before they settled on where those timbers were going.

"Don't you dare take the little ones out there. You've got trucks and timbers and goodness knows what going on," the hospital cook told him menacingly, before shooing him towards the door, and effectively blocking it for the two children to follow.

"But Al's out there already."

Mrs Toombs wasn't going to stand any nonsense from Walker or Maze.

"Al may be, but he got out there without going through *my* kitchen first."

Aggy was about to suggest she took them out the other door of the kitchen, but then heard a slight thudding noise approaching from that direction. She'd never heard that sound before but knew instantly what it was. It sounded like someone tapping the panels of wood that lined the rooms leading into the kitchen with the knuckle of one of their fingers.

"That's Joe," Mrs Toombs recognised it too, and called him in. "Joe, I can hear your dominoes! Come on in, you know the way."

Walker was standing with the biscuit tin in one hand and Maze's hand in his other. Mrs Toombs remained barring their exit through the outside door of the kitchen, whilst Aggy was still standing in front of them, obscuring their view of the door that led from the kitchen to the rest of the hospital.

"You can hear dominoes?" Walker fearlessly doubted the cook.

"No, she can't," came Joe's voice ringing forward. It was loud and seemed to wrap around the entire kitchen before he'd entered the room. He was grinning and striding forward, the walking stick he'd been using, easy in his hand. "I thought you'd hear my dominoes first. Being smaller, your ears ought to be sharper than hers."

Walker immediately released his hold of Maze's hand and with his now freed hand went up to feel his own ears. Why weren't they sharp? He liked the sound of having sharp ears.

"You can hear dominoes?" Maze repeated Walker's question in amazement.

Then suddenly gasped at the sight of the figure that came

into the kitchen, as Aggy stood to one side.

The young man's face was terribly scarred. From halfway across the bridge of his nose, which had obviously been broken, the flesh was buckled and ridged, with red weals creasing into the folds around each of his eyes. The eyes were wide open and gazed ahead. He had no eyebrows, but his forehead was white and clear. No trace of furrows. Ageless, careless. His smile was enormous. It filled his face, dismissing his blindness.

As soon as he felt the kitchen stones beneath his feet. He stopped walking.

"Look." He offered out the hand that wasn't holding the cane, towards the small voice that had squealed in alarm. "See how the dominoes have painted dots on them to make the numbers? You sound small; are you big enough to count them for me? I'm trying to learn to 'read' the number of dots on each of the dominoes. I'm always carrying a few in my pocket, to practise. Mrs Toombs can hear them rattling. Can you see the dots? How many are there?"

"Oh!" Maze peered forward into the open palm at the dominoes there. "I think one has one, one has four and one has three. Is that right?" Anxiously looking up to him. "Can you really feel the numbers? That must be wonderful. How?" Maze asked him boldly.

Walker stood in silent astonishment at the little girl's bravery.

Joe felt the chair to his side. He'd heard Mrs Toombs nudge it towards him and sat down. He showed both children, putting the three dominoes flat on his palm, then with the lightest touch from the first finger of his other hand, he drew it across each tile.

"That's got the one dot, yes?" he asked them.

Maze nodded; Walker spoke for her.

"Yes, sir. That's the one with one."

"Then this has the three dots?" he asked them.

"Yes, sir." Walker was nodding along with Maze.

"Go on, your turn. You try this one." He held his palm out towards the smallest voice he'd heard earlier.

Maze shook her head. "Can't!"

"Why not?" he asked her gently, keeping his hand steady and open.

"I don't do my four and fives at school 'til next week."

"Then you must be very bright. I couldn't read any dominoes at all when I was your age."

Joe moved slightly, gauging where Walker stood nearer to his shoulder. "Then how about I have a piece of that shortbread of yours and you have the last go with this?"

Joe kept his hand open, waiting. Walker took the dominoes. "How did you know about the shortbread?"

"I can smell it, silly. Are you feeling better now?"

Mrs Toombs and Aggy stood in silent admiration of the brave young Lad, holding the two children spellbound.

"How did you know I'd been sick?" Walker asked, as he cautiously exchanged the dominoes for a piece of shortbread.

"Ah, well, those are some of Mrs Toombs special make-you-feel-better shortbread. She only lets you open that tin if you've been poorly. Are you feeling better now?"

Walker suddenly decided. "Yes, sir, thank you," he said, straightening himself and remembering his manners.

He watched Joe break the shortbread into two, taking his half into his enormous smiling mouth, silently offering the other half towards Maze. Walker knew he should have done that. Taking a step forward to stand directly in front of the young pilot, Walker waited until Joe had finished his shortbread. Then he took the Canadian giant's hand in his own and shook it.

"Thank you, Sir. You're blind, aren't you?"

Joe grinned and nodded and kept up the hand-shaking, whilst his words dissolved into more laughter.

"Yes, but I can still play dominoes and I'm going to learn chess soon."

"Oh!" Maze was nibbling at her piece of shortbread. Not wishing to rush it. Not wishing to leave the lovely kitchen. It was large and smelt so much nicer than her mum's. "Can we too?"

Joe looked towards where Aggy stood with Mrs Toombs. "Where to, Cookie?"

"They're not allowed outside, and neither are you without a nurse or a porter. You know that." Mrs Toombs stood her ground.

"I'm allowed in the library, aren't I?" Aggy checked with the cook.

"Oh yes, my dear. You came with books." Mrs Toombs approved. "But if you're going to take the children in there, you'd better try and avoid any of the nurses. Matron will be in her office about this time. The doctors won't mind, but you need to avoid the nurses."

"Ah, yes, we don't want to send the Graces into 'Oh Cripes'," Joe told them. "Avoid doing that at all costs!" The Canadian chortled at the prospect of a conspiracy. "How about I show them the way? Who else are we looking for?" he asked, already getting to his feet and starting to turn back the way he'd come. "There's another young boy in the library already, by the sound of it."

"Oh, good. That'll be Gertie. He'll have my books," Aggy exclaimed, with a happy sigh of relief.

"We ought to find Al, too. He's with Rusty. Do you think they'll have finished unloading?" Walker asked, as he took Maze's hand again, and began to follow Joe.

Mrs Toombs had an opinion on that. "If they're still at it, Old Spot will have got them organised. If they've finished there, he'll have them over in the long greenhouse. He always ends up there, whenever he comes bringing me something for the kitchen."

"Then we'll meet up with them that way. The long greenhouse opens off from the library." Joe led the way.

Aggy waved to Mrs Toombs and mouthed a 'thank you' before stepping into her place behind Joe, with Walker bringing Maze. Joe stopped them a few paces out from the kitchen, hushing them and moving a little nearer to the wall.

"Forgot the names, always doing that, sorry. Mine's Joe. Who's got my dominoes? I can hear you rattling."

Aggy told Joe her name, then looked back to Walker.

"That's me, Sir. Walker. This here is Maze," he volunteered, as Maze looked around at the enormous dark, wood-panelled walls with more doors than she could count and with ceilings as high as the sky above their heads.

"I can hear your friend up ahead. What's his name again?"

Walker spoke before Aggy could.

"It's Gertie, Sir. That's what he likes."

"Ok by me. Sounds like he's with Dotty. She's one of the nurses, but you don't have to worry about her, she's one of the junior nurses. They're a little clumsy sometimes, but never mean no harm."

Joe heard the sound of his feet on the floor change again,

as he walked from the hall into the library.

"Aggy?"

"Yes, Joe. I'm right here."

She stepped beside him as they let the two children run ahead of them, eager to meet up with Gertie and ready to tell him all they'd been through since they'd last seen him.

The first thing Gertie said by way of greeting was, "Phew! You smell a damn sight better. What're you wearing?"

"They're not mine!" Walker informed him.

"And are those not yours, neither?" Gertie queried, pointing to the tin of shortbread.

"Oh, we're meant to be sharing them. They're for making you feel better. They work ever so well, but you're not sick, so maybe you're not meant to have any."

Walker had only just thought of that. Joe heard an argument brewing and called into the cavernous room.

"Don't worry about the make-you-better bit; that only works in Mrs Toombs' kitchen. Once you bring them out of there everyone can have a piece. No harm done."

"There'll be some harm done when Al's mum finds out you've lost your clothes," Gertie reminded Walker with a grin, as he took his piece of shortbread.

They hadn't noticed the young nurse standing to one side. She knew enough to know the children weren't meant to be in the library. Dotty had found Gertie there, but he'd come in with a pile of books, so she wasn't sure if he was meant to be there or not. These two youngsters definitely didn't belong.

"Don't worry, Dotty, they're with me. They're playing dominoes with me. Show 'em, Walker. Show her you're taking care of my dominoes for me."

"That's all very well, but I don't think..." Dotty began to protest.

"Then don't think," suggested Aggy, calming the flustered young nurse. There was hardly more than a year between them, but Aggy seemed to be a decade older in her clear confident manner.

"Don't worry, they're with me. I'm Walker and Maze's teacher and Gertie is simply helping me with my books. Mrs Toombs didn't want the children out in the gardens whilst they are unloading Rusty's truck. Nor did she want us cluttering up her kitchen. We've simply come into the library until it's time to join up with them in the long greenhouse."

"Oh!" Dotty almost bobbed a curtsy before blustering across to Gertie. "Then get down from the library stepladder."

The young nurse then turned to Joe, cautioning, "One game, mind you, and please be quiet. I'll stand by the door. If your teacher will keep an eye on the garden windows to see when they arrive at the long greenhouse."

"Action stations!" Joe called, finding the edge of his table and the box with the rest of his dominoes in. "Come on, you lot, let's have a game. Dotty you're at the door? Aggy you're at the windows? Check."

Joe sat down and promptly tipped out the contents from the box and began turning them over, dots down. Maze came first to sit beside him, soon joined by Walker, then Gertie. By the time Al came in from the long greenhouse, Maze knew her fours and fives, and her sixes, too.

Old Spot was teasing one of the Lads about not having green thumbs, and Rusty was happy with the way the day had gone.

"Come on, everyone in the truck so we can get you lot home before teatime."

Aggy stayed behind. She wanted to have a little more time to choose new books from the library. Gertie had checked them; they all smelt even older than the ones she'd brought with her.

By then Gertie had decided he didn't like playing dominoes. The white dots sort of swam on top of the domino pieces. He was sure they rearranged themselves every time he took his eyes off them.

Al decided he'd had a good day. He might have missed all the excitement with the shortbread and meeting Joe, but soon caught up with both, and was especially satisfied with the salvage bucket.

"You remember why we were going over to Jeepers'?" he asked his friends, as they gathered to clamber back aboard Rusty's truck, this time with Old Spot taking the seat next to his granddaughter in the cab.

"We were going over to Jeepers' for salvage," Maze remembered. She nudged Walker, but he'd long since forgotten that bit of the errand.

"We were going for some old iron nails, and nuts and bolts and such, weren't we?" Al reminded them.

Gertie was just relieved to see his bicycle was where he'd left it in the back of the truck, unscathed by all the timbers getting unloaded.

"Oh yes. Why?" Walker asked, guessing that was what Al was waiting for.

"Because I've filled it!" Al announced, showing them the bucket already waiting for them in the back of the truck. "It took two of the Lads to put it there and it's *really* heavy."

Walker tried and couldn't shift it an inch.

"How d'ya manage that?" He stared at the contents. "And where'd you get it all from?"

"The Lads found it for me. They've got loads of sheds

back there. Sort of sheds in sheds and shelves all over the place," he told his friends. "D'you know, when this was a big house before it became the hospital, they didn't throw anything away? Nothing. Never. Not even when there wasn't a war on! They just put it somewhere else!"

Gertie stood over the top of the scrap metal filled bucket, with the truck starting to move down the drive towards the gate.

"Get down back there. Do you want Sarg on the warpath again?" Old Spot barked back, saving Rusty's breath.

Gertie promptly crumpled back down to his knees and waited until they'd got clear of Sarg's gate, back onto the Long Town Road heading into the village.

"Go on. You can have a go now," Al urged.

Gertie got back to his feet, settling his balance, as the movement of the truck steadied into an easy rhythm, gripping the bucket handle with both hands, arms extended, feet braced wide, and legs locked at knees. For one moment Gertie thought maybe if he gave it one good jerk that would shift it. Then he thought how Walker hadn't done too well with that method. Maybe slowly taking the strain would make the difference. Gertie bent his knees this time and eased the tension in his forearms. He'd been told enough times he had long legs; maybe they were good for buckets as well as bicycles?

Gertie knew how to lift properly. Mrs Tweeny had taught him when he'd helped her with the laundry baskets. He adjusted his grip and bent his knees a little more until he was almost crouching, then keeping his back upright, began to straighten up. It was all going so well, until Maze saw Jeepers coming out from the village in one of his trucks.

"JEEPERS!" she squealed in high-pitched alarm.

No one ever got to the bottom of the reason for the warning. Jeepers didn't know anything. But by then it was too late. Maze had screamed, Al had jumped and knocked Walker, who was still trying to get to grips with the extraordinary length of his shirt sleeves. He'd been trying to roll them up over his elbows, but with Al's sudden movement he'd lost hold and it had all flopped back down over his hands. Walker had tried to stretch his hands out from under the voluminous folds, not realising that took them directly into Gertie's face.

As if the poor lad wasn't distracted enough, that did it! Instinctively, he took one hand off the handle of the weighted bucket to swat Walker's hand away, forgetting he was straining. Losing his balance, Gertie toppled over the bucket, landing unceremoniously into Maze's pram propped in the corner of the truck.

"Cripes! What was that?" Old Spot yelled angrily from the front, whilst Rusty kept on steering steady through the village.

"No, not cripes. Just Jeepers!" came the answer from Al in fits of laughter in the back.

"Oh heck. Did he see us?"

Old Spot got the gist, straining to see which way the other truck might have gone, then noticing something was missing from the back of Rusty's truck.

"Where'd Gertie get to?" realising he'd suddenly lost sight of the lad.

"He's in Maze's pram!" Walker managed between chuckles.

Rusty heard that and yelled back, "Well get him out of there, or it won't be Jeepers we'll be fretting about, the whole ruddy village will be talking!"

Walker had a sudden flash of inspiration.

"Don't worry. If anyone saw him, we'll just tell 'em he was practising for the go-cart."

Al thought that was brilliant. Rusty decided the safest thing for her to do was to see the three youngsters back to their front door before she went any further.

"Come on all of you, out!" She'd pulled over and stopped the engine.

"What do we do about our bucket, it's too heavy to move?" Walker queried. Al hadn't thought about that, and Gertie was just glad to get his bicycle out from the truck and back onto solid ground. Maze didn't care about the bucket, either.

Walker and Al exchanged glances: "We could tip it out." Between them they started thinking just how much of a mess a bucket of scrap nails was likely to make on the village footpath. Old Spot came to the rescue with a solution.

"How about we take the full bucket back to the Yard with us?"

"What?" Walker exclaimed, almost hysterical. "After all we went through to try and get the bucket full *away* from the Yard, you want us to let you take it all back?"

"But you didn't get it from Jeepers' Yard, did you?" Rusty reminded the boys, coming to stand beside her grandfather.

Old Spot had a suggestion at the ready. "We'll take the scrap from the bucket, return your bucket and see if we can find something for your go-cart to boot. How does that sound?"

"Then if Jeepers did see us, we can just say we were doing a deal," Al told Walker brightly.

"We're doing a deal with Jeepers' Yard?" Walker asked, in awe at how such a thing had come to pass.

Both boys then turned back to Old Spot, who was grinning

and offering them his hand on it. Rusty climbed back into her truck and waited for them to finish. Walker positively beamed as he took his turn after Al to shake hands with the elderly gentleman. It was the second time he'd shaken hands that day. Great times.

Rusty took the truck back to the Yard. Jeepers didn't get back until late and never said a word about seeing them in the village. Old Spot was already snoring in his armchair by then. Rusty sat on her own in the kitchen and listened to the radio for a while.

"Thank goodness for Aggy," she smiled, remembering how relieved she'd been to see her and how well Florrie had coped too.

Her grandfather might sound like he was grumpy sometimes, but that was simply because nothing stayed the way he liked it anymore. He was the first to remind her, "Nothing wrong with change, so long as it's in the right direction."

She hadn't intentionally been putting off taking her grandfather over to the House. She wouldn't have done that, but now that it was over, she could admit it had gone better than she'd feared. He might have said a few odd things, but the Lads up at the hospital had taken it all in good humour. If ever there was a place that was able to make allowances, then that was it.

When they'd got back, she'd left her grandfather walking down to his pottering shed. He usually ended up back there before she was ready to call him in for supper. He'd been muttering something about a load of bricks. Rusty didn't ask where he was going to get a load of bricks from. Her grandfather sounded quite content with whatever it was he was planning, and she didn't like disturbing him down in his pottering shed.

There wasn't much for supper. Thank goodness Mrs Toombs had given her a couple of eggs. Rusty walked through the nip-way behind the farmhouse, in between the stacks of stones and slabs, seeming to manage to make themselves into a wall all by themselves, whilst the lengths of old railings and rotten fence posts and props crammed into the space between the hedge that tended to grow that way. Technically, because that area was behind the farmhouse, it all belonged to Old Spot. Jeepers wasn't meant to use that ground. That had been the agreement between the two men. So, *who's* bricks those were would likely boil down to the fact that Jeepers had left them there too long and Old Spot had got busy 'noticing' them. That was the way it usually went.

Her grandfather had been muttering about 'maybe making a pigsty' out of them over supper. At least that's what it sounded liked he'd decided. There might be room for one. Chickens would have made more sense, but Rusty wasn't going to tell him that. Old Spot wanted to work this one out for himself.

She never did hear when Jeepers got back to the farmhouse that night. She might have heard him thumping about but didn't open her door to investigate. He might have been unloading more of his 'keeping' boxes. At least he hadn't disturbed Old Spot. Her grandfather had trained himself to sleep through anything.

Jeepers was there next morning. The supper she'd left for him had gone and he seemed to be in a reasonable mood with no word of having seen the Scamps in Rusty's truck the day before.

Rusty was keen to learn what Walker had got Al to tell his parents by way of an explanation for the state of their return.

Then laughed at herself. Al would never get the chance. Maze would be telling of how Joe had showed her how to count her fours, fives and sixes with those dominoes long before then.

The tea was brewing, and Rusty called out to her grandfather to make sure he washed before coming into the kitchen. He was in a good mood too, talking about his intentions for those bricks.

"*My* bricks, and I'm quite capable of mixing my own mortar, thank you," he informed his son.

Jeepers pulled a face. "*Your* bricks?" he queried, realising he'd forgotten about that stack of old bricks long since. Jeepers wasn't really annoyed. Actually, he was pleased for Old Grumps. It would keep him out of mischief. There was cement sand in the dry corner of his long shed, but he wasn't going to mention that. No telling what he might be finding for himself if the old man got in there.

What Jeepers hadn't reckoned on was the cunning of his father. Old Spot had that bucket of scrap nuts and bolts from the Salvage Scamps. There was a bit of bargaining to be done over the breakfast table. The contents of the bucket for the bags of cement sand, and the use of one of the sack-barrows, and a couple of old crates to boot.

"And you don't happen to have any pram wheels back there?" Old Spot recalled, cheerfully.

Jeepers almost snorted a nose full of tea with laughter at that enquiry. "No, but I could probably find you a couple of wheels from some wreck spares that have come my way. I'll have a look, if you tell me what you want them for."

"I'm making a pigsty." Old Spot winked over the table to Rusty, who grinned and stayed silent.

Jeepers choked on his toast. "What d'ya wanna go and do a thing like that for!?"

"'Cos it's one of the 'bits' I can do, so I'm gonna do it!" Old Spot informed him.

"Seems to me we ought to be giving serious thought to a bomb-shelter? How about you build us one of those out there?" Jeepers was teasing, but his teasing missed its target.

Old Spot took the suggestion seriously. "A bomb-shelter? Hadn't thought of that. You're on!"

Rusty chuckled. Jeepers was laughing himself by then. What else could he do?

"What, you didn't think I could give you a better suggestion than a pigsty?"

"Well, yes," Old Spot admitted, then had another thought. "Can I borrow a couple of your blokes to help me?"

Jeepers gave up on the rest of his meal after that.

"No chance! They're on callout. Can't have them where I can't find 'em. Anyway, you'd better get a shift on if you're gonna be building a bomb-shelter. If France has fallen, then the Germans'll be coming for us next. We're all that's left!"

Old Spot swore and looked suddenly alarmed, checking his wristwatch he scraped his chair away from the table as he scrambled to his feet, looking for his boots.

"I'd better get started then!"

Jeepers would find the crates and the wheels for the Scamps go-cart. He'd leave them by the side path. Then it would be up to Rusty and Old Spot to take them wherever they were needed. He'd leave them the cement sand, too. He wasn't going to let them into his long shed, Germans or no Germans!

"So, you've definitely decided, then?" Rusty queried, when it was just the two of them in the farmhouse kitchen again.

"I think so!" Old Spot told her. He was still a bit shaken by the news that the Germans were coming. That wasn't what his radio had told him.

He would have liked to have kept a pig, even if only for fattening up for winter. He was sure Mr Tor wouldn't mind giving him a squealer, especially in trade for half. He was already enjoying the prospect of a piglet getting loose in Jeepers' Yard. That was a good enough reason by itself, except the bomb-shelter sounded more urgent.

"Then how about we just clear the area and make a start? You always think better when you're working."

Rusty's grandfather nodded as they walked over to where the bricks were stacked drunkenly across the waste ground straddling the patch of land north of his pottering shed, before the working fields began. Old Spot looked out to those fields with a slow sadness in his eyes. "I just want to help."

"We all want to do that," she agreed. She knew her grandfather felt safer doing something on his own land. Rather than fussing about in the village or bothering anyone else.

"From the sound of it," she continued, "Jeepers has got his hands full with the day's dealings. At least we've still got plenty of long days to work by. I won't be able to get out of the Yard for a couple of hours at least, so how about we make a start? Then I can take the Scamp's bucket back with my shopping list, and maybe get you a newspaper."

Whilst her grandfather used his barrow to shift the cement sand bags, Rusty used more of the old flat stones and broken slabs dumped to one side by the loose reclaimed bricks. She could make a higgledy path for the boots and barrow wheels to roll over with those.

"Bit of cobbling called for," Old Spot sighed contentedly a little later, as he leant against the sycamore tree and mopped his forehead.

"Oh, I think there's a lot of that going on. Nothing wrong with that!" Rusty reminded him. They could both hear Jeepers still yelling at his blokes out in the Yard. He was almost finished, sounded like he was running out of breath and patience!

Rusty listened for the sound of the shed doors being locked up again, then the scrape of the gates being dragged open, then finally the sound of cab doors being slammed shut, as the truck engines got started.

She didn't hurry to leave her grandfather. Already she could see him starting to struggle, his pace slowing. The best she could do was bring more of the bricks nearer to the building site for him.

"Are we being ready yet?" he suddenly looked over to her, anxiety furrowing his brow.

Rusty hadn't been listening and wasn't sure what he was referring to. "Probably not!" she answered him honestly.

"No, I didn't think so either."

Old Spot looked out across the working fields again, then back at their farmhouse. It wasn't *that* old, not to his way of thinking. It might have been charming once, but even he could admit it was too ramshackle for that anymore. It was sort of grubby and worn down, rather like he was feeling, but it was still standing, it was still useful, and *he* could still contribute.

Rusty waited for her grandfather to finish saying what he'd been thinking.

"If we're not yet, then we'd better pull our socks up, and tighten our belts and brace ourselves, 'cos we *really* need to be and pretty-damn-quick!"

Rusty burst out laughing at that, looking down at her own boots, no socks and she was wearing the same overalls as yesterday, with one of her grandfather's belts.

"Do we have a plan?" she asked him gently, coming to his side.

Her grandfather was getting too old to be labouring like this. He was getting redder in the face, his breath coming with more puff, and she could see his hands trembling a little when he took them away from the barrow handle.

"Look, we've got it all marked out now," she indicated. "Everything's at the ready and within reach. Jeepers can't take it back anymore, so how about you sit and do your working out, whilst I get us a cuppa?"

Old Spot sat down obediently and tugged at the crumpled piece of paper in his back pocket.

"Just to be sure," he smiled up at her, wrestling the tape measure out from his other pocket. "Any chance of a cup of tea before you go? I'm gasping."

Rusty slowed her pace back to the farmhouse. She wasn't sure if even he knew what he was planning for, only that he was determined to do it, to do his bit for the War Effort. She knew her grandfather was getting more confused, and the long summer days that lay ahead of them seemed suddenly to be all too short.

She brought out the mug of tea with a piece of shortbread from the parcel Mrs Toombs had given her. Old Spot hadn't noticed her approaching. When he did he smiled, and Rusty found the sadness gone.

"Oh, lovely! I'm ready for that. You been baking?"

Rusty shook her head. "Not me. The shortbread's from Mrs Toombs, a thank you for the strawberries."

Her grandfather took the mug and the biscuit. Perhaps he hadn't heard her, but he didn't seem to recognise the mention of visiting Mrs Toombs' kitchen at all.

Before Rusty could get her truck out of the Yard, she'd need to do some clearance of her own. Jeepers' blokes never bothered with the broom, so she'd have to sweep the debris off the lane where they'd dumped it.

"Must remember to take Al's bucket back to him," she reminded herself. Jeepers had been good to his word and left a couple of crates and an odd-looking pair of wheels with no tyres, one only slightly buckled, by the cab of her truck.

What he hadn't left her was any fuel. He kept the jerry cans locked up in the long shed. She climbed up into the cab and started the engine then checked the gauge, it was the wrong side of quarter full. Damn! She could get into the village and around her route with that much, but nothing else, and these days there was *always* something else. Especially if she tangled up with the Salvage Scamps again, best leave the crates and wheels to wait another day. At least, *just* returning the bucket felt less likely to start anything new.

Rusty made sure the crates and wheels were safely tucked round to the side path of the farmhouse. It was neutral territory between her father and grandfather. Neither man used it unless he had to.

Jeepers' Yard at the front was far wider than the width of the family farmhouse. The back garden followed the same width at the back of the house, which meant beside the house on either side there were two broad strips of fallow waste ground. This was not the time for wasting ground. Jeepers seemed to have already taken that to heart, spreading his Yard's domain backwards with an assortment of railings, engine parts, posts and old door panels, with more bricks and roof tiles, by the looks of it.

Rusty hadn't been surprised to discover he'd done that. What had been unexpected were the forlorn-looking potted fruit trees Jeepers had discarded that way. He wasn't usually into anything green, only if the greenery was already included in a load he wanted, as part of a 'to boot' and the first thing he did after that was to boot it back to Old Spot's back garden! The fruit trees seemed to have survived the neglectful treatment, long since breaking free of their pots, their roots finding the earth for themselves, their branches reaching with sturdy summer growth.

It wasn't much of an orchard, but it was nice to see it regardless. If nothing else, Rusty thought it might discourage Jeepers from chucking anything else over that way. She could see how some of the lengths of rusted railings were steadily being swallowed by hedge and deeper back there appeared to be some sheets of corrugated metal. She grinned. That was good to know. Might come in handy.

"Oh, there you are!" Old Spot found her, "What'ya doing over 'ere?"

"Did you know we had a bit of an orchard going on this way?" she asked him.

"Are they meant to look like that?" her grandfather queried, taking a closer look. "Seem to have made themselves at home though, haven't they?"

Old Spot was thinking. "If they get in Jeepers' way, then maybe we can snaffle a few more of those surplus supplies of his."

The smell of the soil filled the air, the sounds of the sky clear above their head, whilst the scuff of rubble dust mingled with old mud and fresh grass, and the songs from the hedge sparrows, and the noises from the fenland fields came easy to their ears. It made the day itself seem eager to Rusty.

"Are you taking my mortar bucket away with you?" Her grandfather suddenly demanded, spying the bucket in Rusty's hand.

"No, this one belongs to Al, the little boy that helped you with the strawberries," she remined him.

"Oh yes, the bright one, not the green one, or the clanky one!"

She thought that last reference might have meant lanky, or maybe clumsy? She wondered what Gertie would make of being referred to as 'clanky'. Al would definitely enjoy being recognised as the 'bright one'. Rusty never thought Walker wasn't bright, only a little too city-quick for his own good sometimes, and he'd definitely been rather green the last time her grandfather had seen him!

"Yes, it's Al's bucket. I'm taking it back to him before he manages to get into any more trouble without it."

"Oh yes!" her grandfather agreed sagely. "Always better to have a bucket with you if you're going to be getting into trouble."

He smiled across to her and she saw the soft summer breeze brushing aside the fine brick dust from his weathered forearms. There were even a few pieces of grit up in his hair.

"How did they get up there?" she asked him merrily, picking them out. "A bomb-shelter, really?"

CHAPTER 5

Maze's Plan, Jam Jars and Rabbits

DOTTY DIDN'T GET INTO TROUBLE for allowing the children into the hospital library, but only because she forgot to tell Pru.

Florrie had hurried her breakfast the morning after, but already knew she was going to miss the bus if she was going to check in on Walker before starting her shift. Dotty would have been happy to cover, only she was late too.

Pru decided the only way she was going to get to the bottom of what her two friends were up to was to miss the bus along with them.

"At least if we're all late, we can use the same excuse!" she reasoned.

"Ever practical Pru!" Dotty smiled, steering her along the village footpath towards the school gates.

"We're going to school?" Pru checked.

"No, we're waiting for one of the schoolchildren. We have a young patient who probably doesn't want the rest of his friends to know what got him so sick yesterday. I don't know if Al has told his parents the real reason for Walker coming back in different clothes."

Pru indicated she understood, but otherwise remained

silent, realising she'd learn more that way. "Oh!"

Maze saw them first and waved them over.

"Did you bring Walker's book?" she was asking Dotty.

Pru and Florrie looked to Dotty.

"Oh yes, I met you both in the library, didn't I? Was he looking for any book in particular? I thought he wanted to play dominoes with Joe."

"I think he was hoping to find one. He told me afterwards he likes books much more than he likes berries now!" The little girl informed the three junior nurses.

Florrie could appreciate why that might be the case, but before any of them had time to response, Maze continued her cheerful chatter.

Al could see his little sister, but didn't reach her in time to stop her, and Walker just waited for the inevitable. He'd learnt quicker than Al, when Maze decided to say something, the best thing to do was to let her get on with it and pick up the pieces afterwards. It was quieter that way.

"When he saw how many books you had, he thought afterwards if he'd been a bit quicker you wouldn't have missed one or two. Didn't you?"

Maze turned to check those were Walker's words. He blushed and rubbed the back of his neck, then scratched up behind his ear, before wiping his nose with the back of his hand and sniffing.

"I did say that, but you wouldn't have missed just one, would you? And I would have brought it back."

"Firstly, none of those books in the library are mine, and even if I was able to let you borrow one, you never asked. Why not?" Dotty asked.

"Because between the shortbread and the dominoes and

the truck I wasn't quick enough," Walker admitted.

"I don't think you were feeling too quick yesterday, were you?" Florrie offered the young evacuee gently. "How did you get on back home? Did Al explain everything to his mum for you?"

Maze was at the ready with her next revelation. "He didn't need to. Mum could 'smell mischief' on Walker. It smelt like soap!"

"That, and he was wearing clean clothes, too," Al added, not wishing to be left out.

Florrie had told Dotty about the 'wrong berries' incident because she'd needed her help rinsing Walker's clothes and getting them back to him. She couldn't ask any of the porters to help with that.

Pru had been too busy with one of the new Lads who'd just been moved on to the wards. He'd been in one of the side rooms since arriving. As junior nurses, they weren't allowed to take care of any of the Lads in the side rooms, unless everyone else was busy and then usually only to sit with them.

"Did you miss your salvage quota that day?" Florrie asked.

Walker was delighted to report, "No, we got a whole bucketful of scrap."

"You didn't. I did," Al corrected him. "Some of the Lads up at the House helped me load it, but I wasn't allowed to keep it though, on account of we couldn't lift the bucket out the truck afterwards, so it got taken back to Jeepers' Yard; but that still counts, don't it?"

"Did you get your bucket back?" Pru picked into that detail.

Maze blinked, looking to her elder brother.

"No!"

The only bucket Florrie knew about was the one she'd asked the porter to find for her to put Walker's stinking clothes in and that belonged to the hospital. Getting his clothes rinsed through and dry enough to fold and return to him involved bringing Mrs Toombs into their confidence, although by then Mrs Toombs seemed to know everything, as she usually did, before anyone told her properly.

Pru didn't know any of this and with neither Al nor Walker willing to tell her everything, she decided on a far more efficient route.

"Come on, Maze, let's make sure you don't miss the start of school. Then you can ask Miss Aggy about getting one of those books for Walker next time she's visiting the hospital library."

Al and Walker were left with the other two nurses.

"Are you feeling better?" Florrie finally got to ask Walker directly.

Al offered, on his friend's behalf, "Mum said he'd bounce back, and he did because she sent him to bed with no supper."

"You're going to feel a bit tender for a few days," Florrie approved.

"I don't feel tender. I feel hungry!" Walker complained. He wouldn't have a word said against Mrs Toombs offering him that cup of tea and the tin of shortbread.

"Mrs Toombs' feel-better biscuits remedy worked much nicer than Al's mum telling me bed-no-supper."

Aggy was coming out from the school looking for Al and Walker by then. Maze had told her where they'd be, but the schoolteacher was surprised to see them still there. Classes were about to begin, and Florrie and Dotty were going to be late for their shift.

"We can't be late again," Pru informed them. "We just *can't* be!"

Gertie came to the rescue. He'd seen them from the other side of the duckpond. He was out of breath, but ready with the solution by the time he got to them.

"Milko's coming round; he's late too. He'll take you. You'll have to sit in the back of the cart with the empties. He's halfway round, but I know his horse!"

Pru almost shrieked, "We couldn't possibly!"

Dotty was all for the idea. Florrie hesitated, looking to Aggy. "What will Matron say?"

Gertie had the answer to that one too. "She'll have nothing to say. Matron won't know you're late if you're not."

Aggy agreed with Gertie, shooing the three junior nurses on their way.

"Come on, then." Gertie waved them to join him on the quick dash to catch up with the milkman's horse and cart whilst Aggy looked back to Al and Walker.

"Goodness, you two don't do things by halves, do you?"

Walker grinned and answered for the pair of them.

"We've all got to do our bit, Miss."

"That's all very well, but I hope you remember to thank Gertie for getting you out of trouble again."

"Gertie got us out of trouble, Miss?" Al asked. "I thought it was Rusty with her truck."

Aggy didn't think so.

"It was Gertie and his bicycle. It was Gertie who knew to get you to hospital, and it was Gertie who showed you the library, too."

That gave the boys something to think about for the rest

of the day. They had plenty to think about even before then. It was in the newspapers: *'The Germans have invaded the Channel Islands.'*

Walker kept thinking of the Vikings with those horned helmets that reminded him of bulls. He thought the Germans were bullies. Al had started off calling him an idiot, then thought about it, until it didn't sound so silly.

Aggy decided it might be time to help the children understand the difference between evacuees like Walker, who would be able to go home one day, and those thousands of refugees from the Channel Islands. She had begun to practise the words she would need to use, but found they broke in her throat. Instead, she took the large heavy classroom atlas in her hands, laying it flat on the middle desk in the classroom, slowly turning its reassuringly sturdy pages, giving herself a chance to compose herself.

The fall of France felt like a long time ago. The German Army was getting closer to their shores, the German planes had already begun bombing some of their coastal towns.

"Told you so, Miss. Bullies!"

"They're not only throwing all the 'fugees out the place, they're trying to sink our beaches, too!"

Aggy sighed. Thank goodness for young sparks like Walker. His classmates soon chimed in with their own opinions. They weren't in the mood for asking her questions.

As well as the arguments regarding the character of the Romans and the Vikings, there were some colourful opinions on the various merits of tanks and aeroplanes, as opposed to what had been achieved with only shields and spears!

They finished the lesson talking about how everyone was ready to do their bit. It would have been a far more stirring end to the school day if Walker's stomach hadn't been growling quite so loudly.

Walker had been wondering if the milkman's horse had kept a couple of apples spare, left over from his recent visit to the village stables.

"He wasn't visiting, he was delivering," Al reminded him.

Between them, the two boys decided the only way Gertie could have persuaded the milko's horse to take Florrie and her friends in amongst the empties, in time to catch the start of their shift, was to use apples.

"Gertie didn't have any apples. We would have seen them in his pockets," Al reasoned.

Walker was adamant that he'd had to have had apples somewhere. That had been when they decided Gertie must have a stash of apples.

Maze had tried to help. "Or carrots?"

Her older brother had told her that wasn't likely, not with Mrs Toombs. "She counts them, you know."

Walker was starting to feel giddy, and it wasn't because of his stomach.

"We really ought to find out if Florrie and her friends got to their shift before Matron found them missing."

When they came out from school there was no sign of Gertie, or the milkman and his horse, with or without apples. Aggy would have happily taken them with her over to the library.

"If you can wait for me?" the young schoolteacher cautioned. "I've a few things to sort out first."

But Walker couldn't wait, and Al didn't want to.

"Takes a lot of sorting out, this 'not being ready' yet, don't it?" Al asked his friend. Maze hadn't waited for either her elder brother *or* his friend. She hadn't even stopped to feed the ducks this time.

Maze had an idea. She was going to do her bit, whether the boys were ready or not, and she was taking her old pram with her!

When they'd mentioned Mrs Toombs, it had reminded Maze of something she'd seen whilst in the hospital kitchen. It had been down in the bottom of Mrs Toombs' larder. Maze had been just the right height to notice, whilst Walker had only been interested in the shortbread tin on the table.

Maze could only think that Mrs Toombs herself was too large to see down that low. In the bottom of the larder there was a cardboard box full of empty jam jars.

"My pram will be perfick for those, not a truck, not a bucket, just my pram and me!" she told them with a little pout and a proper stamp of her foot.

Al could see there was no arguing with his little sister and he for one didn't want to incur the wrath of his mother again. Although the incident with the wrong berries had been all Walker's fault, he'd got blamed for it too.

"OK then, you lead, if you think you can walk that far. You'll have to think of a trade before then, remember."

Maze hadn't thought of that part of the bargain.

"It's not a trade, it's salvage," she told them defiantly, though her voice wasn't quite as confident this time. She hadn't stopped, but her pace had slowed a little by the time they got to the edge of the village.

"What do I say?" she asked Walker, who'd been struggling with that part too. The best he could come up with was 'please might work'.

Al wasn't going to help. He was still sulking about being scolded for the wrong berries and he hadn't even been sick!

Then Walker reminded them about Mrs Toombs.

"Maybe she *needs* someone to collect those jam jars. Maybe we're helping her? Maybe she'll be the one thanking us with more shortbread?"

"We're not meant to be doing this for shortbread," Maze told him sternly, wagging her finger at the pair of them. They might be bigger than her, but she knew what was right.

"Miss Aggy told us it was our *duty*. You can't do duty if it's for shortbread. That doesn't count."

"I can't do duty when I'm hungry," Walker told her firmly, stomping on ahead. "Anyway, Florrie will help us. She's a nurse; she helps everyone," he told both of them.

Al had forgotten that Florrie would be there.

"You like her 'cos she's got the library."

"No, she doesn't," Walker told his friend, with Maze staying silent, pushing her pram. "Dotty has the library. Florrie has the soap!"

"What about Pru? She's very good, Pru is, a proper nurse," Maze informed both boys.

"What d'ya mean?" Al took charge of the questioning. "What's wrong with Florrie? She smells lovely." Turning to Walker, "Better than you did before we took you to her, that's for sure! Anyway, we didn't even see Pru then, so how would you know?"

Maze knew.

"Because Pru gets to the hospital on the bus, properly. She doesn't need to use Rusty's truck and she only went on the milko's cart because Florrie had to check in on you."

That had both Walker and Al stumped.

"Hey there, it's Gertie!" Walker called out, grateful for the timely intervention.

Gertie had his bicycle with him this time. He'd got caught up with the milkman, then got behind with the butcher's deliveries, but was almost done.

Maze was pleased to see him, eager to know how the nurses got on with the horse. Walker wanted to know about the apples. Al wanted to know if he thought Mrs Toombs had any more shortbread. Gertie was just happy to be so popular. Getting off his bicycle, he began pushing it beside Maze's pram.

"You're in the lead, are you?"

Maze grinned and lifted her chin. "It was *my* idea. I'm doing salvage duty," she informed him.

Gertie followed her lead, thumbing back to the two boys behind them. "So why are they tagging along?"

"Apples," Walker offered.

"Shortbread," Al countered.

Walker adjusted his expectations with the next step. "Shortbread first. We can take the apples home with us."

"Can you?" Gertie asked the pair, winking across to Maze.

"Can we?" Walker asked.

Al shrugged.

Gertie grinned brightly. "Don't tell me you've eaten more berries," looking a little accusingly at Walker.

"Haven't eaten anything!" Walker grumbled.

Al nudged him muttering, "Except breakfast!"

"No, he hasn't," Maze called back. "We're going for the jam jars this time."

Gertie didn't know anything about the jam jars in Mrs Toombs' larder, only that they were in demand according to Over-Eager-Edith's leaflets.

"What you going to trade for them, then?" He checked with Maze. Al kept an admirably straight face, whilst Walker was delighted to confirm, "We've already asked her that."

"Shortbread!" Maze reminded them.

"You've got shortbread?" Gertie asked her, peering into the pram.

"No, we're going to get shortbread with the jam jars," the little girl explained determinedly.

Gertie halted the convoy of bike, pram and three children at that announcement.

"Hang on a minute, how does that work? You get the jam jars *and* the shortbread, without poisoning yourself with berries first and no soap?"

Maze assured him she'd got it all straight in her little head.

"I saw them first, so I can have them. Mrs Toombs doesn't want them, or she wouldn't have put them down where she can't reach them, and she'll give us shortbread for helping her not waste them."

Gertie was impressed, Al and Walker were too, now Maze had explained it like that.

By the time they'd got to the gate leading up to the RAF hospital, everyone was taking orders from the five-year-old. Gertie knelt down beside her.

"OK, you going to tell Sarg, then, or shall I?"

"Which one's the sergeant?" Maze asked, looking at what seemed like an entire regiment standing at the gate to the drive that swung up past the stables to the main entrance of the grand old house.

"The one in the middle," Gertie whispered. "The one looking daggers at me right now."

Maze wasn't having that. Sarg looked like a bully. Gertie

was only a weed of a lad. A tall weed, admittedly, and his glasses were on wonky again, but that didn't warrant 'daggers'. Maze didn't like bullies, but she didn't know how to return the daggers look, so she coughed to get Sarg's attention, then charged at him with her old pram. The front wheels rammed into his shins.

"Oy, miss, you can't be doing that! Is she with you?" Sarg glared at Gertie.

Gertie had one hand holding on to his bicycle, whilst his free hand had tried in vain to be quick enough to grab for Maze to halt her charge. Sarg had noticed his efforts. He didn't blame Gertie for missing; the little girl was quicksilver.

Gertie didn't have time to answer Sarg's query, as now he was fully employed struggling to restrain both Al and Walker, who'd rushed forward to Maze's defence.

Sarg amended his initial question.

"Are they *all* with you?"

"No, Sarg. I'm with *them*. They're the Salvage Scamps. You remember Walker, Sarg?"

Sarg took another look at the boy in the oversized clothes. "You?"

"Me." Walker came to Maze's side, whilst Al took care of the now toppled pram, righting it and bringing it back to face Sarg.

"No berries this time?" Sarg checked.

"No, Sarg. We're here for the jam jars," Maze informed him.

"Urgent, is it?" Sarg queried, managing to bend down, nose to nose with Maze, whilst surreptitiously rubbing his bruised shins.

"I didn't eat any of the berries. He did." Maze pointed to

Walker.

"Just him? You weren't an idiot?" Sarg checked.

"No, Sarg. I was on the bicycle," Maze explained, "and Miss Aggy took me into Mrs Toombs' kitchen."

"Oh, you're with your teacher?" Sarg straightened up, starting to look behind them.

"No, Sarg. I came with my pram this time."

Maze proved the point by resecuring her grip on the pram from her brother, who'd realised she was well capable of handling this situation without him.

"Walker's very sorry for using up your soap!" Al tried to help.

"I didn't want any soap. The nurse made me. Florrie did it. It was her fault!" Walker spluttered.

"Ah, but I bet the nurse made sure you got a cuppa and a bit of Mrs Toombs' shortbread after, didn't she?" Sarg flicked Walker's ear, then Al's, so the other boy didn't feel left out.

"Please, Sarg, salvage duty," Al spoke up.

"Do you know where you're going?" Sarg checked.

Gertie grinned. "Kitchen, Sarg."

Sarg pointed at each of them in turn. "Kitchen *only*. Got it?"

"Yes, Sarg."

Gertie led with his bicycle on to one side of the driveway, Maze with her pram just behind, turning back to her dawdling brother and his friend, informing them loudly, "See, he *wasn't* a bully. Not really!"

Gertie decided Maze had walked far enough. The drive was a long way and her voice seemed to have got louder since challenging Sarg.

"Come on up on my bicycle. I'll give you a lift. Al can take his turn with the pram. Walker can do his bit on the way back, when it's full of jam jars."

That was the plan. Gertie said it just loud enough to assure Sarg that he would make sure the Salvage Scamps didn't get distracted any further than Mrs Toombs' kitchen. Walker was the first to ask about the stables in the grounds. Gertie knew about that place.

"Oh, very fine it used to be. They don't use the carts anymore, now they've got the cars and the trucks. I think there might be a motorbike about the place, somewhere. Although I know Shark-shoulders still likes to ride his horse regular every Saturday."

"Shark-shoulders?" Walker gasped.

Gertie had their attention now, which was what he'd been hoping, at least until he'd steered them safely round to Mrs Toombs' kitchen door.

"Shark-shoulders. He's the consultant for the clinic. He helps the Lads when the doctors can't."

"Oh!"

The two boys followed as Gertie walked with Maze on his bicycle. Gertie wasn't quite sure what the difference was between the doctors and the consultant. He only knew that Shark-shoulders was the consultant over at the clinic because he'd heard one of the porters saying that.

"What was the porter doing?" Al wondered aloud.

"Ah!" Walker knew this one, he'd seen them at the train station. "Porters are there to be moving things."

"What about Matron?" Maze asked. She hadn't forgotten the one that Florrie had been worried about. Gertie wasn't brave enough to hazard a guess at that.

"How about we ask Mrs Toombs? She'll know."

Maze gleefully approved of that notion. They were already safely through the gate and no one else seemed interested in their intentions. There were a few people about, at least a couple of individuals they could recognise as nurses, and a porter was spotted in the distance with a wheelchair, walking it across the grass, seeming intent on returning it to the house, confirming Walker's description. No one saw any doctors.

"They must be upstairs." Al had heard about that when he'd been helping Rusty unload the truck with some of the Lads. "The doctors only come down when they're 'ready to be a nuisance' again."

Mrs Toombs had heard them approaching. She'd been expecting Aggy, or perhaps Rusty at least, to be accompanying them. Seeing Gertie coming in with Maze made her tut.

"What mischief has brought you up here today, then?"

"No more berries," Walker blurted, "but if you've got any shortbread, yes please! Just without the soap, please?"

Al kicked him. "That's not what we agreed. You said apples!" he reminded his friend.

"I only said apples because of the horses," Walker corrected him. "You were the one that said shortbread. I just didn't want any more soap. It wasn't my fault, and it was your bucket anyway!"

Mrs Toombs had remained perfectly motionless during this exchange. Maze had brought her pram into the kitchen and had steadily begun to move it towards the larder.

Gertie had been in a quandary as to whether to follow Maze or deliver those last couple of butcher's parcels to the kitchen table first, and somehow at the same time stop the two Scamps in front of him going further.

"These ones, Mrs Toombs!" Maze called out from the bottom of the larder, trying to pull out the large heavy cardboard box full of empty glass jars.

"What do you think you're going to do with those, missy?" Mrs Toombs took one gigantic step and immediately towered over the crouching child.

"We're going to salvage them for you."

"They're already salvaged right where there are, thank you," Mrs Toombs informed her firmly.

Maze was devastated, and promptly stopped her tugging and sat down on the floor of the larder. "Oh!"

It had been such a lovely idea. All her own. No jam jars meant no shortbread and she had walked so far and been so certain of what to do. Finally, she let got her grip on the box, abandoning her lovely plan.

"I wanted to do my bit because the Germans are bullies. They don't deserve any jam."

Mrs Toombs leaned down now and helped the little girl back up to her feet. Maze was already sniffing and close to tears. Her enormous girth prohibited her from getting far into the larder cupboard, but she was more than capable of scooping up the little girl into a massive hug and bringing her to the nearest kitchen chair.

"Now, don't you worry about those jars. They're quite safe where they are, I assure you. And as for those nasty Germans getting our lovely jam, our boys are seeing to them."

Maze sniffed again. She knew the RAF were doing their best, but it had been such a lovely idea and she had so wanted to do *her* bit.

Mrs Toombs did her best to shush the little girl's sniffs. "Maybe if we sit here and you let me think about it for a minute, we'll find something else for you to salvage. Did you walk *all* the way over here?"

Maze nodded.

"Yes, and we didn't even have an apple. The milko's horse ate them all."

Mrs Toombs found her own handkerchief and handed it to the little girl. The two boys and Gertie stood where they were. Maze blew her nose loudly and smiled weakly, before handing it back to Mrs Toombs, together with the query, "Why do they call him Shark-shoulders?"

"Oh heck!" Gertie gulped.

"Shark-shoulders is the one that rides the horse on Saturdays, isn't he? Gertie told us," Maze explained.

Mrs Toombs looked across at Gertie. "Did he, now?"

Sarg must have had time to walk back to the house by then and send a message to find Florrie, quite certain the nurse would be well advised to visit the kitchen.

"Ah, Florrie, are these with you?" Mrs Toombs looked across the table, as the nurse entered her kitchen.

"I wasn't expecting them. Has school finished already?"

"Ages ago, and we're still hungry," Walker assured her.

Florrie looked over to the cook.

"Have we got anything for them? I thought you had everything all sorted with the salvage, Mrs Toombs. Did you send for them?"

"No, we walked over all by ourselves," Maze chirped up.

"I just helped, before she got to thumping Sarg," Gertie cheerfully added, without being asked.

"We just came for the apples and shortbread," Al blurted, whilst Walker looked a little apprehensively towards Florrie.

"Without the soap, please."

Florrie didn't have time to take care of them. Gertie might be able to cycle back to the village, but Maze and Walker definitely weren't fit enough to walk that far back.

"How about I see if someone can take them back in one of the cars?"

"Well, they can't wait here. I dare say I might be able to find something for them, but they can't stay here. I'm working," Mrs Toombs stated categorically, although the strength of that statement lost a little of its vigour, due to the fact that Maze was still perched happily on her lap.

Florrie didn't have the answer. Maze did.

"If it was Saturday, Shark-shoulders could take us home on his horse, couldn't he? Except it's not Saturday."

"Who?" Florrie went red. "Who called him that?"

Maze, Al and Walker all pointed to Gertie. Mrs Toombs tutted, and Florrie shook her head. Gertie's only defence was, "One of the porters told me."

"Then stop listening to the porters. They're terrible for nicknames," Florrie instructed the children.

"Oh, but you're meant to do that," Walker reminded her. "Using codenames is safe. We have codenames for *everyone*."

Florrie smiled over to Mrs Toombs' unspoken query. "Yes, they do."

"How about if one of Lads took them over to feed the pigs? Would that be all right? That would count as part of the War Effort, wouldn't it Mrs Toombs? Salvage or no salvage today, they'd be doing their bit, wouldn't they?" Florrie continued, as no one seemed to be interrupting her or coming up with a better idea. "That should earn them a lift back into the village."

"Are any of the Pennies going that way?" Mrs Toombs asked the young nurse, over the heads of the children.

Gertie heard that one. "The Pennies?"

"Oh yes, the Pennies are the junior doctors, all bright and shiny like new pennies!" Mrs Toombs described, to the children's delight.

Whilst Florrie had been coming up with the errand, Maze had started looking for the biscuit tin and Mrs Toombs had started making a fresh pot of tea.

"Why in heavens didn't you wait for Miss Aggy to come over? I know she's coming back to the library."

"We thought it was urgent. Walker's stomach was grumbling so loud I couldn't think straight, and I couldn't stop Maze, as she'd already grabbed her pram," Al explained.

"Never mind, no harm done. The buckets are outside the back door. Andy'll help you."

Mrs Toombs sent Gertie looking for Andy, any of the porters would do, as she poured their cups of tea, then put down two pieces of shortbread very particularly on the plate in front of them, looking directly at Walker.

"Share them properly, then when you come back, I'll see if I can find you two more. I'm sure I've got a few old magazines around here for you to take back. Will that do?"

She was looking to Maze by then. Maze was smiling, waiting for her piece of shortbread. "Oh, yes please, thank you."

Mrs Toombs didn't have any time for jam-making. She could see Maze was still disappointed about leaving the box of jars behind.

"How about I use the magazines to wrap a couple of those jars in and see how you get on with taking those back, first?

Precious things jam jars, these days."

"Everything's precious now, including soap and shortbread, and I know which one I prefer," Walker muttered, hoping no one noticed he'd broken the piece slightly in his favour.

Gertie came back with one of the porters.

"Andy?" Florrie asked, looking to Gertie. "All the porters are called Andy. Nice and simple, ain't it? 'Cos they're 'andy to have when you need 'em."

"Quite right!"

Mrs Toombs shooed Florrie back upstairs, the junior nurse needed to be getting on with her own duties.

"Now what about those buckets?" Mrs Toombs scanned the youngsters in her kitchen. "Whose taking them over to the pigs?"

"We're not meant to know where they are?" Gertie reminded her, with a mischievous grin.

"No, we won't tell anyone," Al assured her eagerly. "It's all coded. We don't tell them you've got any pigs; we just call them rabbits and no one's any the wiser, you're allowed to have rabbits."

"Oh," Mrs Toombs smiled inscrutably, but her second chin trembled with mirth. "I always keep a bucket of plate scrapings ready for anyone who comes asking, to show them we *only* have rabbits here."

The porter grinned and helped them balance the buckets on Gertie's handlebars.

"No coffee grounds and no rhubarb tops. Can't go poisoning the rabbits!" Andy checked cheekily with Mrs Toombs, before starting out with the Scamps.

Florrie hadn't gone directly upstairs; she'd checked the library first. Joe was in there – he usually was – and a couple of the other Lads, but no sign of Aggy. The best she could do was try and find when the next truck might be heading back through the village.

Joe heard her and called the young nurse in.

"What's the problem? I can always tell when you've got a problem, because you stand in the doorway and tap your fingers on the doorframe, as if you can't decide which way to turn from there."

Florrie told him about the Scamps. Joe couldn't drive a truck, not anymore, and he didn't think any of the Pennies could help, not with all the recent arrivals, but had another thought.

"What about Humfrey? He's due by on his way back home. He lives in the village, doesn't he?"

"Humfrey?" Florrie wasn't sure she knew who that was.

"Aggy's husband, the librarian. The one that was here the other day. Humfrey works over at the Army camp, drives one of the trucks in between here and there. What with him being church warden and Home Guarding and all, he needs the truck for all that to-ing and fro-ing."

How Joe had learnt all that without ever leaving the hospital was a wonder, but Florrie knew if Humfrey was the village church warden, then that meant he was definitely Aggy's husband.

"He doesn't like driving an empty truck. You'll be doing him a favour," Joe offered. He was still thinking it through. "Always coming by here with deliveries over from the camp. You know what they're like for paperwork and Humfrey works in their clerking office. He'll see it all gets delivered properly. Camp to hospital, every day, regular as clockwork, that's clerk work."

"Humfrey?" Florrie repeated.

"Tell 'em they can come and meet me out on the front steps of the main entrance, I'll keep 'em happy until Humfrey turns up. That way no one is getting under anyone's feet. How does that sound?"

Joe smiled, and Florrie could feel the tension leave her fingers.

"Thank you."

CHAPTER 6

Joe's Story and the Work Crew

JOE SHRUGGED A GRIN AND nonchalantly reached to the side of the door where he'd rested his cane. The library was easy for him to navigate; none of the furniture moved. Getting across the open expanse of the main hallway was a little less straightforward; no telling who'd left a wheelchair or a trolley in an awkward place. He could feel Florrie's gaze following him as he walked steadily, his cane following his steps, whilst his other hand felt a little away from his side. He could hear where the stairway was, from the echo of his own footsteps, and knew where the doors were from that direction.

Joe felt the fresh air hit his face, the sunshine and the sounds of summer, then heard the distant laughter of children, already returning towards him.

He could hear the empty buckets clattering against the side of Gertie's bicycle, they were still a fair way distance yet. Joe took another step and felt the surface change beneath his boots. The top step. He'd wait for them there. They could help him 'watch' for Humfrey's truck.

He could hear them calling ahead to one of the porters that they'd finished 'feeding the rabbits'. Joe guessed they'd twigged the code. Quick kids, these country Scamps! It reminded him of home. The city kids had always looked down their noses at him and his country cousins, but where the city college had taught him how to be smart, it hadn't been so quick to pick up on what was really happening on the other side of the world.

America wanted to isolate itself, insulate itself away from the war over here. It was happy enough to help with trade and loans, but American industry couldn't afford to lose its workforce. That's what they were saying the last time Joe listened. That was America for you. All about the almighty buck. Joe was Canadian, and he wasn't going to stand idly by when there was fighting to be done. That wasn't the Canadian way!

He'd started in a small town, then gone to the city to work and hadn't liked it. The buildings were ugly and the people rude, and they all thought they were smarter than him. Maybe they were, but that didn't make him an idiot, just not with the same smarts they had. He wasn't going to call them selfish or arrogant about what they'd said about the English. Every Canadian could make up his own mind and that's what he'd done!

Don't ever try and persuade a Canadian he needs to change his mind. You try that, and the only thing that's pretty much damned guaranteed to happen is that he'll dig his heels in and stop listening to you. That's what Joe had done.

Plenty of opinions in Canada, just as many as in America. Only difference was in Canada most of the men wanted to get into the thick of it. America wanted to keep it all at arm's length. Maybe they'd manage that and maybe they wouldn't. Joe wasn't a man with that much patience!

He'd been able to read the newspapers and listen to the radio as well as the next man. Last time he'd looked France wasn't going to stay standing for long and England would be out there on its own. Joe wasn't going to let that happen.

Oh, sure, they had the supply ships coming across the Atlantic and the guys were doing their best to protect those supplies. Joe had watched them loading up a couple of those ships at the docks. They had dry stores, tractors, trucks and everything all crated up safe. Defended. That's what America was doing, helping England defend itself.

That was defending, but Joe knew what *really* needed to be done. Got to take the fighting over to the Germans. Can't wait for them to come to you.

Joe knew all about the Depression, twenty years of despair and desperation. He'd heard it all from his uncles. They'd told him all about tough times and how the small businesses were only just getting back on their feet. He'd heard them telling him how they couldn't afford to fight a war. As far as Joe could see, no one could!

Maybe America could support the War Effort with their trade and ships, but that wasn't *fighting* the war, not to Joe's way of thinking.

He'd seen a lot in those months whilst he was deciding what to do. He'd seen for himself in that small Canadian town where he'd grown up. Empty shops, boarded-up homes, streets where people shuffled along in the shadows, almost afraid to be out in the sunshine and walk tall again, in case they got knocked back down on their behinds. He could remember seeing men sitting on the steps of a tall building, waiting for the doors to open, waiting to get to work.

Joe wasn't going to wait anymore. He couldn't do that. He didn't want to go back to that small town where everyone was telling him there was nothing they could do, they had enough problems already, and they didn't need anyone else's. England wasn't just 'anyone else'.

Joe hadn't wanted to get stuck in any of those city offices either, or even in one of his uncles' workshops. He wanted to get over to England and start fighting.

Maybe he'd been a bit idealistic. OK, maybe he'd been a bit idiotic!

Maybe a bit naïve in the way he'd looked at the problem. Joe wasn't going to sit here and regret it now. He grinned at his own thoughts, stiffening his jaw. That was something every Canadian would understand, the stubbornness. He wasn't going to regret a moment of what had happened.

Joe's thoughts came clear, as his ears 'watched' for the sounds that would tell him of anyone approaching.

'Rabbits', he smiled as he sat on his own on the steps of the grand old entrance up to the RAF hospital. He was blind. No way of avoiding that fact. His ears did his seeing for him now, whilst his nose listened to the smells and his fingers were as sensitive as any whiskers might be. It had been the thought of his fingers being whiskers that had made him think of the rabbits.

When they'd first used that word 'blind', he could remember being so calm. It was almost a relief, knowing that was it, no longer expecting anything else. The Canadian stubbornness had kicked in big time then. The doctors had done their best, the nurses were wonderful, and the Lads were a great bunch of fellows. Joe knew where he was and what he was doing, and that was probably a damn sight more than some of the men.

He'd got used to the words they used and the way they spoke. Joe could even notice the expression on their faces from the way they formed their words.

He liked their spirit. That's what it was, the spirit around these parts. It was sort of contagious. Not just the men, but the women, the nurses, even the children. They were indomitable, that's what they were, and incorrigible!

No getting away from that. No matter where he was in this country he'd never heard a complaint. Grumbling, yes, but every sentence that sounded like it began with a grumble ended on a note of determination. Generous they were, too, even with so little, they still managed to be unfailingly generous.

Maybe his family back home would call them 'quaint', he'd heard it all before. Maybe some of the local ways were 'charming and old-fashioned' compared to the big business and heavy-duty drive of the Canadians, but there was that same can-do attitude here as he'd known back home. Home? Joe was wondering whether he really wanted to go back. Here everyone did their bit, the best they could. Everyone, even the kids.

"Rabbits?" he asked them when he heard them charging over to where he was sitting. "How were they?"

He could hear them giggling. That must have been the little girl. He'd forgotten her name. He could remember Gertie, but he wasn't the little girl.

"OK, guys? Gertie, how did ya find those rabbits today? Getting fat enough for your liking?"

"Almost as big as Mrs Toombs!" Gertie told him confidently.

"How you guys feelin' today, then? No more wrong berries?" he checked.

Walker was quick to tell him, "Abso-ruddy-lutely not!"

"Ah, but I can smell shortbread crumbs. Who's been visiting Mrs Toombs' kitchen?"

"We weren't visiting, we were salvaging," Maze informed him brightly.

"You only wanted the jam jars from the bottom of her larder, Maze, 'cos you thought she'd give you the shortbread as a thank you," Al teased his little sister.

"Hang on!"

Joe spluttered and stumbled to his feet. He'd heard Gertie's voice and 'Maze' mentioned. She must be the little girl, so as far as he could remember there were two other young boys. The one speaking wasn't the one who'd got sick. That only left the one who'd been out in the back gardens with the delivery truck. He hadn't heard a truck come by yet.

"How did you all get over here?"

"Boots," Al confirmed:

"Are you a 'fugee?" Maze blurted.

Joe turned his face back towards the little girl.

"No, I volunteered. Why did you think I was a 'fugee', a refugee?"

He was holding his hand out now, to get the little girl to sit beside him on the steps, and waiting for the boys to stop moving about, so he could place their voices with the names he was starting to get familiar with.

"You're not from around here, are you?" Maze was trying to work this one out for herself.

"No, but some of us still wanted to do our bit, and we didn't mind coming over here, to get started early at it," Joe explained.

"That's what we wanted to do. We walked all the way over here to do our bit," Al told him.

"It was *my* idea," Maze added, just to be clear on that.

"Why are you sitting here?" Gertie asked, tapping the step with the toe of his boot.

"I'm waiting for your truck to arrive," Joe told them with

a smile.

"We've got a truck coming for us?"

Joe could hear the relief in Walker's voice.

"Humfrey comes by every day in one of the Army camp trucks, with the paperwork from his clerking office over there. Very good at making sure all the t's are crossed and the i's are dotted, and the paperwork is in the proper place is Humfrey."

"He's a postman?" Maze wondered.

"No postman 'post'," Joe happily corrected the misunderstanding. "Humfrey deals with the clerking paperwork."

"Paperwork only, not the messages, they come by motorbike," Gertie seemed to think that might help clear up any lingering confusion.

Joe agreed. "These are files and folders, no post, no messages. He uses the camp truck, just in case there's anything else needing to be coming or going, from the offices at the Army camp to here and back. Very efficient fellow, that Humfrey."

"Is it secret?" Walker asked, starting to get the gist of what he was saying.

"I don't know. I wouldn't, now, would I, not if it was secret?" Joe reasoned. "I think it's just anything needing to go through official channels and that means Humfrey's truck."

"And we're going in Humfrey's truck?" Walker checked, just to be clear.

Joe nodded.

"So, we're going through official channels too? See, told you we needed the codenames!" Walker jabbed Al in the ribs. "Like Shark-shoulders."

Joe laughed. "Shark-shoulders, hey? You've clued them in?"

He could feel Gertie's uncertainty in the way he fidgeted. Joe didn't want them getting restless. The truck would be arriving soon. He just needed to keep them all together and out of mischief a little longer.

"I'd better tell you the rest of 'em, but only the ones you can mention in front of the nurses. That way we're not going to be giving away any sensitive information."

Joe could feel their curiosity bringing them shuffling closer. Gertie put his bicycle down to one side and sat with Maze. Al and Walker were already agog, sitting on the steps beside the blind Canadian pilot, waiting for Humfrey.

"The clinic consultant is Shark-shoulders. He's a very important guy, a surgeon. Very clever with them knives that one. He can get inside you and out again before you even wake up." Joe could hear the squirms and gasps from the youngsters around him, Maze whimpered at the thought.

"You still can't see. He didn't make you better," she reminded him.

Joe nodded.

"No, I still can't see. The surgeon did the best he could and made sure nothing else went wrong, it could have been worse." He sighed, reminding himself with the same breath, "Sometimes knowing it could have been worse is the best you can manage."

"Why Shark-shoulders?" Maze asked.

Joe smiled at that.

"That's because of the way he walks."

He got to his feet. Walker put his hand under Joe's elbow, just to steady him down the remaining steps. Feeling the gravel beneath his feet, Joe tapped the final step behind him with the heel of his boot, to give him an idea of the area he had available.

"He walks like this when he's not at his operating table. No one sees him at the operating table. That's one of those rooms you go into and out of and never know about. Best way to my thinking. When Shark-shoulders walks he looks like this." Joe hunched his back and reached his hands down, clasping them together low behind him. "You've got to remember he's taller and narrower than me." Joe kept his hands low and locked behind his back, shoulders hunched forward, his chin out, taking very small quick steps. "He walks like this, circling your bed after the operation. I couldn't see him do it, but I heard him. Like a shark circling."

"Tell us another one," Walker requested, with eager murmurings from Al beside him.

Joe was getting into the swing of it by then.

"Mrs Toombs you've met, haven't you? Never give a cook a nickname. Never tease a cook; very unwise to do that," Joe warned them.

The children nodded obediently, appreciating the blind Canadian was a wise man.

"Let's start at the top then. Matron, she's Crag 'n' Cap. Formidable lady, all matrons have to be! Can't be a proper matron without being formidable. They're fully trained to be that. Takes years of practice to get them into such fine formidable condition. It's very difficult to maintain so they tend towards getting a bit craggy, I guess."

Joe hadn't given it much thought, but as he explained it in a way he hoped the children would understand, it sounded entirely reasonable to him.

"What about the cap? Why do they need to wear those? They're silly perched up there," Maze queried.

"Oh no, don't you ever go saying that. You'll hurt their feelings," Joe immediately guarded the little girl from saying anything so foolish. "Remember, all matrons, nurses and doctors, they're all in uniform. That's what this war means, everyone knows what everyone else is meant to be doing. Don't need to do too much talking that way, and Matron's uniform most definitely includes the cap."

Al was getting bored with all the talk about caps and sharks.

"Who's next?"

"Next? Oh, I wouldn't want to say which comes first between Matron and Shark-shoulders, but definitely next after them comes the senior doctor at the hospital. He doesn't do the surgeoning, that's all done over at the clinic. The senior doctor doesn't do the running of the hospital, but he's in charge of all the other doctors and their doings, until the nurses can take over. That would be 'Beanpole 'n Whiskers'. He's the tallest man in the hospital. Have you seen him?"

The children shook their heads. Gertie thought he might have, but only a glimpse and he wasn't meant to have been there at the time, so decided not to admit to that.

"Nor have I," Joe told them with a chuckle, giving the children a moment to realise what he'd just said. "The Lads tell me about him, though. Very tall that senior doctor is. Must be something to do with his standing! Although, it's the width of his whiskers that make the first impressions. I bet they're wider than those handlebars on your bicycle, Gertie."

Joe waited for the children to look back at the bicycle and try to imagine that.

"Tall enough to hit the top of the upstairs doorways, he is, and I've got a theory about those whiskers of his." Joe brought them in closer. "I think he doesn't like for us to know when he's coming. Very gentle sort he is, soft spoken, so you have to really listen when he talks to you. I think those whiskers of his make him light on his feet, so we don't get worried by the sound of him coming over when it's time for him to talk to us."

"Oh, that's nice of him," Maze murmured. "I wouldn't want to worry you either," she blurted. Joe gave her a little hug and thanked her, then put his finger up to offer a caution.

"It's very kind of him to be considerate like that, isn't it? It also means he can sneak up on those junior doctors of his, when they're not paying attention."

"Oh, they're the Pennies, aren't they?" Walker knew that codename. They'd learnt that one already, "The Pennies, because they're all bright and shiny."

There was plenty more to be said about the resident nurses, known collectively as 'the Graces', unless they were on the warpath for one of the Lads, then they were the, 'Oh Cripes'. The junior nurses were the 'Little Graces' whilst they were completing their training.

"We're all a bit of an experiment to them," Joe admitted. "We all need to be glad for 'small mercies' these days."

"And all the porters are called Andy, on account of them being 'andy when they're needed!" he remembered. They all knew that one.

"Any more?" Al checked.

Joe smiled. "Oh yes, but I can't tell you those."

"Why not? Are they all secret?" Walker whispered.

Joe chuckled.

"No, because I can hear Humfrey's truck coming up the drive and you lot need to get home. Have you got everything you need?"

They looked up from their position. There *was* a truck coming up the drive.

"How d'you know it's Humfrey's?"

Joe smiled.

"Got to be. He's due, ain't he? Sarg wouldn't have let any old truck come through, not without good reason."

"He let Rusty come through when she was bringing a delivery for the Lads and Old Spot's strawberries," Al wondered.

"There you go, then. Can't think of a better 'good reason' than that!"

Joe waited for the children to stand up with him, before starting to walk forward across the gravel, his cane resting at ease by his side, waiting for the truck to stop in front of him.

"Well, that wasn't what I was expecting," Humfrey observed ruefully out from the cab window as the truck stopped a couple of yards short, "a welcoming committee."

"You're Miss Aggy's mister, ain't you?" Walker checked.

"We're going home!" Maze gave the direction.

"And waiting for you," Al explained.

"Can't fit them all on my bicycle!" Gertie added his reason for being there.

"And why?" said Humfrey, looking over to Joe, who was grinning broadly.

"Don't look at me; I was just keeping them company until you arrived," Joe told him, sensing Humfrey's gaze had turned to him. "Florrie was worried about them walking all the way home again. They're the Salvage Scamps. Mrs Toombs had a few pieces for them, and they've already been over to see the rabbits. It's about time they got back and the best I could come up with was to wait for you."

"Um, thanks for that!" Humfrey snorted, looking down and across at the motley assortment of children and articles.

"Yeah, got to admit, I can't see Sarg agreeing to sending a car for this lot either."

"You're not going to mess with my loading, are you?" He looked down at their faces, scrutinising them. His face was more careworn than weatherworn, his nose was quite red and his eyebrows heavy with studious furrows above them. He couldn't be as old as Sarg and he didn't shout like Sarg, but his face had a threatening thunderstorm sort of an appearance, just for a moment. Then the storm lifted, as Humfrey's eyes crinkled in merriment, accepting the commission. The children were still vigorously assuring him they wouldn't dare do any such thing.

Humfrey had heard plenty about the Salvage Scamps from Aggy. He could work out who was who from her descriptions. The old pram and the bicycle simplified that exercise, as did the state of Walker's oversized clothes.

"No Rusty today?"

Joe shook his head. Humfrey was about to swear, before he remembered the company and stopped himself in time. The sound wasn't lost on Walker.

"What d'ya need Rusty for? She doesn't work for you, she's with Jeepers' Yard and Old Spot."

"I was hoping she'd help with the delivery for the Home Guard office at the village hall. Can't be organised without an office. Can't have an office without a desk. Got to get everyone organised, mobilised."

Humfrey knew Joe didn't need to see the wink to hear it in his voice.

"We'll do that for you, Mister," Al volunteered. "You going to see Miss Aggy?"

"I'm going to try to," Humfrey confessed, "if I can trust you lot to get the desk into my office. Then I'll have five minutes to say hello to my missus and grab a bite to eat before starting my wardening rounds."

"If you're grabbing a bite to eat, can you grab us some too, please?" Walker begged.

"Didn't Mrs Toombs give you something to eat, shortbread?" Joe checked.

Walker grumbled, "We had to share."

"You're gonna need to give your stomach a chance to toughen up. It'll soon stop growling once it gets used to the rationing," Humfrey told him plainly. He wasn't a fierce man, but he was rather stern. Al thought maybe as a warden he had to be that way. Humfrey wasn't gentle and smiling like Joe. He was sort of stout without being jovial, sort of straight-faced, at least until he smiled. Then Al realised maybe there was plenty of jovial tucked inside of Humfrey, only that he wasn't allowed to show it on duty.

"You lot get in then. Don't disturb anything and stay down, whilst I go and sort these out. Joe, keep an eye on them for me, will you?" This was said smoothly, without a flicker of a grin from Humfrey at the phrase he'd used.

Joe responded with a confident, "Right-ho." Stepping up to the side of the truck, he felt along its length until he found the flap of back canvas.

"Come on, you lot, climb in. Maze and pram first. You've got the magazines and jam jars in the pram, haven't you?" He could hear them. "Best get them in and out of the way, before you start scrambling about back there."

Walker and Al went in next, Gertie last. Joe handed the bicycle up to him.

"All in?"

"There's a load of sandbags back here!" Walker queried.

"There'll be for the village hall?"

"Looks like Humfrey's got his work crew sorted," Joe told them, before closing the canvas back.

Humfrey returned to the truck and climbed into his cab without a word to the 'crew' behind. All he'd heard was a shuffle as Gertie tried to steady the pram wheels with one of the sandbags as the truck moved off.

Joe had done his bit and went back inside. Next time he saw the young salvagers he'd give them a bar of chocolate. He still had a couple up in his locker. They deserved it; they'd done him a lot of good with all that talking. Joe always found he made more sense when he was trying to explain something to someone else.

Sarg waved Humfrey back out through the gate and within twenty minutes the church warden was pulling up outside the village hall, yelling, "All out that's getting out!"

By the time Humfrey had got round to the back, Gertie was already down with his bicycle and leaning it against the doors to the village hall.

"They're locked."

"Of course they are, got to be now. Can't be keeping them open. Can't have us doing our Home Guarding duties with the doors open. That don't sound very secure to me." Humfrey took the ring of keys from his pocket and fed them through his fingers until he'd found the one he needed to unlock the doors. He hadn't yet turned to see the expression on Gertie's face.

"You mean I'm responsible for them? You're leaving all three of them with me?"

Humfrey turned now to stare squarely at the lanky lad.

"Who else? I can't stay with them. You all got in the truck;

that means you're my crew. That means when I'm not here you're in charge. IC sandbag crew."

Gertie was stunned into silence for a moment. How did that happen? Just a couple of months ago, the butcher wouldn't even trust him with his second-best bicycle, and now he was in charge of three children and a truck full of sandbags!

Humfrey didn't hang around to wait for Gertie to figure it out, guessing he would in his own time. He'd shown them where to put the sandbags, either side of the hall doors.

Gertie took just long enough for Maze to squeal out from the back of the truck that they'd forgotten her and her pram.

"You're IC. ICs don't leave prams in the truck, I heard him say so," she reprimanded the lanky lad.

Gertie reached in to bring the old pram safely out. By then, Rusty had pulled her truck alongside Humfrey's and called over, waiting for someone to respond. Whoever's voice Rusty had been expecting to hear in response, it hadn't been the squeal from Maze.

"Good Lord! What on earth are you doing there?"

"We got bored waiting for you!" Maze blurted.

"Were you waiting for me?" Rusty queried. It wasn't like Maze to tell fibs.

"Mrs Toombs said we couldn't have all her jam jars, but we were allowed to take the buckets to the rabbits and then Joe told us all about why Matron has to wear a cap and why the one you don't know is coming has wide whiskers."

"Goodness, I'm sorry I missed all that!" Rusty laughed.

Maze's story, as far as Mrs Toombs, gave Rusty enough of a clue, and the pram offered the rest of the story. With Gertie there too she knew they were all safe enough.

"So, Humfrey brought you back with him, did he? Is he about?"

"No. He left Gertie in charge. We've got to get all these sandbags banked up before he gets back, and they're ever so heavy," Al informed her.

"Don't forget his office desk, too!" Walker reminded his friend. "That's why we've got to get the sandbags out, because the hall is going to need guarding, 'cos it's got a desk in the office."

"Oh!" Rusty wasn't feeling quite so sure about following that bit, but the children seemed to know what they were doing. She had a message for Humfrey, but it could wait. Al was right; those sandbags looked heavy, and Gertie looked a little flustered already.

She sent Gertie with Maze in with the desk first. It wasn't a proper desk, no drawers, no substance really, just a regulation table. Her thoughts were to give Gertie a chance to calm down and Maze an opportunity to see that the empty village hall wasn't as scary as she feared.

Rusty watched the mismatched pair handle the desk, a lanky fourteen-year-old and small five-year-old. Unwise, but hilarious! It also slowed the pair of them down, enough so they missed the corners and managed to find the right room.

This gave Rusty enough time to get Al and Walker 'fully mobilised', Al in the back of the truck, Walker on the path just outside, with Rusty near the hall doors.

"Right, that looks more like a work chain, doesn't it?" she asked the pair of them.

Admittedly, it wasn't much of a chain, but none of them had too far to lift and shift. It started off well with the sandbags nearest the open back of the truck, then Al's arms started to falter.

"I can't lob them from back here."

Rusty sent Walker in after him with the instructions, "Just

get them out of the truck for starters."

Gertie returned triumphant.

"Right room, proper office," he reported.

Maze emerged reluctantly from the hall, seeming quite happy to stay and explore more of the rooms.

"Oh no you don't, miss," Rusty called her out into the sunshine. "You're in charge of that pram, remember? That means it's your responsibility until you deliver the salvage. You can make sure our banking is straight." She showed the little girl where to stand. "There."

By now all the sandbags were offloaded from the back of the truck. So, too, were Al and Walker, with Gertie standing by. Rusty looked at the three of them.

"Maze is in position. What are you three waiting for?"

Rusty started heaving the sandbags across to either side of the doors to form the start of two barriers, then looked over to Gertie.

"D'you think that'll be enough?"

"For what? Oh cripes, I guess we're all hoping we won't find *that* out!" Gertie offered.

Rusty thought how Gertie had a way of making spot-on sense at the most unexpected moments.

"Right, you lot, start banking them up. We need to get them high enough to protect those doors."

Gertie started. Al and Walker followed. Maze kept checking they were stacking them straight and Rusty helped with the heavier ones. Gradually, the walls of sandbags grew. They were well past Maze's height, by the time Humfrey and Aggy returned.

"Goodness, you all still here?" He grinned back to his wife. "Thought you'd have finished that ages ago."

None of the work crew had strength to answer. They were red faced and out of puff. At some point one of the bags must have split, as there seemed to be a grubby coating of sand everywhere. It was matted in their hair, daubed across their faces, and smeared along their arms. Their hands were stained by the old jute and throbbing from trying to handle the weights. Rusty and Gertie were still managing to lift and position the sandbags by themselves, whilst for Al and Walker it was a combined effort.

"Are you there too, Maze?" Aggy called out.

Maze popped her head around from the other side.

"Yes, Miss."

Aggy had already got a message prepared.

"Will you take your pram over to Brisket's for me? He's expecting you."

"Me, Miss?" Maze was speechless with delight, bringing her pram out from behind the wall of sandbags.

"You can leave the magazines and jam jars here. I'll put them in the office and the WVS can collect them with their next meeting," Humfrey suggested.

Maze did as she was told and scuttled off by herself, along the village footpath to the butcher's shop, gripping tightly to her old pram and the piece of paper.

Humfrey had waited for Maze to get out of earshot, before turning to the rest of the work crew.

"As for you lot, let's see how you've been doing? Looks like we'll be needing a plank up there soon, you need to build over the top and join the walls together."

Walker had already thought of that but was too exhausted to say so.

"Didn't I put one in the back?" Humfrey checked. "Yep,

still back there. Come on Walker, give me a hand."

Rusty could see a problem with that plan.

"You're gonna need a ladder, Al, I've got one in my truck. Come on, this is a combined effort, plank and ladder and sandbags. We can do it."

Gertie couldn't work on his own. For a moment he felt quite abandoned and the pile of sandbags in front of him was daunting. He sat down and took a breath.

"You all right there, Gertie?" Aggy stepped forward whilst the rest of the crew was busy.

"I was only going over to Mrs Toombs to deliver the last of the butcher's parcels, Miss Aggy. How did I get into this?"

He wiped a filthy sleeve across a sweat smudged forehead.

"Poor lad, you do have a knack of being in the right place at the right time."

"Come on, crew," Humfrey started barking at the children and Rusty.

The ladder went up and, being as how it was hers, Rusty climbed up whilst Humfrey handed her the plank. Al and Walker got ready to start sending up the sandbags.

"Gertie, you good with heights?" Rusty checked down.

Gertie hadn't got a clue. "I'm all right up in my attic. Does that count?"

"Good enough," Rusty assured him, stepping to one side for Gertie to climb the ladder, and sit on the plank in place atop the two walls. "You're in charge of settling them in place along there, whilst we all do the handing up."

Rusty checked with Humfrey.

"That's OK, isn't it?"

Humfrey winked.

"Gertie's in charge!"

Sat on the plank, Gertie realised he had four of them passing up the sandbags. All he had to do was grab each one, steer it to sit next to the one before it, then shuffle along the plank until it was covered with a row of sandbags, then sit on top of those and start on the next row. By then, from his lofty vantage point, Gertie could see Maze returning. Aggy heard her and clapped for the crew to come back to her.

"That's enough. Humfrey, if there are any more sandbags I think your lot can finish off."

"My lot?" he chuckled.

Gertie waited for Rusty to hold the bottom of the ladder. He could have jumped but decided not to. The children and Gertie sat down on the last few sandbags heaped beside the village hall. Maze seemed to have an announcement.

"Look what I've got. Mrs Brisket said the message told her to prepare enough food to feed the sandbag crew. Working rations!" The little girl was beaming. "Thank you, Miss. We were starving."

"I can imagine." Aggy turned to her husband. "Really Humfrey! What were you thinking? Not even giving them a chance to get home and have some tea, before putting them to work?"

Humfrey looked down at his boots, contritely.

"Sorry Miss," he muttered, before raising his head with a lovely smile, that reached from his chin to his eyebrows. "I'll lock up and take the truck back," he told her whilst the children were eating.

Brisket's wife had even got Ol' Creak to send over a couple of bottles of pop for them.

"Oh, don't worry, Miss Aggy isn't paying for it. They're

work crew rations, so they have to send the bill to the Army camp," Gertie grinned, checking with Humfrey. "That's right ain't it? Paperwork?"

Rusty shared a few sips from Maze's bottle of pop but was quite certain the little girl could manage the sandwiches all by herself.

"Before you get on, any chance I could have some of the sandbags for my grandfather?"

"What does Old Spot want them for?" Humfrey asked, not entirely sure he wanted to know the answer.

"It might be a bomb-shelter. I don't think he's decided yet."

Rusty guessed it might be wise not to mention her grandfather's notion of a pigsty, seeing as how Humfrey was Home Guard.

"Does he know something we don't?"

Rusty smiled, she knew Aggy and Gertie would understand her response. "Always!"

The tea sent over from the butcher's wife was consumed in double-quick time. The next task, as far as Aggy could see, was for the children and Gertie to have a bath. She couldn't send them home in *that* state!

"You'd better come back with me. I'll get the bathtub out. Rusty, I think you'd better come, too," giving Rusty just enough time to put the ladder back into her truck.

The most presentable amongst them was Maze.

"I think we can send you home directly," Aggy decided. "You let your mum know Al and Walker are getting cleaned up after salvage and sandbag duty."

"Yes, Miss."

Maze assured her she could remember that and skipped

off with her pram, more than happy to be the one to tell her mother first about everything.

Aggy led the way, Al and Walker behind her, with Gertie trailing wearily and Rusty pushing his bicycle for him. The old bathtub was in the back garden of the church warden's home and was soon filled with water. Whilst the boys washed, Aggy fetched them some of her old towels, while Rusty made herself useful brewing up a fresh pot of tea.

"We'll have to send them home in their own clothes this time. Do you think we can get Humfrey to bring over some spare overalls next time?" Rusty wondered.

Aggy was smiling as she looked out the kitchen window into her back garden at the three boys mucking about with the water and the towels. They were clean and getting dry, their clothes were rough and filthy, but they were all safe and well and happy.

"One day at a time, hey, Rusty?"

Rusty drove back to Jeepers' Yard, wondering if she might be able to persuade him to spare a few surplus overalls. She knew he had some tucked away somewhere and those Scamps were going to need them, the way they were getting through this summer.

Rusty was also wondering what her grandfather had finally decided he was building on that waste ground at the bottom of his garden. Old Spot was certain it was definitely going to be a shed of some sort.

"Can't have too many sheds, war or no war!" he assured her confidently.

He was still considering the bomb-shelter but wanted to listen to the radio again.

Rusty felt happier just knowing her grandfather had everything down where he needed it, not cluttering up the path or annoying Jeepers.

Old Spot sat down at the kitchen table, putting the paper and pencil down in front of him.

"Shall we get started?"

It seemed Old Spot had got himself in the mood for a spot of clearing whilst she'd been out and discovered not everything in his pottering shed was where it ought to be. Apparently, it had somehow got to overflowing! Her grandfather had been rummaging through the undergrowth ever since and looked like it.

"You could donate some of those extra-spare garden tools of yours to them that's new to digging in the village, those ones you've been 'rescuing' from Jeepers' hoard over the years," she suggested.

"Some of them might have been down there a while, might have got a bit settled-in," he muttered stubbornly, down into the depths of his mug of tea.

Rusty wasn't going to have any excuses. "They'll still be needing 'em."

She followed him down to where the blackberry branches were fiercely tangled, reaching much further than the quarter-depth her grandfather had managed to clear so far. He seemed to have started by dragging them away from the side of his pottering shed windows. Just enough for him to start finding the stuff he'd 'set aside' down there. There seemed to be far more than he remembered and not in the best of condition.

Not quite scrap: "It's salvageable," her grandfather told her resolutely, trying to find a thicker pair of gloves, whilst Rusty began trying to retrieve what had been uncovered so far into a wheelbarrow.

"We can load this into the back of my truck with those surplus spades. After all, you can only dig with one at a time.

I'm sure the church warden will be able to see them fairly distributed," she suggested.

Old Spot wasn't ready to be distracted. Tugging at the brambles, he growled back at her, "Stop rushing me. I've only got started on this!"

Rusty suddenly felt those knots in her chest again. She wanted to help him, but at the same time was never sure from one moment to the next what he wanted her to help him with, or if he wanted any help at all!

"How about we let the cuttings wilt a bit? You'll be able to separate them a little easier, then, and the sooner we get those bomb-shelter walls up, the fewer bricks we'll be tripping over."

She hoped her joke landed lightly. It seemed to work. In a moment the scowling expression fell away from her grandfather's face. He looked over to her and grinned.

"Little 'n' often sounds better than a slow rush, don't it?"

"How about I see if we can find those spare overalls Jeepers has got tucked away, get them aired and the kettle singing again? You open up your pottering shed and if we time it right, we can load up those idle overalls into my truck before Jeepers even notices them missing."

Rusty gauged it well. Suggesting a sneaky bit of snaffling through the long shed was too much mischief for her grandfather to resist. She didn't mention those old tools again. Her grandfather would decide about those when he was ready.

Rusty's thoughts felt as clear as her arms felt weary. If she asked about his garden, it always cheered up the chatter.

"What was your garden like before?"

It had been a long time since that first vegetable garden and Old Spot hadn't been the one doing most of the growing then, too busy working in the fields.

"Gardens used to be for those that had time for 'em. Now we've all gotta be doin' some digging-in for winter, ain't we?"

The way he looked at his granddaughter, she could feel his thoughts struggling to stay with her.

Old Spot had more urgent considerations than overalls, reminding Rusty they'd be needing to clear more of those toppled blackberries.

"Too much bramble, not enough berries, and we need more room for the rhubarb. You know how it likes to spread."

Before Rusty could respond, her grandfather recalled how his parents grew both. "Pies and crumbles in autumn. Autumn's *meant* to be muddled; tastes better that way."

"Rhubarb and blackberries together? Surely not!" Rusty gave her grandfather a look of mock horror at such a suggestion. He chuckled wryly.

"Aye, but it's all about the apples along with 'em and the pastry around 'em!" the elderly gentleman assured her. "Apples," he explained, patiently. "Apples is what makes for a benevolent autumn."

"Oh, that sounds wonderful," Rusty agreed. "That's what we need, isn't it? A 'benevolent autumn', but first we need to salvage this summer!"

She knew Jeepers and his men were out on business, the Yard was clear, and she soon had those spare overalls tucked down in the corner of her truck.

"Now, what about those blackberries?" her grandfather was asking her. "We're only cutting back those that have already toppled. Plenty more branches ripening up back there." Taking a longer look at the state of the ragged hedge, "It's blocking the way to that parcel of land. Can't waste a yard of land. Not with a war on, not even for a few pretty blackberry flowers."

Rusty watched silently as her grandfather's hand paused, whilst he gazed in ageless joy at the bees going about their business, just a few inches from him.

"I like clearing things back, makes more room for thinking!" he suddenly told her. The bomb-shelter building site looked clumsy, but well supplied. Haphazard, but at least now there was a definite path to it.

"Just be careful of the ditch down behind it. Goes round that corner somewhere," Old Spot chuckled.

"What's funny?" Rusty asked, as she helped him search for his gloves amidst the clutter and debris of overgrowth and scrap.

The bottom of his back garden was 'developing nicely', according to Old Spot's reckoning. Losing the gloves seemed to be a good indicator of that fact!

They found the gloves down by the water bucket. He must have taken them off to wash his hands. That made about as much sense as it needed to for the day. Rusty took the bucket to fetch more fresh water, whilst Old Spot rubbed his hands on the thighs of his trousers, scuffing off the worst, before putting his work gloves back on.

"I could put some of those old boxes of tools up in that spare bedroom," he shouted over brightly, then realised what he'd said and looked a little sheepish. That 'spare bedroom' was his granddaughter's!

"Between the two of you, Jeepers' Yard and *your* garden sheds are gradually taking over the whole farmhouse," Rusty joined her grandfather, with a sad sigh. "Sooner or later we're not going to be living in a house at all, just another store shed."

She'd once had hopes of making the farmhouse a home

again, but the War Effort meant sacrifices for them all. Rusty sat beside her grandfather and drank her tea in thoughtful silence for a couple of minutes.

"How about we tackle one box at a time? That way we won't miss anything useful. Then you can decide if you really need it, or if we can contribute it to the Effort."

"That works!" her grandfather agreed.

"What about the rest of the stuff out there?"

He scanned his back garden. It seemed well balanced to his eyes. The building site was forming a good huddle and the pottering shed was overflowing healthily. As for the bramble hedges, compost heap and rhubarb, it was starting to get difficult to distinguish one from the other. Not to mention the pieces of fencing down that way and whatever else had migrated back there from the front yard.

"It does need a bit of work, don't it? You say you're looking for salvage?"

"The more we can find, the more we can help," Rusty reminded him. "The more I can use my truck, the more often I might be able to sneak into one of Jeepers' sheds."

She knew how to persuade her grandfather. Old Spot was enjoying that prospect.

"Sounds like a plan."

She watched him, standing quietly for a long while after that, listening to the lanes and the fields around him, leading out to the farms and back over to the village. Tractors working. He was hearing them more often these high summer days. They sounded more urgent than he remembered they had before, suddenly looking back to his granddaughter.

"Gotta hope they can bring in enough. It's gonna be tight." His voice sounded anxious and tired. She wanted to reassure him, but couldn't, so instead changed his attention.

"Some of those packing boxes have been there longer than me."

He laughed at that truth and wondered what on earth he'd been keeping them for. Then there was such an aching sadness in his eyes, as he tried to remember when he'd first taken those boxes down to the pottering shed, when those working fields had been his, and he'd worked them long and hard and well.

Rusty suddenly found herself wanting everything to slow down, to hold on to this quiet little piece of summer, to hold on to her grandfather.

Then in the next moment Old Spot came to her side. "At least we can see where we've been," putting a reassuring arm around her shoulder. "That's always a good start in getting where we're going."

He was right, Rusty knew that. It felt easy to keep things simple in Old Spot's back garden. Bricks and mortar, buckets and gloves, boots and garden fork. Lift, shift, settle and lay, two pairs of hands, strong shoulders, steady backs and loud laughter. These were precious summer days, warm and bright and well met. Time enough, she hoped.

There was plenty to be done yet, before the shed-cum-bomb-shelter would be ready, but no more today. Old Spot was in the mood for talking, as his eyes looked far back. His thoughts clear, aware of every detail, his voice sounded almost happier to be back in that uncomfortable sounding place.

"Far too hot, far too much. We slept where we stopped or dropped. They were good lads, then. Didn't really sleep until we got back; too much to keep watching out for. We were young, didn't need to sleep. We'd get back, wash where we stood, dry off walking to our tents, then crawl as far as a bed and sleep for days."

He seemed able to still feel the cold water splashing at the grime baked on to his skin, to hear the rustle of the humid breeze lift the tent flap, to smell the camp and remember so many faces.

It was getting late, and the Yard had been quiet for hours. No telling where Jeepers and his blokes had got to. Rusty and her grandfather had returned to his pottering shed.

"We'll just go through one box at a time. Then you can decide what to do with it."

Old Spot pulled his stool up to his bench, looking over to the boxes.

"They do tend to accumulate, don't they?" he admitted ruefully. Then suddenly sounded cross, "You're not taking them away from me?" he accused her.

Rusty realised he'd already forgotten what they'd agreed: tools in the shed, boxes in the house, anything salvageable to be salvaged, and surplus shared with those that didn't have enough. She could see her grandfather was listening to the tractors again, nodding in agreement to their intentions.

"No time for tucking ourselves away," he told her, shaking his shoulders. "Not unless we're ducking from the bombs. Glad we got that new shed started now, ain't you?"

Rusty was starting to recognise the signs. She could make allowances but wasn't expecting Jeepers to be so tolerant.

If Old Spot wanted to build a bomb-shelter in his back garden, Rusty was sure he wouldn't be the only one. If he took it into his head to sleep down there sometimes, at least then she'd know where to find him. Later, over supper, as they listened to the radio together, her grandfather offered a few more amiable grumbles, then started midway through another story.

Rusty was smiling as she fell asleep that night, recalling the details of the summer day coming to an end, with building sand knocked from their work boots, and more sand drifting under the door.

CHAPTER 7

Surplus, Supplies and a Bit of Practice

THE DAY HADN'T STARTED WELL. Her grandfather had woken deciding Rusty should have brought back some of those village hall sandbags, and before she'd managed to get out into the Yard, Jeepers had already locked his sheds again.

Fortunately, Rusty had been quick enough the day before not only to swipe a few of those surplus overalls, but also to take advantage of the unoccupied Yard to sneak out two of the jerry cans, using half from each before putting the remainder back where she'd found them, a lesson she'd learnt from one of Jeepers' blokes.

Rusty knew better than to be the one to empty any of the jerry cans. Jeepers would have hit the roof at that, but if there were a couple of half-empties discovered, then no one knew who was to blame. Jeepers would swear at everyone, but no one in particular, so everyone was happy. All of Jeepers' blokes knew better than to put back an empty can.

She decided to get Old Spot on to a cheerier subject before Jeepers came in for breakfast, and started asking what the prospects were for his rhubarb?

"Oh, pink and fine," he assured her, picking up the old newspaper, before Jeepers decided he hadn't read it yet. It was at least two days old. Jeepers didn't rise to the bait; he was far too busy with business to notice newspapers and a few less overalls in the pile at the back of his long shed.

Jeepers hadn't said much until then but was now reminding Rusty he might be needing her and the third truck that morning.

"Oh no you don't. I've got her this morning!" Old Spot declared, glaring at his son, who promptly teased him about the building site at the bottom of the back garden.

"Another shed, Grumps?"

"Maybe, but it ain't yours and that's all that need concern you! So don't go getting no ideas about it. It's mine and Rusty's." He dared his son to answer that!

Jeepers just took his second mug of tea and stomped out into the Yard to yell at a couple of his blokes who were taking too long about getting out onto the road.

"Damn!" Rusty's grandfather swore as the front door slammed behind his son. "Forgot the sandbags, didn't you?"

"Did I? When was that part of the bargain? I was just meant to be getting the overalls for the Scamps." She smiled as she saw that impish grin again. "What are you up to?"

They both knew Jeepers kept a stash of old sacks somewhere in the back of the long shed, but it was too late to look for them.

Old Spot still hadn't explained the reason for needing Rusty's truck but was fully occupied for the next few minutes trying to locate his boots. Sleeping downstairs on the sofa and sometimes in the armchair should have limited the range of his search, except he seemed convinced he'd left one of them outside in the back garden yesterday 'to cool off'. Rusty didn't argue.

Whilst her grandfather searched, she checked her backpack and toolbag were ready for a working day. With the Yard clear, she could add a couple of working gloves the blokes had left behind.

"You want to sit in the back or up beside me?" she offered, when Old Spot was ready.

It was her truck and her wheelbarrow. That was good enough to persuade her grandfather she'd be the one taking him and not the other way around.

Standing in the early sunshine, it was already warm. A few leaves had appeared on the porch step, windblown and faded, fallen from their fragile stems. The leaves reminded Rusty of those young apple trees she'd found growing where their pots had been dumped down past the side path. There were a few pathetic fruits still clinging to their bending branches, requiring only the slightest twist to come away in the palm of her hand.

"Enough for a few pies, perhaps, or a cake, maybe? I like the sound of a cake," Old Spot suggested eagerly at her elbow, making his granddaughter jump.

The few apples she'd been able to find from their feeble orchard hardly covered the bottom of her bucket. Her grandfather looked down into it, then chuckled.

"I'm guessing we'll just have to make-do with apple sandwiches this time."

She laughed with him: "Maybe later," and put the bucket down. There was work to be done. She pushed her sleeves up over her elbows, the fine, fair hair on her forearms already lifted by the warmth, and her freckles putting in an appearance to chime with the sunshine. The sweet smell of bruised apples lingered on her hands, whilst the trace of crumpled leaves stuck to her boots. Late summer, surely not? Already the first notes of almost-autumn were finding their subtle rhythms upon those long days.

They were soon out in the truck and driving along the country lanes. Rusty found her thoughts wandering back to those young trees and those old buckets, old memories softening the truth of current times. The notion of making a cake made her smile just for a moment, a bittersweet hope that one day maybe it might be possible to make their old farmhouse smell like a home again and less like a musty storeroom or a worksite.

Rusty had only managed to get to the real reason for her grandfather wanting to get into the village as she turned out from the Yard heading towards the village. That was her regular route in, and he'd immediately begun to tell her she needed to take the out-back route.

"Why would I want to be taking the long way? I'm short on petrol. Unless you want to walk the rest of way into the village?" she challenged him, after he suggested the turn for the second time in as many minutes.

She wasn't that low, not since the double half-snaffle, but it was the only way she was going to get to the truth of her grandfather's intentions.

"I was gonna have a word with Mr Tor about a pig." He saw the grimace on his granddaughter's face. "Just a little one, a squealer. What d'ya think?" Scratching his chin, realising maybe he ought to have mentioned that sooner.

Rusty had already had time enough to consider the pig and decided not!

"Bomb-shelter and store shed makes more sense, a toofer. You've always told me you prefer that sort, haven't you?" She could see he was listening. "What's the point of keeping a pig, when we both know Jeepers has got two whole crates of tinned meat in the back of that side shed? You can get some of those out of him any time you want. You're better at that sort of bartering than I am, so I'm relying on you."

She'd learnt a while back the best way to persuade her grandfather was to compliment him towards an alternative venture. Distraction was far easier to cope with than disappointment.

Old Spot cheered up at the prospect of getting one over on his son. He'd always preferred the idea of a bomb-shelter, anyway. What's the point in keeping the pig safe if they all got blown up? If the bombs started coming their way, they'd have more to worry about than a stray pig running about the place!

That was when he began asking Rusty about those village hall sandbags again.

"Rather like full jerry cans, you can never have too many sandbags about the place. Never know when they'll be coming in handy," he told her cheerfully.

Heading into the village, Old Spot caught his first sight of the precautions put in place outside the village hall.

"They didn't hang about, did they? What exactly are they protecting in there?" He wondered loudly.

As far as Rusty knew, there was just a desk, a chair and a cupboard of some sort. That didn't sound very impressive, but her grandfather corrected this delusion.

"You'd be surprised how much damage you can do with a desk and a chair!"

They were both laughing by the time they climbed down from the cab.

"Mind you, I'd have gone for the food supplies first. What about the village shops? No sandbags. And the school?" He was right. Rusty hadn't thought of that, and nor had Humfrey.

"They're probably expecting a fresh delivery of sandbags. They're working on it," she hoped.

"Wardens, camp trucks, sandbags coming through," Old Spot snorted. "Should have brought my ol' tin helmet with me."

The school was right next to the village hall, so his comment about protecting the school had been picked up by numerous small, inquisitive ears with eager questions.

One of the children had shouted they'd be much happier with tin helmets than with the gas masks they'd been issued with.

Old Spot was more than happy to shout back at them. "Gas masks? You've gotta be kidding! What about a siren? Do you need one of those? Better than the school bell any day. Might have one of those in my pottering shed, somewhere." He turned back to Rusty. "I do, don't I?"

"Probably," she smiled, and steered him towards where Aggy had come out, seeming to be waiting to have a word with them both. "I wouldn't be surprised, having seen the state of your pottering shed and that old tumbledown barn behind it. What does a siren come under? Useful-scrap, working-tools or something worth-keeping within reach for later?" Rusty knew her grandfather's shed filing system well.

Old Spot wasn't rising to that. He'd seen Aggy and nudged his granddaughter, asking loudly, "She's one of the schoolteachers, ain't she?" Then turned to Aggy, wagging his finger at her. "I've been meaning to have a word with you about that there school of yours. You'll be needing sandbags!"

"So I hear!"

Aggy kept the level of her voice steady. He hadn't alarmed any of her children. In fact, from the sounds of it they were rather delighted by the prospect.

"Were you waiting for us?" Rusty wondered.

It was true the young schoolteacher had heard the truck approaching and paused her own errand, but she'd actually been looking for her husband.

"Sorry to disappoint you. It's just us, Miss!" Old Spot laughed.

Rusty's original errand had been to deliver the overalls to the Scamps. Finding Aggy in the school playground meant Rusty was likely going to find the Scamps sooner.

Aggy saw she was carrying the overalls and half guessed the rest.

"It looks like you've come prepared."

Rusty nodded. "They're for the Salvage Scamps."

"Do I get a pair?" Gertie asked behind them.

"Looks like you could do with a pair! What *have* you been doing?"

Aggy and Rusty both stared at the lanky lad in disbelief. How was it possible to get in such a state so early in the day?

"Delivering!" Gertie told them.

Old Spot had to ask, "What?"

"One of Mr Tor's sows. She was having problems and Brisket told me to get over there first thing. I just arrived in time!"

"Strewth!" Old Spot coughed. "Lad, you've got a mighty fine habit for getting grubby! We've got enough overalls, haven't we?" he asked Rusty.

Aggy decided for her.

"I think you'd *better* have!" catching Gertie by the tip of his ear and causing him to freeze. The young schoolteacher checked with Rusty.

"Got a bucket in the back of that truck of yours?"

Old Spot volunteered, "Always. What d'ya need it for?"

"Give it to Gertie. Gertie, take that bucket and fill it with clean water. Take one of those overalls off Rusty's pile with you. I shall expect you back here in five minutes, washed and re-dressed, with *those* clothes you're wearing in *that* bucket."

"Yes, Miss Aggy."

"Don't worry," the schoolteacher told him a little less sternly. "We'll wait for you. You won't miss anything."

"Right-ho, Miss Aggy. Thanks, Rusty." Gertie could see the question in Old Spot's face. He hadn't asked and didn't need to. Gertie was happy to tell him.

"They're all doing well and squealing, even the one Mr Tor almost missed!"

He could hear Old Spot chuckling as he ran with the bucket and overalls. Aggy had given him five minutes, Gertie reckoned he could do it in half that time. It was only his front that really needed washing anyway.

Rusty didn't think it was worth mentioning where she'd got the overalls from, and Aggy knew better than to ask. Old Spot was interested in developments in the village.

By then Gertie was racing back over to join them. Rusty hadn't realised she was still standing there with the other overalls.

"Them for the Scamps?"

She nodded.

"They'll be needing those. They'll be their siren suits," Gertie approved. "I saw some like them in one of Brisket's missus' magazines."

"In what?" Old Spot spluttered.

Gertie told them what he'd heard on the radio, too. Not

his radio, mind you. He lived in the attic. No radio up there, 'but a lovely view,' and no one up there to moan about the state of his clothes or the stink of his feet, either. Gertie was evidently on a blurt.

Old Spot decided he wasn't interested in attics or overalls, and strolled over to where the children were playing, inspecting their playground for where to put the next delivery of sandbags and happy to tell them when he'd last had to use his siren. Aggy and Rusty took charge of Gertie and his jabbering.

"Must be the overalls," the schoolteacher suggested kindly. Gertie had outgrown her classroom a while ago, but she still had time for Gertie.

"Oh yes, Miss Aggy. I do like the overalls. Much nicer than those old trousers; don't sit well in trousers!"

The two ladies took a moment to digest that extraordinary fact, before Aggy lowered her voice and enquired, "You like wearing overalls then?" She wasn't quite sure she should be asking Gertie but was relieved it was only herself and Rusty listening to his response.

"Oh yes, Miss, but I prefer those dungarees the Land Girls wear over at the Totters' farm. They look lovely."

"They do?" Rusty asked. She'd never thought dungarees could be considered lovely. Practical, maybe, comfortable, quite possibly, but lovely? That was a first.

"Good gracious!" Aggy spluttered, immediately correcting herself, looking around and checking no one else heard that outburst. "I beg your pardon, Gertie. Land Girl dungarees?"

Rusty was grinning, Gertie was too, not the slightest embarrassed to admit it.

"Oh yes, Miss Aggy. Always admired them Land Girl dungarees the best. Plenty of wriggle room and no belt, and I can roll the legs up to save them getting caught in my bicycle chain."

Rusty felt like hugging the lad. There was something adorably understandable with that blurt. The revelation, once considered for a moment, came as no great surprise to either Aggy or Rusty. That was the way Gertie felt. In fact, it made a great deal of sense.

In the few minutes it took for the mayhem in the school playground to settle down, Gertie was able to tell them more about what he'd found in his favourite magazines. Sometimes whilst he was waiting for Brisket to finish wrapping the delivery parcels, the butcher's wife would allow Gertie to look through them. She didn't seem to think it a good idea for Gertie to take the magazines away with him, not unless they were wrapped around the sausages she gave him to take home at the end of the week. Gertie told them how the butcher's wife always wrapped his sausages very thoroughly, with the most interesting of magazine pages!

Fortunately, Old Spot hadn't heard any of that. He'd been pacing out the playground.

"You're gonna be needing more bomb-shelters!" he informed them as he came back to where they were talking, before giving Gertie a sniff. "You smell a mite better lad. Ready for some work?"

"Ready when you are, Sir," Gertie informed him, with a happy smile and a nod to both Aggy and Rusty. "That all right, Miss Aggy?"

"Quite all right, Gertie."

"If we're talking about needing a siren, then I suppose we *do* need a shelter to go to when it sounds, don't we?" Aggy asked Rusty, who immediately looked to her grandfather, shaking her head mournfully, with a big grin on her face.

"Now look what you've started!"

"Maybe we ought to know *how* to build one, just in case the bombs reach us before the delivery trucks," Rusty suggested.

Aggy couldn't find fault with that.

"We're not going to be able to build much if we don't have any sandbags."

Old Spot stood triumphant. "There, told you so!" reminding his granddaughter this was all her fault! He turned to the schoolteacher.

"Don't worry about the Scamps, Miss Aggy. Some of your children told me they're on their salvage round at the moment." Then turning to Gertie, "weren't you meant to be keeping an eye on them for me?"

Gertie never got a chance to remind him about Mr Tor's sow. Old Spot brushed the excuse aside.

"Don't worry, I've sent a few of the other little'uns off to bring 'em in. Those overalls are going to be needed. The sooner we get started with the sandbags the better."

Old Spot was clearly up for a session of bomb-shelter building. That would keep him happy. It only took an exchange of glances between the two young women for Rusty to know Aggy would keep him in check whilst she finished her errands.

"Sandbags don't need sand. If we can get the sacks, we've got plenty of earth around here. That'll do won't it, Miss?" Gertie offered.

The young schoolteacher agreed fenland earth was as good as any.

"We still need the bags, though."

Old Spot knew where to get some, if he could wrangle the keys off Jeepers.

Gertie suggested a simpler and far less devious plan. Humfrey had not only delivered enough sandbags to protect the entrance to the village hall for the Home Guard meetings, but he'd also brought over the desk for his new office. Gertie and Maze had taken the desk into the office and they'd found a big cupboard already in the room.

"Just like the school stationery cupboard, Miss Aggy," he informed those gathered around him, "only this cupboard was full of sandbag sacks, just sitting there. I don't think they liking having empty cupboards in the office. Don't seem right, does it?"

"Sounds reasonable," Old Spot agreed.

Gertie was still working it out. It was the overalls! So much easier for him to think right in overalls, the Land Girl dungarees would be even better, but the overalls would do him nicely for now.

"If it works like the school stationery cupboard, then the only time you're able to reorder fresh supplies is when you've used up the current batch. That's the way it works isn't it, Miss?" Gertie checked across to the schoolteacher.

Aggy had to agree that was certainly the way it worked in the village school. She would inform Mr Pegg if they were getting low on any supplies, he would check, then put in an order.

"There, so it's office paperwork and that's what Humfrey does, don't he?" Gertie turned to Aggy again. "So, we need to use up those sandbags first for him, then Humfrey can bring over more. Can't he, Miss? Joe said Humfrey's very efficient. He knows how an office cupboard works."

Aggy wasn't the only one smiling and nodding. "Quite right, Gertie. He does that."

Gertie was at ease and seeming to be doing all the

making sense so far. Those overalls were doing him a power of good. Rusty had already decided as soon as she could get hold of some more, she'd see to it Gertie got a second pair, at least, bless him. Bright lad, bit clumsy at times, and maybe a little awkward around the edges, but his thoughts were enlightening.

Gertie might not have a radio up in his attic, but he'd heard the one at the back of the butcher's shop. The German Luftwaffe had begun attacking British supply convoys in the English Channel.

"I hope we've got enough supplies, 'cos it sounds like we're not likely to get more for a while." Old Spot seconded that. He'd read the newspapers.

"What about those trucks you mentioned, Gertie? Those ones bringing the corrugated metal sheeting for building the Anderson shelters?" he queried.

"They'll get here."

Gertie wasn't sure who'd told him that. It might have been when Ol' Creak yelled at him for reading along the top of the newspapers shelf again.

"Humfrey will know when, won't he, Miss? He'll know when the trucks are due this way with our bomb-shelters. Official channels and all?" He checked with the schoolteacher, before turning back to Old Spot.

"What if the bombers come first?"

Old Spot decided if he was being asked, then he'd better come up with an answer.

"We build our own and we'd best be quick about it, lad!" he replied, with a voice loud enough for the entire playground to hear him, "'cos those bombers aren't going to be waiting for no trucks!"

Rusty knew her grandfather was only saying what they were all thinking.

Florrie had arrived by then. There was quite a crowd assembling, as the considerations had got clearer and more widely broadcast. Florrie had already heard stories from some of the Lads at the hospital, the ones who'd arrived since the first bombers had begun coming over. The hospital would be all right. It had cellars and the walls were at least three times as thick as any in the village.

"Why would they want to bomb the hospital?" Rusty asked her.

"I don't want to find out!" Florrie admitted.

Some of the children were already tugging at Old Spot. He'd been bragging. "Come on, tell us how you did it. You've built a bomb-shelter. We've only done a doorway. Show us what to do."

Rusty was chuckling, muttering under her breath to her grandfather, "Gotcha there!" Handing the rest of the overalls to Gertie, "You see those get distributed to the Scamps and Old Spot'll stay here to give bomb-shelter building practice. How does that sound?"

Aggy was already organising the children by the time Dotty came over, looking for Florrie. Al and Walker were heading towards Gertie, who was waving them over, his hand full of their overalls.

"Come and get 'em. You're gonna need 'em!"

Rusty was relieved to see Al and Walker, with Maze sitting in their wheelbarrow.

"We came prepared," the little girl announced.

"How d'ya get to know so quick?" Old Spot asked them, suspiciously.

Walker reminded him, "We were collecting paper today."

"Is that what your wheelbarrow's for?" he teased them. "Mine's not!"

"What's yours for, then, Mister?" Walker challenged.

Old Spot grinned and stepped up with the wheelbarrow he'd taken off the back of Rusty's truck, facing the city-quick boy.

"We're gonna be building bomb-shelters, in case the Anderson trucks miss us by and the German bombers don't!"

Maze had a proviso. "Only if I'm the one to stand straight and do the measuring."

Old Spot stood his wheelbarrow to one side and got down on one knee, until his face was level with the little girl's. Maze had yet to climb out of their wheelbarrow. The old gentleman reached out his hand, taking hold of hers and shook it enthusiastically.

"Done!"

Then returned to his feet to proceed to duly shake the hands of Al, Walker and Gertie, too, before checking over to the two young nurses standing with Aggy, "You staying then?" Florrie and Dotty seemed to think they 'ought'.

"Looks like we're set," Old Spot reported to the schoolteacher.

Aggy needed to get them all organised. "Who's fetching the empty sacks?"

Maze could do that. A slip of a thing, and she knew where they were kept.

Gertie couldn't help, not yet. He still had to get back to Brisket and let him know how Mr Tor's pigs were doing.

"We'll be needing both barrows for loading the earth. Al and Walker, you go start on that."

Old Spot could borrow some of Aggy's teaching chalk to mark out the footprint of the shelter. "Where d'ya want it then?"

"In the playground," she offered. What would Mr Pegg the headmaster say?

"School's gotta set a good example, doesn't it?" Rusty reasoned gently. Aggy couldn't argue with that.

"Just so long as you've got a good sturdy broom about the place, Miss. If he don't like it where we put it, we can soon remedy that," Old Spot offered.

Mr Pegg, the headmaster, wasn't about and Mrs Parr was occupied. That meant in the playground Aggy was in charge.

Rusty's grandfather was looking directly at Al and Walker when he'd mentioned that broom. Walker might be city-quick, but Al knew a hint when he heard one!

Gertie had his errand over to Brisket's, and Maze had her errand over to the Home Guard office cupboard, Al felt more than able to fetch a broom.

"Bracket's always got a few about the place," he said, dragging Walker by the arm. "Come on."

Old Spot chuckled as he watched the two boys heading for the village ironmongers. "Two Scamps, one broom; sounds like a plan!"

Rusty had already decided she'd best go over to the village hall with Maze, retrieving her wheelbarrow from where her grandfather had left it.

"We'll be needing this and this," she said, tucking the overall she'd saved for Maze under her arm. "Come on, let's get you ready."

Aggy went to fetch the chalk and warn Mr Pegg.

Bracket's shop was almost directly across the road from

the school. There was a path down the side of the shop that separated it from the village pub. The path ought to have been wider, but Bracket's shop had spread a bit since then. He'd once had a rather nice little front garden but that had long since been buried under stock.

The shop comprised basically the whole of the front garden and the downstairs of his house. It wasn't so much a shop as a hoard of useful things. Bracket could find anything he wanted to, if you gave him enough warning of what you might be needing.

He'd had a wife once. Those who needed to know knew what had happened to her; those who didn't at least knew enough not to ask! That was a good seven years ago. The only time a washcloth or duster had moved in Bracket's home since then was when he flicked it across the counter to check how much he was going to charge for it.

Bracket wasn't good at spur-of-the-moment decisions. Al knew about Bracket, not everything, but he knew what Ol' Creak at the village shop thought of him.

"It's all about the timing and the approach," he warned Walker, who was keeping up beside him. It would be even better if they could see what they wanted and fetch it first, before Bracket caught them. That seemed to be the crux of their plan. By then they'd taken all of the half dozen paces from the footpath outside the school to across the width of the village road. Bracket wasn't a large man, shorter than Gertie, though not as scrawny. Walker felt confident that between the two of them, he and Al could stand up to Bracket.

"No, don't try and do that!" Al warned him. "You'll be all right, he likes talking. Just don't get within reach if you see his hand itching for the yardstick!"

Bracket didn't mind children in his shop. They were always

the most eager to pick something up and ask him about it. It was true Bracket liked talking.

Bracket knew where he'd put everything once upon a time. However, he wasn't so good at putting things back after he'd brought them out for a customer to consider. There were no shelves in Bracket's shop. 'Always lose things when you have shelves,' he would tell anyone who asked him why.

The front room was a bare wooden floor, no furniture in the place except for his counter, which was comprised of the kitchen table and chair. The counter was dominated by a set of large, heavy-duty cast-iron weighing scales. Behind the chair was an upturned crate with two biscuit tins. One had biscuits in, the other held Bracket's day-cash coins. He had a yardstick leaning beside the biscuit tins and a tape measure sitting on the counter beside the scales.

The yardstick had many purposes, one of which was for measuring lengths. Few of the village residents had seen Bracket ever use it that way. Most had heard stories of him using the yardstick for swatting the knuckles of anyone who picked something up and started messing about with it.

Best thing anyone could do, before going into Bracket's shop, was to know what they wanted. If they didn't know what they wanted, they needed to be very clear what the problem was that they were trying to remedy.

The stock Bracket held in his shop was only half of his business; 'fixing the problem' was Bracket's other venture. That was why it was always best to do your own searching before disturbing Bracket.

The majority of Bracket's stock was contained in either bundles in barrels, or in crates sat on their side with more crates stacked on top. The longer items were kept in the barrels, whilst the smaller tubs were kept for the sharper items. The prices were always on the side.

When anyone had decided what they wanted and found it, and Bracket had approved their choice, he'd asked them what the price was. They'd tell him and he'd consider that: "Sounds about right."

Nothing was sold at Bracket's, not good and proper sold, until he knew what it was needed for. Bracket had a system to his stock, which relied on the crates. The crates, if anyone was interested enough to inspect them, would have given a hint as to the source of Bracket's original stock.

Al and Walker had a plan.

"We're going for a school broom," Al reminded his friend, before adding, "That means for starters he can't ask us to pay for it."

"He can ask all he likes, won't do him no good!" Walker agreed.

"Don't we need a bomb-shelter broom?" Walker wondered, as they made their way a little more hesitantly, since leaving the footpath outside the playground, on the other side of the road. "Or should that be a sandbag broom?"

"Hang on, I've got another plan. Put your overalls on." Al halted and thumped his friend's shoulder. "Go on, quick."

"What here, in the middle of the road?"

"No, you idiot, behind the back of the pub wall. No one down that way and Horace is too fat to get out that far and Rosie doesn't let him keep anything back there, not anymore. The only thing back there is the rear of the stables, and the only reason any one wants to go down there is to collect fresh horse manure."

The two boys did a rapid sidestep, Walker following Al's lead. He could see what Al had meant. The back of the pub had two large wooden doors and there were the remnants of a cobbled path from them down to what smelt like the back of the village stables. It reminded Walker of some of the city back alleys he'd played down before being evacuated. Not that there were many stables down those ways, but the smell was somehow similar enough to remind him.

They barely stopped walking; two strides and they were stripped from the waist up, one pace missed and trousers off, overalls skipped into. They were large enough to step into, shoes and all. Swivelling on their heels and scooping up their clothes, stuffing them down at the corner of what remained of Bracket's fence.

"Ready?" Al asked, with Walker beside him and already appreciating the effects the overalls were having. He didn't feel like a schoolboy anymore. He and his mate were heading into a man-size errand in man-size overalls.

"Ready."

Both boys felt bolder.

"Now what?" Walker asked. "We still need to get a broom for any sandbags we spill. How are the overalls going to help with Bracket?"

"Told you I had a plan, didn't I? The overalls are our disguise. We're sandbag stackers. Remember Humfrey called us that and he's in uniform. Can't argue with uniform, can you?" Al told him.

"Yes, but Humfrey wasn't the one to tell us we needed to get a broom. I think you volunteered," Walker began to suggest, then shut up, suddenly realising he wasn't convinced that part hadn't actually been his idea. Fortunately, by then they were already in the start of Bracket's shop. If that was the best plan they could come up with, then that was it!

"OK, I'll find the broom, you do the talking," Walker

decided, shoving Al ahead of him.

"What are we looking for, a school one or a sandbag one? Do you know the difference, 'cos I don't!" Al checked under his breath.

Walker grinned, "I'm just looking for the biggest one."

"Good idea," agreed Al. "It's a big playground and we're going to be stacking a lot of sandbags!"

"What you looking for?" Bracket called forward.

Al began, "School broom for Miss Aggy."

"For the school, hey? Haven't they got one?"

"That's the schoolroom broom. We need one for the playground," Al could think that quick, but he was still hoping Walker would hurry up and make his selection before Bracket delved any deeper into the details of their plan.

"Found it!" Walker called.

Al was impressed. "Ruddy heck, that's twice the size of you!"

Bracket was evidently equally dubious. "Think you can handle that?"

Walker was happy to explain. "Oh, we're not doing the sweeping. We're on stacking duty."

"Are you?" Bracket queried.

"It's for the school. Miss Aggy sent us," Al repeated. Walker held up the broom just to be sure Bracket could see what they'd got, deciding it might be helpful to state the obvious. "It's a broom for the playground."

"Miss Aggy sent you?" Bracket queried.

"It was Old Spot's idea. He said we need a bomb-shelter in the playground, for practice," Walker blurted.

"Old Spot's idea, hey?" Bracket queried, getting up and inspecting Walker's choice. "For the playground, you say?"

Both boys nodded, attempting to back away from the counter. "Old Spot's building a bomb-shelter for you, is he?" Bracket's interrogation ratcheted up a notch.

"He's got more practice than we have, *and* he's got a bigger barrow!" Walker explained.

"Got the sandbags ready, have you then?" Bracket checked, solicitously.

"Maze and Rusty are fetching the sacks and we've got to fill them before we stack them," Al explained.

"You'll be needing spades – or did Old Spot bring over some of his spares?" Bracket had got the boys stumped on that one. They didn't know. Neither of them had thought to look in the back of Rusty's truck.

"Do you two even know *how* to sweep a playground?" Bracket queried.

That caught both boys on the back foot. The only thing Al could think of was to repeat, "We're not on the sweeping duty, we're stacking. They just sent us over to fetch the broom, 'cos we've got the overalls!"

Walker held a little tighter to the broom. He didn't know why, but it helped.

"Come on. Let's see what Old Spot's cooked up this time." Bracket looked over Walker's choice of broom. "I can do better than that," guiding them further from the daylight. "Best brooms are out the back."

"Why?" Walker had to ask, not letting go of his first choice.

Bracket explained. He had time for the two boys. They weren't fiddling about with anything, and they had come in knowing what they wanted and why they needed it. That always boded well for Bracket.

"You always sweep from the top to the bottom. You always sweep from the back forward. So the dust comes down and out. Only way to do it. So, I always keep the best brooms out back, where I need 'em!"

Al knew the theory of how Bracket's shop got started was connected, in some way, to when Horace first arrived to take over the village pub. It was a relative of Rosie's who'd had it before then. Rosie had stayed. Previously they used to have guests staying upstairs at the pub when the carriages and coaches came through the village. Rosie lived upstairs now and no one else stayed there. Horace was too fat for the stairs, which suited Rosie nicely. She'd been itching to give the place a fresh coat of paint and before she allowed Horace to take over the pub, she made him 'clear everything out from the cellars that don't belong.'

She wouldn't allow him in until he'd promised that. She'd even had the vicar over to make sure he kept his promise! Horace and Rosie shared the pub's business between cellar and upstairs, with Rosie in charge of upstairs. The story went that she got one of the farmer's carts down below the upstairs windows and just chucked everything out, 'clean sweep, top to bottom.' It had been Bracket's words of advice about the broom that had reminded Al of what he'd heard.

The farmer's cart had only been put there for the catching. Bracket's shop started when his wife left him, or thereabouts, with the cartload of furniture from the pub's upstairs and all those old crates that held the lost property cleared out from Horace's cellars.

Only one question remained in Al's mind: where did the farmer's cart go? Did the farmer get it back, or did Bracket have that stashed out the back somewhere, beyond those best brooms of his? Al never got a chance to ask Bracket about that. Bracket was doing all the asking, striding back with the two boys across the village road to the front of the school.

"You wanted a broom, Miss?" he checked with Aggy. Florrie was with her and was admiring the overalls. "You both look ready for business."

Walker beamed. "Barrow and stacking duties, at the ready."

"Where's Old Spot?" Bracket asked both ladies. He wanted to find out what they had in mind for the school bomb-shelter. If it was going to be properly equipped, he'd likely have a few more items they'd be needing beyond the broom. Aggy could only direct Bracket out to the back of the school.

"We've got plenty of land back there for filling those sandbags."

"You've left Old Spot in charge of the digging and filling?" Bracket queried, giving the impression he didn't think that entirely wise.

Aggy invited him to go and see for himself. Bracket took a couple of steps into the playground, then began to shudder.

Florrie noticed, immediately coming to his aid. "You'll be needing to take the side path, not through the school."

Bracket breathed a sigh of relief, then swore. "Should have brought a spade."

"Yes, you should have," Walker agreed. "Want us to fetch one for you?"

"You'll be needing a spade for the digging," Al agreed with his mate.

It was the first time in a long while that anyone had offered Bracket advice on what he needed to get something done. Bracket didn't like the way it sounded, twisting round he reached to cuff the side of Al's head, but missed. Al was quicker. The overalls were proving their worth.

"Tell you what, how about we fetch *more* spades?" Al offered, tugging Walker's sleeve to follow. "Instead of sticking them all upside down in those barrels of yours? The whole village would appreciate that. Get them working for the Effort," the village-smart local boy told the shopkeeper.

Bracket paused mid step, still with his hand reached out and swore again. "Damn. Should have thought of that!" Then remembered where he was. "Sorry, Miss, you too miss, Nurse. Sorry."

Turning to Al and Walker, "OK, you know where they are. You'd better get 'em. Nothing else mind you." Bracket turned back to Aggy and Florrie. "How much is this Effort going to cost me?"

Walker could answer that. "Less than if you don't make the effort before the bombs start dropping!"

Florrie tilted her head, a half-smile winking in approval at Walker's city-quick thinking. With a solemn 'tut' to Bracket, that told him the boys in the overalls knew what they were talking about.

Dotty seemed to be doing most of the running around keeping the children organised. Old Spot knew what to do, but not how to tell the younger children. Maze was quite happy where she was standing. With the chalk marks having been made, she was patiently waiting for the filled sandbags to begin arriving.

Al and Walker came back over with what must have been a full barrel's quota of spades, before Bracket had caught up with Old Spot.

"Ready for stacking duties," Al shouted ahead.

"What kept you?" Old Spot called over.

"Reinforcements," Bracket informed him. "Looks like you've got a ready 'n able bomb-shelter building crew there."

"No, we haven't," Maze informed him. "We're missing Gertie!"

CHAPTER 8

An Errand or Two and a Tug Too Hard

"I THOUGHT HE WAS ONLY meant to be checking in with Brisket."

Gertie had been as good as his word and gone directly from the playground to the butcher's, to let him know how Mr Tor's sow was doing. He also wanted to see what Brisket's missus thought of his new overalls.

Gertie's next stop was to fetch a copy of the day's newspaper for Old Spot. Rusty might have mentioned he hadn't had a fresh one for a couple of days. It was late enough in the morning and most of Ol' Creak's regulars would have fetched theirs by then. The shop keeper wouldn't be needing many more. Gertie didn't have any money, but that didn't stop him asking.

"Who's it for?" was Ol' Creak's first question. The second was noticing what Gertie was wearing. "What you got them on for?"

Gertie stood tall. He was a lanky lad at the best of times, but when he stood tall his whole frame seemed to stretch an extra couple of inches.

"Rusty issued us with them."

"She 'issued' you with them?" Ol' Creak was intrigued. As keeper of the village shop it was his duty to be fully aware of anything remotely interesting in the village. He had a reputation to maintain. If anyone needed to know anything they came to his village shop to be told what everyone was talking about, first!

"They're overalls," Gertie explained.

"I can see that," Ol' Creak confirmed.

"Rusty gave us them. Miss Aggy said it was OK and Humfrey needed sandbag stackers."

"He did, did he?" Ol' Creak queried. If Humfrey was involved then likely it was official, so maybe he shouldn't ask any more questions. If he needed to know anything official, then it ought to come through official channels. Ol' Creak took another look at Gertie. Gertie didn't look like he worked through official channels!

"Tell you what, have you still got your bicycle?"

Gertie nodded, waiting for the errand he could hear was coming.

"You can have the newspaper for Old Spot if you take over the smokes for the consultant at the clinic. It got missed off from the order heading to Mrs Toombs this morning."

Gertie grinned he knew better than that. Ol' Creak might have said 'missed', but he meant 'forgot'. Gertie wasn't going to say anything, and the shopkeeper knew that too.

Ol' Creak lowered his voice.

"Just do me a favour, Gertie. Take the smokes over for the sawbones. He's got some surging to do this afternoon and needs them urgent-like. Wouldn't want a shaky sawbones working on any of Our Lads, now, would we?"

Gertie hadn't been intending to go over to see Mrs

Toombs. Brisket hadn't given him anything for the house. He'd been hoping to get the newspaper directly over to Old Spot and join in with the bomb-shelter building. Gertie was still hopeful of having his own shed one day and a bit of bomb-shelter building practice would stand him in good stead.

But if Old Spot was happy enough reading an old newspaper over his breakfast, then today's could wait another hour or so. Gertie was also thinking Ol' Creak was right. He didn't like the sound of a shaky sawbones 'surging' on one of their Lads!

Gertie couldn't imagine what sort of 'surging' might be called for up at the clinic. He only knew Brisket had a bone saw and he didn't smoke!

Gertie had another query. He'd already picked up the packet of cigarettes from the counter, but was he meant to be taking them all the way over to the clinic, because he wasn't allowed over there. He'd been told that enough times. Maybe he ought to mention it to Florrie first, before heading out to the hospital?

Gertie took the newspaper and the packet of cigarettes. Another reason why he liked the overalls: plenty of pockets! Then he hurried back to the playground with Ol' Creak's warning ringing in his ears. Florrie was still there.

"Oh, thank goodness, I've got this to deliver for Shark-shoulders."

Florrie was pleased to see him. "We've been wondering where you got to." She'd been startled by the reference though, "Who?"

Aggy had heard the two of them whispering. "Everything OK?"

Florrie explained for Gertie, "I think I need to go over to the hospital with Gertie, a sensitive delivery."

The schoolteacher was intrigued, but guessed she'd learn

the details in due course. In the meantime, it sounded urgent and *not* the time to ask questions.

"You can borrow Humfrey's bicycle," she suggested to the young nurse.

Gertie waited. It only took Florrie a couple of minutes to get over to the church warden's house and grab the bicycle.

"We'll be back before you finish, Miss Aggy," Gertie assured the schoolteacher, before giving a thumbs up to Maze. "Smashing job!"

Maze was walking backwards and forwards with chalk in one chubby little hand and the tape measure in the other. As the children got on with filling the sandbags with the earth from the waste ground behind the school, Al and Walker were shifting the wheelbarrows. Old Spot and Bracket were directing the digging and filling. Aggy and Rusty were staying in the front, with Dotty doing something with more buckets!

Gertie was engrossed, until Florrie rang the bicycle bell.

"Come on, no time to waste," the young nurse prompted, and they both started pedalling. Florrie was right; when it came to Shark-shoulders and cigarettes, 'No time to waste!'

Florrie didn't know anything about the cigarettes but did know the surgeon did most of his surgical work at the clinic in the afternoon. The only time he operated in the morning was if it was absolutely vital or an unscheduled emergency had arrived.

"I don't know what he's doing, I haven't been allowed in there yet. Pru might know. Maybe I ought to go with you to give them to him."

Gertie hadn't been intending to hand them to Shark-shoulders personally. He'd just thought that giving them to Mrs Toombs would suffice.

One thing Gertie noticed about his new overalls, they seemed to make a good impression with Sarg at the gate. "Come to do some work this time, then?"

"Yes, Sarg," Gertie grinned, and gave him the thumbs up as he cycled straight through.

Florrie would have explained everything, but Sarg didn't seem to need to ask her. The overalls made Gertie feel like he knew what he was meant to be doing. Maybe Sarg knew that, too.

Sarg recognised the pair of them. Nurses on bicycles always made him smile; they reminded him of his mother. Gertie wasn't a nurse, but from a distance there was a remarkable resemblance!

Mrs Toombs would know where Pru was, Florrie told Gertie, as they wheeled their bicycles off the path and hurried round to the kitchen entrance.

"She's likely upstairs, if she's not over at the clinic already," Mrs Toombs hazarded a guess. "They brought the patient directly over in an ambulance, a referral. Pru's probably still upstairs getting the side room ready."

"Oh." Florrie understood what that meant. She took a moment to make sure Gertie understood.

"We keep the side rooms ready for the Lads that need some quiet time, maybe when they need a nurse to sit with them during the night."

Gertie understood what that meant. No one needed to tell him what night-sitting meant.

Gertie had forgotten to give Florrie the cigarettes, and the young nurse was already upstairs before he remembered. Gertie knew he wasn't allowed upstairs, at least he hadn't been when he was in civvies, but he wasn't in civvies anymore, he was in overalls! Sarg hadn't even asked him what he was doing.

If the overalls were good enough for Sarg at the gate, then they were good enough to get Gertie upstairs to find which side room Florrie and Pru were in.

Gertie had one foot on the first stair. It was quite thrilling, then alarming, as he realised he was standing in the way of someone coming down! Beanpole 'n' whiskers was coming down the hospital stairs.

"What are you doing here?" The senior doctor recognised the young man from somewhere. Not one of his staff, but a regular about the place. "Do you work here?"

"No, Sir. Not much, Sir. Sort of. Overalls, Sir," Gertie blurted, then decided a more succinct explanation might help. "Shark-shoulders' smokes, Sir!" Handing the packet of cigarettes to the senior doctor.

"Urgent then?" Beanpole 'n' whiskers suggested.

"Yes, Sir," Gertie confirmed.

"Shark-shoulders?" the senior doctor checked the packet.

"Yes, Sir. Can't be having him with shakes before surging, Sir," Gertie's overalls were bolstering his blurts!

"No, we can't be having that now, can we?" Beanpole 'n' whiskers agreed. "Shall I take them over for you?"

"Yes, Sir. Thank you. I'll let Florrie know you've taken care of it, shall I, Sir?" Gertie queried.

"You do that." The senior doctor solemnly took possession of the packet of cigarettes, placing them in the top pocket of his jacket, patting it to be sure he knew they were secure, before giving a second opinion. "Urgent, indeed."

Gertie was tall, but Beanpole 'n' whiskers seemed to tower over him, although that might just be the effect of the moustache! Gertie stepped to one side and allowed the senior doctor to continue on his way, just as Florrie and Pru reached the top of the stairs, staring down in disbelief at the exchange.

"You never!?"

"I did. You didn't, so I had to!" Gertie told both nurses. "It's all right, I've got me overalls on." Recalling what the doctor had told him, "Beanpole 'n' whiskers gave me permission to tell you he'd take care of it."

Pru didn't know what to make of that statement. All she knew about the patient scheduled for surgery was his name, Art. He had burn injuries. That was on his notes. He'd got them at Dunkirk; the porter had told her that much. Art had been in another hospital for a few weeks, but they'd decided to send him to the clinic for special surgery on his hands.

Gertie instinctively glanced down at his own hands, turning them over and rubbing his thumbs over his fingertips, murmuring under his breath, "No wonder Shark-shoulders needed his smokes!"

As shocked as Pru was that Gertie had asked the senior doctor to complete the errand, she was glad they'd got there in time. Florrie would stay with Pru in case she was needed for the night-sitting, too.

Gertie couldn't do anything else to help, except to deliver Old Spot's newspaper, which was still stuffed in the back pocket of his overalls.

"Do you think they'll have finished the bomb-shelter yet?"

Pru hadn't got a clue what he was talking about, but she was used to that where Gertie was concerned. Florrie doubted the sandbag stacking crew would have had enough time to finish the job.

"You'll catch Old Spot. He won't want to leave until it's done."

Florrie hadn't forgotten the bicycle Aggy had lent her; it

was still parked outside Mrs Toombs' kitchen. "You'll give her a message, won't you?"

Gertie grinned. "I'm good at messages."

It turned out Aggy didn't mind Florrie keeping the bicycle for another shift. It was her husband's bicycle, and she hadn't seen him yet to tell him anything!

"I don't suppose you saw Humfrey on your way in?"

"No, but I'm glad Old Spot's still here."

"You looking for me? Need any truck driving, do you?" Old Spot seemed to have overheard just enough to decide it was to his advantage to be listening.

"If I let you do the driving, you'd have missed the turn and ploughed through the hedge by now," Rusty told him pointedly. "Where are your glasses?"

She could see he'd already begun to squint and was holding the newspaper that Gertie had given him at arm's length, to get the headlines into focus.

"Have I read this one already?"

"This morning's newspaper was a couple of days old. If you were reading that, you must have had your glasses then." Rusty couldn't remember seeing him with them at the kitchen table.

"I wasn't reading it, I was just stopping Jeepers getting hold of it. Does him good to start the day with a bit of a stomp in his belly. What's the point in me having my glasses?" Old Spot reasoned, tucking the newspaper into his own back pocket and returning his gaze to his granddaughter. "I knew you wouldn't let me do any driving."

Aggy decided she needed to stop this before it got any sillier. "Where *are* your glasses?"

"Somewhere safe, I guess. If the bombs start coming

down around our ears, I don't think I'll need my glasses to know where to go, will I?"

The 'tut' came better from Aggy. Being a teacher, she knew just how to do it.

"How we gonna test it? To see if it'll stand up to a bomb dropping on it?" Walker shouted up. Al had almost forgotten about the bombs. Building the shelter was fun, a good test for the overalls, but he didn't like the sound of the bombs messing up all their hard work.

"Need to test it, don't we?" Walker brazenly checked with Bracket, who was still trying to find the last of the spades he'd counted when they'd been filling the sandbags. That must have been a good hour ago. Since then, it had been all hands to the stacking.

Bracket had to give it to Old Spot. He might talk rubbish sometimes, but when it came to building a bomb-shelter, he knew what he was doing. Maze seemed to be in charge, though!

Every time a sandbag was placed in position, she checked it lined up with its predecessors, in accord with the chalk markings on the floor of the playground. Bracket had even been toying with the notion of sending Al back over to fetch his yardstick to help her keep it steady, especially once it got too high for her to reach anymore.

"Don't worry, it only needs to be a practice one, just until the trucks arrive," Old Spot calmed her frets when she couldn't see the top anymore.

Walker came to the rescue with her pram. "Put it inside the walls, then Maze can stand in it and look out over the top, at least until we start on the roof."

Al would have suggested that sooner, but he would have used the wheelbarrow.

"Idiot! Can't do that. We still need the wheelbarrows for the rest of the sandbags."

Al couldn't think of an answer to that, so volunteered to fetch Brisket's yardstick before he asked, "Didn't we put planks on top of the roof over the village hall doors?" he checked with Rusty.

"Humfrey would know," Aggy told them, but Humfrey hadn't been seen all day.

"We don't need Humfrey and his truck for a few planks," Gertie told them. "Plenty over behind Ol' Creak's shop. He uses them when he's got more trays than table space out front."

Walker knew where he meant. "Over where the allotments have got started?"

"That's it. Can never have too many planks or sheds on an allotment!" Old Spot agreed, sending Gertie and Walker to scramble them up, before checking over with Bracket. "Half dozen do it?"

Bracket would have preferred his yardstick to check the reckoning, but he'd make-do with Maze's tape measure. She wasn't ready to relinquish command of the tape.

"I can do it from up here. How long do you want it to be?" she asked the shopkeeper.

Bracket couldn't help himself but smile at the little girl's way of asking. "A half dozen should do it."

He came to stand by the bomb-shelter wall, as Maze stood up in the pram in the middle of the construction, reaching the tape from her side to his.

"I know six. Six is half a dozen. I know that because of the eggs and shoes," she told him. Bracket was just starting to feel like he was keeping up with this count. Eggs he could follow. "Shoes?"

"Feet?" Old Spot wondered, stepping over to see how they were getting on.

"No, not feet. Shoes," Maze corrected both men. She had been quite clear on that. "Shoes. Six shoes. Two each, me and Al and Walker. Six."

Old Spot scratched his head, Bracket chuckled, and Rusty came over to see if they'd got it sorted. Maze yelled loud enough for everyone in the playground and likely half the village to hear.

"HALF DOZEN PLANKS PLEASE!"

Walker and Gertie had already been sent to fetch that many. They could find half a dozen planks easily, but not in a condition that would hold the weight of a couple of rows of sandbags on top, never mind a bomb drop.

"We need the ones that have been kept dry and no splinters, like the ones Humfrey had in the back of his truck for the hall doors. They were lovely straight bits of timber; that's what we're looking for," Walker instructed Gertie.

Gertie knew where to find such timbers, but the allotmenteers weren't going to like it. "The best planks are always kept in their sheds for shelving. If we take them, they'll have nowhere to put their pots."

"What do you think is more urgent, dropped bombs or dropped pots?" Walker reasoned. "Anyway, we're in overalls, aren't we!?"

Gertie nodded, waiting for Walker to continue. "Then we're as good as in uniform and you said Sarg didn't even ask you." Gertie nodded again, still waiting. Walked continued. "Then if Sarg ain't gonna argue, the allotmenteers can't, can they?"

Walker was right. Gertie agreed.

"Dropped bombs it is, then! Come on, take these old planks with us. We can put those in the sheds. They'll just have to make-do with soggy wood and splinters with their pots. Pots don't weight as heavy as sandbags anyway."

Gertie took his end of the stack of planks as Walker led the way back over to the playground, handing the planks over to Old Spot and Rusty. Bracket was lifting Maze out from the middle of the bomb-shelter, then the pram.

"Can't leave you behind in there," he told her gently. "You're vital, you are. Can't be having wonky walls. You have a wonky wall to start with and it won't take much of a bomb to send them tumbling!"

"Quite right!" Rusty agreed, coming over and helping the little girl bring the pram out of the way, as more of the children were preparing to start lobbing the sandbags up to the roof of the shelter. "Gertie, you getting up there, again?"

Al and Walker handed the planks up, and they were duly laid across from one side wall to the other, back to where the bomb-shelter wedged up against the old outhouse. It hadn't been in use for years and butted up against the side of the village hall, so that wasn't going anywhere. With the planks in place, the remaining sandbags needed to be brought up. The fact that Gertie could sit up there and not break through the ceiling was a reassuring sign.

"But those bombs will be coming down heavier than you, Gertie," Old Spot reckoned.

"Looks like you've been getting ahead of yourselves there!" Humfrey shouted, as he walked over from the camp truck. He was late. "Have you lot been hearing something I missed?"

"We're practising," some of the children told him.

"So I see." Humfrey came closer.

"That should do it!" Bracket informed him, as Gertie clambered down.

"You sure about that?" Humfrey asked the shopkeeper.

"How d'ya know?" Old Spot wasn't convinced either. "We need to test it, don't we?" he asked the children and Gertie.

Humfrey beckoned Aggy quietly to his side, glad to spend a few minutes together. It wasn't very private, but at least there was laughter and silliness around them. Those had been rare for Humfrey these past couple of days. The news wasn't good, but he wasn't going to tell his Aggy that. Rusty and Gertie seemed able to take care of things in the playground for a little while.

Bracket had retrieved every one of his spades and one of his brooms. He was eager to get them back to the shop and back into his selling barrels.

Walker had a quick think. "I'll help you." He grabbed the wheelbarrow and clattered across the road, keeping up with Bracket, then tipped the contents out unceremoniously on the pavement. Walker then grabbed his and Al's clothes from where they'd stashed them earlier and dashed back. He'd only been gone a minute at most, but already some idiots had decided battering the sandbags would be test enough.

"A bomb's not going to hit it like that! Bombs drop down, then blow up!" Walker was stating the obvious, but it felt like a few of his fellows needed reminding.

"Then what do you suggest?" Al asked the question Walker had been hoping someone would.

"Only one way to test a bomb-shelter and that's to drop something heavy on to it," Walker declared, looking over to Rusty. "What you got that's heavy enough in that truck of yours?"

"Old Spot!" she suggested.

Old Spot didn't think so, but he did have an alternative. "Your toolbag!"

"Don't you dare!" Rusty glared at him.

"We could drop Maze from the shed roof on to it, but I think she'd bounce too easy. You want more of a thud drop, don't you, not a bounce drop?" Al wondered, teasing his little sister. Maze grabbed her pram and scampered nearer to the school gate. Gertie calmed her down and stepped in front of her. Mr Pegg and Mrs Parr had finished the school day long since. The playground was getting busier.

"Definitely got to be a drop," Old Spot agreed. "Anyone got a ladder?"

"Don't need a ladder, just climb up on that old shed roof. What are we taking up to drop down?" Walker asked them.

Al had the idea. "How about if we put Rusty's toolbag in the wheelbarrow? That way it'll stay in one place."

Al was sceptical. "How you gonna manage that?"

Gertie had already fetched Rusty's toolbag. Old Spot was right, it was heavy.

"You'll never get this up there, not with the wheelbarrow too," he told them.

"Al and me can manage the toolbag. You can hand us up the wheelbarrow," Walker explained the plan.

Old Spot and Rusty took a step back at that point. Whatever was going to happen next, they weren't going to be able to stop it. Their only hope was that either Aggy or Humfrey would come back soon. After all, this had been Humfrey's idea to start with!

'The Scamps', Rusty grinned, as she rubbed her aching arms. They certainly deserved that title. She was proud of her grandfather too; he'd done well today, with all that digging and filling, keeping the children organised and occupied. No squabbles, no tears. They'd talked about bombs and no one seemed to be frightened. Her grandfather was good at that, taking the fear of what might happen and turning it into something useful. Old Spot had simply suggested, 'Right then, we'd better do something to be ready for that,' and the children had got themselves ready.

Al and Walker were fully occupied trying to work out how to climb up on to the top of the old outhouse roof and throw a wheelbarrow down on top of the new bomb-shelter. Even before Al could pass up Rusty's toolbag, never mind the wheelbarrow Gertie had ready, Walker took one step off from the top of the roof of sandbags on to the old tiles of the outhouse and went straight through!

Shouts and a cloud of dust and mayhem immediately ensued.

"What the HECK was that!?" Old Spot shouted.

Al knew exactly what that was. "Walker's jumped on top of the privy."

"Oh cripes!"

Al was still holding Rusty's toolbag. Putting it down, he took the wheelbarrow off Gertie and turned it over, using it to step up and lean in to the dusty mass of rotten splintered rafters, crumbled ancient bricks and shattered tiles.

"You all right in there?"

There were a few choice oaths and a healthy measure of shouting coming back from Walker.

"Woops!"

Gertie could already see what was going to happen next if he didn't intervene. Rusty and Old Spot were laughing too much to be sensible. As for the children, they were enjoying the ridiculous sight, and Maze was resolutely holding on to her pram.

It was down to Gertie to stop Al going the same way as Walker. Two strides and he was back up on the roof of the bomb-shelter. It was sturdy enough to take his and Al's weight. Gertie grabbed the collar of Al's overalls before he leaned any further into the ramshackle remnants of the privy roof, and yanked him out of the way.

"You stay there and make sure no one else does anything any *more* stupid!" Gertie told him, before getting down on his hands and knees and peering into the dusty grubby depths.

"Walker, you OK?"

"Think so." The boy coughed and looked up, his face a picture of smudges of ancient dust. He had bruises forming where he'd caught his knee and shin going down and both his elbows were scraped where he'd had the sleeves of his overalls up, but otherwise it was just grime, cobwebs and a whole lot of rubble down there.

"Can you stand?" Gertie checked.

"I am," Walker informed him.

"Oh. Give me your hands. I'll pull you out, straight up," Gertie instructed. Before he took hold of Walker's upstretched hands, he got Al behind him to make sure they were both steady.

"This is going to be a heck of a heave," Gertie warned back to Al. "Got to get him out in one go, or he'll get stuck." Gertie checked both boys understood what was about to happen. "When I say so, Walker, you jump up. I'll have your hands and pull. Al, you grab the middle of my overalls, back and steady! Got it?"

Walker had loosened one of his hands from Gertie's grip, in order to move some of the sharper edges from his route.

Gertie took a firm hold of the one remaining hand. "Got it," Walker called up.

"Ready." Al confirmed.

"NOW!" Gertie yelled.

Walker duly jumped, but his brushing-aside hand seemed to have a mind of its own and shot up alongside the one in Gertie's grasp, swinging wildly, punching his fist up to catch Gertie's chin.

Gertie swore and the shock of pain caused his grip to tighten. Walker yelped as Gertie yanked him so violently, the boy almost flew out from the roof of the old outhouse, up into Gertie's face. By this time, Al, true to his word, had grabbed Gertie's middle and pulled with all his might, which was more than sufficient to take all three of them off the roof, tumbling to the floor of the playground.

There was swearing, shouting, yelling and blame all round. A brawl seemed imminent, until Maze came over with the bucket and broom.

"That worked well, didn't it?"

CHAPTER 9

An Irregular Day and a Spot of Snaffling

"YOU'RE NOT TAKIN' THIS ONE. I haven't finished with it yet!" Old Spot snapped at Jeepers across the kitchen table.

Jeepers had made a half-hearted grab for the newspaper. "Suit yerself! I'll get one from the shop, fresh."

Rusty had the distinct impression both men rather relished their sparring over breakfast. Not that it was much of a breakfast, nothing like Rusty could remember her mother presenting them with each morning when she'd been alive, a full plate of a 'proper cooked'. Rusty did her best with what she'd got, but there wasn't much. Not that she got any complaints from either her father or grandfather. They drank what she poured from the pot into their mugs, and they ate what she put on the plate in front of them.

"Did you say newspaper?" Rusty queried, as Jeepers took his second mug out into the Yard to start getting his men working.

"Why, do you need something?"

That caught Rusty off guard. She wasn't used to her father offering to do her a favour like that. That made her hesitate. "Why?"

He grinned a little sheepishly. "Might be needing the third truck today." They both knew that meant he would.

"Why?" she persisted.

Jeepers shrugged, but replied honestly, "Can't be taking you with us on this run, but the third truck'll come in handy." Rusty knew better than to ask for any more details. "You can have the bicycle," he offered.

"Well, thanks for that!" They both knew Rusty was the only one who used the bicycle.

"Sorry." Jeepers' voice lowered. It wouldn't do for his men to see such a sign of weakness. He wiped his mouth with the back of his hand and managed to conceal the apology to his daughter in the gesture.

"Shouldn't be too long; might be able to get your truck back to you by this afternoon." He hesitated, before continuing, "Actually, you could do me a favour and take it over to Abe, then."

Rusty smiled at her father's discomfort. Being considerate didn't come naturally to the man. She appreciated the thought and hadn't missed the fact he was starting to recognise that third truck as *her* truck now.

"Can you manage that in the basket," Jeepers pointed to the parcel of waste paper, which currently seemed employed as a gate wedge. "Thought the Scamps would appreciate it."

"What, you couldn't drop that off at the village shop when you get your newspaper?" she queried.

Jeepers started to wind up to a bluster.

She calmed him down. "Don't bother, I can manage and you're right, it would come better from me, wouldn't it?"

"Just a minute." Rusty nudged her father out of the way from heading towards her truck cab, scrambling ahead of him to haul her toolbag and backpack out from the front and the tarp from the back.

"These are mine. I know what you're like. They'll get caught up in one of your dealings and dodgings and won't be there by the time I get my truck back."

He didn't mind her talking to him like that. She was probably right, too, about her toolbag. It wouldn't be the first time that had happened. He rather admired her spirit. As for it being *her* truck? That third truck was the oldest and he was expecting a couple more to be coming his way any day now.

By then Rusty had taken her stuff out and safely stowed it under the kitchen table. The bicycle was in good working order and the stack of paper would just about fit in the basket, although she'd have to be careful on the bends.

"Can you manage?" he grudgingly checked, as he saw her struggle to lift the weight and get it loaded.

"It's only got to get as far as the Scamps, and I'm going to try and get some eggs for supper. So, if you're not back you'll miss them," she told him. That was as near as a 'see you later, have a pleasant day' greeting between Rusty and her father.

She waited until the Yard was clear of trucks, the sheds were all locked and she could hear her grandfather working the wheelbarrow round the back garden. He sounded as if he was set fair for the morning.

Rusty knew where to find the Scamps. It was paper collection day. The paper was 'needed for munitions'; that's what Over-Eager-Edith had told them when she'd put that notice on the board outside the village hall. The paper salvage was for shell containers, cartridge wads, mortar bomb carriers and demolition cartons. If she was going to contribute to that paper salvage, for the time, Rusty just needed to stay upright and pedalling.

Al and Walker did the paper-round for Ol' Creak early out from the village shop. He didn't like the two boys cluttering up his shop when his customers began coming in. He hadn't wanted to give the job to them. They were too young, but they ran as quick as the older boys and between them got it done sooner. Early out meant early gone from under his feet.

Gertie knew which day it was too, and was waiting outside the shop for the boys after their round, ready for salvage duty. He'd got Brisket's delivery bicycle. The boys only had Ol' Creak's rotten bicycle between them, and Maze had her old pram.

"Shouldn't we fetch the wheelbarrow?" Al offered.

Maze reminded them they were meant to be waiting for Rusty.

"You're not expecting us to collect a whole truck load, are you?" Walker asked her.

Maze knew he was teasing her, although she wouldn't have minded collecting a whole truck load of paper, or even just having a ride in the back of Rusty's truck; but that wasn't why they needed to wait for Rusty.

"She said if we wait for her, she might be able to get us some eggs." Maze seemed very clear on that point.

Gertie was a little uncertain how that was going to work. Bicycle baskets and eggs didn't mix so well in his experience, but thought better of mentioning that and waited with the rest of the Scamps outside the village shop.

Al suddenly decided he definitely ought to get the wheelbarrow. "Feels like a good day for collecting and I don't like wasting time."

Rusty had taken it slow coming in. The scrap paper was a block of weight that kept threatening to tilt the balance of the bicycle into the hedge every time she took the turns heading into the village. Once she'd got to the tail end of the church's stone wall, she'd got off and walked, it was safer. Seeing the Salvage Scamps, she waved and called them over to her.

"How's this for a start for you?"

Maze was impressed. "We ought to take that over to the village hall first thing, before we start fetching from the doorsteps, or we'll be full before we start. Where's your truck?"

"Don't ask!" Rusty told the little girl.

Gertie checked, "Jeepers?"

"Three bicycles, one wheelbarrow and a pram. Should be enough, shouldn't it?" she asked them.

"Would have been better with the truck," Maze observed. Al and Walker laughed. They both knew why Maze had wanted Rusty to bring her truck.

"You'll just have to ride in my bicycle basket instead," Rusty offered.

"Oh, yes please!" Maze agreed.

Gertie had both his own bicycle and Ol' Creak's, whilst Al pushed his wheelbarrow with the pack of old papers in it and Walker got stuck with Maze's pram. Maze got to ride in Rusty's bicycle basket, just until they got along the village footpath, past the vicarage.

Gertie being the tallest and quickest to notice such things, called behind him to the rest of the Scamps.

"Seems to be a bit of fuss up ahead. I think it's one of the nurses. No, I think it's all *three* of them! Has Mrs Tweeny thrown them out?"

"What? No!" Rusty scrambled, pushing her bicycle ahead of them, still with Maze in the basket gleefully punching forward. "CHAAAAARGE!"

Pru, Florrie and Dotty had been brought back into the

village after being on duty for a double shift, twenty-four hours and then some. One of the doctors had offered to bring them that way, after seeing them at the bus-stop and taking pity on them.

The fuss was about the fact that it was after 8 am. Mrs Tweeny was going to refuse them breakfast! Everyone in the village knew she kept her habits 'clean and regular'. Mrs Tweeny had breakfast ready and on the table from 7 am to 8 am only, ever. After that her kitchen was closed until supper was ready and on the table at 7 pm.

The fuss seemed not to have originated from any of the young nurses, but rather from the village doctor, Dr Hastings, who lived in the house next door to Mrs Tweeny.

Mrs Tweeny had shut her front door, girls or no girls. It was 8 am and she always started her housekeeping chores at the doctor's house at 8 am. When the nurses got to Mrs Tweeny's, her front door was locked. Dotty was so tired she just burst into tears.

Florrie guessed where Mrs Tweeny was and knocked on the doctor's front door. Dr Hastings didn't know anything about the state of the young nurses, only that Mrs Tweeny didn't do doors. He'd opened his door and Florrie had told him they couldn't get in. He'd then called Mrs Tweeny down from upstairs.

It had been about then when the Scamps reached them, with Dotty on Mrs Tweeny's doorstep in tears, Dr Hastings shouting, Florrie standing on his doorstep, and Pru in the middle of the footpath not quite sure what to do with herself, but already feeling slightly faint from having not eaten anything since yesterday afternoon.

Dr Hastings wasn't waiting for Mrs Tweeny to get all the way down his stairs and out the surgery front door.

"You can't be so heartless!" was as much as Gertie had heard so far, enough to prime the Scamps and scramble Rusty to investigate.

"It doesn't matter what time of day it is. That's not the point!" Dr Hastings was informing Mrs Tweeny, who must have said something, but her words had been lost within the doctor's house.

She now emerged with her cleaning basket still in her hand, Dr Hastings right behind her, with Florrie taking a couple of steps back to stand beside Pru on the footpath between the two front doors. Florrie had noticed Pru starting to sway. So had Rusty, who'd propped her bicycle up against the railings and lifted Maze out, before coming to help Florrie with Pru.

"Is she alright?"

"Just hungry and tired. We all are," Florrie explained.

Rusty realised the time. Everyone knew Mrs Tweeny's habits. "Oh dear!"

Dr Hastings wasn't backing down. He was in full outrage rant. "We can't have our girls fainting on duty for lack of sustenance, Mrs T!"

"I don't like leaving them in the kitchen when I've got to get out for chores. You like me here on the dot at 8 am, and that's where I am," Mrs Tweeny objected. That sounded perilously close to Mrs Tweeny blaming the good doctor for her locking the three young nurses out from their rooms. Dr Hastings was about to blow his top. Gertie was glad he hadn't missed this!

"Mrs Tweeny, how *can* you be so uncharitable!"

Rusty and Maze were fanning Pru with some of the old newspapers. Florrie had steered her back to Mrs Tweeny's front doorstep. Dotty was already there and still sobbing quietly. Rusty had found her handkerchief and given that to

Dotty.

"This is *not* what I want to see," Dr Hastings now pointed over to Mrs Tweeny's own front doorstep, then looked sternly at his housekeeper. "They're asleep on their feet. Look at 'em," he commanded.

Mrs Tweeny obeyed, putting down her cleaning basket, she returned to her doorstep. She didn't like having to unlock her front door once she'd started her working day, but doctor's orders were doctor's orders. "Sorry, Doctor."

"You don't need to say sorry to me, Mrs T," the good doctor informed his housekeeper steadily.

Mrs Tweeny scratched at the lock with her keys. She wasn't used to being shouted at and Dr Hastings never shouted. Gertie could see that and took pity on the poor woman. "I'll do it for you, Mrs Tweeny," matching action to his words. Swiftly opening the front door, he put Mrs Tweeny's keys on the hook where they belonged, before walking back out to follow the events now unfolding.

Mrs Tweeny starting shooing Dotty inside. She didn't like to be out in the middle of the village with everyone looking at her and hearing what Dr Hastings had just said.

Rusty had something to add. She didn't shout but spoke loudly enough to let the doctor know her opinion. "You can't send them to bed hungry. You just *can't*!"

Rusty and Gertie both knew that Dr Hastings' own son was 'out there', somewhere, doing his bit. Neither of them had any doubt that if Dr Hastings senior was a younger man, he'd have been right 'out there' with his son.

This sounded like fighting talk coming from Rusty. Gertie had already scooped Maze out from the line of fire and pushed her back to where Al and Walker were with the pram, wheelbarrow and bicycles. At a safe distance, but from an angle where they weren't likely to miss anything.

Mrs Tweeny cowered as Dr Hastings raged over her. "They're *Our* Girls," he reminded her, "and they're in *your* charge, Mrs Tweeny. Now, what do you think the rest of the village will make of this?"

"But there's isn't anything!" the housekeeper whimpered. "My cupboards are as bare as everyone else's. It's not that I don't trust the girls in my kitchen. I'm ashamed for them to see the state of my cupboards!"

The wind was blown out of the doctor's sails at that. His mind went blank. That had never occurred to him. Mrs Tweeny was almost in tears by then, taking up the corners of her apron and trying to waft some cooling air over her flustered cheeks.

Florrie and Pru were still outside. Dotty was inside, but only just. Rusty had managed to calm her. Gertie had already got as far as the kitchen and was filling the kettle to set it boiling. Sensible lad.

It wasn't the way Mrs Tweeny liked the have her tea served, but Gertie came out with a tray filled with every mug from the kitchen, and the cups he trusted himself to balance alongside them.

"Tea up! Sit down and let's get this sorted out! If you wait, I can get the stash of biscuits I've got up in my attic, Mrs Tweeny. Would that help?"

That was it; that was the last straw! Gertie's kind thoughtfulness broke Mrs Tweeny's defences and she sat down on her front doorstep and sobbed.

Maze, Al and Walker all surged forward, with the intention of getting between Dr Hasting's wrath and Mrs Tweeny's obvious distress. Dr Hastings was not a man to get angry easily, and he wasn't angry now, only perhaps a little annoyed by Mrs

Tweeny's stubbornness. He was also beginning to appreciate there was more to this than simply his housekeeper sticking absolutely to her 'clean and regular' habits.

Mrs Tweeny began to tell the village doctor, and everyone else who seemed to have gathered around, of Brisket the butcher. If Dr Hastings considered her rules tough and inflexible, then he should wait until he had to fetch his own rations from the butcher's! Did the doctor not realise how the rationing had been tightening? The doctor had never fetched his own food. It just appeared in his kitchen from time to time. Mrs Tweeny had always made sure it was there for him, just as she did her own and the three young nurses'.

The doctor hadn't given it any thought. If it was there, he ate it; if it wasn't, he didn't. Of course, when he was called out, he was always offered a cup of tea, sometimes even coffee, and usually something to eat, so he was seldom more than peckish when he got home. But the young nurses were growing and busy girls. They had healthy appetites and Mrs Tweeny was struggling to keep up!

Bread was unrationed, but Mrs Tweeny went to church and knew 'man cannot live by bread alone', even less three young nurses! They needed their vegetables and fruit, and they weren't going to grow themselves, but Mrs Tweeny didn't have time to go digging up her garden. She needed that for drying the laundry every day. But it was in the butcher's shop where she was really struggling.

By now, Maze was feeling sorry for the poor lady. The little girl delved down into her overall pocket. It wasn't easy, being so small, there was a lot of pocket fabric to wade through.

"Will this help? I was saving it for the milko's horse. Nag likes carrots, but I can soon tug up another one. We don't have any washing out on our line, not until after bath night."

The carrot wasn't a particularly impressive sample of its ilk, but as it was solemnly presented to Mrs Tweeny, who managed to regain her composure sufficiently to put down her mug of tea and accept the donation. "Thank you, deary. That's very kind of you."

Gertie offered to take the carrot back to her kitchen, as Mrs Tweeny picked up her mug, and took another long sip before continuing.

"The bacon is tightly controlled, and the sausages are impossible! There's offal if you're lucky, but I'm never there in time for that."

It seemed Mrs Tweeny hadn't been lucky for quite some time. She was the first to agree it was all done very fairly, even before Dr Hastings started to say so. He was out of puff anyway and glad of Gertie's tea. The lanky lad made a good strong brew.

Rusty took the lead, agreeing with both parties. The fuss and fluster had gone. Everyone was calm, and really just trying to decide what to do next, even the doctor.

Dr Hastings was already wondering if he ought to increase Mrs Tweeny's housekeeping allowance. He'd read the papers and kept up with the news and instructions but hadn't given domestic expenses a thought. Oh dear! Suddenly it was the doctor who was feeling awkward.

Rusty was explaining what every woman in the village knew, for the doctor's benefit. "Any meat is the most you can make from the cheapest cuts. Anything prime is already sold out. It might be the middle of summer, but Old Spot's happy with stew and Jeepers only cares there's something on the plate waiting for him, when he comes in at the end of the day."

"That's what I was trying to do," Mrs Tweeny confessed.

"I think I must have miscalculated somewhere last week. I always have bread and tea, but butter is half the ration of lard, and either is better than nothing. I was hoping for some jam, but it's too early for that." She sniffed, as Maze sat next to her and patted the housekeeper on the hand. She'd seen Miss Aggy do that to some of the other schoolchildren, herself included, when they'd taken a tumble or scraped a knee or got frightened. This seemed to be one of those times, Maze wasn't sure which, but it definitely felt like one of those hand-patting 'there, there' moments.

Rusty approved. "Good girl." Al and Walker weren't left out of that praise. They were already talking about taking the bicycles and getting over to see what Abe and the Totters had available. One of those bicycles they were proposing to use to get out to the farms was Gertie's, the other was Rusty's, and she needed that for getting back to the Yard. Ol' Creak's bicycle certainly wasn't capable of that sort of a trek.

"How about you wait until I've picked up my truck? Jeepers will have finished with it soon enough. We should be able to manage something between us," she suggested.

"That's it!" Dr Hastings decided.

"What, Rusty's truck?" Walker asked, more than glad to agree to that suggestion.

"No." Dr Hastings grinned and came to stand beside Mrs Tweeny. "We should be able to manage something between us. *All* of us!"

"Oh." Mrs Tweeny sounded like she was edging close to another bout of blubbing. Maze kept patting her hand. Florrie was still sitting with Pru, who wasn't feeling quite so lightheaded, more weary-headed but with an empty stomach. Dotty had come back outside into the sunshine, since being offered the cup of tea. It had helped.

Since this had all started, those who could hear the reason for the fuss had fetched Brisket. It sounded like it was *his* turn to do some explaining.

The butcher couldn't do anything. He was only following orders like everyone else!

"They're not even waiting for me to turn the sign round, anymore. As soon as they see me in my shop, they start tapping on the door with their baskets. It's intimidating! I can only give them what it says they're allowed, and I've only got what I've got, and when it's gone it's gone. What am I meant to do? Muster up some extra grub from thin air?"

Glancing from Dr Hastings to Mrs Tweeny, to Florrie, Pru and Dotty, Brisket wondered, "Aren't they meant to be getting their meals up at the hospital, where they're working? Like Humfrey does, when he's over at the Army camp office-clerking?"

Brisket had said that loud enough for Aggy to hear. She'd been wondering something similar.

"That's all very well, but what am I meant to do when they come home hungry?" Mrs Tweeny pleaded to the gathering crowd.

Dr Hastings had the answer for that. "You feed them, Mrs Tweeny. That's what you do. You feed them! No one is going to say a word against your routines. We all respect that you have 'clean and regular habits', Mrs Tweeny, but they're *Our* Girls and they're taking care of *Our* Lads."

Dr Hastings realised he was addressing more than his housekeeper and the Salvage Scamps, on the footpath in front of the two houses that morning. It felt like half the village had gathered by this time, and rather a lot of them were carrying those intimidating, tapping baskets Brisket had mentioned.

Dr Hastings intentionally raised his voice. "Our Lads get

sick and injured at the most inconvenient times, and when it comes to their healing, it takes as long as it takes. We all need to make allowances! Our girls need their strength to keep on doing what needs to be done, and it's *our* duty to see to that."

Al cheered and Walker impulsively lunged forward to shake the unsuspecting doctor's hand. "Right you are, Doc. Where d'ya want us? We're at the ready, overalls and all!"

Maze stopped patting Mrs Tweeny's hand to stand in front of her, assuring the housekeeper, "We're *all* ready to help. You only had to ask. That's what we're here for."

"Oh, bless you, deary," then looking up over to Rusty, "Bless you." The housekeeper sounded almost as shaky as her girls by that point.

Aggy took charge of Mrs Tweeny's kitchen, taking the three young nurses and Mrs Tweeny herself inside. It had given them all something to think about.

It had given half the village something to think about, and the other half would hear about it soon enough.

Brisket had to get back to his shop. There were tapping baskets waiting for him. Except they weren't tapping anymore. His customers silently parted to allow him to open his door and waited for him to get himself settled behind the counter.

His missus came out from the back to stand beside him, as yet unaware of what had just transpired. The first three ladies came into the village butcher's shop, took their baskets forward and without a word said between them, all gave the same instructions.

"Two-thirds for us, one-third you put into Mrs Tweeny's basket, for *our girls*."

The butcher's wife did the paperwork as her husband did the portions and wrapping. There was a little bit of sniffing and a lot of chin-lifting going on at the butcher's shop that morning.

The Salvage Scamps had also decided what they were going to do about the morning's developments. Rusty was included in the plan by then and they were going to be needing her truck.

Gertie suggested, "Old Spot, too, give him an airing. Never know we might be needing him." Rusty couldn't follow Gertie's thinking on that but couldn't fault it either. "Can't do any harm," she agreed.

The Scamps finished the first round of their paper salvage delivery to the village hall, and were hoping Rusty would catch up with them as they began to head out towards Abe's chicken orchard farm. They still had Ol' Creak's bicycle and Gertie with his bicycle, and whilst they'd been salvaging, they'd been talking. Maybe they could go out and scrump their own apples and berries whilst they waited for Rusty and her truck.

The apples wouldn't be properly ready yet, but Gertie didn't mention that; the Scamps would figure it out for themselves.

"We can scrump enough for everyone, more than enough for our girls, can't we?" Al was keen.

"If it doesn't fit in your pocket then it ain't scrumping," Maze reminded her brother. He'd been told off before for doing that. "The allowance is pocket-sized scrumping only."

Walker was quicker. "They said we're allowed to pick more than our pockets-full if we're foraging for berries. They told us that on the poster on the village hall door, except we have to give them over, 'cos that's for the Effort. If we eat them first, then that don't count!"

"Well then, that don't help, does it? Idiot!" Al told his friend, before whispering so Maze couldn't hear. "Good to know for later, though."

Gertie could hear what they were plotting. "No scrumping today. We're going to be doing a spot of snaffling!"

Gertie had a plan, as he pushed his bicycle with Maze on board. He would be needing the Salvage Scamps to help him, and Rusty's permission.

Jeepers must have had a good start to his day. They could hear Rusty coming back into the village already, and they hadn't even got halfway over to Abe's long-gate yet. She was coming with the truck and Old Spot, too, by the sounds of it.

Even before Rusty had stopped the truck, the children were telling her grandfather their intentions. Old Spot was up for it. "Snaffling, hey? Haven't been able to enjoy that for a while. I'm in!"

Rusty was a little more wary. "Firstly, snaffling what?" she asked Gertie pointedly. He appeared to be the one with all the details. She didn't want to discourage them, especially as her grandfather seemed delighted by the prospect. "The snaffling, I can work with," she told them. "I just need to be a little clearer on exactly where this 'spot of snaffling' is going to take place."

"That's why we need your permission," Gertie informed her. "It's Jeepers' Yard."

"You mentioned the tinned meat he's got stashed, and that's what we need for our girls, isn't it? Meat, something substantial?" Gertie asked.

Old Spot was already nodding enthusiastically. "Abso-ruddy-lutely!" Then added his full opinion on the argument, just in case Rusty was in any doubt. "Mrs Tweeny needs our help. Empty cupboards ain't healthy! It's all very well to be 'clean and regular' in your habits, but a little bit of something in reserve at the back of the kitchen cupboards wouldn't go amiss."

That rather nicely brought everyone back round to Rusty's truck. Maze was satisfied. As far as she was concerned, she'd been the one to start the notion rolling, with that tugged-up carrot, and was now riding in the back of Rusty's truck!

By the time they had piled in, bicycles and all, with Gertie and Rusty in the cab, there was more than one target agreed upon. They were going to do a raid on Jeepers' Yard. Old Spot was already gleefully formulating his own plans, happy to have the backup of the Scamps at the ready for some 'lickety-spit snaffling'.

Before they got to the Yard gates, Old Spot was poised. He was going to set up a diversion by demanding extra sandbag sacks, and when Old Spot decided a diversion was necessary, he gave it full steam ahead!

Al, Walker and Maze got themselves out the back of the truck. They hadn't seen any sign of Jeepers in the Yard yet, so felt bold enough to make their own way over to the long shed. Gertie was to do the actual salvaging of the sacks, whilst Rusty kept watch, making sure the Yard blokes didn't look too closely at what they were all doing.

The children were running in and out of sheds with blurts and queries more than sufficient to send the blokes scatty, with Old Spot standing there in the middle of the Yard, a-shouting and a-hollering. He'd already fetched his tin helmet for the occasion, 'to add authenticity', he muttered to Gertie. Even Jeepers' blokes didn't want to argue with Old Spot hollering in a tin helmet!

Jeepers wasn't there, but Old Spot was Jeepers' dad, so it was his Yard, one way or another to their reckoning! Their trucks were out of the way and Jeepers wasn't there to tell them to do anything else. Old Spot even got them to help with loading Rusty's truck, once Gertie had got hold of the sacks. That gave Rusty the opportunity of taking advantage of those refilled jerry cans.

Al and Walker were further back in the long shed. It wasn't easy to tell what they were scrambling around and over, but they had their mission to find those crates of tinned meat.

"Mrs Tweeny will need to know where it came from. Otherwise, she'll be handling stolen goods," Al pointed out.

"We're not stealing it, it's from Rusty's own Yard, ain't it?" Walker reasoned. "It's just like the baskets in Brisket's shop. Jeepers is contributing to the War Effort, only he don't know it yet!"

"So, if Jeepers asks, you're going to tell him it's his 'bit' to refill Mrs Tweeny's kitchen cupboards?" Al queried, still not convinced.

"You don't need to tell Jeepers anything. He's not going to ask *you*," Walker sounded certain.

Al wasn't convinced. "Why won't Jeepers ask about the missing tins?"

"I didn't say he wouldn't ask. He might. But he's not going to be asking you, is he?" Walker reckoned. Al could see that sounded about right.

"He'll be asking his own blokes first. Then Rusty, most likely. She'll be able to tell him, she hasn't touched it. She hasn't, has she?" Walker reminded his friend, who realised that was true; Rusty hadn't touched the tins of meat.

"Oh, that's clever."

As for the Yard blokes noticing what the two boys were doing, that wasn't likely. Between Gertie and Old Spot they were fully distracted, and goodness only knew what Maze was doing!

Gertie had heard Al and Walker's argument, and suggested

they put the tins into a couple of the sacks.

"We can put them in the bicycle baskets. That way there'll be no 'handling' involved!"

Rusty heard that last bit of the scheme, adding for good measure, "Just because I don't have the keys to the sheds doesn't mean I don't know where Jeepers keeps them. If he really didn't want me to know, he would have hidden them properly."

Maze was in the farmhouse kitchen, clattering about with some pots and pans by the sounds of it. Old Spot was waiting for her.

Rusty was starting to suspect her grandfather had another scheme alongside the one they had already agreed upon. "Have you got a 'to boot' brewing?" she quizzed him.

His grin widened with his answer.

"Always. Whenever possible! Even better when the 'to boot' involves annoying Jeepers into the bargain!"

They had plenty of empty sacks loaded into the truck by then. With Al and Walker checking there were still plenty more remaining in the long shed.

"He won't even notice the difference!" Rusty agreed. "It's not like he keeps any paperwork on them. The only time he'll notice is when he needs them in a deal, and I can't think of any deals where they're going to be asking for exact numbers of empty sacks, can you?"

Gertie couldn't imagine any deal like that but could see another problem.

"We need another bicycle!"

"Why?" Rusty checked. The Yard was clear of Jeepers' blokes by then. They'd scarpered out on their afternoon runs and Jeepers still hadn't returned, but Rusty had her own truck run to do. They had Rusty's bicycle, Gertie's bicycle and Ol' Creak's bicycle, but there were four Scamps and Old Spot, too.

"Five backsides and only three bicycle seats," was the way Gertie reckoned it.

"You're right we need another bicycle," Rusty agreed, scanning the Yard, doubting there was anything remotely like that.

Maze had come out from the farmhouse and was helping Old Spot fill his backpack when she heard the problem. "A wheelbarrow will do. Walker, you're good with a wheelbarrow, aren't you? You can manage. It's not far."

"Far enough and my legs aren't as long as Gertie's!"

Rusty was losing track of what they were planning. She looked over to her grandfather, who was enjoying the riddle unravelling immensely. He was halfway to the solution, but hadn't quite figured out the last bit that Maze had come up with.

The five-year-old girl explained for everyone's benefit. "Old Spot takes your bicycle, Rusty. Walker take's Gertie's bicycle, with the sacks of tinned meat. Al takes Ol' Creak's bicycle, with the backpack in it. Gertie, you're with the wheelbarrow for everything else, and I'm going with Old Spot, in his bicycle basket!"

No one else spoke for a moment, stunned by the brilliance of the plan. Maze hadn't finished yet. Just for clarity, she decided to add,

"Old Spot needs his balance, so I'll be doing the steering up front for the bends. Walker, you've got the best bicycle, so can manage the tins. Al, you know Ol' Creak's bicycle and the pots and pans won't get damaged too badly if you fall off. Gertie, you can really run better than any of us, and Rusty will need you round at the village hall when she gets there and restocks the Home Guard stationery cupboard."

"Ruddy heck! That's what I call village-smart there, girl!" Old Spot beamed with pride.

The bicycles had long since been unloaded from Rusty's truck, and the wheelbarrow was quickly brought forward.

Gertie didn't mind giving Walker his bicycle just for the next hour or so. What with Old Spot and Maze steering up front, and Al with Ol' Creak's bicycle behind, how much mischief could Walker get into? He didn't even mind being the one stuck with the wheelbarrow. It was a lovely afternoon. They'd had a good day so far, although maybe not the one he had imagined when he'd first come down from his attic that morning.

Gertie remembered those young nurses. "We're going back to Mrs Tweeny's first, aren't we?" he checked.

Walker spoke up first. "Abso-ruddy-lutely."

Rusty saw them all out from the Yard and safely heading back towards the village before she got herself into the cab and out on to the lane. The gates were left open. Jeepers would get back when he was ready and see all the trucks gone. For him that was a good sign; good enough to keep Jeepers happy. If the trucks were out from the Yard, then they were all doing business. He wouldn't think to check the back garden for Old Spot.

Rusty smiled to herself, as she hoped Maze hadn't got too enthusiastic with the snaffling of the reserves in her farmhouse larder, or it would be Jeepers going hungry that evening. Then laughed at the ludicrous notion.

Rusty hadn't asked what Old Spot was planning with that backpack of his. Maze had only mentioned pots and pans, but Rusty was sure there was more in there than that. Her grandfather seemed to know what he was doing, and he had Maze in the basket, so he'd have to behave himself!

Whilst they waited for Gertie to catch them up with the wheelbarrow, Al and Walker took the packed sacks round to Mrs Tweeny's kitchen. The door was wide open. Mrs Tweeny's habits had gone 'irregular' for the day.

Old Spot and Maze were only a few minutes behind them. They'd been having such a fascinating conversation on the way over that Old Spot had forgotten about the pedalling a couple of times. No harm done, and everything and everyone arrived intact, with no scrapes or dents.

Gertie was ten minutes behind Old Spot. Maze was right, he could definitely run faster than any of the others. As per instructions he'd taken the wheelbarrow over to the village hall first. Rusty hadn't arrived yet.

By the time Gertie was walking back to Mrs Tweeny's, he was relieved to see all the bicycles had arrived safely and could already hear Old Spot making himself at home in Mrs Tweeny's kitchen.

Gertie decided this might be a good time for another pot of his tea. Al and Walker had unpacked the pots and pans, whilst Maze had gone directly into Mrs Tweeny's sitting room and pulled her to her feet.

"Come and see what we've got for you." The little girl hadn't waited for an answer and led the way, still holding on to Mrs Tweeny's hand, tugging her into her own kitchen. It had never been so cramped and cluttered. The extraordinary thing was that Mrs Tweeny didn't find it as disturbing as she had always feared.

Dr Hastings had told her he wouldn't be needing her for the rest of the day, and she was rather at a loose end. It was a little unnerving. The basket had been sent over from the butcher. Aggy had brought it along with news of how it had got filled. That had been about when Mrs Tweeny had needed to sit down quietly in her sitting room.

Soon after the earlier doorstep incident, Aggy had seen Rusty take the Scamps with her and suspected there might be a mission underway from that direction. As soon as the schoolteacher noticed the bicycles collecting outside Mrs Tweeny's front door again, Aggy made her way back over and could hear the commotion starting to rise from the kitchen.

"Oh dear!" It seemed Mrs Tweeny didn't know what to do with tinned beef, except put it into a sandwich.

"A sandwich!?" Old Spot spluttered, almost having a fit at the thought of such a waste. He'd immediately started ordering Al, Walker and Maze about the kitchen cupboards. Mrs Tweeny had sat down at her own table and Gertie had made them all a pot of tea. By the time Aggy had arrived, the corned beef cake making was well underway, even utilising Maze's carrot into the bargain.

"Nothing wasted!" Old Spot declared with relish.

Aggy didn't enquire where the bag of flour had come from, guessing Old Spot would know, and she might feel more comfortable in ignorance of the answer.

Mrs Tweeny had sent the young nurses upstairs as soon as the Scamps and Dr Hastings had left them. It had been a few hours since then. Aggy could hear the bathroom water running, which was a good sign.

"That OK, isn't it, Mrs Tweeny?" she enquired gently, bringing a second cup of tea to the doctor's housekeeper.

The sound of bathwater, and only early afternoon, and not even Wednesday, was a little disturbing. Some of Gertie's strong tea would help, with sugar! Aggy was about to mention the wondrous appearance of that precious commodity on Mrs

Tweeny's table, when she caught a wink from Gertie.

"Good lad, smart thinking."

Mrs Tweeny sniffed and sat back a little further in her kitchen chair, sipping at the tea. Feeling a little better and glancing around at the industry surrounding her.

"Yes, Miss Aggy, thank you. It's all OK. I never imagined it would be, but it is. Our girls are rested, washed and returning to a meal fit for them." Mrs Tweeny sighed.

"Bless you." She took Gertie's hand, it was the nearest within her reach and began patting it, repeating. "Bless you, my dear."

"Pleasure, ma'am. Honour to help. You taking care of our girls, it's the least we could do." Gertie's heartfelt response sent Mrs Tweeny back to her handkerchief. Aggy sensibly suggested she didn't forget her excellent tea, returning the cup to her hand and shooing Gertie to help with the washing up.

The schoolteacher also managed to hand him the eggs she'd brought over. They were hers' and Humfrey's rations for the week, and the baker's wife had made sure there was a fresh loaf. The vicar had given the remainder of his butter ration and there was a half-bottle of milk from Rosie over at the pub, too.

The table was laid and Mrs Tweeny, Aggy, Old Spot and the Scamps left the girls to enjoy their very late breakfast in peace, and the doctor's housekeeper didn't tut once!

By then Rusty had got round to the village hall. Aggy sent the Scamps over to help her with taking the restock of sacks into the Home Guard office.

It was too soon to be sitting listening to the radio, so the two ladies sat in the housekeeper's sitting room together, drinking their cups of tea, until the young nurses were ready to tell them all about what had kept them so busy up at the hospital. Everything was late getting done that day, and some chores had been missed entirely. It had been a very 'irregular' day in places, and neither Aggy nor Mrs Tweeny knew the half of it yet, but these were Mrs Tweeny's girls, and she was going to see them properly taken care of!

CHAPTER 10

Art's Story and The Reckoning Begins

THE RAF WERE GETTING THEMSELVES more organised, they had fighters, bombers and coastal-command, and they were *all* going to be called upon to tackle what was heading their way from Germany! The radio had begun to give clear warning: Hitler was preparing for a landing operation against Great Britain. He just needed to knock the RAF out of the skies first!

The newspapers had quoted them: *'We cannot resist invasion by fighter aircraft alone. An air striking force is necessary not only to meet the seaborne expedition, but also to bring direct pressure to bear upon Germany, by attacking objectives in that country.'*

In other words, the RAF would be carrying out raids on the ports where Germany was assembling its invasion fleet, and targeting the Luftwaffe's airfields and industries too. The RAF was busy, and the RAF hospitals were going to need all their nursing staff at full strength.

Dr Hastings had been too busy to notice whether or not Mrs Tweeny was at her housekeeping 'station', but he'd had time enough to think about what he'd said, and the way he'd spoken to her. He might have been a little hasty. He couldn't do anything about easing the workload up at the hospital, but he could at least make it a little easier for Mrs Tweeny to maintain her routine, without causing the young nurses to skip their breakfast in order to catch the bus to their shifts. Dr Hastings sent his own bicycle over to be permanently billeted with the nurses at Mrs Tweeny's. He had his car and was rather ashamed he hadn't thought of it sooner.

Florrie was the one best able to explain their earlier state of exhaustion to Mrs Tweeny and Aggy, when they joined them in the housekeeper's sitting room later. It was Art; all three young nurses had taken their turn sitting with him throughout the night, after his surgery.

He'd woken many times, in pain and anger, restless and needing to talk. The doctors couldn't give him anything more to ease his pain, it was too deep for that. The only way the nurses could keep him calm was to let him talk and reassure him they were listening. Florrie had been the one to do most of the listening.

Art's hands had been badly burned. He'd been shot down over France, behind Dunkirk. Going down hadn't been so bad; the real damage had been done when he'd been picked up. Coming back on one of the 'little ships', they'd never been designed for such a task, some were no more than tug boats, the engine blew and the boat had caught fire. Art and most of the fellows onboard had been rescued.

Florrie did her best to remember everything he'd told her, in those long low hours before daylight had come again. He could recall every moment of those days reaching the beaches and waiting there with thousands of other men, and those hours of wading out and waiting again, waist deep in freezing water for the next pick-up, only to be told, 'We're full mate. There'll be another soon.' Dragging themselves back onto the beach, trying to dry themselves out, amongst those endless dunes of men, waiting for the next boat. And there was, Art had told her, thousands of those 'little ships' coming into the beach, picking up a few dozen men each time and ferrying them out to the bigger ships waiting a safe distance off shore.

"They just kept on coming back for us. Didn't matter what those Germans threw at 'em, they just kept on coming back. That was the ruddy miracle of it all," Art had told her.

Art couldn't remember much of the weeks he'd been in the other hospital before the surgery. He hadn't even been aware they'd moved him from that first hospital to have the surgery at the clinic. The room didn't register. There were names and faces, but he didn't try and make sense of that. It was the voice of a young nurse speaking to him through the haze of his pain that got through, soft spoken and calm, with a steady warmth behind her words; and that kind hand holding a cup to his lips to help him drink, to quench the grating, hot thirst of agony at the images in his mind, that would never leave him. He would clench his fists, not in the spasms of pain, but in impotent fury.

"We got out of that hell. I still don't know *how* they managed it. We'd already heard the big ships had gone. We could only hope they'd come back. All those trucks, we saw them lined up along the sides of the roads leading into Dunkirk, wrecked by their own men. We left too many men behind. No helping them. Even before we got to the town of Dunkirk, we knew if we got that far, we were only going to get back home by the skin of our teeth."

"They were sending the Luftwaffe bombers across the lines of refugees on the roads. They didn't need to bomb them; they were saving those bombs for the beaches. France was beaten, nothing in reserve. They had nothing left and we couldn't help them because we had nothing left either! We had to try and get out, so we'd have something to come fighting back with."

"Took us three days and nights on those beaches. I couldn't count how many were out there, for miles, on those blasted dunes. Blasted dunes! Just stuck there. The buggers were screaming those bullets down across us. They'd hammered and kicked and beaten us all the way out of France. We were standing in the water, waiting for the next ruddy rowboat. We didn't care. Anything. You could have given us a bathtub and we would have tried to have rowed ourselves off those damned beaches in it!"

"Cold and dark. The stink and the screaming. Brave men, bloody brave men! Couldn't see the rest of 'em, who they were, where they'd come from. Didn't matter. We were all stuck there together, with the Germans at our heels and over our heads."

"The grit in your mouth, that wasn't sand you were tasting."

Florrie could recall almost every word of that long night-watch. Not all of it made sense, but she understood that didn't matter, only that Art knew there was someone there with him, listening. He wasn't alone and he could hear his own voice. He still had strength enough to speak, to tell of what he'd seen.

Florrie was rested, washed and fed, and wanted to get back over to the hospital. Dr Hastings' bicycle was waiting and ready for her. She wasn't due back on duty yet, but she needed to know Art had been moved and settled in, to see him realise he was in a ward, amongst other men who understood what he'd spoken of, in a way she never could.

The Home Guard office cupboard had been refilled, and the wheelbarrow returned to the back of Rusty's truck, together with her own bicycle and all the Scamps, Old Spot included.

Ol' Creak's bicycle had been hastily taken back to the village shop, whilst Gertie's bicycle rested outside Brisket's shop. No one would bother them there until tomorrow morning.

Rusty hadn't intended for Old Spot to be with her on this run, but he was already there. It should have been a straightforward delivery of three bundles of chicken wire over to Abe. With her grandfather and the Scamps onboard, Rusty doubted it would be anything so mundane!

From the sounds of it, the Salvage Scamps hadn't forgotten their earlier offer of picking berries to supplement Mrs Tweeny's larder cupboards. Rusty drove steadily. Everyone else was in the back, enjoying the afternoon sunshine.

"Does looking for chicken eggs count as foraging? Like looking for blackberries?"

"Can we bring back more than a pocketful?"

"Are we allowed to keep them this time?"

It was a smooth drive straight out from the village, past the church, not stopping until the turn to the long-gate entrance of Abe's chicken orchard farm.

Abe had been expecting her much earlier. He was ready for a rant.

Rusty was about to let him know she'd had her fill of those today, but Old Spot was shouting ahead of her. "Go on then, what's the problem? We're in a problem-solving mood!" he assured the rattled farmer.

Abe had been expecting a truck driver with a delivery of chicken wire, not Rusty and her grandfather and a whole truckload of children and Gertie, too. "What are you all doing back there?" he blustered.

Gertie grinned. "Helping. What's your problem?" In four words managing to take the lead in the situation.

Old Spot chucked down the bundles of chicken wire, which bounced and rolled for the children to catch, whilst Abe explained the paperwork he was tackling. The Ministry of Agriculture controlled everything that went on 'in' the farm; the Ministry of Food controlled everything going 'out' of the farm. They were happy for the apples and the eggs, but they didn't want him keeping so many chickens. How was that going to improve the situation?

"I need my chickens to produce the eggs. What's their problem?" Abe ranted. "It's not like I feed them the same food as we eat. Most of the time I just let 'em scratch for it! I don't know what the scratching does, but so long as they keep laying, why should I stop keeping 'em?"

Old Spot was listening as hard as Gertie was. "Scratching?" Gertie checked. "Peckin'!" Old Spot explained. "If they're laying, they're worth keeping." He agreed with the farmer.

"That's it!" Abe clapped his hands together, relieved that someone realised the absurdity of the instruction.

"Then all you've got to sort out is which ones ain't layin'," Gertie suggested helpfully. Both men looked to the lanky lad, amazed at how they'd missed that. "He's right!"

"He usually is," Rusty informed them cheerfully.

Abe's primary businesses were his eggs and his apples, but they weren't the only considerations to be found on his chicken orchard farm. Abe was mad about motorbikes, although they weren't so much a business venture as a weakness, and there was an old motorbike he was hoping someone would be able to have a look at. He showed the pile of metal to Rusty. "Not Jeepers. I know him and he'll only take it as scrap, and if it goes in as scrap, it ain't never coming out."

Rusty didn't disagree with him about her father's dealings with motorbike parts. There was a fine line between usable surplus and scrap. Abe's words seemed to be appealing to her to offer him an alternative.

"You could try the blacksmith. Maybe he might be able to do something with those parts, but it's not all there, is there enough to rebuild?"

By that point Gertie was having a gander through it too. "Where's the rest of it, and how'd it end up like this?"

By the time the pair had finished asking the questions, Abe had already realised he wasn't going to be able to remedy this particular motorbike, no matter from how many angles he tried looking at the problem! By then he also had an audience waiting to hear his answer to that last query.

"How did it end up like that?" Old Spot repeated, just to be clear what they were all interested in learning about. Abe had thought he'd picked up all those pieces, but if Rusty could already recognise there weren't sufficient to recover a working engine, then maybe he'd missed a few. Old Spot and the Scamps waited for the rest of the story.

"The officer walked away from it – well, limped away. His friends picked him up and just left it behind. It was *his* fault. What did he think was going to happen, trying to bully a tractor to get off the road with a motorbike!"

Gertie decided someone had to state the bleedin' obvious. "We're here. Truck and Salvage Scamps. We can take it away, as a favour," he offered cheerfully. "It'll give you and your laying hens a bit more space."

Maze was the one to remember to suggest a trade. "And some of our girls could do with a few extra eggs. They're nurses and need their strength."

Gertie gave Maze the thumbs up. "Good girl, smart thinking."

Walker had been thinking too. "If you keep on driving like

that, Abe, you're gonna be glad to be in a nurse's good books one day."

Abe looked down at the scars across his hands, deciding some work might be due before the dealing could get underway proper.

"I'll be needing that chicken wire in place, if I'm going to keep those Ministry chappies happy. My hens tend to wander when they're scratching, then they go laying in the most awkward places and I can't always reach them. Then how am I meant to know which are laying and which aren't?"

Al didn't want to be left out from this scheme. "We can herd them for you mister, but you'll have to sort out the chicken wire. That'll take posts and hammering and we're weak from hunger and too many sacks!" That might have been overegging the pudding a tad, but he got the message across.

Walker came to his friend's side, "We're smaller and quicker, we can round 'em up and find the awkward eggs for you."

That sounded a little more sensible. Abe was happy with that. Gertie called out he'd get the buckets. "You'll need two, one with water and one with straw."

"We will?" Walker was still learning village-smart.

Maze explained, "One for putting the eggs in for carrying and one for testing which eggs is fresh for eating."

Al and Walker followed Maze and waited for Gertie to catch them up with the buckets, whilst Rusty and Old Spot followed Abe back to where he kept the posts and hammers.

Salvaging eggs was a new skill for some of the Scamps to learn. Al had done it before. Last year Maze had been too young, but she'd grown into the task since then. Gertie had an unusual technique of his own for finding eggs, but it seemed to be no less effective for that.

They went out to the furthest point of the orchard, then started clucking and stomping, sending the hens strutting and careering in front of their boots and hands. All four of the Scamps, bent down until their hands were just in front of their knees, stomping their boots and clapping their hands and clucking their tongues. Gertie wasn't surprised at their success. "Works with the pheasants, so I thought it might work with chickens."

"I've never seen it done that way before," Abe observed. Gertie definitely had a different approach to problems. "How do you know where the eggs are, then?" That didn't seem so obvious.

"Ah, learnt that from the pheasants too," Gertie grinned up across to the farmer. "They think they can distract you by making a fuss opposite to where they've laid. You look for where all the noise ain't, and a little way off from there."

"Really?" Abe wasn't convinced he was any the wiser. Old Spot was happy though. "Eggs for tea, then, Abe?"

Abe wasn't sure of that either. Those were meant to be his market day eggs.

"Maybe so," Old Spot pointed out, "but we only came to deliver the chicken wire, not to help you herd the chickens and put the borders up, and if you'd collected the eggs yourself, you'd have missed half of those."

"That's right," Walker stepped in. "So, if you'd have missed half, then if you give us half of the second half, you've still got about twice as many as you would have had for market!"

Abe wasn't sure about the maths, but it was near enough and he wasn't going to argue. Old Spot was right; if it had been any other delivery driver, they wouldn't have stayed and helped.

"You're going to make sure the nurses get some of those there eggs?"

Gertie wagged his finger at the farmer. That wasn't what he and Maze had figured.

"How about you put aside a half dozen extra for Mrs Tweeny's girls, *every week*?"

There was something in the way Gertie spoke, clear and slow, simply indicating the farmer was contributing to not only the energy reserves of the young nurses, but also their morale.

Maze added, just to be absolutely clear, "They're *our* girls; *we're* responsible for them."

Abe couldn't argue with that. Glancing over to Rusty, he admired, "You've got them well trained there," chuckling, nudging Old Spot in the ribs, "ain't she?"

"That she has! Grandest bunch of Salvage Scamps I've ever worked with," the old gentleman assured the farmer sincerely.

Maze packed the eggs destined for the Scamps in a small box with more straw, whilst everyone else helped Abe with the remains of the motorbike, destined for Jeepers' Yard. Gertie even swept the yard clean for the farmer, before climbing into the back of the truck and slapping the side to indicate they were all in and ready for the next stop.

That put Rusty in a quandary. She hadn't been figuring on doing a 'next stop'. Old Spot was sitting next to her in the cab.

"I guess that means the Totters. We've got the eggs sorted for our girls, we really ought to try for some extra milk, don't you think? A pint should do it."

Al had overheard from the back and yelled forward, "Butter would be better!"

"Done!" Old Spot laughed. "Butter it is then," he informed

his granddaughter. "What have we got to trade?"

Gertie was already explaining to Walker who the Totters were. They ran the dairy farm over at the Grazing Meadows. They were an elderly couple who kept two of the local lasses to help with the milking sheds. Mr Totters did the tractoring and Mrs Totters knew her butter and cheeses, and she'd be expecting some 'real work' for that butter, he cautioned wisely.

How to get into Mrs Totters' good books? Figuring that out would keep the Scamps quiet in the back all the way over, Rusty was fascinated to discover what plan they came up with and was impressed with its simplicity: they'd sweep the yard.

"It's a dairy farm. The yard always needs sweeping!" Gertie reasoned. "We're not asking for nothing, but if Mrs Totters has a pat of butter, we wouldn't say no to that. She doesn't know about the nurses, does she?" he asked Rusty, before continuing, "by the time you've told her, she'll know more than Ol' Creak at the village shop, and you know how happy that makes her. Almost as happy as she'll be when we've swept the yard, whilst you're talking!"

It sounded like Gertie and the Scamps had done a lot of thinking it through, whilst Rusty had been doing the driving over to the Grazing Meadows.

"Mr Totters and the lasses will be busy, so it's not like we're going to be getting in anyone's way," Walker added, happy to reassure Rusty they'd figured that out too.

Fortunately, there was more than one broom. In fact, once the Scamps started looking for them, there seemed to be as many brooms as there were sheds around the yard.

"Almost as many as Bracket's got!" Al wondered.

Gertie was already making steady progress by the time Al and Maze joined him. Walker was left with the chucking bucket.

"Got to put it all somewhere," Gertie explained. "We can sweep it up but got to put it all somewhere."

It took Walker a couple of minutes to figure out what he was talking about. He would have been happier with a broom, but at least it didn't stink as bad as the pile behind the rear of the village stables.

Mrs Totters was happy to admire their effort. "I haven't got any butter, it's too late in the day, but I'll have some ready for market day. Will that do?" She checked over with Old Spot.

"Just remember it's for Mrs Tweeny's basket, for our girls."

"Right you are, dearie. I'll do that." Mrs Totters was well pleased with the clean yard. She was even more delighted to learn she was up on the village gossip ahead of Ol' Creak. Mrs Totters was already planning an 'urgent' errand that would take her into the village shop to inform him of such!

"We just need to get to Tuckly then?" her grandfather reminded Rusty, as he climbed into the cab next to her.

"Why?"

"Well, we've got to take the Scamps back home again, haven't we? And Maze took the last of your flour bags, unless Jeepers has got any upstairs? We might as well take the long way out back and round in to the village, and see if Tuckly's boys have got any flour sacks in their dry store. You know what they're like!"

Rusty knew *exactly* what Tuckly's boys were like, they were Al and Maze's older brothers, and the same two farm-bullies that had tried to drag Gertie off his bicycle a while back. She didn't like them one little bit! They'd done their best to turn Al away from school learning, according to Aggy, fortunately Maze was too young to understand. Rusty wasn't relishing the prospect of dealing with that pair. "I'll manage without the flour for a while, I think we've done enough 'salvaging' for one day."

Old Spot was still muttering about Tuckly and his Far Fields farm, reminding her of those 'wide, vast, flat measures of dark, fertile fenland soil'. Rusty could already hear her grandfather was forming a plan.

"Versatile fields, much in demand," he reminded the children in the back of the truck. Tuckly would be needing more help than those two boys could give him when harvest time arrived. "Best to trade when the tractors start working. It's not like you're gonna have time for baking any time soon, is it?" Old Spot wondered, turning back to Rusty.

Rusty nodded, keeping her eyes on the way the lanes were winding ahead of her truck. They both knew Tuckly preferred working the land with machines, not animals. The only problem with that was Tuckly had two tractors, which meant he could only be driving one at a time, leaving the other in the far less capable hands of those farm-bullies of his.

"They'll likely be needing a mechanic near to harvest time," Old Spot reckoned. "You're the best around these parts and Tuckly knows it. You won't have long to wait."

With that decided, Rusty turned her truck towards the village.

"Home time, you lot," she called out from the cab. It was getting late and she could hear the tiredness in her grandfather's voice. She doubted he'd get further than his armchair tonight. He wasn't the only one. Maze was almost asleep before she got out of the truck, and Al and Walker were quieter too.

"It's been a long day," Gertie agreed, steering the younger children towards their home. His own attic room wasn't far.

Mrs Tweeny's front door was closed. It all looked calm over there.

"Do you think our girls are OK?" Gertie asked Rusty, as he took his bicycle out from the back of the truck. She could hear the concern in his voice. Bless him, sensitive lad.

"We're gonna do our best for them. We're all in this, and they need *our* help as much as we need *theirs*."

CHAPTER 11

Bookshelves and Haybale-Stew

THE VICAR WAS STILL CONFUSED about what was due to go in the paper collection. Bracket had been teasing him that they wouldn't allow him to keep his crossword pages anymore.

It was still early enough for Al and Walker to be out before school that morning. They didn't usually listen in on the vicar's conversation. Whenever Walker heard the vicar's voice, it made him think he ought to be sitting very still on a hard wooden pew somewhere, hearing someone snoring behind him.

It reminded the two Scamps of the sound Grouch made whilst he was waiting for his horse to move the milk cart the next few doorsteps over. It was too soft for a snort and too long for a tut. Could have been a snore, only louder. Grouch had been doing the village milk round for long enough; it wouldn't have surprised either of the boys to discover he was doing it in his sleep, except for the milk bottles on the doorstep bit, but then that would explain why he liked to have a lad along with him.

Al was still trying to persuade Walker that the vicar did a lot more than just the Sunday sermons. After all, with Humfrey as church warden, he had to be 'wardening' more than just Sunday services. What was he doing?

The vicar helped with the 'visiting', according to Al. "Not like the doctor, but he does his best. Dr Hastings does the sort of mending way, and the vicar does it another way. It's not all about talking. With the vicar it's more about the listening."

Walker wasn't convinced, although he could see the vicar didn't carry a bag like the village doctor. Walker was more interested in the mention of the crosswords.

Joe had said about those crosswords too, over at the hospital. The Scamps had been able to catch up over there a couple of times since Florrie had told them about Art. He was feeling better and settling in with more of the Lads.

They'd expected Art's voice to sound smoky on account of his burns, like the bus-driver did from his cigarettes. The bus-driver's voice sounded like it was rasping over sandpaper and gravel, but Art's voice didn't sound like that at all. His voice was lighter, full of air. He breathed deeply before he spoke and allowed the breath to lift the words out of his mouth. That was how it sounded: sometimes almost like laughter, sometimes almost like a relief to let go of those sounds and only occasionally was there any harshness to what he had to say. Art wasn't angry anymore. Florrie's listening had helped him, although sometimes his voice began to fracture into sadness, the young nurse recognised this too was part of the healing.

What with Joe being blind and Art being unable to use his hands yet, neither of them were up to getting much done outside. But the Scamps had found Joe still trying to keep Art cheered up with his antics, not too far from the house so they didn't bother the nurses.

"The nurses and porters are busy taking care of those that need them. We don't!" Joe had reminded Al and Walker when they'd been bold enough to ask why.

Joe and Art could walk and talk, but not much else, at least not on their own, but together they seemed to make a capable team.

They sat together at one of the tables just beyond the conservatory in the sunshine. The porters always brought a few of the easy chairs out from the library on to the grass there, once the days had begun to get reliable. They'd have the newspaper and 'read' it between them. Joe would turn the pages and Art would read it. When it came to the crossword, if any of the Scamps were in the vicinity, Gertie included, then the Lads would get them to do the scribbling and test them on the clues.

Gertie was going over to the hospital more often since he'd got his overalls. Sarg and Mrs Toombs no longer tried to work out why he was over that way. The lanky lad seemed to be forever going between one errand and another. Sometimes he might know both parts, sometimes only the one way, but with every confidence the second half would present itself by the time he was ready for getting back over to the village.

Mrs Toombs wasn't quite sure what to make of him but had to admire his confidence. Sarg liked him, against his initial misgivings, Gertie had a cheerful resilience that Sarg had seldom seen in one so young.

Sarg had seen it in some of the Lads at the hospital and in his own men, but he expected that of them. Gertie was only fourteen. He'd known nothing except life in the village, as far as Sarg could tell. Even so, there was something about the boy that made Sarg believe him older and stronger than his frame and face would first suggest.

Sarg could see a change in Gertie in the past few months, possibly more clearly than many others up at the hospital. Sarg never thought doctors were the quickest of individuals in that department. They'd looked for the symptoms of the problem. They'd look from the injuries to their prescriptions and miss the most important part! They seldom looked at the person and notice the changes beyond the wounds and scars.

It might have been the overalls, but Sarg wasn't convinced of that!

Gertie had got the Scamps to think differently about those newspaper crosswords in recent weeks. He wasn't so good at getting the answers from the clues, but he was good at finding a different way of looking at the problem and finding an answer to fit anyway.

Joe liked him, Art found him slightly unnerving and Florrie was pleased to know that. Art needed to have something interesting to focus on. Whatever Gertie and the Scamps were doing they were helping, and that was as good a diversion as any. It had worked before!

Gertie had been interested in helping Al and Walker with the next waste paper salvage from the vicarage, because there were always magazines over there, as well as the newspapers to be collected. The vicar didn't have time for reading magazines, but it seemed many of his visitors felt he might. The vicar always remembered to put the newspapers he'd finished on the doorstep, so there was no confusion. The vicar didn't cope well with confusion. Bracket had already called him a 'right Charlie!' for forgetting the magazines previously.

The Scamps found the vicar's used newspapers ready for their salvage collection. It wasn't that the vicar had forgotten about those magazines he'd been given, he knew where they were, only he hadn't been so sure how to handle the delicate matter of throwing them out!

There were all stacked up in piles behind the back of the vicar's sofa. They'd been accumulating back there for years. The vicar had never quite decided if they were a donation or a gift. If they were a gift, then he really ought to be keeping them somewhere, but couldn't fit them on his bookshelves. The only other place that he wasn't going to trip over them was behind that sofa. No one looked behind there, except Bracket when he'd come to help with the blackout curtains, and the village ironmonger had been quick with his opinion on the matter.

"If they brought them to you Vicar, then they intended for you to donate them. They're not doing anyone any good down there, are they? They need salvaging."

The vicar hadn't thought of them that way and was pleased to have that clarified, although he could have done without being called a 'right Charlie'. Nor was he so pleased to learn that, according to Bracket, he needed to clear out more of his reading books, as well as all those carefully saved newspaper crossword pages.

The vicar had protested, weakly, 'but I haven't finished with them yet'. He had every intention of re-reading some of those books and had been carefully saving those puzzle pages for winter. The Scamps could have all the other pages of the newspapers for their salvage, just not the pages with the crosswords on.

Thankfully, Al and Walker had come over in the nick of time to help the vicar with his dilemma.

The first thing Walker told the vicar was, "Don't listen to Bracket. He only ever uses his newspapers for wrapping and packing and he never reads any of them. Bracket thinks if it ain't on the radio then it ain't worth knowing."

Al had learnt what Bracket had said about visitors bringing donations to the vicarage. "That's true enough, no one brings anything to the vicarage they want to keep. That wouldn't make sense, would it?"

The vicar nodded. That sounded extraordinarily reasonable. Al nudged Gertie, who promptly picked up the reasoning.

"Then if they don't want it, they're not *giving* it to you, they're *donating* it to you, so you can do whatever you want with it!"

Gertie always had string in his pocket. "You'll need this for the magazines," he offered the two younger boys. "The magazines won't stay stacked so well as the newspapers. Slippery blighters, they are!"

None of the Scamps were so sure about the vicar's reading books, though, but there were definitely too many for the vicarage bookshelves!

Gertie checked his copy of the salvage leaflet from the back pocket of his overalls. It definitely referred to 'old books', although it wasn't so clear on the *how* old. "Maybe they're not old enough if you're still reading them," Gertie checked, finding a different way of looking at the problem.

The vicar had heard mention of Gertie's alternative ways. No one had an unkind word to say about the lanky lad; a few sideways glances, perhaps, but not unkind. Most were simply making an observation. They all seemed to think he looked more comfortable in the overalls. At least, Gertie seemed 'less awkward,' was the general consensus of opinion.

Rusty had given Gertie one of her colourful handkerchiefs and ever since he'd had it tucked half in half out from one pocket or another. Aggy had given Gertie her husband's old satchel. Humfrey hadn't used it in years, and it was too unwieldly for the schoolteacher to manage, but she didn't like to see the satchel idle. Gertie had assured her it wouldn't be idle with him, and it never was!

It hadn't gone unnoticed that Gertie was keeping the

butcher's second-best bicycle. The butcher's own best bicycle was kept in his back shed, for high days and holidays, though there hadn't been time for many of those recently.

Gertie had earned that bicycle, and those overalls suited him. It was the *way* the lad carried himself these days. He seemed to know what he was doing, and it had been noticed! The village could always do with more of that sort.

"Oh dear!" The vicar agreed, Gertie's leaflet definitely mentioned 'old reading books'. The Scamps looked back across at the vicarage bookcases. There were a lot of old reading books.

"You can't be re-reading *all* of them, Vicar?" Al queried. "There's more here than at school and we don't even want to be reading most of them, for the first time!"

"There must be some way of deciding?" Gertie wondered, before offering. "It's always easier after the first couple of decidings."

As an evacuee, the vicar realised Walker must have needed to decide to leave a lot of things behind. He was likely the most experienced amongst them on this matter. "Where do you think I ought to start?"

Walker started walking along the length of the nearest of the bookcases, one shelf at a time. The vicar's office was the largest room downstairs. Most people would call it their sitting room, but the vicar preferred to call it his office. Somehow it made the vicar feel more useful. The large bookcase went from the floor to ceiling along half of the back wall of the vicar's office and was tightly packed with books. There were two smaller bookcases against the wall opposite his sofa.

Gertie grinned. "Cripes, Vicar! If you have read all those no wonder your sermons are so long. You've got to put all that learning somewhere, and you only get an hour on Sundays."

Gertie didn't attend church, at least not in the normal way. He'd always liked listening to the bells, but they'd been stopped since the start of war. He didn't like all the sitting and kneeling and standing so much, preferring to stay quietly sat on the church stone wall outside and listen to the singing from there, with the birdsong and the grass growing between the standing stones of the churchyard.

The vicar hadn't thought his sermons to be so longwinded, until Gertie had mentioned it.

"Oh no, Vicar, I didn't mean *you* were longwinded. I mean, you tend to use a lot of longwinded words, but that's only because you know so many of them, they sort of crowd out the shorter ones!"

Gertie tried a hasty explanation to his blurt. It got the vicar chuckling. It was quite refreshing the way Gertie put his opinions forward; clear, considerate and unexpectedly enlightening.

Walker was still trying to decide which books could be put into the salvage barrow. They hadn't brought Maze and her old pram this time, she had her own errands to get done before school.

"How about I see if I can find a boxful for you, whilst you take what's already out on the doorstep? That will take you at least two trips to the village hall," the vicar suggested kindly, hoping to delay the inevitable.

He wasn't successful. The mention of the box triggered a notion in Walker's head. It got him thinking about cardboard. "How about we start with the paperback books, Vicar? You don't want to keep those, do you?"

"I don't?" the vicar asked, taken aback by how certain the boy sounded.

"No, you don't," Walker informed him. "If you'd wanted to

keep the book for more re-reading, you wouldn't have bought a paperback. I know that because they sell them at the train station and they're not for keep-reading books, they're just for travelling-with reading."

The vicar's polite smile broadened into a grin of relief. "Done!"

Al looked amazed at his friend's skill.

"Did you just do a deal with the vicar?"

"Sounded like it to me," Gertie told the pair of them, then checked with the village cleric. "That's right, isn't it Vicar? We take all the paperbacks?"

"Quite right, Gertie. I'll start taking them off the shelves and putting them on the front doorstep for you. That way, if you take longer than you think, they won't get muddled up with anything else, or with any more visitors to the vicarage!"

"Done."

Al had already decided to scold Bracket for teasing the vicar, muttering a stern 'not meant to do that sort of thing!' At least, he would tell him that, next time he was in Bracket's shop, and no one else was listening, and before Bracket could get his hands on that knuckle-rapping yardstick of his!

Gertie had his bicycle basket, Walker had the wheelbarrow and Al took hold of another bundle to carry from the vicarage at one end of the village, over to the collection point at the village hall at the other.

Walker was still wondering what else was in that leaflet of Gertie's.

"What about any letters? Are we meant to take them? They're paper, aren't they?"

"No letters." The vicar was adamant on that point.

On the way over to the hall Al had started talking about

those 'secret message warnings' he'd heard about from the radio. "They're hidden. Have you checked the newspapers? They could put the secrets in them."

Gertie listened to them teasing each other, before reminding the pair, "If those secret messages are printed in the newspaper, they can't be *that* secret. We can all pick up a newspaper and read it."

"Might be in code, like those crosswords," Al suggested. The teasing lightened the task. "The cleverest thing would be to hide the secret messages in the cartoons. No one would be able to find them there. Maybe we ought to check the cartoons, before giving them in at the hall, just to be sure?"

Al and Walker were almost late getting into school that morning. Gertie had managed to rescue a handful of the cartoon pages from the vicar's newspapers and put them in the bottom of his basket. They wouldn't get in the way of the butcher's deliveries down there and would be ready for Al and Walker to check through for clues to coded messages later.

Mrs Parr and Aggy were at the school gates, ready to take the children out from their classrooms over to the allotments for thinning duty. "We need all those little fingers!" the teachers informed them.

The area of village ground put aside for the allotments was where the playing fields had used to be, behind the village shop. Ol' Creak was glad to see the back of those playing fields; the balls annoyed him. It had been a safe place for the children to play. The only traffic down Furlong Lane were the horses and they didn't come as often as they used to.

Scar and Hatchet kept the village stables. They hadn't been particularly happy about the allotments, until someone had mentioned the possibility of free carrots in exchange for the fresh manure. Scar was all for having the allotmenteers fetch it themselves, until Hatchet pointed out they didn't want anyone else poking around the sheds behind the stables.

Hatchet was happy with them needing to do all that digging, though. A lot of digging on rough ground meant a few of the forks and spades broke. Bracket would have new, but Hatchet could repair the old ones 'just as good as, for a fraction of the price'.

The ground behind the village shop had been used as a playing field for good reason. It was an old field in an awkward place and not good for regular working, but fenland soil was always good for digging!

Those in the village with large enough gardens had already had plenty of practice. It was easy to dig in the summer, but autumn was coming and that meant they needed to get on with the growing before winter.

The Parish Council had arranged the allocations fairly, so fairly that no one was entirely happy, but everyone was determined to make the most of what they'd got! Most of the children knew about the allotments, if only because they'd been told they couldn't play there anymore. Having a school day down at the old playing field sounded like a lovely way to avoid classroom lessons.

Furlong Lane started between where the village shop ended and the church warden's house stood. It went down past the village side of the allotments, all the way back behind the Long Terrace of old cottages, until it found the village stables, then a bit further round to almost meet up with the backyard doors of Horace and Rosie's pub.

The little stream that flowed through the centre of the village puddled at the duckpond in the middle, then wound wide around behind the broad banking, safely back past the church stone wall and slowly out on beyond the church meadow. After that the little stream seemed to have got lonely, deciding to trickle its way back towards the village again, coming alongside the outer edge of the allotments, and flowing from there down to the low ground of the boggy bottom field, from there no one seemed able to decide where it went.

Hatchett liked having the boggy bottom field right where it was. It lived up to its reputation and flooded regularly, saving the village. It was common ground over that way, south of the village. It was also common knowledge how treacherous the ground was for walking, so Hatchett never got bothered by anyone creeping over to his stables from that direction, and if anyone came along Furlong Lane, he could hear them coming on the cobbles.

The children could play football along the length of the lane, so long as they remembered to avoid it when Scar and Hatchett needed to use it. There weren't so many horses being kept at the stables anymore, and Grouch the milko kept Nag in his own back garden shed.

Gertie had always thought it was a good place to put the allotments. It balanced out the village, with the market at the other end!

The church had its yard, now the shop had its allotments, and at the other end there was the village hall one side of the road and Bracket's ironmonger shop the other. Yes, Gertie liked the way that felt.

He'd finished his earlier deliveries. Likely there would be more, depending on what Brisket had got coming over from Mr Tor. In the meantime, Brisket's missus wanted to see Mrs Parr, and Gertie knew better than to ask what for. He just delivered the message to Mrs Parr with the children over at the allotments and stayed after that.

When Aggy asked why, Gertie grinned as he reasoned, "Only fair, Miss. Got to keep the numbers right, so I'll take her place."

The schoolteacher didn't have an answer for that, except to offer Gertie one of the spare buckets. "Is this for Mr Tor's rabbits, Miss?"

"No, Gertie, not this time. These are for *us*. I thought we'd have a go at making one of those thinnings stews. I thought you'd have read about that in one of your leaflets."

Ah, Gertie realised what the schoolteacher was telling him. Al and Walker had been talking. Gertie had a copy of every leaflet that ever came his way. That wasn't wasting the paper, that was using it! They wouldn't have printed the leaflets in the first place if they hadn't intended them to be used.

Gertie liked the bucket-idea, and the young schoolteacher seemed to be trying to help the younger children with deciding the differences between what was meant to be tugged for the pot, what was to be tugged for the heap, and what was meant to be left in the ground for growing. Most seemed to know already, except Walker, too city-quick, not enough village-smart, still a little slow on the country wisdom.

Gertie brought his bucket to the row beside where Walker was working. The young boy hissed across to him, "I haven't got a clue what I'm doing. What am I doing?"

"Tug two for every three. Then the best of what's in your hand put in the bucket for the stew, and what's left in your hand for the heap," Gertie suggested, wisely.

That sounded simple enough.

"How do you know we've tugged the right ones, and kept and lobbed what's needed?" Walker wondered. He wasn't arguing, just intrigued how Gertie figured it, and how the soil seemed to be able to keep count better than he could.

"Not difficult really. If you're thinning, that means you're making space for the growing. As for which thinnings go into the bucket and which into the weed heap, we're eating the one direct from the stew and the other's either going to the pigs, or back in the ground for more growing, so it's coming to our stomachs one way of another, ain't it?"

That was such a revelation, Walker almost lost his balance and sat down on the row of young tender vegetables.

Gertie wasn't finished yet. "Anyway, if it's good enough for the rabbits, then it's good enough for us!"

"You mean we're going to eat pig food?" Walker's voice had got louder in alarm. Al had come over and shushed his friend.

"You're not meant to be talking about Mr Tor's rabbits like that. We don't know who knows that's code for his pigs!"

"I wasn't talking about Mr Tor's pigs," Gertie told both boys. "I was talking about the really-rabbits, like the ones over on the edge of Abe's orchard and the ones that have been bothering Tuckly's farm boys."

That was news to Al. If anything was bothering Tuckly's farm boys, be it really-rabbits or pigs, he was happy to hear it. They were bullies. "Good!"

"Good which? The really-rabbits or the pigs?" Walker asked, feeling like he was getting swallowed up in this confusion.

"I think Mr Tor might be going over to sort out Tuckly's rabbit problem. You know they don't like animals in those working fields," Gertie told them, much to Al's delight.

"There aren't no pigs this side of the village, only the really-rabbits that have come over from Abe's orchard. Rabbit stew is lovely and goes even better with fresh-picked thinnings." Gertie informed them of that lovely little snippet of country wisdom.

"All you have to do is think either this is going to be thinnings stew, with rabbits or without rabbits!" Gertie helped the reckoning along.

By then, many more of the schoolchildren were listening in. Aggy was trying not to, but it was fascinating the way Gertie made it sound so simple.

Maze led the way after that. "So, it's three then, Miss?"

Aggy looked along the rows. She wasn't sure if she could tell the difference either, but the rows were already looking tidier. As for maybe a few of the weeds finding their way into the pot, she doubted anyone would notice. It also gave her an idea of how to maybe improve on her original recipe.

She wasn't going to expect the children to take the pig-bucket over to Mr Tor, not this time. She could leave that to Brisket to organise.

There were just two of the allotment crew in attendance at that time of day, and they'd kept to their sheds for the past hour, which Aggy thought was a wise precaution. By then, Rusty had come round that way. She had an unscheduled delivery of bricks, ideal for spacing the shelves in the allotment sheds. At least that was her suggestion for what they might be good for, but she left it up to the allotmenteers to decide. All Rusty knew was that Jeepers didn't want them in his Yard and Old Spot had enough!

Jeepers had got lumbered with them when a delivery driver messed up his drop. From there, the Yard-owner had promptly re-dropped them into Rusty's truck with the hay, due to go over to Abe's, and she was still hoping to make it over to the Totters' farm.

Rusty was happy to deliver the spare bricks to where they could be useful, and found she was intrigued by Gertie's really-rabbits theory but didn't think much of Aggy's bucket of ingredients so far.

"That's not going to make much of a stew."

Whilst the allotmenteers came out to do their inspection of Rusty's delivery, the children shared the corners of their cheese and salad sandwiches. The bread was dry, but the tea from their flasks was strong, and the little cucumbers and spring onions tasted wonderful.

Walker had never tasted anything so delicious and so green before! As for the baby carrots, one of his elders showed him they were sweet enough to tug out from the ground, rub the crumbs of mud off between their fingers and just crunch straight into their mouths.

No one had seen any rabbits yet that morning, so it seemed it would just have to be thinnings stew this time. As for what was in the bucket, that could be sorted through before it went into the pot.

If Rusty could spare one of those haybales that would be useful, though. Aggy knew what she was doing, and Rusty recognised the plan. "Yes Miss Aggy, of course." They both enjoyed the looks of bewilderment on the children's faces.

It was Walker, city-quick as ever, who had to ask, "Are we having hay in our stew? That's going to be a bit chewy, ain't it, Miss?"

Rusty wondered if she might borrow the Scamps for a while, a few extra hands for an hour or so? They had their overalls, and she had some extra working gloves with her; never move bricks nor hay without them, and was overdue out to Abe's farm to deliver the rest of those haybales.

Gertie liked the sound of that, yelling over to the young schoolteacher confidently, "Don't worry, Miss. We might have some rabbits for that haybale-stew of yours, yet."

Al and Walker didn't need asking twice, dropping the weeds and grabbing the proffered gloves, they were at the ready, with Maze tugging at Gertie to help her into the back of the truck. "Got room for a few tiddlers, Rusty?" he called forward, merrily.

CHAPTER 12

Buckets, Piggy-Backs and 'That's the Way, Walker!'

ABE COULD ALWAYS USE THE extra haybales, but the chicken orchard farmer needed Rusty even more urgently. He'd received another notice from the Ministry, very clear this time, and it wasn't about his eggs.

"Need you lot to help me catch some of the old uns." He noticed the little heads popping up from the back of Rusty's truck and didn't waste his words. "I know which ones they are, and I can point them out for you. They may be too old to lay, but they're still too quick for me to catch!"

Now Abe's hens were a little more contained by the chicken wire, the children found it easier to corner them. Maze stayed well back, just shouting encouragement. Rusty stayed until they got the hang of the 'approach, grab and tuck the head under' technique. "If they don't know which way is up and which way is down, then they won't try to fly away."

Walker had been reminded enough times that morning he wasn't village-smart enough, but he was still city-quick, and as far as he could tell being quick with those chickens was going to be the best way to tackle the problem. Lunging into the fray, he grabbed the first hen he could. He somehow managed to grab it by its beak first, which stopped the pecking, with his other arm now wrapping around the widest part of the hen's body, wings and all, then grabbing at the feet underneath. The last thing to do, as Rusty had instructed, was to tuck the beak downwards under the wing.

"Crikey! It works!" No one was more surprised than Walker to have accomplished the mission so seamlessly.

"Bet you couldn't do that again," Al challenged.

"Bet you I could!"

The gauntlet had been thrown and Maze would keep score between the boys.

Abe had a lot of chickens and most of them were going to be able to stay, at least until next spring. The catching was down to the children; the despatching was down to Abe and Rusty. Gertie could have told the Scamps what they were doing in that shed behind the farmhouse, but Rusty felt maybe they ought not to see this time. Walker definitely wasn't ready for that bit of country wisdom.

Whilst Abe and Rusty got on with that, they left it up to the Scamps to 'gather dessert'. Everyone was checking which berries Walker was heading for. They hadn't forgotten the incident with the wrong berries up on Jeepers' lane.

Abe had plenty of buckets all over the place for eggs, apples and rabbits.

"A farm should always have too many buckets," he told them.

"And haybales," Rusty reminded him.

Abe was grateful for the delivery and the extra hands. "You must have got one of those leaflets," he wondered to Rusty, "over at *your* farmhouse?"

Gertie struggled to think of Jeepers' Yard as being a farm

with a farmhouse, and Rusty couldn't help. The only paper Jeepers was interested in were the ones that he could fit in his wallet.

"Oh, money!" Gertie's snort of disapproval startled Abe.

"What, you got a problem with money lad?"

"Just got no time for it. I like paper leaflets though," Gertie offered. "Plenty of ideas in those leaflets. Money just leaves a nasty taste in the mouth. I'd much prefer bread and cheese, although sausages are even better!"

Abe didn't try and make sense of that, instead shooing Gertie over to check the children's hedge-pickings, whilst he helped Rusty with the truck.

The hedge was just for keeping the chickens off the road as far as Abe was concerned. He'd provide the buckets for the Scamps' berry-picking efforts and a couple of old hens for the school stew pot. Even the Ministry leaflet hadn't told him not to do that! It had plenty of 'Do this' and 'Don't do that' but hadn't mentioned the school stew pot anywhere.

Abe was busy with more to do in his back sheds and Rusty had the rest of her round to finish. The Scamps were to make their own way back into the village.

Gertie led Al, Walker and Maze, now each with their own buckets, steadily along the blackberry hedges. "This isn't foraging, not if you've got a bucket," Gertie had heard them earlier and thought a little more explanation might help. "Pockets are for scrumping, baskets are for foraging and buckets are for picking!"

"Why don't those leaflets make as much sense as you do?" Walker asked.

Gertie grinned. "Because leaflets don't wear overalls!"

Abe was the sort of farmer who always had something for market, no matter what the season. It might be chickens or eggs or apples or rabbits, now blackberries were added to that list.

By the time Gertie and Al were ready for the long walk back from Abe's farm to the village school, Maze was flagging and Walker wasn't too keen on the trek back either.

"Can't we just wait for Rusty to come back this way from Totters'?"

"You'll be waiting a long while if you do," Gertie reminded him. "She'll likely have finished by now and be waiting for us to get back to school for that stew."

"You can get on my back," Gertie gestured to Maze. "I'll carry you, and Al and Walker can have two buckets each."

Al was happy with the challenge, nudging Walker encouragingly with a timely reminder 'it's all Effort, gotta do our bit'. Gertie had already lifted Maze into position, waiting for the two boys to set the pace.

"Ready?"

This was country wisdom, and Walker was starting to like the way it felt. It made his feet feel steadier and his head taller on his shoulders, his hands felt stronger and his back broader.

The thought of chicken and thinnings stew waiting for them gave the pace a stride sufficient to set the boys' buckets of blackberries swinging.

Gertie approved. "That's the way, Walker!"

Walker liked the way that sounded, too – 'That's the way, Walker' – and grinned across to Al, matching his friend stride for stride. The buckets of blackberries got to the village school, where they found the dairy lasses from Totters' farm had brought over a jug of cream in anticipation of a decent haul from Abe's hedgeways.

Humfrey was there, too. He'd been setting up a bit more kit in his Home Guard office.

Gertie wondered, "More leaflets?"

Humfrey smiled. "Worse than leaflets, Gertie, brown card folders and envelopes!"

"Oh, that does sound worse! Can't go stuffing brown card folders down into your back pocket, can you?"

Humfrey had a whole list.

"They need a typewriter to start with, and extra copies to file, files need shelves, shelves need cupboards, and my cupboard is already full of sandbag sacks! I've even had to put trays on the table for more paperwork they're sending me, telling me what paperwork I'm meant to be sending them!"

"If you've got a typewriter and trays on the table, that makes it a desk, don't it?" Al queried.

They'd already handed in their buckets at the school, and the crate had been packed with straw, ready for Mrs Parr's stew pot to keep stewing in until everyone was ready for eating it. Al was already ready for a bowl of stew, but helping Humfrey sounded better than waiting for it! Even Walker could make sense of that notion and tagged along.

Something had happened somewhere along that walk back into the village, back from Abe's chicken orchard farm. It might have begun sooner than that, maybe Walker hadn't noticed the beginning before then, but he'd noticed it on that walk back into the village. It had been about when Gertie had said, 'That's the way, Walker.' It had made him want to stride into more of that country wisdom!

Walker had begun to appreciate you couldn't study it, you sort of strode or maybe ambled on from one day to the next and stumbled into it. Although the likes of Gertie seemed able to breathe it!

Walker had also realised his friend Al had plenty of village smarts, but neither Al nor Gertie had what Humfrey had: a radio! It was there in front of them, in his Home Guard office.

"You can't make sense of what's happening if you don't know what's happening," Walker reasoned.

Al agreed.

"Can we help unload the truck for you?" both boys offered in unison.

Humfrey was a little surprised at their eagerness. "Haven't you done enough today?" He'd seen the weary plod of their steps across the schoolyard with the buckets.

"Oh, that was farm work. This is office work! Can't plod in an office, can we?" Gertie reckoned.

"Paper don't weigh as heavy as buckets," Walker offered.

Humfrey laughed at their eagerness. "Don't you believe it! But if you want to unload everything, then I'll be glad of the help. It'll give me a few minutes to say hello to me missus. Just don't touch anything, OK?"

Walker was only a step behind, with a little of his city-quick cheek bubbling forward.

"How are we meant to unload the paperwork without touching it?"

Al had already climbed into the back of Humfrey's camp truck by then, to see what was due for their unloading. His voice came up from the depths.

"Hey, there's a proper filing cabinet back here. Crikey, Gertie are you ready down there? This is all sharp corners and slippery drawers!"

Gertie had seen how a filing cabinet worked before. At least it would be empty this time, if it was coming off the back of Humfrey's truck, and it wouldn't be too heavy between the three of them. Gertie had helped Ol' Creak move one years ago, and it had left a lasting impression on one of his shins.

"You need to carry it out with the back down and drawers up. That way they can't slide out," Gertie directed.

That was the first thing they dealt with. Humfrey had already got the office desk in the right place, with the chair. The cupboard was in one back corner, and it looked like the filing cabinet could go into the other, behind the desk.

"There must be something else in the truck to fill that space between the cabinet and the cupboard. That doesn't look right," Gertie queried, thoughtfully.

"How do you know what looks right in an office?" Walker checked.

"An office is all about keeping everything running smoothly, isn't it?" Gertie reasoned. "Well, how can you have everything running smoothly if there's a ruddy great gap between the cabinet and the cupboard?"

Walker didn't have an immediate answer to that riddle, but the more he considered it, as they unloaded the truck, the more he realised Gertie's way of making sense tended to make more sense the more you thought about it!

And Humfrey was right, too. The paperwork *was* heavy! There were not only office supplies, like those kept behind the post office counter in Ol' Creak's shop, but Home Guard supplies too. They could recognise some as having come from the Army camp.

"Can't get much more office-cial than that," Gertie admired.

They'd almost finished emptying the back of the truck by the time Humfrey got back to them.

"Well done lads. Couldn't have done better myself." He'd

brought them over mugs of tea. "Miss Aggy says the stew will be ready soon." He looked over to the state of the Scamps and their overalls. "I don't suppose you want to bother about washing before then? I'm guessing you'd rather enjoy your brew whilst I get the radio up and running, off duty, in the Home Guard office?"

"Yes please, Sir."

Walker was first to step forward, taking the mug Humfrey handed him.

"Glad to hear it. Then you'd better learn the first rule of the office. See that second box over there, marked 'Belts'?"

Walker followed Humfrey's directions and opened it without waiting. The belts filled half the cardboard box, the biscuit tin filled the other half.

"If you're going to be working in an office, you need to know where the 'essential equipment' is kept."

"There I told you!" Gertie slapped Walker on the back. "I told you there had to be something between the cabinet and the cupboard before the office would be able to run smoothly!"

Al was ready to argue that point.

"Can't be cardboard boxes, they don't count as furniture. They're for moving, like the vicar's magazines."

"You told them there ought to be something between the cupboard and the cabinet did you, Gertie?" Humfrey checked, ignoring the squabble between the two younger boys, as he offered the tin to all three of them.

They each took two biscuits in one hand with their tea mugs in the other, whilst Humfrey got the radio crackling into life. Only then did Humfrey take another look at the space where the cardboard boxes were temporarily sat.

"You're right, Gertie. They're wrong there, aren't they?"

He allowed the three boys to sit and enjoy the radio for a while, whilst he settled the files and sorted out the contents of the other boxes. Time enough for him to remember what Al had said about the vicar's cardboard boxes.

"Why did the vicar have so many boxes?" Humfrey finally found himself compelled to ask. As church warden, amongst his other responsibilities, he needed to keep an eye on the state of the housekeeping over at the vicarage. Even Humfrey had to admit the old vicar could be a 'right Charlie' at times.

It didn't take much to keep up with what the vicar was doing, and if Humfrey wasn't about, he knew Aggy was more than capable of checking in on him, but those cardboard boxes were news to Humfrey.

"Paper salvage!" Al explained, reminding Walker. "We need to go back for those paperbacks."

Walker had forgotten that, and Al's words had an immediate effect.

"That's it!" he pointed to middle of the back wall of the Home Guard office. "That's what's you're missing over there. It's a bookcase! That's what you need in an office, don't you? I knew there were three things in all," Walker blurted.

"Three things?" Humfrey queried, exchanging confounded expressions with Al, who grinned and shrugged whilst Gertie sipped his tea in silence, patiently waiting for Walker to follow the thinking through. He could already see the question in Humfrey's face: was this one of Walker's city-quick thoughts? Gertie didn't think so.

"Three things?" Al repeated the question to his friend.

"You can't count the desk and chair, can you!" Walker asked Gertie, who was with him on that, and waiting for the boy to explain for the benefit of the others.

"It's like you said about the 'essentials'," Walker started. Humfrey was none the wiser and waited with Al for Walker to explain about the 'need for three'.

"Stationery cupboard, filing cabinet, the third thing that goes with them? It's the bookcase! Fits, doesn't it?" Gertie slapped Walker on the back for a second time that day. "That's the way, Walker!"

Humfrey chuckled; the boy was right. Standing and looking at the space at the back of his office. "It *needs* a bookcase. Any ideas?"

"One of the vicar's," Walker offered. "He's got too many books. If we take away *all* his paperbacks for salvage, then he'll have too many shelves for the books he's keeping for re-reading, and he's got *plenty* of bookcases!" Walker sounded very certain of that.

"Shall we go and ask him?" Gertie offered.

Humfrey was about to say he ought to be the one to do that, but realised the Scamps were already halfway out his office and on the way with that errand. He also suspected they might have started to wonder whether their share of that haybale-stew was ready.

"I'd better go with you. If – and I mean only if – the vicar is happy for us to relocate one of his smaller bookcases to the Home Guard office, then we can move those paperbacks for salvage you mentioned at the same time, can't we?"

"We'll need a wheelbarrow," Al suggested.

Gertie seconded that. "Bookcases are almost as tricky as filing cabinets. They don't slip so quick, but they topple easy enough."

"It sounds like you know what you're talking about," Humfrey checked with Gertie, as they waited for Al to return with the wheelbarrow.

At the thought of moving a bookcase Gertie was already rubbing his left shin. "Didn't have a wheelbarrow that time. Maybe this time it'll be easier."

"With all four of us, that should be enough," Humfrey reckoned.

"Should be, Corp, should be!" Gertie answered without thinking and liked the way it sounded. Humfrey didn't say anything, but they walked together along the footpath, shoulder to shoulder, towards the vicarage at the other end of the village. Both men in uniform and on a mission, to finish setting up the local Home Guard office. They didn't pause outside the school. They could hear the calls and noise, but they were working. That stew would have to wait.

Many things had changed that summer's afternoon. Maybe it had been the walking that had done it, and the thinking along the way of it. Maybe it had been the listening, and the figuring out between them.

Aggy wouldn't forget them. There would be bowlfuls of stew enough for the Scamps when they returned. Gertie could guess Maze would be sure to do enough reminding for that!

They could see Al and Walker returning with the wheelbarrow, heading over to join them at the vicarage, but for the next few minutes it was just Humfrey and Gertie, striding along the village footpath.

Humfrey had been wondering about something for a while, and if he didn't ask the lad now, he might never get another chance.

"Gertie. Why is it Gertie?"

Gertie grinned. "Maze gave it me."

Humfrey had heard that part of the story, but he'd always thought there was more to it than that. "Maybe Maze *did* give it to you, but you've *kept* it, Gertie?"

"I like it. It makes everything simple," Gertie offered.

Humfrey wasn't sure he understood. "It does?"

"It's like the overalls," Gertie offered.

Humfrey felt like Gertie was trying to tell him more than he was saying. He remained silent and slowed the pace, giving the fellow by his side a chance to say more, but Gertie didn't seem to feel the need. Humfrey gave a quick exasperated, "Phew," before muttering an, "in for a penny in for a pound," to himself.

"OK Gertie, so you're happy with the overalls… um?"

"Oh yes, very comfortable," Gertie returned, cheerfully. "It's always easier to be useful when you're comfortable, isn't it?" he checked back.

They'd almost got within listening distance of the vicarage door, where Al and Walker were waiting with the wheelbarrow for them. Humfrey couldn't ask him anything more, even if he could find the right words for the question.

"Have you asked him?" Walker quizzed the church warden, jerking his head pointedly towards Gertie. They surely couldn't have heard him asking Gertie about his name? Humfrey didn't respond for a moment, uncertain how to.

"Was I meant to be asking him?"

Al knocked on the vicar's door before giving his opinion.

"Of course you were! We weren't sure. We thought you'd know?"

"I would?" The church warden was feeling suddenly very awkward and clumsy with his words, not a state to be meeting the vicar in. He took a step away from the front door. Taking a breath and composing himself.

"What was I meant to be asking Gertie about?"

"The stew bowls! What did you think we were talking

about? Walker says stew bowls are bigger than soup bowls and I said they weren't. Gertie's been up to Mrs Toombs' kitchen more times than any of us, so he'd know, wouldn't he?"

"Oh!" was the only response they got from the church warden, before the front door was opened and the vicar was standing there looking at two bright boys, a contented lanky lad and a blushing church warden!

"Can I help you?"

"We've come for the paperbacks and the bookcase, Vicar!" Walker informed him, as he proceeded to walk briskly passed the cleric into the hallway, and immediately started looking at which of the candidates might be suitable for requisitioning by the Home Guard's office.

"Do we want a tall one or a wide one?"

Walker called back to where the vicar was already standing to one side, allowing Al to catch up with his cohort. Gertie was eager to join them and yelling advice.

"Needs to be short and fat, 'cos it'll need to be useful for more than books, hey, Humfrey?"

The church warden was laughing, calming the vicar as he did so. "We need something to fit between the filing cabinet and the stationery cupboard in my office, Vicar," he explained.

"Oh yes, then quite right." The vicar could appreciate the requirement, "it needs to be short and fat, definitely. With deep shelves and plenty of space for shuffling papers on. I know what you need, I've got just the thing," the vicar confirmed happily, then turning back to scan the hallway of his vicarage, glancing across at the three boys in his study, then up the stairs. "I'm just not quite sure where I last saw it."

"You can't have hidden that down behind the back of the sofa, too, Vicar?" Walker called over.

The vicar thought it unlikely. "Probably up in the back bedroom. That's where most of the larger wooden donations end up, eventually."

"Do you get a lot of donated bookcases?" Al wondered, as he bounded up the stairs behind Walker, with Gertie keeping up and no less keen.

Humfrey sensibly staying down with the vicar. "I think they can manage."

"I think you're right," the vicar observed, then revised that estimation. "With Gertie? Undoubtedly!"

They left the Scamps to the matter of finding an appropriately short, fat, deep bookcase for the new Home Guard office, whilst they delved into deciding which paperbacks could be sent for salvage first.

It seemed Humfrey's missus had correctly guessed the vicar would have plenty of extra bowls, "Miss Aggy sent me," Maze explained loudly, having found the front door of the vicarage conveniently left wide open for her.

"Always too much crockery in a vicarage kitchen. No one likes throwing away odd bowls and plates, so they donate them," she informed Humfrey, who found the little girl already helping herself, when he was startled by the clattering sounds coming from that direction.

"Miss Aggy said you wouldn't mind," she told him brightly. "Just borrowing, not keeping, and we'll wash them up before bringing them back."

The vicar couldn't find fault with that, and Maze was right, he did seem to have accumulated rather an extensive collection.

"You can't manage all those, Maze. I'd better help," Humfrey offered, he didn't feel like he was being particularly helpful anywhere else at the moment.

Leaving the vicar to diligently bring out stack after stack of faded paperbacks, Al and Walker took one end of the bookcase and Gertie the other – "Ready!" – before bringing it down the stairs.

Gertie managed the wheelbarrow with the paperbacks. The empty bookcase was easier 'on the straight' of the footpath, between the two boys. The boys were a similar height and Gertie still recalled the difficulty he and Maze had experienced with moving that desk into the Home Guard office.

Humfrey led the way carrying the majority of the 'spare' vicarage bowls, with Maze taking her share and keeping up, right beside him. The boys with the bookcase followed, Gertie at the back struggling a little with the weight of the paperbacks in his barrow. It had been a long day.

The vicar was standing on his front doorstep watching the procession along the footpath, when he suddenly remembered that large ladle.

There were some curious glances coming from a few of the locals at the sight of their elderly vicar running along waving a ladle up in the air, calling to a lad with a wheelbarrow.

"You forgot this!"

Humfrey found himself wondering who amongst the spectators might attempt to make the connection between the wheelbarrow full of books and the soup ladle. He wasn't going to say anything. He was rather enjoying himself.

The bowls were delivered first. The bookcase fitted almost perfectly, just a little short.

"The right side of wrong," was Gertie's observation.

Humfrey didn't say anything. He just smiled and waited for them all to settle themselves and enjoy the bowls of blackberry crumble they'd brought with them back to his office. The stew had gone down well and quickly.

"We'll take our pudding back to the office please, Miss," Maze had informed the schoolteacher, who had exchanged knowing glances with the church warden over the little girl's head.

Humfrey had solemnly picked up a tray and waited for Aggy to fill it with the servings.

"Supper in the office, hey? You make sure he doesn't work too late," she instructed Maze, as she counted the spoons into her hand.

"Yes, Miss."

Now all the Scamps were sat cross-legged on the floor in the Home Guard office, with their bowls in their laps and spoons in their hands, listening to the radio, whilst Humfrey finished working at his desk.

In recent days and weeks, the radio had given many in the village cause to think more about those Lads up at the RAF hospital. The Germans had realised the British were using radar and had been attacking those stations along the coast. Some had been put out of operation for a day or so, but the radar vans had nipped in quick whilst the repairs had got done. The Germans had also been attacking airfields and aircraft factories, but the recent bad weather had worked in Britain's favour. *'Fighter Command is offering stiff resistance, despite coming under enormous pressure.'*

Gertie, Al and Walker listened transfixed, whilst Maze finished off her crumble. The radio was assuring them that Britain had a *'highly effective air defence network, bringing together the technology of radar, ground defences and fighter aircraft into a unified system of defence.'*

"They'll have the Observer Corp up and awake with that lot," Humfrey muttered to himself, as he listened to the report with them.

"Once they see which way those ruddy raiders are heading, and how many there are up there, they'll send that down the line to the plotters and planners and we'll be getting our boys up and at 'em in no time."

Humfrey had spoken those words without thinking. *Our boys.* He'd forgotten who was with him in the Home Guard office. These weren't his Home Guard men. These were children, even Gertie. He was just a boy, no more than fourteen. What would he know?

Gertie had looked up from where they'd been huddled with their supper bowls around the radio. He'd heard what the church warden had said, and smiled in that way he had, his head slightly tilted, somehow managing to make those freckles of his dance across his nose. "Don't worry, Corp."

Humfrey hadn't realised he'd allowed his cares to show so clearly.

"You're right. *Our* boys will see 'em off, 'cos it's not just them up there that's doing the fighting. We're *all* in this. Every one of us is doing our bit as best we can. We'll see *our* boys stay fit and fightin'."

Humfrey couldn't turn his face away from the fresh-faced eager boy, looking up at him in oversized overalls, looking like he'd been dragged through a hedge backwards, with scuffs on his knees and straw in his hair, so earnestly telling him they were 'all in this now'.

"Good grief, Gertie," he sighed, muttering quietly under his breath. "What are we gonna do with you?"

They'd listened to the rest of the radio programme and talked about the news. It was a comprehensive discussion, although Walker didn't sound convinced. He was still trying to figure out how they managed to make a whole chicken stew out of just a few grubby thinnings.

Al winked across to Gertie. "Village-smart."

"Not only did you manage to make a stew from a few weeds, you also managed to make an office from the vicar's old cast-offs," Humfrey teased them, relieved to have something else to talk about.

Gertie wasn't fooled. "Always good not to have too much of an idea of where you're heading when you start. That way you're so much happier with what you've got, when you're finished!"

Not for the first time that day, Humfrey found himself impressed by the wisdom of Gertie's observations. The lad's notions might come from unexpected angles, and he had a strange way of expressing himself sometimes, but once you got past that and gave it a little consideration – eventually and invariably – Gertie made remarkably good sense!

The vicar had been called over to the hospital and had come by the Home Guard office to see if Humfrey could take him over in the truck.

"It sounded a bit urgent."

The vicar didn't need to say more.

"Right you are, Vicar. The office is settled in and we've already made good use of your bookcase. Gertie was right about that."

The vicar smiled and patted the church warden on the shoulder, leading him away from the youngsters, still seated contentedly chatting amongst themselves. "He usually is, you know."

"Yes, but I am worried about him," Humfrey confided. He wouldn't usually admit such a thing, but felt he could with the vicar, and he *had* to ask someone about Gertie.

"You're worried about Gertie?" The vicar needed to be clear. They were outside the village hall by then, beside Humfrey's truck, where no one could overhear what they said. "I wouldn't be."

"He's going to get called up soon, isn't he? He's not ready for it and they're abso-ruddy-lutely not ready for *him*!"

Now Humfrey had started all his fears for Gertie came out.

"Come on let's get in and you can talk as you drive. It'll be easier for you to say more that way. I'll sit and listen," the vicar told him steadily.

Humfrey knew he was right, but hesitated, looking back at the village hall. "They going to be all right if we leave them there, on their own?"

"They'll be fine. Gertie will take care of them," the vicar assured him.

Humfrey smiled, then scrubbed his chin before climbing into the driver's seat of the truck beside the vicar. He started the engine and moved away from the village, on to the Long Town Road heading for the RAF hospital, before speaking again.

"You're right, vicar. Gertie *will* take care of them, but who's going to take care of Gertie? The Army? The RAF? The Navy? Oh, damn it, Vicar! We understand him. They *never* will."

"They won't have to." The vicar sounded quite certain on that point.

"Doesn't he want to join up?" Humfrey checked. He might have misunderstood after all. "I thought he wanted to join the RAF? I thought that was why he's been helping so much over at the hospital?"

"He's been helping because that's what Gertie does. He helps anyone who needs it," the vicar reminded Humfrey. "But no, he's not interested in joining the RAF." Again, the vicar sounded very clear on that point.

"I give up, Vicar! Tell me, for Gawd's sake, how are we going to take care of Gertie?"

The vicar realised Humfrey wasn't wearing any of his official hats at that point. There was genuine concern in his voice.

"As far as I understand it, he wants to be a Land Girl."

"WHAT!" Humfrey almost missed the turn through the gate onto the hospital drive at that point. "Sorry Vicar, he wants to what!?"

The vicar wasn't going to repeat that statement in front of the men at the gate. Humfrey collected his wits and indicated the vicar was expected. Sarg waved them through. Only then did Humfrey feel able to turn back to the vicar. "Are you sure? How? Is it all sorted, for Gertie? Is he gonna be OK?"

"When he's ready. We'll always have a place for Gertie."

"Then why is it he seems so happy coming up with errands for the RAF hospital, and not so much to the Army camp? Is someone bullying him over there? You tell me, Vicar." Humfrey's brows were thunderous, his eyes flashed lightning and his voice was menacing. "I'll not be having that, Vicar. No one's going to bully our Gertie!"

"Oh, bless you, Humfrey." The vicar solicitously patted the shoulder of the tortured soul beside him. "Not at all, not at all. Gertie just likes the scarves, and he's told me the RAF have wonderfully warm socks, too!"

"He WHAT!?"

The vicar chuckled at the expression on Humfrey's face. It wasn't often he managed to get his church warden speechless.

"But the Land Girls? Really, Vicar!?" Humfrey almost stalled the engine trying to park the truck.

"Oh, you'd be amazed," the vicar informed him.

"With Gertie nothing would surprise me!" Humfrey muttered under his breath.

The vicar ignored that remark and continued his comforting manner.

"He's thought it all through. He's told me he's very comfortable in his overalls but thinks the Land Girl dungarees would suit him better than 'uniforms'. He says, 'uniforms' don't fit him."

"D'ya know what, Vicar?" Humfrey found himself bursting into laughter, as the tension left his shoulders, *"That* actually makes sense!"

The vicar climbed down from the cab and began to walk towards the hospital steps, then turned back to his church warden.

"It usually does, Humfrey. Where Gertie is concerned, it usually does."

CHAPTER 13

Old Tyres and Fresh Paint

RUSTY HAD COME IN TO help the Scamps with the rubber salvage.

"Nothing's going to be that simple," Old Spot had warned her.

They were already late. It had taken them over an hour to persuade Jeepers to allow them to take away a few 'useless' old tyres from his Yard. They were just taking up much-needed space, at least that was Rusty's argument.

Jeepers was still hopeful of getting those extra trucks but at the moment he was relying on being able to call in a few favours, whenever he needed more men and trucks, and he wasn't happy about it. Having to call in favours always made Jeepers uncomfortable. It meant he had nothing in reserve.

"Then you'll be catching up with the rest of us!" Old Spot had told his son, unsympathetically. That attitude wasn't going to help Rusty get those old tyres into the back of her truck any easier.

Jeepers was yelling over at his father, and Old Spot was yelling right back at him, getting redder in the face by the second, whilst Jeepers seemed to be winding up to lob something at someone and already had a bucket in his hand.

Rusty saw it first and distracted him by reminding him that bucket was hers and he could "go right ahead and lob it into the truck, thank you very much."

Jeepers didn't want the ruddy bucket anyway. That was getting in his way too. He flung it in Rusty's general direction, she ducked, and the bucket rattled down into the back of the truck.

"Go on, you've started now. You might as well chuck the rest of those old tyres over to me. Then I can take Old Spot out of *your* Yard," she offered.

It was a persuasive argument.

Old Spot was happy with the plan. He'd been getting fed up in his back garden. Rusty had been leaving him to get on with building the rest of the bomb-shelter by himself, and the fact he'd insisted on doing so had nothing to do with it!

As for those boxes that were cluttering up his workbench in the pottering shed, Rusty had told Old Spot she would help clear them out of there for him, but he could swear there were just as many boxes now as there had ever been. Maybe there was a bit more room at the back of his shed, where all the boxes had been moved forward, but that was just shuffling up. He could have done that without her help. It was the sorting that took the time, and no one could help him with that.

Rusty had tried, but Old Spot had his own system that 'would take too long to explain'. Her grandfather was cantankerous at the best of times and obnoxious at the worst, but somewhere in between he was kind, considerate and patient, with a never-ending array of stories at the ready to offer for every occasion. Unfortunately, he had recently seemed to be saving those up for when Rusty could next take him down into the village, or even better over to the RAF hospital.

It never failed. It might be the most ridiculous or outrageously impractical notion of a reason for tagging along, but if her grandfather could tell Rusty with a straight face, then she was defenceless! This time, however, there was no way she was going to take her grandfather on a 'salvage raid' over to the hospital, but if he wanted to tag-along with her and the Scamps through the village?

"Done!" Old Spot agreed instantly. "The village'll do me nicely."

Then Jeepers had started winding him up. Rusty had been about to assure her grandfather that he'd be just as able to get into mischief with the Scamps, as he would with the Lads. Only Old Spot was already threatening to start flinging those tyres right back at Jeepers!

Rusty didn't need to get exasperated. Jeepers was ahead of her on that score, picking up one of the wellingtons he'd just tripped over for the umpteenth time and chucking it at his father.

"Will you get outta the way, or do I have to make ya? I've more of those where that one came from!"

"Damn."

That was all Rusty needed, a brawl in the Yard. She was already late keeping her promise to help the Scamps, but Jeepers' warning had given her an idea. She scowled at her father, then winked over at her grandfather.

"Go on then, Jeepers. Let's see what yer aim is like. Let's see how that shoulder of yours is holding up?"

She knew he'd pulled it a couple of days earlier. She'd heard him swearing about it to his Yard blokes from halfway down the back garden. Since then Jeepers had been grumbling about it, trying various remedies.

Rusty had tentatively suggested he tried going to see Dr

Hastings, but his response to that idea had been vehement. "What would a doctor know? He'll just tell me to rest it. There's a war on, can't do that!" At that point Rusty stopped making suggestions, and just let him get on with rubbing and swearing at it. As for her grandfather swearing in his pottering shed, that was simply part of his sorting system!

It was a fair bet Jeepers' shoulder would be playing him up by now. Rusty knew he'd already had at least two lorries coming into the Yard that morning, so Jeepers wasn't going to be fit to do much flinging of anything at his father.

Old Spot was quite safe, and Rusty and her grandfather knew it! Those wellingtons would come in useful, and Jeepers was always more idiotic when he got angry. He always kept a couple of pairs of wellingtons about the Yard. 'Never know when you'll need 'em, between leaks 'n stinks!'

He'd forgotten that detail by then though. All he could think of was that he'd nearly tripped over again, and his shoulder ached, and his father was being annoying, again!

The first wellington boot skimmed the corner of the truck, bouncing off at an angle. Old Spot jeered at the pathetic ricochet. He'd caught the wink from Rusty, picking up the wellington boot, threatening to lob it right back at Jeepers, but instead stepped to one side and dropped it neatly into the truck, alongside the bucket.

That was deliberate. That was just provoking Jeepers. Snatching at the second boot a couple of yards from the first, and noticing Old Spot had moved position, Jeepers adjusted the angle of his throw. But his shoulder let him down, the sharp jab of pain as he brought his arm up caused him to release the hold and he kicked it instead.

This time the wellington fumbled under the truck. Rusty could pick it up from there, at the same time pointing out where Old Spot needed to go next, then pointing out to Jeepers where the next nearest boot was to him.

"Go on, you can do better than that!" Old Spot banged on the side of the truck, for a split-second checking over his shoulder how close he was to the front window of the farmhouse.

Jeepers was wise to that manoeuvre. He switched hands with the next boot and flung it over the truck, a high, slow lob. Plenty of time for Old Spot to avoid that one. It caught the pots by the side of the front door. Oh, that was plain infuriating!

Jeepers snarled as he grabbed at the last of the wellington boots he could find, flinging it wildly in the general direction of the cab of Rusty's truck. It was a mighty swing and missed entirely, hitting the side of the door to his work shed, bouncing off that and denting the corner of his caravan.

"Damn it, you two! Now look what you've made me do! Go on, get outta here and take that lump of rubber with you. I told you weeks ago to get rid of it!"

Jeepers hadn't said any such thing, but it was near enough what Rusty had hoped for.

As for Old Spot, if he was being told he couldn't do something then there was never going to be a better reason for doing it! "We're taking the tyres over to the Scamps then?" he asked cheerfully.

Rusty took a breath and watched until her father had stomped off into the work shed, to see how much space he'd freed up, having got rid of those 'flamin' old tyres' at last! She could hear his muttering becoming muffled in the shed's depths. They should be clear to move out now.

"Come on, let's load up. You and I can do better at the lifting and shiftin' than Jeepers anyway, what with his knackered shoulder." Old Spot didn't have any sympathy for his son's injury. "He should know better than that, you never jerk a twisted lift like that."

"Do you know what he was lifting when he did the damage then?" Rusty was interested. She hadn't seen it happen, and as far as she knew her grandfather hadn't either.

"Didn't need to. Seen the injury before, and it always happens from when you jerk a twisted lift. Don't need to know any more than that."

The tyres, boots, buckets and barrow were all loaded in the back. The gates to Jeepers' Yard had been left open, so it only took as long as Old Spot needed to fetch his toolbag. Rusty already had her own in the cab. She guessed her grandfather would prefer travelling in the back. He always preferred being in the back when he'd got the better of his son: "Better gloating distance!"

Rusty could hear her grandfather cackling with laughter, as her father hollered oaths at the empty lane outside the Yard gates. Rusty expected nothing less from those two. When it came to teasing and tantrums, she saw better behaviour in the school playground.

She was tutting for the first half mile of the journey into the village, but no one was hurt and they had got a good haul from the Yard. Rusty was soon smiling at the thought of what the Scamps would make of it all. Jeepers would have calmed down by the time they got back, and likely decided it had been his idea from the get-go, well pleased with himself for making space in his sheds for some up-coming deals he had in mind.

Old Spot was in fine form in the back of the truck, singing loudly.

Rusty couldn't quite make out the lyrics of the song. He'd

gone heavily into his childhood coastal accent, which he always did when he started singing. The louder he sang the less she understood. Rusty had learnt a long time ago it was wiser not to try to listen too closely when he sang, but her grandfather sounded happy, and her truck rattled and bounced between the ruts and the bends merrily enough.

She caught up with Gertie coming into the village from the direction of Abe's farm. "What've you been up to?" Rusty called a cheerful greeting to the lad.

"Fetching the eggs for our girls." Gertie reached forward into his bicycle basket, showing her the bag of eggs. "Can't be fresher than that. Still warm!"

"You'd better come up here with those," Rusty suggested. Gertie lifted his bicycle easily up to the waiting arms of Old Spot.

"I'll be havin' that, then!" The elderly gentleman rubbed his hands together gleefully. Gertie wagged a finger at him.

"Don't you dare. It's not scrap day." Leaning back into the cab, he asked Rusty, "It isn't scrap day, is it?"

"No, your bike's safe. It's meant to be rubber salvage today," Rusty told him.

"Oh, that explains the tyres," Gertie had noticed. "I guess if you've got Old Spot in the back singing like that, then plenty of soft tyres is a sensible precaution."

Rusty wasn't following the connection, until Gertie joined her in the cab. "Last time I could hear Old Spot singing like that it was a late night before market day. They got him home, but he must have hit at least two lampposts on the way."

Rusty was surprised Gertie knew so much. He was younger than her by at least six years. She was about to ask, then realised when he might have been referring to, when her mother died. She hadn't come into the village much that year, or the year after, so she could only guess what Old Spot had got up to in those years. As for Jeepers, he'd literally thrown himself into the Yard and kept out of the farmhouse altogether. He'd only started returning to the farmhouse when he'd run out of space in his sheds, taking over the upstairs rooms, all except for Rusty's own. The arguments hadn't been in those years; they'd come after, when Jeepers had started talking to his father again.

Rusty could remember standing in that lonely farmhouse kitchen, with the sunshine streaming through the open windows, and the smell of laundry powder softening the air, and the sounds of shouting rushing through the fabric of the building, from front yard to back garden, seemingly unhindered by bricks and mortar. It had been going on for years.

Old Spot was all for Gertie joining in the singing with him, but Gertie wisely suggested that the rough 'long lane' song he'd been singing might not be quite so appropriate, what with them fast approaching the village church.

"Cripes, I hadn't noticed," Old Spot grinned a little sheepishly. "Don't think I alarmed anyone, did I?"

"Only those two fellas that were with you in the back there, looks like you frit them right out of their boots!" Gertie had seen those old wellingtons in amongst the tyres.

Old Spot was laughing loudly at that for the brief journey through the village to where Maze was waiting with her old pram outside the hall.

Rusty could see it had been wise to suggest Gertie sit beside her in the cab. If she'd let him stay in the back with her grandfather, no doubt by now they'd be teasing each other on how far they could fling those wellington boots across the duckpond! Maze wouldn't have liked that.

Aggy had told Rusty how much the little girl enjoyed feeding the ducks. Not today, though. She had her old pram with her, which meant she was on salvage duty too. Climbing down from the truck, Old Spot greeted her with a salute to the overalls. Gertie did a little bob before dashing over to make sure Mrs Tweeny got those fresh eggs.

"Where have the boys got to?"

"They're over at Bracket's and I won't go in there because I'm the smallest, so he would have hit me with the yardstick first."

Rusty was pleased to hear that. Not about Bracket's yardstick, but at least the Scamps weren't so likely to get as far as pestering the poor vicar again, quite so soon.

Mrs Tweeny was pleased to see Gertie. "If you're heading over to the hospital, would you give a message to the doctor?"

Gertie guessed she was meaning the village doctor, Dr Hastings, not any of the other doctors at the RAF hospital. Gertie knew better than to suggest Mrs Tweeny might pass the message on to the good doctor herself, seeing as how she was *his* housekeeper. He knew Mrs Tweeny didn't do doors, books, errands or messages, but she was an excellent housekeeper!

"What's the message?" He had a piece of paper somewhere in one of his pockets and Rusty would have a pencil.

"You'll never remember it for that long," Mrs Tweeny decided. "I'd better come with you and tell Rusty."

Gertie didn't mind that notion either, he was going that way anyway. They walked back to where Rusty and Old Spot were waiting for Maze, who seemed fascinated with the pantomime unfolding on the opposite side of the road. Al and Walker were arguing with Bracket as to what he might *not* be needing anymore.

"I'm going to sell *that*." The ironmonger was attempting to explain the principles of having a shop, while Al and Walker seemed equally decided. "No, you're not. You haven't yet!"

Al was already calling his little sister to come over with her pram.

"Hurry up. Once we've loaded it, he can't take it back."

There was a scuffle, then the two boys scrambled across the road with Bracket wielding the yardstick over his head. Walker had something in his hand, a couple of somethings, or perhaps pieces; it was difficult for Rusty to tell until he got back over to her. Maze, sensibly, hadn't moved from her spot next to Gertie.

"Oh, they're old leather buckets!" Old Spot laughed. "That's not rubber!"

Walker had been so pleased to have got away from Bracket's grasp unscathed, he hadn't realised. Al was already laughing at him. "Idiot!"

They apologised to Mrs Tweeny, who'd been so rudely interrupted, whilst trying to ensure Rusty had the details of the message due for Dr Hastings.

Gertie showed Walker the tyres from Jeepers' Yard. "This is rubber. This is what we want."

"Well, how was I to know that? Bracket has it all packed back there in those crates. Couldn't really see what I was grabbing, but it smelt rubberish!"

"Idiot," Al pointed out to Gertie. Mrs Tweeny had stayed long enough to hear this part, and suggested Gertie ought to fetch another of those leaflets from the baker's wife.

"She'll know. She's WVS. They have all the leaflets for everything."

Gertie was always happy to have more leaflets to read.

Mrs Tweeny was approving the tyres from Jeepers' Yard, then noticed the wellingtons that Old Spot was about to include in the salvage stack.

"Oh no you don't. You can't put those into the salvage!"

"Why not?"

"Because they're already boots," Mrs Tweeny explained.

Old Spot looked at what he had in his hands, then back across to the doctor's housekeeper. "I know that, missus. Rubber boots is rubber. This is for rubber salvage, ain't it?"

"Yes, but they're already boots!" Mrs Tweeny insisted. "We need boots as boots. We don't need them to be anything else!"

Old Spot was confounded by that, but Mrs Tweeny seemed to have decided she'd said quite enough and didn't have time to add anything further.

"They want the tyres, but not the boots?" Walker asked, even more confused than Rusty's grandfather. "What about the buckets, then?"

Old Spot knew the answer to that.

"We need all the buckets we can get."

Gertie was in agreement with that. "Can't ever have too many buckets!"

"What are we meant to be asking for at the doorsteps then, for the rubber salvage?" Walker was struggling. "Isn't that a vegetable? Rubber grows on trees." He hadn't seen the leaflets but could remember a poster somewhere.

"No. Fruit grows on trees, not vegetables," Al corrected his friend, before adding helpfully, "they come out of the grounds."

Gertie felt it necessary to point out to the pair of boys: "Trees grow out the ground too, roots and all!" That wasn't helpful, but the Scamps seemed to find it hilarious, as Old Spot and Maze sat together on the village hall steps and enjoyed the show.

"So, if we grow trees, why aren't we doing that instead of collecting all the old bits left over and worn out already?" Walker asked them.

"Because we can't grow rubber here. They bring it in on ships and those ships are needed somewhere else more urgently. We have to collect the rubber, like the saucepans," Al explained.

"Don't tell me *they* grow on trees, too? Rubber saucepans would be worse than useless! It's like those leather buckets. No wonder Bracket couldn't sell 'em!" Walker picked up the items he'd managed to grab. Old Spot got up at that gesture.

"Don't you go being too quick about that. Leather is leather, just like rubber is rubber."

Walker put the buckets down and went over to join Gertie. He was the one with all the leaflets and the bicycle.

"Right, what are we meant to be doing?"

Gertie grinned, giving Maze a wink. "We're going fishing!"

"What?" Al and Walker queried in unison.

"We're going fishing. Come on." Gertie wasn't waiting for them. "Rusty, you've got rope in the back, and I bet Bracket's got a ladder hook, we'll only be borrowing it. What's the betting we fish out at least a couple of old tyres from where the stream catches between the duckpond and the bridge?"

Maze was immediately 'in' on the plan. "I can feed the ducks."

"Yes, you do that, and you can make sure Old Spot doesn't fall in while you're at it." Gertie gave the little girl her orders, at the same time giving due warning to Rusty to keep an eye on her grandfather.

Rusty sent both the boys back to Bracket to apologise, and to return the old leather buckets, if he wanted them back. At the same time, they were to ask if he had such a thing as a ladder hook. She hadn't heard of it, but apparently her grandfather had. Walker came back triumphant.

"Bracket was just pleased someone had asked him for it! We told him it was for fishing, and he seemed to think that was a very good idea. Why do we need it for the fishing?"

Rusty let Gertie explain. "The ladder hook is what keeps it up on the roof, when you get it that far. It's just for grappling and holding secure when you're yanking on it or clambering over it."

Gertie had fetched the rope from the back of the truck by then and tied the hook to the end. "You'll take it in turns, except you, Maze. You're too light for flinging duties, or we'll be needing to fish you out. You're happy with the feeding the ducks and keeping an eye on everyone else from there for me, aren't you?"

Maze nodded happily.

Gertie and the rest of the Salvage Scamps got themselves assembled between the flooded puddle of the village duckpond, and just before where the stream's flow was captured to steer it under the bridge.

Old Spot was the most successful fisherman that day, but it took all the Scamps to haul the old tyres out from where they'd got bedded in to the soft mud. It was proving a rather entertaining distraction for some of the other village residents, so much so by the time they were heaving out the third old tyre, the spectators were cheering their efforts.

Perhaps it provided a little too much of a distraction for one of the village residents.

Mrs Tweeny saw the smoke first when she was opening

the doctor's upstairs windows. The vicar had been trying to cook himself a chip butty again! The smoke was a chip pan fire. Mrs Tweeny was doing enough shouting to raise the alarm through the entire length of the village, from Ol' Creak's to Bracket's and back again, with the baker, the headmaster and even the milkman coming out to see what was happening.

"Is it a bombing raid?"

"Better than a siren any day," Old Spot cackled, but got himself running just as fast as Al and Walker, with Gertie picking up Maze and keeping her at a safe distance.

Rusty was ahead of them all, getting to Mrs Tweeny first who was standing on the doctor's doorstep by then, with one of his flannelette pillowcases still in her hands.

"He's done it again!"

The vicar was being a 'right Charlie' about it and panicking all over the place!

The village schoolchildren had always thought Mr Pegg was elderly. They'd presumed he was half deaf from the way he shouted at them in the classroom, but he'd heard Mrs Tweeny's call to arms, just as quick as Aggy and Mrs Parr had done, all the way over in the playground.

Dashing out and straight over, Mr Pegg was reaching for one of the two school buckets and calling over his shoulder for Aggy to fetch the other one. He knew what to do. Everyone else streamed out from the school, behind the headmaster.

Suddenly everyone seemed to be shouting from all corners of the village, whilst the vicar was running in circles in his front garden, coughing and flapping, unable to think straight, with his eyes watering and his handkerchief wafting feverishly in his trembling hand. Not mopping his eyes, nor covering his mouth, but attempting to send the smoke billowing in the other direction with his handkerchief!

Mrs Tweeny's flannelette pillowcase could have done better than that!

Mr Pegg got the school buckets to the duckpond and showed everyone what to do. Then left Mrs Parr and Aggy in charge of the children, whilst he got to organising the other residents.

Gertie got shouting to Al and Walker – "Scram and scramble, bucket brigade!"

Old Spot was hollering as loud as any of them. "Don't roll those old tyres out the way. Kick 'em! If you roll 'em, they'll roll right back into the water!"

The headmaster dashed past the vicar into his vicarage kitchen, grabbing at one of the tea towels and plunging it into the washing-up bowl, drenching it and wringing it in one single movement, then throwing the sodden tea towel over the flaming chip pan. With another sopping tea towel wrapped around his hand, he made sure the stove was off. Then he took hold of the pan handle, flames diminished but not yet fully quenched, with the towel dripping and smoking. Gertie was right behind him.

"I'll open the window, you fling it!" he called.

The headmaster nodded and made ready. The curtains were burning, and the windowsill scorched. Gertie reached and wrenched, glad of his long limbs. Mr Pegg was equally grateful, needing both his hands on the pan handle to provide enough power in the lob, throwing the whole package out of the window and on to the vicarage lawn.

By then Aggy and Rusty had everyone ready from the edge of the village stream to the front gate of the vicarage, up the garden path to the front door, handing along dripping buckets. It was a 'scoop and slosh' system.

The flames had been contained to the stove and window

mostly, the curtains having come off by far the worst, but there was a lot of damage, as much from water as from smoke, before they were finished.

With the last remaining flames safely isolated to the patch of scorched ground on the vicarage front lawn, and before anyone else could get to it, Old Spot had stomped over from his position by the duckpond and retrieved two of the ancient wellington boots from Rusty's truck. He wasn't going to wait his turn for a bucket. He could do very well with what he'd got!

Promptly dunking both boots into the water, before barging past those in his way over to the vicarage, he emptied the contents across the spread of charred grass and smoking pan. Then stomped energetically with his own boots, cheerfully obliterating the last trace of the conflagration, and shoving the jabbering vicar into Mr Pegg's arms.

"Take him to Mrs Tweeny. She'll know what to do." Only then surveying his progress, he muttered to himself, "Yep, just as good as a bucket any day!"

Mr Pegg was so surprised with the speed of the elderly gentleman's response he did as he was told. The headmaster wasn't used to being told what to do.

No one knew Old Spot's actual age, although the headmaster gauged it to be about ten, maybe fifteen years older than himself. He only hoped he'd be as spry when he reached that number. Mr Pegg could have happily retired a couple of years ago, but then the war had come and everything had changed. He steered the vicar towards where he could see the doctor's housekeeper and Florrie waiting with a blanket to wrap around the drooping figure in the headmaster's arms.

With the vicar safely out of the way, Aggy had a chance to check the damage in the kitchen. "Oh dear!"

Old Spot came in from the garden to view for himself. "Yep. That's what happens. Stinks, don't it? First thing we're gonna have to do is have the rest of 'em down. You'll need those buckets for rinsing out the smoke and staining," he recommended.

Aggy was still staring at the battered old wellingtons Old Spot was carrying. "Why?"

Old Spot grinned. He knew what she was referring to, but chose to ignore it, answering the alternative query. "Well, we've gotta start somewhere, Miss Aggy!"

Aggy suspected the vicar was going to have rather more than just rinsing to do to put the damage right. The walls in the kitchen looked awful and the hallway didn't look much better. The smoke-blackened, soot-smudged smears seemed to have got everywhere!

No more stream water was needed. Now was the time for buckets of clean warm washing-down water. The scent of carbolic soap was already arriving into the vicarage! Everyone was mobilised for the rinsing and scrubbing duties, with Gertie and the children each freshly equipped with their wash rags and, by the looks of it, a couple of Mrs Tweeny's scrubbing brushes to boot.

"Excellent practice," Gertie applauded.

Bracket was fuming at all the upset he'd had that afternoon.

Gertie wasn't going to let him start moaning, no time for that. "We'll be needing more brushes, scrubbing and painting. You've got those haven't you?"

Bracket was soon sent scuttling back to his hoard to fetch them.

Mrs Tweeny knew exactly what to do with the vicar. With the village doctor still called out somewhere, she had one of her girls with her. Florrie had been comforting the vicar with the blanket around his shoulders.

"Something to calm his coughing fits!" she suggested, looking over to Mrs Tweeny. "We'll be needing some of your tea, please. Plenty of your tea, please, best make it strong and sweet."

Mrs Tweeny handed Florrie the pillowcase she'd been clutching to continue wafting the vicar's spluttering, then duly disappeared into her own kitchen to follow nurse's orders. Florrie glanced at the eager faces surrounding her, spying Maze. "You're quick and little, just the thing. We need some of Ol' Creak's cough drops."

Gertie handed the vicar his handkerchief. "Cheer up, it could have been worse. It was only the chips. Just think of the mess if it had been bacon."

The vicar's face crinkled into a smile. Taking the offered handkerchief he dabbed at his eyes, before realising how wet they were and smearing the soot further, until he finally blew his nose.

"That's better, Vicar. Always helps me whenever I've done something stupid. Blow your nose real hard! Always helps clear the head to start it up thinking again," Gertie offered helpfully.

The vicar chuckled into another cough. Florrie had Mrs Tweeny's cup of tea in her hands but held back until the vicar had stopped. Gertie realised the problem.

"Don't worry, Florrie, I've got this one!" Leaning forward and taking a swipe, he slammed his hand into the middle of the vicar's back. "There you go, Vicar. Cough it out and get that tea down your neck. Smoke's out, tea's in. Sorted!"

Old Spot joined Gertie, Rusty and Aggy, checking that the vicar was able to stand. Mrs Tweeny was ready to ask if any more tea was required?

"Always!" Old Spot assured her, before presenting her with the battered, old, dripping boots he'd retrieved, and shouting over to the Scamps and the rest of the village children.

"Ok lads! Keep your boots on and your buckets at the ready. We ain't finished yet!"

It would take a few days, but between them they'd get the vicarage cleaned up. No one seemed to be in the slightest doubt about that, though Bracket was dithering about whether it would be wise to supply the vicar with a replacement saucepan. "Maybe we ought to ask the church warden to have a word with him, about not attempting the chips anymore."

Aggy agreed they would be needing Humfrey. More specifically, she would need to be asking her husband about where the vicar was going to be staying for the next few days, whilst the restoration works were underway!

Aggy and Florrie saw to it that the vicar was returned to his normal composure before attempting to move him, then gently guided him over the road to the church warden's home, allowing Mrs Tweeny to get on with her chores.

Dr Hastings still hadn't returned. She wasn't worried, only a little concerned as to how she was going to explain the state of his best pillowcase!

Mr Pegg and Mrs Parr began calming down the excited children. Rusty got the Scamps to help her with the discarded tyres that had been dragged from the stream. At least they'd had time to drain. Gertie accompanied Old Spot to the truck, his bicycle still in the back.

The vicar would be staying with Aggy and Humfrey at the church warden's home. Everyone in the village knew that, and Humfrey would be duly informed of the fact, just as soon as he came by on his regular route with the camp truck.

Humfrey was later than usual, but that was happening more often these days.

"It's starting to get a bit hectic over there," he informed the doctor's housekeeper. Mrs Tweeny had a good mind to inform the church warden things had been getting 'a bit hectic' in the village that afternoon, but decided it wasn't her place to tell him. Aggy would no doubt enlighten Humfrey when he got home for his supper.

Humfrey had come over to see Mrs Tweeny first, before going home. He had a message from Dr Hastings.

"He's fine, just rather involved with something over at the hospital and wanted me to let you know not to expect him back until tomorrow morning, at the earliest."

"Thank goodness I didn't waste supper on him," Mrs Tweeny harrumphed appropriately, but was rather relieved. That would give her an opportunity not only to catch up on her interrupted cleaning of the good doctor's house, but also to get over and help with the clean-up at the vicarage.

The other message Humfrey needed to deliver was round to the village stables. He would have liked to have gone to see his missus first but knew it best to get the errands done soonest. That was, if he could find Scar or Hatchett down there at the stables. He had a suspicion that the pair tended to avoid him later in the day. Humfrey could understand why, likely something to do with the fact that by then he'd returned from the camp and tended to be on either 'village-constabling' or Home Guarding duties. Scar and Hatchett much preferred to meet him earlier in the day when he was just the church warden.

This wasn't Home Guarding business; nor did he have any particular constabling intentions. The message had come from the RAF hospital.

"They're going to knock the old stables down up at the House!"

He couldn't see either of the stable fellows, so stood at the entrance to the village stables with his back to Furlong Lane and shouted out the message. Humfrey had tried this technique a couple of times before. If it was to their advantage, then they'd acknowledge the shout. If it wasn't, then they wouldn't. Fair enough. Humfrey knew what to expect and could work with that. He'd delivered the message. What Scar and Hatchett did with it was up to them.

He took a step further into the barn. There were a couple of local horses. He knew whose they were, and the animals hadn't been disturbed by his message which meant at least one of the stable fellows was close by.

"Do you want the details or not?" Humfrey offered and made to spin on his heels to head back up the cobbled lane, to his own home and supper with his wife.

"For sure, this time?" Scar asked causally, as he wriggled out from behind the stack of haybales wedged up between the stalls and the tack bench.

Humfrey smiled and noticed how the stable fellow hesitated, checking where he was keeping his Home Guard cap. If it was tucked in his belt, then Scar could say what he liked. If it was more obvious, then caution was advised. He saw the furtive scan and patted his belt; the cap was safely stowed. Scar breathed a sigh of relief.

"Sorry, Hatchett's been having some bother with one of the RAF Lads."

Humfrey knew better than to ask for *those* details. All he needed on this occasion was to discover whether the pair were interested in helping clear out the old stables up at the House or not. Scar looked suspicious.

Humfrey grinned. "It's official. They're going to knock it down. Need more room for the ambulances."

"That don't sound good." Scar had the good manners to sound concerned.

"No, it don't!" the church warden muttered under his breath, but waited for a proper response to his query.

"About ruddy time. Been falling down for years! State of that place not fit for man nor beast!" Hatchett growled emerging from his own hiding place. "If any of 'em had any sense up there, they'd have taken a sledge hammer to it months ago."

Hatchett didn't like brick buildings much. To his way of thinking the village stables were the only proper working stables for miles. "Timber and straw, that's what you need for stables, not all those old bricks. Horses don't like the taste of brick dust."

Scar had already heard all this.

"What they gonna do with all that good rubble and scrap?"

Humfrey didn't know anything about that part of the plan. He only knew as much as he'd been told. Now he'd delivered the message, he wanted to get home to his supper and, hopefully, his armchair for a couple of hours.

If they were interested, then they'd have to get over to the House in the morning and make their own enquiries.

"Does that mean going through official channels?" Hatchett checked.

Humfrey couldn't stop himself from grinning at that query.

"It means going through Sarg at the gate, if you want to get any further."

There had only been the one horse staying over at the house stables for the past six months at least, and Hatchett had always said that was a bad idea.

"Horses get lonely and putting a motorbike in there don't count as a companion. Shark-shoulders should know that."

Humfrey could hear the squabble bristling between the stable fellows behind him, as he happily left them to it and headed for home. Scar sounded like he was more interested in finding out who got to knock it down.

Humfrey could still smell the smoke from the vicarage chip pan fire, mingling with soapsuds and the evening air cooling the grass. Strangely, it made Humfrey feel like autumn couldn't be far away. It had already been a hell of a summer and it wasn't finished yet.

He wasn't going to get involved in the stables, either of them, beyond the message. Humfrey had enough on his plate and hopefully, in about ten minutes, on his supper plate!

He could already guess Aggy would have taken care of the vicar, otherwise he'd have heard all about it from Mrs Tweeny. Humfrey had hoped for a couple of hours rest, but a half-hour of sitting down quietly would do him a power of good whilst Aggy got the vicar settled up in the second bedroom.

By the time Aggy came back downstairs she knew Humfrey would be ready for a cup of tea and brought it to him quietly, just in case he'd dropped off to sleep. He had, almost, but heard her soft footsteps, opening his eyes and smiling up to her as he accepted the offered cup. Humfrey briefly mentioned the news about the house stables and ambulances to his wife. He could see it came as no surprise to her.

"We should have expected that," she suggested.

Sadly, Humfrey had been thinking the same thing. What he hadn't been expecting was Aggy's next suggestion.

"Gertie's good with the horses. He could walk the surgeon's horse over to the village stables, if he's got time. Hatchett would be happier with that. No reason for Hatchett to show his face where it's not wanted. You might want to mention that to Gertie."

Humfrey smiled. He should have guessed Aggy would have something to say on the matter. She always did, bless her. He was glad he'd married her. She knew when to go gently and when to be loud and clear, when to make a soft suggestion and when to deliver one of her schoolmarm scolds!

He appreciated that, just the sort of woman a man needed at a time like this.

"Yes dear, I'll do that. I'll mention it to Gertie." He grinned and blew her a kiss, then returned to enjoying his well-earned cuppa for a few more minutes as she bustled about with his supper. "It's amazing what that lad can do on a 'mention'," Humfrey muttered to himself.

It took a couple of days of cleaning before the fresh lick of paint could start going up on to the walls in the vicarage kitchen.

The vicar's office wasn't too badly affected, although it was decided the sofa would benefit from a spot of airing out on the front lawn. Gertie and the Scamps had just seen to the sofa and were now enthusiastically giving the vicarage cushions a good pounding to knock any residual smoke out from them.

The vicar and church warden stood together, admiring the youngsters' efforts through the open window.

"Adds to the character," the vicar observed.

"Plenty of that going about these days," Humfrey agreed, glancing over to Gertie, "character."

"And our days are all the more capable for it!" the vicar reminded him.

Humfrey sincerely wanted to believe that. From the way the news was sounding recently, they were going to be needing all the 'capable characters' they could get!

CHAPTER 14

'Good Grief, Gertie!'

THE NEWS COMING THROUGH ON the radio in recent days had been both difficult to hear and compelling. Humfrey had been allowing Gertie to listen with him to the set in his office most evenings now.

Humfrey was still getting caught up with his Home Guard paperwork, whilst Gertie seemed remarkably adept at sorting out cupboards.

"Had a lot of practice with Old Spot's shed," the lad revealed when the church warden admired his technique.

Gertie was still wearing those surplus overalls Rusty had brought over for him and seemed to have no problem growing into them.

It suddenly reminded Humfrey how call-up for Gertie surely wasn't far away. He also realised how fervently he was hoping the vicar's confidence in the plan to keep Gertie in the village wasn't misplaced.

The radio had marked the days: 15 August, a day that had seen the heaviest fighting of the battle over English skies so far. The Luftwaffe had flown over 2,000 sorties and lost 75 aircraft. Fighter Command had flown 974 sorties and lost 34 aircraft. 16 August 1940, the Prime Minister, Winston

Churchill, had offered the words: *'Never in the field of human conflict was so much owed by so many to so few.'* 17 August, Hitler had declared a blockade on the British Isles. 18 August, a hard day. The Luftwaffe had mounted largescale raids on targets across southern England. In the intense fighting, Fighter Command had lost 68 aircraft, the Luftwaffe 69.

The newspapers had been printing plenty, but to hear the voices giving the reports, and the speechmakers themselves, made it feel far closer, inspiring … and unsettling. Humfrey knew there was a great deal to be thankful for, but there was also much to dread, in the months ahead of them.

That was the day before Humfrey was due to lead the local Home Guard out on a night exercise. The timing of the exercise was rather a relief, a chance for Humfrey to feel his training wasn't being entirely wasted. Even with his injury stopping him being in active service, his days felt active enough, between one desk and the next, with a truck in between and, very occasionally, the necessity for the church warden's bicycle.

He couldn't tell Aggy anything about the exercise, except that he wouldn't be back until breakfast time. She knew better than to ask.

As for Gertie? He already knew.

Humfrey had only told the men it was an overnight exercise and to prepare themselves accordingly. The orders had been simple enough and he'd made sure his men understood them.

They'd had similar exercises before, although it had been a while. It was likely even the same truck and driver that would be dropping them off to get started. This time it was the 'target' that had got Humfrey more rattled than the prospect of outwitting the other team, trying to get there first. Maybe it would be better if he didn't mention that particular detail yet, Humfrey decided. So, he kept the 'pep-talk' to the basics of, "we need to get there before the other team stop us, simple. Any questions?"

"Why've we gotta take the boy out with us, then? He's not Home Guard," one of them had queried Gertie's inclusion. Humfrey was prepared for a little resistance to that part of the plan. "Because the other team won't be expecting him, and it's not against the rules." There was still a residual murmur of dissent. "And if any of you know your way around those out-back lanes better than him, *and* in the dark, then you step forward now and tell me!" Humfrey challenged. The murmuring stopped.

They could all hazard a guess to the distances involved. No more than a Sunday stroll, under normal conditions, except these weren't normal conditions. It was dark and damp, and they were meant to be avoiding anywhere with the slightest hint of being comfortable! Because that would be precisely where the 'other team', another Home Guard group from one of other nearby villages, would assuredly have got themselves sitting in wait.

Humfrey's men were all local and knew more or less where the truck had dropped them off at the start, even with the driver refusing to tell them. One of them could already tell from the smell they were only about a half mile over from one of the out-back barns.

"Mr Tor does some of his best work at night."

"Why isn't he on our team, then? He's not on the other team, is he?"

"Don't be an idiot. He's working. You've just said so."

"Reserved occupation?" another man asked.

Humfrey told them to shut up.

"If we can smell him, he can hear us. Orders, remember."

"Yeah, but you've just said he's not on the other team, so can't he help us? With Mr Tor on our side, we could get anywhere. No one's going to argue with *him*!"

"You offering to ask him, then?"

"Don't be stupid. I'm not an idiot!"

Since the drop-off they'd maybe managed a half mile, since realising the proximity to some of Mr Tor's barns. The muttering and banter had subsided significantly, for which Humfrey was grateful.

He'd also appreciated that Gertie had stayed silent so far. The lad knew how to keep up without being obvious. Humfrey was already glad he'd agreed to bring him along.

Some of Tuckly's fields should be ahead of them. They were vast open arable fields and went broad around both Tors' barns and Jeepers' Yard.

Humfrey couldn't see any lights coming from that particular direction. He'd been half expecting to hear some dodgy business dealings going on by torchlight, or Jeepers unloading. It wouldn't have surprised him.

Whispering over to Gertie, who'd come to his shoulder by then, "You hear anything?" Gertie kept his response concise. "A good country night? Plenty. But no wheels, no voices and no boots, if that's what you mean?"

"Thanks, Gertie. That's what I thought." It was a relief. The only voices Humfrey could hear were his own men already objecting to the trudge. They were going to be even less happy with what he was going to suggest next.

The margins of the summer working fields were dense with high grasses, rough and uneven beneath their boots, but safer than along the roadside. There was a run-off ditch alongside it. It didn't have much water in it, but enough to remind the men how near they were to it. "We'll follow this."

No one had asked him yet. Humfrey was waiting until someone got fed up. It only took a few more paces across, before one of the men behind him tripped, swore and yelled forward.

"OK, Corp. What the heck are we meant to be doing out here?"

"Cover of darkness," was the first part of that answer.

Humfrey hazarded that gave them about three or four hours before daybreak. The truck wasn't going to wait for more than a half-hour after that. It wouldn't want to get tangled up with the early traffic from the farms.

Humfrey brought the men round him into a huddle. There were six of them, counting Gertie and himself. They were three men short this week, what with the extra shifts over in town.

"Got to be cover of darkness and got to be off the beaten tracks," he explained.

The idea was they were meant to attack an old hut that was located on the edge of one of the upper Grazing Meadows.

"The RAF have taken over one of the Totters' old fields. They're using it for training. We've got to keep clear of that, and avoid the other team, and get round to where that hut is," Humfrey informed his men. "The other team are looking for us. They win by stopping us getting to that hut."

There were a couple of impulsive queries as to what the RAF or the Army were intending to do with the requisitioned field. All Humfrey could tell them was that it was for 'training'.

"Aren't we training?" one of the men at the back called forward.

"This is different," Gertie spoke up. Humfrey remained silent; the lad could explain this part for him. "We need to stay out of their way."

"Why's it different?" the same man checked, recklessly.

Humfrey spun round and told him to shut up, but Gertie kept his voice low, which somehow managed to make it even more compelling.

"Because we're the ones training *without* ammunition."

They were still stumbling low through the high grass, perilously close by the run-off ditch. Humfrey could tell there was a little water in it, but no more than a trickle. Unfortunately, the sound had begun to have an effect on both himself and one of the other men.

The grumbling and muttering had started to run out of steam behind him, and he needed them to focus. Avoiding the 'active' training field was straightforward enough. The rest of the exercise wasn't quite as ridiculous as it had first sounded.

"The idea is we should be able to find them before they find us. If the Germans get this far, then we've got to expect they have maps as good as ours," Humfrey explained.

"Our advantage is that the Germans don't know what's not on the map!" Gertie added.

"Even with the signposts painted out, when they get to the village, they're going to notice they've arrived at the village, aren't they?" one of the men asked.

They'd fallen into a steady pace and the banter came with the boots.

"They'll know they've reached *a* village, but not which one. We're going to make sure they don't get that far!" Humfrey answered. "It's going to take every village all the way across England to stop them."

He could hear his men listening.

"They might *think* they know what they're doing. We're

going to make sure they don't know what *we're* capable of doing, until it's too late," Gertie offered. There was a murmur of approval at that notion.

"Are we allowed to use the gate?" another voice piped up. "Were we expecting a gate to be here, Corp?"

"If you can find it, use it," Humfrey began, but Gertie's hand went across to his arm, a timely reminder, a quiet voice with wise words.

"Problem with using a gate in these parts is it means, like as not, you'll be crossing a path straight after."

"Path?" Humfrey realised what Gertie was telling him and raised his own voice. Time to remind his men of their training. "Paths mean we could be getting into the line of sight of the other team. And your boots, even on a muddy path, are going to give enough sound to alert someone who's listening for 'em. Don't be stupid. We don't know how much they know," he cautioned, acutely aware he probably didn't know as much as at least one of the men trudging alongside him.

The path the other side of the gate turned out to be no more than a track. That was useful. It gave Humfrey the hope they were a bit closer to the target hut. If they were still on the tractor side of the working fields, then the path would have been wider. The lanes might be on the map, but not the farm paths, nor the rough tracks.

Gertie had sat with him before they'd set out and helped add a few local details to the regulation-issue map. There was a hedge just across the width of the track. No more gates though, by the looks of it.

"OK, Corp. Which way? Follow the hedge?"

Humfrey crouched down and used the torch inside his jacket as cover to check the map again. He was sure that hedge was going to be helpful.

"All right, until we get to the next ditch." He didn't want to tell them any more than that. They weren't going to like it.

"Should have kept this better trimmed," one of the men observed. They weren't wrong, but a ragged hedge was going to be helpful.

"Come on, Corp. We can just keep to this side of the hedge and no one will be any the wiser."

"We could, if the hedge was going the way we are."

Gertie nudged Humfrey again.

"It's not, look!"

Humfrey showed them how the hedge and the tracks veered away. However, down amongst the hedge roots there was the beginnings of the next drainage ditch. That was what Gertie had been looking for.

"Through here," he whispered across to Humfrey.

"You've gotta be kiddin'!" One of the other men heard the softly spoken suggestion. "Through *that*?"

The channel was only a couple of feet deep and not much wider. It was going to take some wriggling, and that was before they took on the brambles and those murky banks. Gertie grabbed at some of the soft damp soil, rubbing it between his fingers, then sniffing it. "This year's digging."

"It won't be on any of the old maps," Humfrey hoped, leading by example. "Down here. Keep moving."

They were cold and scuffed by the field trudge and scratched from where the hedges had already caught them, now it seemed they were going to be dunked for their troubles.

There was the sound of the boots splashing, then knees crunching and hands grabbing, whilst the swearing got louder. The digging might have been fresh that summer, but the water was already stinking green.

Someone was making cheerful gibberish, as they half-waded, half-crawled under and through the hedgeway, into the open field the other side.

"Oh, that's a good sign for the crops. What's Tuckly growing over this way? Gotta be green from the smell."

"Stay down." Humfrey signalled for them to quieten down. "This is the field before the barbed wire starts."

"Barbed wire, Corp? You didn't tell us about no barbed wire. We didn't bring any cutters."

"No, the barbed wire marks the perimeter of the 'No unauthorised entry' area, remember? That RAF training field, I mentioned? The one *with* the ammunition? We need to get around that. No wire-cutters needed. The target hut should be on the far side," Humfrey made that clear, before muttering out the side of his mouth, to Gertie by his shoulder, "Problem is, the others are likely to know that much, too."

Someone made mention of the fact that, "If we smell like damp undergrowth, maybe it'll throw the other lot off our whereabouts."

Another voice further back offered, "If we smell any more like damp undergrowth, I'm going to throw up, never mind throw off!"

It was a cheerful grumble and Humfrey was glad to hear it. If they had energy for that, then they had energy for the rest of the route – apart from the idiot who suddenly had the impulse to clamber out from the ditch and stand up in the middle of the field to relieve himself. Gertie was nearest and immediately reached up to the back of the man's belt and yanked him back.

"DOWN!"

This caused the unfortunate culprit to send a midstream of urine in a fine arc of spray, before he fell backwards into the ditch.

"If you need to do that, do it!" The sudden harshness in Gertie's voice stunned even Humfrey. The bedraggled wretch stumbled an apology.

"Sorry Gertie. Don't need to now."

His fellows congratulated him on the display, whilst Humfrey kept them moving steadily forward. Both he and Gertie had heard noise from the active training field. That area was categorically out of bounds to both teams in the exercise. The noise from there was more or less what Humfrey had been expecting. Not entirely dissimilar to the Army camp where he did his clerking, only on a lesser scale, and more tightly contained. It had only been set up a few weeks earlier, maybe a couple of months. Humfrey didn't know any more than that, not for certain, although now he was close enough, it sounded like they were definitely RAF not Army.

That wasn't the sound Gertie was focusing on. He tapped Humfrey's shoulder, redirecting his attention. Someone was approaching their position.

"What the devil!"

It was coming across the middle of the open field, in the dark and at speed. Not a tractor, nor a truck; too small and fast for either. A motorbike?

"Damn it, Gertie! Who is it?" Humfrey hissed loudly at the man beside him.

"It's Abe, the twit."

Humfrey stood up from the ditch and his men followed. They were wet, stinking, chilled to the bone and almost at their goal, and Abe was about to blow their cover. They were furious.

"Does that moron even know where he's going?" Humfrey queried back to them.

Gertie grinned in the darkness. "More to the point, does that moron know there's a ditch here?"

"Oy, ABE!" Humfrey had to do it, yelling and waving his arms until the motorcycle slowed.

"What in heaven's name d'ya think you're doing?"

The chicken orchard farmer brought the front wheel of his motorbike to a juddering stop. The back wheel took a little more skidding before it got the message. Humfrey's men all held their breath waiting for Abe to fall off again.

"Good grief, Gertie! Why'd you go and do that? I had a nice bit of welly going on there. Now it's gonna take me some churning before I can get going again," Abe screamed at Gertie, who was the nearest man to him, and the only one helping him to keep the bike upright.

Humfrey remained silent for a moment, and appeared even more menacing for it, as he took another slow deliberate step towards the farmer, this time ignoring Gertie, who could see Corp could handle the situation from here.

Abe didn't hold on to his bluster for more than a heartbeat.

"I was trying to avoid getting told off for riding my motorbike out on the roads," he said, defending his actions brazenly. "Every time I do that, your lot tell me off."

"*My* lot," Humfrey checked.

"You're Army, ain't you?" Abe peered into the dim beam of light flickering precariously from the slit of his headlights.

"Is that you, Humfrey? What you doing here? Is that a ditch? Wasn't there last time I came over this way!"

Humfrey briefly explained about the night exercise, then asked the farmer if he'd seen anyone else from his long-gate on the other side of the village road, to this far over, that might look like they were on a similar mission?

"Oh, you mean the *other* lot? They're down by the turn off to the lower Grazing Meadows. They must be thinking you'll be coming along the village road. Don't think they're expecting you to take the soft and smelly route!" Abe was looking in particular at the sodden individual who'd been flung back into the ditch by Gertie. "Cripes, mate! My week-old hen hay smells better than you!"

Gertie hadn't heard any change to the sounds coming over from the 'active' field. He could only hope those currently stationed there were already sufficiently aware of Abe's night-time antics and weren't paying any heed to such an idiot!

"Hey Abe, how about we get you out from the middle of this muddy field, and you give us some covering noise?" Gertie suddenly suggested, with his hands still steadying the motorbike.

Humfrey's men weren't going to argue with any suggestion that kept them out of that ditch, whilst Abe was all for a bit of extra muscle power where wheels and mud were concerned! There was also the fact that if it hadn't been for Humfrey standing up and hollering when he did, Abe would have very likely written off another motorbike.

The men clambered over and began pushing, managing to keep their grunted oaths and more general objections to a hushed mumble, as they followed Gertie's example.

Not a man amongst them felt the slightest need to question the lad's sense of direction. Humfrey wasn't the only one to notice that. Abe could be heard muttering something along the line of, "about ruddy time."

They trudged in silence after that, hauling the motorbike already heavily clogged with mud, as they were themselves, until they were within a few yards wide of the wire. From there, Gertie indicated 'go low', and everyman silently crouched and hunched as best he was able whilst keeping the bike upright and moving. They followed around to where the perimeter wire seemed to catch up with what seemed to be an old footpath.

"Any ideas?" one of the men whispered.

Abe could take a guess. "Probably one of Totters' old uns, maybe older."

Humfrey was relieved to concur with that estimation. It didn't appear to have been used in a while.

"No wheel tracks neither, and even more importantly, no recent boot prints!"

"We're ahead of them this far," he offered to Gertie, who nodded and kept moving. They were still following the ancient footpath. No one had asked him, but Gertie gave his reasons regardless.

"Hut's older than the RAF, so the farmer would have used the path for it. We follow this we'll find it."

"You alright?" Humfrey queried a few minutes later, when he realised the lad had stopped. Gertie grinned and pointed up ahead. It was the old hut and it didn't look occupied.

"Call it, Humfrey. You're in charge."

The church warden very much doubted that, but took the lead anyway, straightening up and raising his voice.

"OK, Abe, do your thing! Let everyone know where you are. Just give us five minutes' head start."

Abe didn't need telling twice. As for the rest of the men, they were just glad to get out of the fields. Humfrey was trying to get them organised, at the same time calculating how long it might take before the pick-up truck came by, and what was he meant to do if the other team got to them before then?

Gertie wasn't waiting for him to figure that out, helping Abe to get his motorbike cleaned up sufficient to be rideable again.

"You take this path over and on a ways," he directed, giving the farmer a push. "It'll meet up with Totters' Lane down on to the village road. You'll be heading down the same way as the other lot will be coming up." Both men checked across to Humfrey, before Gertie continued, "Feel free to tell 'em whatever you like. We'll have done our bit by then."

Abe liked that plan. "You giving me permission?"

Gertie shrugged; it wasn't his place to do that.

Both men turned back to Humfrey. Humfrey gave a weary grin. "What the heck, Abe. The cows'll likely be awake by now anyway. Go for it!"

The hut had clearly been abandoned many years previous. Certainly, the only thing that had disturbed it recently was the wildlife. It was much closer to the barbed wire than Humfrey had anticipated and he wondered if the men using that 'active' field knew about the Home Guard exercise. They certainly knew all about Abe's motorbike by the sound of it!

Humfrey handed the flag to the man Gertie had dragged back into the ditch earlier, giving him the honour of planting it on the hut.

"You deserve this one."

By that time, they were near enough to the field lights to appreciate the state they'd got in.

"Hey Humfrey, do you think your missus would let us borrow her old tin tub? I don't think mine would appreciate seeing or smelling me like this. Too many questions I don't want to have to answer."

Humfrey could hear Abe's motorbike stopping in the distance. He'd either already reached the turn off or caught up with the other lot and they'd stopped him. Their flag was planted. Mission accomplished.

If the other lot were busy swearing at Abe and his blasted motorbike, then they weren't getting any nearer to where Humfrey and his men were, but nor was their pick-up truck!

"Damn."

The occupants of the training field had definitely twigged to their location by then and it was one of *those* trucks that was heard approaching soon after that.

"Oh dammit! Now what?" Humfrey looked for an answer to his men, some of whom were already starting to make a run for it, but Gertie slammed his hand across the chest of the first runner.

"DON'T." He reminded them that was one of those trucks *with* ammunition. "I wouldn't give them a moving target to aim at if I was you."

"How about we see what they want?" He threw that suggestion in Humfrey's direction, whilst steering the rest of the men to tuck themselves behind the old hut.

They waited for the RAF truck to get near enough before a voice boomed across to them. "Come on, you lot. Let's get you back. Some of us have got work in the morning."

Peering out from the cab over at Humfrey was a smart-looking young RAF Flight Lieutenant, taking a dubious sniff at the men in his headlights.

"You're all going in the back, aren't you?"

"Yes Sir," Humfrey grinned, thankfully, and thumbed for his fellows to follow the orders.

"Was it *your* idea with the motorbike?"

"No Sir. Just lucky," Humfrey admitted.

The driver laughed and thumbed them to get in. "Where

to?"

"Church warden's house, first right in after the village shop."

The Flight Lieutenant drove the rest of the way in silence. They never did see what happened to the other team or what happened to their own pick-up truck. Humfrey would have to ask Abe about that next time he saw the farmer.

Aggy was woken by the sound of the truck stopping outside, followed by the sound of her husband's voice amongst others. She'd known they were out on exercises and to expect him when they got back. Shivering a little as she wrapped the dressing gown over her nightdress, thinking to herself, 'whatever they've been up to, two things are certain to be needed; hot tea and clean water!'

She was looking out of the kitchen window as she filled the kettle, smiling at her ever-reliable, battered old tin bathtub out there. She could hear Humfrey trying to keep his men quiet, shushing them loudly, with a stern, "Don't wake the neighbours," as she recognised his boots thudding up the front path, then making a racket at opening the front door!

From the state of them, they weren't going to be able to clean off all of it, but at least they could rinse off the worst and warm up.

"Good grief, Gertie, what are you doing with this lot?"

"Volunteered, Miss," Gertie grinned, cheerfully.

Aggy glanced across at Humfrey with a look that spoke volumes.

"Don't look at me, Aggy. I couldn't stop him."

"Yeah Miss. Don't scold the poor lad. We couldn't 'ave done it without 'im."

One of the other men came to Gertie's defence. "Yeah, even that RAF chappy thought the ditch and the motorbike were a good idea!"

Another chimed in, "Don't worry Miss, we looked after the young'un!"

Aggy gave Humfrey a look that asked, 'what *were* you thinking!?' But said no more of the subject. Instead, she poured the tea, then left them to get on with the rest of it.

The following week, it was Humfrey's turn to think up an exercise. He and Aggy had their heads together over the kitchen table, trying to decide what it might entail.

"We could take it to the other side of the village this time," he started.

Aggy could see the sense in that. If they were going to avoid the working fields, dodgy barns and open roads, that really only left the hospital grounds or the boggy bottom field, or the village itself, for them to practice in. Aggy shuddered at the thought of that last possibility. She could already imagine Mrs Tweeny getting into a tizz at the prospect, fretting that her 'girls' sleep would be disturbed before their next shifts; whilst the ladies of the WVS would be wanting to get involved just to make sure it was done properly. Rosie would want to know what time it was kicking-off so it didn't get in the way of her business and the milko would want to know what time they'd be done-by, to be sure he and Nag could get started on their rounds without getting 'caught up in all that nonsense'!

"Maybe not in the village, dearest," Aggy suggested. She could also guess none of the Home Guard men would be wanting to repeat their experience of that ditch-detour any time soon. Not if it could be avoided. It was something about the mention of the hospital grounds that gave Aggy an idea.

"What about trying to get a message through there? They've taken down the old stables over there, haven't they?"

Humfrey didn't need to explain to his missus why they

were widening the drive, to allow for more vehicles arriving at the hospital. He'd also heard mention they might be needing to extend the clinic; a sign of things to come? But he wasn't going to mention that, not if she didn't know.

"Let's see if they can get a message past Sarg's gate," Aggy suggested, and that was the proposal Humfrey took with him to the next Home Guard meeting.

"We'll have a go too. Only fair," Humfrey informed his men, recalling his wife's recommendation.

"What! With Sarg on the gate?"

None of his men thought that was likely. Humfrey had already asked Aggy the same thing.

"If Sarg agrees, he can leave it to a couple of his men to decide who gets through. He'll be in on the exercise, sort of the judge," Humfrey explained. Aggy was right, that did sound more reasonable.

Sarg agreed. The two men had walked away from the main entrance of the hospital, over to what remained of the old stables. There wasn't much left, only rubble, but at least they could see the entire driveway from that point, from the gate to the steps of the hospital.

"Anything usable has been taken out. Just needs sweeping before the ambulances start arriving," Sarg had informed Humfrey. That sounded ominous.

The church warden had seen for himself how most of the larger pieces had been cleared away by one of Jeepers' trucks. The smaller debris had been moved to one side to be broken up as a base layer for where the drive was being widened.

Personally, Sarg was glad to see the back of the stables. He'd never thought horses and hospitals mixed. As for the proposed exercise? It sounded as useful for his own men, as for Humfrey's Home Guard lot.

"It'll keep 'em on their toes. Can't fault that. As for the rest ... what's your thinking?"

That was going to take some explaining. So far Humfrey had only come up with ways *not* to do it.

"I'll get back to you on that, Sarg. Give me a couple of days. We've got another meeting before the exercise. We'll come up with something."

Humfrey sounded more confident than he felt. Surely they could come up with something! Aggy had even volunteered to take the message in with her library books. Humfrey had categorically put a stop to that notion.

"It's a Home Guard exercise," he reminded her.

Aggy looked squarely at her husband.

"We're *all* Home Guard now."

Humfrey still couldn't bring himself to let her do that. He'd think of something.

"It needs to be someone no one thinks to notice, or who never seems out of place," Aggy suggested carefully. She didn't want to give Humfrey too much of a clue. He needed to get there by himself. It was about time he realised!

For some inexplicable reason the church warden found himself thinking of Gertie. He'd been hearing quite a bit about that lad, from one source or another recently. Not the most obvious choice for a mission, but there was no denying the lad seemed remarkably adept at taking one errand and turning it into something else, that's for sure!

If the Home Guard were ever needed for the real thing, then messages would need to be made into something that didn't look like a message at all, and the messenger likewise, surely if anyone fitted that bill, then Gertie did!

Gertie would need to volunteer for the mission, and

Humfrey would have preferred to have done the asking a little more discreetly. He'd been intending to have a quiet word with the lad the next time they were listening to the radio, in the Home Guard office together. That would have been the right place for such a conversation. But as soon as the church warden caught sight of Gertie and the Scamps over by the village green, he realised someone had already been 'mentioning' something.

"You looking for me, Corp?" Gertie waved him over to where Walker and Al were all ears, right behind him.

Humfrey ummm-ed and ahhh-ed awkwardly, not sure who knew what and how much, until Al suggested he never try and hide anything from the hospital porters!

"They knew something was up the moment you and Sarg went muttering off together over by where they're making space for those extra ambulances. The only reason you two went that way was to be 'private', so of course they were listening in! Those porters have even bigger ears than us!"

Walker wasn't going to be left out. "Those porters just want front row seats to the mischief, and they know if there's any mischief going Gertie's bound to be in it somewhere."

Humfrey couldn't help himself but smile at that. "He is, is he?" That sounded very similar to something his wife had mentioned. Humfrey still hesitated, but Gertie was already making more sense of the suggestion than the church warden was.

"If I don't look obvious to you, I won't look obvious to them!"

It was going to be a daylight exercise this time, Humfrey reminded them. Al could see an immediate problem with that.

"You're too tall, Gertie. They'll see you a mile off. You'll stand out like a sore thumb!"

"Maybe, but sometimes the bleedin' obvious works best. They'll be thinking. 'That's too bleedin' obvious, couldn't possibly be that one'!" Gertie countered.

Maze settled the argument.

"You can't have the 'obvious' both ends of the puzzle, Gertie. If you do that, it won't work!"

The church warden and the two school boys stared at the wisdom of the little girl, but Gertie was already nodding. "Right. That's decided, then."

"We could *all* do it," Al volunteered.

Walker wasn't saying 'no'. All he needed was a bit more clarity on the 'how' of it.

"You're not borrowing my bicycle," Gertie informed the pair of them, smiling in that quiet knowing way of his. He'd had an idea. "I'll need that," with a wink across to Maze. "They'll be expecting me on the bicycle."

"Oh yes, that's right Gertie. Village errand-boy heading for the kitchen? They'll be expecting you on your bicycle," Maze confirmed. "Nice and obvious."

"OK, so how?" Humfrey asked, for his and Walker's benefit this time.

Al seemed to have an inkling but waited for Gertie to make it a little clearer.

"You could play football," he prompted.

Al beamed, grasping the gist a little more firmly now.

"You mean put the message in the football and kick it about along the grass to the gate, then kick it over?"

Gertie nodded, waiting for the two boys to work it out between them. Walker was catching on. "They'll let us go in and fetch it."

Humfrey could well imagine that happening. "They're not going to want to be distracted from their exercises by a couple of boys playing football, and an over-chatty errand-boy, are they?"

"If we put the message in the football it'll be deflated, won't it?" Walker asked his friend, but was checking with Gertie who gave him a slight nod.

"Yeah, but by then they'll think we're too stupid for them to worry about," Al reasoned, giving Gertie the thumbs up.

Humfrey laughed at the ridiculous plan, but Gertie didn't.

Gertie's face was steady, causing Humfrey to reconsider. "Actually, that's not so stupid at all!"

Gertie winked over to Maze. "There you go! So long as it's too obvious at one end and too stupid at the other, the balance tips in our favour."

"Has the message got to get up to the House, Corp?" Gertie suddenly queried.

Even Humfrey wasn't clear on that part, but it sounded like it ought to.

"Then I can just pick up the ball and tell them I'll take it out of their way, round to Mrs Toombs' kitchen. Bound to be a patching kit somewhere in the kitchen. It's a hospital after all," Gertie declared.

Al and Walker both had their mouths open, but it was Humfrey spluttering, "but Mrs Toombs wouldn't ... would she?"

Gertie's chin lifted, as his head tilted slightly. His eyes seemed to have a far-knowing in them, unfathomable, but undeniable. Humfrey wondered why he'd never noticed it before.

Had he missed something in the plan? What did the

Scamps know that he didn't? "What!?"

"War effort, Corp," Gertie reminded him. "We're all in this. Together. That means hospital cooks and errand-boys and all!"

Humphrey whistled softly, as he shook his head. He should have guessed.

Al and Walker were already congratulating Gertie. "Brilliant."

Maze came to his side and took the scrawny errand-boy's hand, looking up to him with a beaming smile. "Think we've earnt our overalls?"

Humfrey could answer that one. "Abso-ruddy-lutely!" The church warden still wasn't too sure about Gertie's hankering for those land girl dungarees, but he wasn't entirely against the notion either, not if they helped Gertie come up with more ideas like those hum-dingers he'd been having all summer.

Shooing the children on with their own errands, Humfrey invited Gertie to walk with him over to the church. "You're going to let Rusty know what you're up to?"

Humfrey wasn't sure why, but it felt important to know.

"Always do," Gertie confirmed with a lop-sided smile.

Humfrey found himself rather comforted by that thought. Rusty was a sensible lass, plenty of common sense there. He'd often heard his wife speak of her warmly, 'patient and pratical'. Yes, Humfrey decided, Rusty would be able to steer Gertie out of mischief, then started chuckling at the thought.

"Not a chance." The church warden hadn't meant to mutter those words quite so loudly and felt the need to explain them away.

"Had a bit of a rough start to this summer haven't you, lad?"

"I think we all have," Gertie reasoned, ignoring the earlier comment and glancing over to the war memorial, taking Humfrey's attention with him. "They had it worse. We can't let them down."

Humfrey murmured his agreement, but remained quiet, sensing Gertie hadn't finished his reckoning.

"And we haven't had it as rough as those Lads up at the hospital."

Humfrey couldn't fault that statement either.

"We're all in this, that means those Lads are *our* responsibility. Just like Mrs Tweeny is taking care of 'her girls'. Then it's up to us to get those Lads able to appreciate the sunshine and birdsong again. Sometimes all it takes is to notice the way a fresh morning finds the old stones."

Before Humfrey could respond, Gertie continued, as if no one was listening. His hand brushing lightly along the wall.

"Best way round though. A rough start. Reminds us it's going to be better … all we've got to do is keep on trying … no harm in trying is there? No telling what you can do if you try."

"And you do plenty of that, don't you, Gertie?" Humfrey felt like he was almost intruding on the lad's thoughts.

Gertie suddenly looked up into the church warden's face, his soft eyes earnest, his words certain. "Got to, Corp. Nothing else to do. Just keep on trying. Any way we can."

"Salvage?" Humfrey queried.

"Any way we can!" Gertie grinned.

It was the morning after the exercise when Rusty found Gertie waiting for her in his usual place, perched up on the church stone wall, with his legs dangling down and his bicycle leaning up against the ancient stones. She brought the truck to a stop.

"So, the Scamps are Home Guard now as well, are they?" Rusty greeted him with a cheerful wave.

"If we're going to salvage this summer and those Lads, then yes, Rusty. It's going to take all of us, doing whatever we can, and that includes the ridiculous, outrageous and absurd."

"And the brilliant and inspired," Rusty reminded him, with a tender kiss on Gertie's forehead. She'd already spoken with Aggy about it.

"Can't afford to waste anything," Gertie murmured, with a little sigh of contentment, as a blissful blush rose through his cheeks, the grin across his face causing those freckles to start dancing over his nose again.

"No, we can't," Rusty agreed. "I'm glad Humfrey has recognised how invaluable you are, Gertie. He's a decent bloke, just needs a hint in the right direction sometimes."

No one had actually told Mrs Toombs about the exercise, or the plan the Scamps had in place to tackle their part of it, but she seemed to guess there was mischief afoot, as soon as Gertie appeared at her kitchen door.

"Just trying to be useful, Mrs Toombs," was his explanation. How could she argue with that!

The hospital porters had told most of the Lads by then, on the strict understanding they weren't meant to know, and there was to be no out of the ordinary activity for the day of the exercise, so that left them with plenty of scope!

For those that couldn't get out or over to the windows to witness the antics, it was Florrie and her young colleagues who relayed the various developments.

It wasn't really a fair contest, with so much going on, Sarg's men knew something was 'up', which put them on alert. But that worked in the Scamp's favour. According to Gertie's plan, slipping the 'too obvious too stupid' in amongst the mayhem was 'simple country wisdom'.

Sarg had to admit, however the lad had figured it, it proved remarkably successful.

Gertie could guess how the morning-after would go up at the house, glad to be able to bring Rusty in on the notion.

"Sarg will rant at his men. The Lads will tease him relentlessly and then he'll stomp into Mrs Toombs' kitchen. She'll cluck and scold him until he's calmed, then offer him a cuppa and it'll all be right again."

Rusty was laughing at the image. Oh, Gertie could listen to that sound forever.

"And Mrs Tweeny will see her 'girls' have had a flustered day. She'll make them a pot of tea and invite them into her sitting room to listen to the radio. They'll listen to the lovely music, then to the news, and by then they'll have talked-it-all-through and agreed: 'It's got to be done and we're glad to do it'."

Yes, Rusty could imagine that was precisely what Mrs Tweeny would have done. "She'll tell them off for staying up so late after their long-shifts, but you can be sure she'll see them off again this morning with pride in her heart."

Rusty's features softened into concern for the scrawny scruff sitting on the church stone wall. There was just something about Gertie that made her want to protect him.

"We need to stick together and stay strong. That's the only way we're going to get through this."

Gertie nodded and shuffled down from the wall. "I'll stick with you, Rusty. Always. And give me half a chance," he straightened his shoulders, "I'll get stronger."

"You'd better," Rusty smiled gently, reminding Gertie, "Salvaging the summer is one thing, but we've got the autumn-harvests and winter will be coming soon-enough... we've got our work cut out for us."

Rusty opened the cab door of her truck, then stood to one side.

"Let's put those overalls of yours to work."

Gertie grinned and grabbed his bike and made ready to put it in the back.

"Right ho, Rusty, I'm with you."

The Salvaged Summer Trilogy:

All for Overalls
If the Sock Fits! (late 2022)
Raids, Rallies & Reserves (early 2023)

All for Overalls

With the news from Dunkirk a scrawny 14-year old errand boy called Gertie is spurred into action. For a lanky lad with borrowed specs, smelly feet, awkward elbows and big ears; who liked to keep things simple, perhaps he wasn't the most obvious choice as a go-between. Plenty in the village had shrugged him off as 'can't make him out'. Then the war had started, things had begun to get desperate and they couldn't afford to waste anything, not even Gertie!

As the local residents adapt to wartime-ways, the old village and the new RAF hospital have plenty of characters and best-intentions between them, but country wisdom and military efficiency doesn't always rub along smoothly …

"Just because you're out of the way, doesn't mean you're not in the middle of it!"

If The Sock Fits!

Churchill had been right about 'the Few' being the ones to save them through the summer, but it was going to take 'the many': the Land Army and the locals, bringing in the harvests of autumn 1940, that were going to get them through the coming winter.

The Battle of Britain might be over in the skies, but the cities were still struggling to cope through the Blitz of Hitler's bombs. The airfields were being rebuilt, but the men were taking longer to recover and in the meantime the farmers needed help.

The Lads up at the RAF Hospital were getting concerned about what was giving the surgeon a twitch ... and Gertie couldn't be having that! It was only a matter of time before he managed to scoop up the patients and nurses in the escapade.

Rusty soon smelt a rat, but with no sign of the village constable, Aggy was called for with Gertie running interference. The Scamps proved themselves equally adept at sabotage as salvage, even if the delivery driver hadn't got a clue! Anyway, with stray bombs and wandering buckets, they were ALL Home Guard now.

Salvage, Sabotage and *"Good grief Gertie, was this your idea."*

*"You get them to believe they can fight back
and they stop feeling beaten."*

Raids, Rallies & Reserves

The village was gearing up to 'get it done', through 1941. Yes the aeroplanes and tanks were doing the fighting, but the tractors were doing the feeding. They were already getting blasted by the winter winds and there was a shortage of overcoats!

Doug did his best, but his 'lovely lady' still managed to plough up the grazing meadow and send a piece skipping the hedge to knock Riggs from his post. The RAF pilot walked away with nothing more than a few scratches and a sandwich, leaving Riggs with two broken legs and a wounded heart, and Gertie's theory on how they were going to win the war managed to open a few eyes into the bargain!

Matters came to a head with the news about Pearl Harbour. Mr Tor went missing down a rum bottle and there were a dozen geese to throttle, pluck and deliver. The best Gertie could do was feed the pigs and drag the delirious farmer along for the ride! By the time the convoy reached the new RAF airfield they could see the wiring was wrong, Riggs did the yelling and Gertie did the bowling. It wasn't regulation by any stretch of the imagination and as for Sarg wondering about that officer? Gertie could explain:

"Oh don't worry Sarg, he's just there to stop the others falling out!"

Also, becoming available by the same author in Spring 2023

Three Sides Out, One Way Home (Malaya 1956-58)

The story of three Englishmen during the Malayan Emergency, each with very different priorities. The driver was also a sniper, the porter was also a thief, and the Padre had come open-minded and empty-handed and turned out to be remarkably versatile!

From building an airfield to opening up a mission house, from dump trucks to chicken soup; they'd be working with trackers, traders, head-hunters and river-pirates. For Porter it started with a crowbar and a motorbike; but Driver needed to allow the jungle to take a piece of him if he was going to survive it; whilst the Padre had been hoping for somewhere 'colourful'. Be careful what you wish for! It was going to be a three-alarm clock job and the satchel prompted the negotiations.

Three men: one of them had been sent there, one thought he ought to be there and one of them really should have known better!

It wasn't until the hillside hospital when the agreement was made: there were plenty of ways of getting home, but for one of them, only one way to do it 'right' ... and it was going to take ALL three of them going off the rails to get it done.

It was always understood: *"No one volunteers, ever, for anything ... but sometimes ... you're asked!"*

Further information available from queries@gertiespath.co.uk